Brian Jameson doesn't even get a chance to pick a college before a worldwide pandemic breaks out—and his home is Ground Zero. After losing his parents and sister in a whirlwind of devastation, Brian's war-veteran grandfather takes him under his wing. But when desperate looters attack Brian's new home, he and his grandfather must flee into a wintery Midwestern wasteland now populated by intelligent infected known as "Stalkers."

These ghoulish creatures don't shamble in hordes—they hide in the darkness waiting to strike, teeth bared in ghastly grins. And they laugh while they're ripping you to shreds.

But with his grandfather's training, Brian makes it to the home of his estranged childhood friends, twins Louis and Eva. And Brian gets a chance to experience something else he nearly missed: falling in love. Drawn to the determined—and ruthless—Louis, Brian escapes with him in search of an island paradise away from the relentless snow and infected.

But even if they make it there, it may not be the haven they're hoping for.

STALKER/S

L.J. Hasbrouck

A NineStar Press Publication

Published by NineStar Press
P.O. Box 91792,
Albuquerque, New Mexico, 87199 USA.
www.ninestarpress.com

Stalker/s

Printed in the USA
First Edition
January, 2019

Print ISBN: 978-1-949909-84-5

Also available in eBook, ISBN: 978-1-949909-83-8

Warning: This book contains sexual content, which may only be suitable for mature readers, scenes of horror and gore, and the deaths of secondary characters.

Chapter One: The Attack

12/19, TOPEKA, KANSAS

Jameson Residence
1:06 a.m.

The light from Brian Jameson's tablet danced across his face in varying degrees of intensity: somber blues, soothing greens, and sometimes the alarming tinge of blood-red. The show's layered soundscape coursed through his earbuds. Drizzling rain enveloped the muted dialogue of two detectives, their shoes crunching against gravel as they hunted an elusive killer. Somewhere offscreen, a gun exploded. Brian's pulse pounded so hard it blended with the strengthening downpour.

Jesus, I didn't expect that.

Brian waited for the scene to change, for stunned gasps, for those dainty footsteps to accelerate into a frantic sprint, but the pair of detectives continued their discussion as if they were taking a stroll through a scenic garden.

Brian paused the video and plucked out his earbuds. Silence. Darkness. A small square of light with an image frozen in time tilted against his knees.

Am I going crazy? I swear I heard a gunshot.

Abrupt knocks shook his bedroom door. Brian's tablet fell to the bed as he swiveled his legs over the edge, muscles tensed—

"Bri! I heard a buncha loud sounds an' I'm scared!"

Brian clicked his lamp on and rushed to open the door for his younger sister, stumbling over a still-packed suitcase. After he ushered her in, he shut the door. His racing heart slowed as he gripped her fragile shoulders. *We might have heard the same thing. Thunder, or maybe fireworks from the redneck neighbors.*

"It'll be okay, Becks. Tell me what happened."

Becky's thin eyebrows knit above glistening pale-blue eyes. "A *boom* woke me up an' I ran to Mommy and Daddy's room, but I heard another boom in there an'—"

"Wait—*in* their room?"

Becky nodded.

Brian jerked his cell phone from the charger. He pressed the "9" from the emergency screen, Becky's fearful gaze locked on his. A whimper escaped her as footsteps creaked in the hall outside. Shadow sliced the sliver of light beneath the door.

Brian abandoned the phone to reach for the door lock—but someone twisted the knob before he could get to it. A sturdy figure burst in and knocked Brian back. Becky cried, "Daddy!" and flung her arms around their father's stocky legs. Their mother pushed into the room after him, collapsing to her knees as their father slammed the door and locked it. Brian caught the glint of a gun wrapped in her shaking hand.

While his father paced the room, phone pressed to his ear and daughter wrapped around his legs, Brian guided his mother onto the edge of his bed. Her distant gaze frightened him—she seemed to be looking at something only she could see. A memory, perhaps, something keeping her from the present. Her auburn waves clung to her shoulders in sweat-matted strands. Blood spatter stained the pink and yellow flowers of a nightgown. It framed four crimson gashes gleaming from her porcelain chest.

In the background, Brian's father spoke to a muffled dispatcher. "My kids are terrified, we're locked in my son's bedroom, and there's a fucking dead guy on my bedroom floor! Why? My wife shot him, that's why! All I know is I woke up to gunshots, my wife screaming, and some nut springing out of our closet. He scratched her—even tried to *bite* her! He was out of his mind, stank like...I dunno. I dunno. Can you hurry, please? I'm worried about my wife."

Brian's father slumped onto the bed and ran a hand through his close-cropped hair. Becky squeezed between their parents, tiny hands clutching their father's flannel pajama sleeve while he listened to the dispatcher. His free hand curled into a fist above his bouncing knee, knuckles tightening to white.

Brian's skin grew clammy. Tingly. He tuned out the sights and sounds around him until they became a blur and buzz, a spinning funhouse tunnel of disorientation. *She shot him. This crazy guy that broke in. God, he could've come after me and Becks if she hadn't...*

Distracted by the motion of his mother setting the gun on his bedside table, Brian looked at her. He recognized a forced smile he'd seen many times before. "We'll make it through this one step at a time. We always do." She glanced down at the bloody slashes, then back up to Brian. "I know this looks nasty, but it's only a couple of scratches. I'm okay. I promise."

She pulled Becky to her, giving her the attention their father couldn't. Despite his muscular build and booming voice, Brian's father often wilted in stressful situations—like the time he lost his job at the Topeka mall and Brian and his mother found him foaming at the mouth with an empty pill bottle beside his outstretched hand.

Brian's father lowered his phone and looked at his wife and children, scoffing. "We have to stay in here and wait for them, barricade the door. The dispatcher said we'll be *safe* and that we shouldn't disturb the scene. Can you believe that? They made it sound like you were more of a criminal than the asshole you shot, Ellen!"

"Joel, language." Brian's mother covered Becky's ears. She rested her chin atop Becky's head and lowered her hands to stroke Becky's lank hair. Brian's father sat beside them, staring at the thin blue carpet between his bouncing knees.

"Brian, move your desk in front of the door."

Any other time, Brian might've found his father's condescension infuriating, but he was happy to have a distraction from the questions stirring within him. He dragged the desk over to the door, hyper-aware and jittery like he'd had too much caffeine.

When he finished, Brian sank onto the foot of his bed. He swept his tablet away, certain he'd never want to finish the episode frozen within it, and curled a quaking hand around his mother's shoulder. "Mom, tell me what happened. *Please.*"

She nodded, taking in measured breaths as she threaded her fingers through Becky's auburn curls. Becky took after their mother both in appearance and spirit. Although Brian possessed the same golden-blond hair and tan complexion as his father, he'd also inherited his tendency toward escapism.

His mother kept him going. She kept them all going. Even though she'd been hurt, she still held her daughter to her, still gripped her husband's hand in hers, still smiled at Brian.

"Someone must've broken in while we were at Nana and Poppa's," she whispered. "He hid in our closet, waited until we were asleep... I-I don't know why he attacked me. But I...I had to protect my family, so I..."

She didn't say anything else. Becky's unbearable whimpering forced Brian to voice the panic bashing against his skull. "Who the hell *was* that guy? Was he some homeless guy that broke in to get out of the cold? Why would he hurt Mom?"

"Bri, if I told you what I saw, you and your sister would have nightmares." Brian's father finally looked up and met Brian's gaze. "Your mother and I will already have them, I'm sure of it. All I know is it was self-defense: they'll clear your mother, get her checked out at a hospital, and we can go back to normal." His lips tightened into a strained smile. He'd been fighting to earn Brian's trust back ever since they found him on that locker room floor, but the sacred trust built between parent and child had been shattered irrevocably.

Brian's eyes fell from his father's. They drifted into silence and awaited the police. His gut soured and every nerve in his body tingled until the tips of his toes and fingers felt numb. One second, he'd been watching a by-the-numbers police procedural, the next he might as well have been starring in an episode of his own.

FROM THE JOURNAL OF BRIAN JAMESON:

12/20

> It's been a long time since I wrote in this, but some awful stuff happened. A crazy guy broke in while we were at Nana and Poppa's for the weekend. He hid in Mom and Dad's closet and ambushed Mom for some reason while she was asleep. She had to shoot him. Dad called 911 and we waited in my room until the cops showed up. They ordered us to put our hands in the air and asked Mom where the gun was, then loaded her into an ambulance and drove away. They took the rest of us to the station for questioning.

> It all happened so fast I didn't really have time to process it until now. It felt like some horrible dream I'd wake up from, but I never did.

12/21

> They let us go home. We all took showers and tried to nap, but Dad was pissed they left a bunch of tape and stuff in his room. I've been sticking close to Becks while he vents.

> Mom's still in the hospital for observation. They won't let us visit her yet. Hopefully tomorrow.

12/22

We got to visit Mom today. It seems she'll get off on self-defense like Dad said. She might even be home for Christmas. Now that Dad knows she's coming home, he's chilled out. It's the first time I've ever been more worried about her than him. As tough as Mom is, I can't imagine what it must be like to kill someone. Poppa could tell me, I guess. He always talks about 'Nam.

12/23

They tested the dead guy's fingerprints and got an ID: Jim Sullivan, from Wichita, Kansas. He disappeared after he murdered his wife and three kids. One was a baby. He plucked out their eyeballs and chewed off their noses and ears.

When I think of that happening to Mom, to Dad or Becks or me, I feel sick. I guess the guy snapped. When I searched for Jim Sullivan online, a bunch of results came up with news articles. They have headlines like: ATTACK ON ALL-AMERICAN FAMILY and JAMESONS WEREN'T SULLIVAN'S FIRST VICTIM. The descriptions of the guy are pretty gross: he "emitted a half-rotten stench like week-old garbage stuffed with meat," "clawed into his victims with jagged talons," and "his skin was scratched raw, peeled back, and his hair thinned into grease-clumped strings." Worst of all, they mention his clouded eyes, the blood streaking his cheeks, and the "Glasgow smile stretching so far it tears the flesh, exposing molars and entrapped strips of meat from his victims."

It's so fucked up—like something out of a horror movie. How can this stuff happen in real life?

At least they let Mom out today.

12/24

Dad's trying to get us excited for Christmas, but it's not working. Mom won't get out of bed. Dad practically has to force-feed her. When I go in to talk to her, she lays there staring at the wall. She doesn't even notice I'm there.

Dad said he'd take Mom back to the hospital after Christmas. I wish he'd take her now, but he says they'll be busy and we should enjoy our last Christmas before I leave for college.

12/26

Christmas was a bust. While we sat around the tree opening presents and listening to cheesy music, Mom sat on the couch and stared. She didn't even open her gifts, just kept staring and smiling like she was keeping some secret to herself.

She started to smell like rotten fruit mixed with really bad BO, so Dad had to bathe her. But her hair's still thin and greasy and those scratches look infected. The rest of her skin is pale and covered in sores and cracks. It reminded me of what they wrote about the guy who attacked her, so I made Dad read the articles. He actually listened to me for once and took her to the hospital immediately.

They ran some tests, expedited the results, and said she had anemia. As for the other stuff? PTSD. In other words, they think she's traumatized by what happened and retreated inside herself. Bullshit.

Dad keeps saying "we have to do what the doctors say." Yeah, right— pills don't fix everything. Sometimes they cause more problems.

12/28

Mom's getting worse.

Now she crouches in the corner of her bedroom, rocking herself and smiling. Sometimes she giggles. She tugs chunks of her hair out. Her eyes have gone all wide and crazy. Bloodshot. She smells like sour milk, vomit, and shit.

I'm aching for her. I don't know what to do. Whenever I try to talk to her, she ignores me. She ignores all of us. She squats in the corner smiling, giggling, staring, scratching her skin and pulling her hair.

Dad says we'll take her to the hospital tomorrow, but he keeps sighing as if it's a hassle. Um, no, this is the woman you married, for better or worse, who you vowed to protect and support, who supported and protected you when you decided it was easier to kill yourself than accept that you lost your job. You owe her.

Maybe I'm being too hard on him. I don't know what it's like to vow to spend your life with someone or what it's like to watch them suffer and feel helpless.

I just want it to end, for things to go back to normal, but deep down I know they never will.

BY SUNRISE, RENEWED determination shaped his father's voice. "Wash up. Get dressed. We're taking Mom to the hospital." He went outside to start their battered old truck and get the heat going. Since it was the dead of winter, snow had already piled on their lawn and reduced the temperature to unbearable, teeth-chattering depths. Flakes still drifted down with deceptive fragility.

While Brian and Becky sat in the living room on a threadbare beige couch, staring at a Christmas tree still strung with ornaments and wrapped in glittering lights and tinsel, something shuffled into the kitchen. The refrigerator door opened. Brian whipped his head to see his mother withdrawing a package of ground beef their father was thawing for himself and the kids. Brian's mother was a vegetarian.

She clawed into the container of raw meat, shoveling bloody chunks into her mouth. While she chewed, a strange, low sound came from her throat: something between a growl and a giggle.

"Hi, Mommy! Do you feel better now?" Becky called, leaning past Brian. The horror of what he was seeing kept him glued to his seat—unable to move, to breathe, to *think*.

Their mother turned, rivulets of red liquid dripping down her grinning face. Her bloodshot eyes focused on Becky. A tendril of wormlike meat dangled from her lips. She fell to her knees and crawled underneath the table on her hands and knees. Rasping snickers escaped her bloodstained lips as she stared at Becky.

The intensity of her gaze sparked some primal instinct in Brian. He shot up from the couch and snagged his sister's hand, swiveled on his heel and rushed for the door as the table skidded across the linoleum floor. He flung open the front door—but something dragged him back. Becky's hand clung to Brian's as their mother wrapped her arms around his flailing, shrieking sister.

Brian pulled Becky with as much strength as he could muster, but his mother was winning the ghastly tug of war. Adrenaline surged through him, giving him a momentary edge until she let out a feral growl that stunned him. It reminded him of a dog guarding its food bowl.

How can this be my mother?

It only took one second of Brian's hesitation for their mother to snatch Becky and dash for the master bedroom. Brian rushed after her, his gaze fixed on Becky's frantic eyes and tear-streaked cheeks as the door slammed in his face. He jerked on the knob, tried to kick the door in—despite the *crack* of splintering wood, it didn't give.

Did she push something in front of it?

While Brian puzzled over what kept him from breaking the door down—how his mother still had the forethought to *keep him from getting in*—a shrill wail penetrated the sturdy wood. His sister screamed his name, begging for help he couldn't offer, making his gut curdle and summoning stinging tears to his eyes. He kicked and punched until his fists were bloody, until his legs ached from his knees to his feet, until he couldn't bear to listen to the hysterical screeching coming from behind that door anymore.

Forced to accept momentary defeat, Brian dashed for the front door and stumbled down the steps. He met his father midway to the truck and grabbed his shoulders, tears streaming down his cheeks as the icy winter air pierced his exposed flesh. "Dad, i-it's Mom. She...oh, God—she took Becky a-and locked her in your bedroom. You have to...you have to help her!"

He would've slumped to his knees right there in the snow, but his father gripped him by the arms. For once, his father's eyes showed the strength and focus of a leader. A role model. Suddenly, Brian was a toddler on the seesaw again, knowing his father stood behind him, ready to catch him if he tumbled. "Bri, go sit in the truck and call the police, then call Nana and Poppa. If I don't come back, drive to their house."

Brian trudged over to the truck. Before he opened the door, he glanced back at the house. His father dashed toward it, a mirage fading in and out of the snowfall.

When Brian finally entered the cab, he locked the door and sat, trying to control his heaving chest and choked sobs. A man crooned through the speakers about how it was beginning to look a lot like Christmas. Brian lowered the volume, withdrew his cell phone from his pocket, and dialed 911 with shaking hands. He tried to articulate a detailed description of what happened but ended up blubbering a bunch of indecipherable nonsense that made the dispatcher repeatedly attempt to calm him. Eventually, he got the address across and hung up, and then dialed the number to his grandparents' landline.

Nana picked up. "Hello?"

"N-nana, it's Bri—"

"Oh, hi, Brian! You hardly ever call us! How was your Christmas? Joel said—"

"Nana, you have to listen: you know Mom…Mom's been sick ever since that man hurt her. She…she took Becks and locked them in her bedroom. D-Dad's going after them a-and the police are on their way—"

"My God…" Nana's voice quieted to a whisper. "Oh, Brian… Are you… are you okay?"

"No. No, not really." Brian wiped his snot-riddled nose and dried his sticky cheeks with his sleeve. "Dad told me to wait here for him. But if he…if he doesn't come back, I'm supposed to go to your house." He shuddered, taking in a shaky, sharp breath. "I guess I'll see you soon."

Silence lingered over the line. Brian pictured his sister trapped in the bedroom with their mother, relived her chilling screams and imagined the fear she must've felt, the confusion, the pain—

A blur of motion smacked against the driver's side window. The truck lurched sideways. Brian jumped and dropped the phone.

Dad!

Brian leaned over to unlock the door. Before he could open it, his father scrambled in and knocked Brian back. He slammed the door shut behind him. His shaking hand clung to the pistol. He had a nasty injury on his neck and blood streaks pooling down into his collar. Glistening red gore covered his jacket.

"Dad, where's Becks? Is she hurt? What'd you have to do to Mom? You had to shoot her, didn't you? Oh, *God…*"

Brian ran out of breath, but his father didn't answer him. He put the truck into gear and peeled away, losing traction on the icy roads. Brian curled against the door and tried to look out the window, to see anything other than the raw memories repeating in his mind's eye, but dense fog obscured the scenery. His father stared ahead, his mind in another place.

The truck lurched forward, the radio filling the grim silence with ironic cheer. Brian muffled his sobs until the song abandoned him, fading out on the loop of the word "Christmas" almost as if it was taunting him.

THE TRUCK SQUEALED into his grandparents' yard. They waited at the porch door, their little black mutt yapping and wagging its ragged tail as it jumped against the screen. Nana pulled Brian to her as soon as he trudged up the steps, wrapping him in a warm blanket of security. His father and Poppa spoke in whispers. Brian's vision distorted, and the voices drifted further away, made nonsensical by the Doppler effect of dreams.

Once they stepped inside, Brian slumped into his favorite chair, a soft brown one with a loving dent worn into it. Flickers of conversation drifted into his ears as the dog tried to jump up with him.

"What about Becky?"

"Did what I had to—enough pain—"

"Can't tell Bri—"

Brian's father broke down into choked sobs soon escalating into mournful howls. Brian didn't want to hear more. He shoved the dog off the chair. It yelped, racing away with its tail between its legs while Brian swatted at the ornaments still dangling from Nana and Poppa's Christmas tree.

Nana wandered into the room, resting on a wooden cane. "Brian, your dad is going away for a little while. You're going to stay here with us until he gets better, okay?"

Brian skirted her cool gray gaze. "You don't have to sugarcoat it. I know he's never going to *get* better."

Poppa moseyed into the room as Nana sighed. Her eyes flitted from Brian to her husband as she wrung her liver-spotted hands. "Is Joel going back to meet with the police first?"

Poppa nodded. He scratched his reddened nose and sniffed, an old hunting cap clutched in his other hand. "Son, you want to say goodbye to your dad? I know you might not feel like it, probably relivin' a lot of things you never shoulda lived through even once, but you might regret it if you don't."

Brian's hands tightened into the velveteen material covering the chair's arms. He tried to fight back his resentment and remind himself his father had been there for him as a kid, that he'd tried to be there for both of his children in the end. His failures had to hurt *him* more than Brian— whatever he'd seen in that bedroom, whatever he'd had to do to his wife and daughter, was worse than the slideshow of images transitioning through Brian's mind.

Brian stood and followed Poppa, freezing at the metal strip between living room carpet and kitchen tile. His father sagged against the front door, his hands shielding his eyes as if confronting something unbearably bright. His shoulders bounced with every sob—a grim parody of private laughter.

"Dad," Brian tried to say, but it came out as a stifled whisper. He cleared his throat and tried again. "Dad, I know…I know you're sick. A-and I know why you overdosed: you felt helpless." He paused, struggling to keep his thoughts together, to keep his voice from cracking and the rising tears from falling. "You did what you could, and that's all that matters. You tried."

Brian stepped forward with the intent of approaching his dad for a hug, but his father lowered his hands and shook his head. "Bri, stay away. That's the best thing I can do for you now."

His father stepped forward. His ruddy cheeks glistened below puffy eyes. Brian's lips quivered, and his vision blurred. He swallowed, wiping his face, wanting to hide his weakness.

"Don't give up like I did, Bri. You might feel like you're alone, but Nana and Poppa will be here for you. And down the road, other people will be too." Brian's father managed a strained smile, a painful reminder of the woman they'd both lost. "I love you, kiddo."

He turned, opened the door, and stepped through it before Brian could see the tears fall. Brian ran after him. His hands gripped the doorframe as his father disappeared into the flurry of snow. "Dad!" he shouted, his cries muffled by the gusting winter winds. "I haven't told you this for a long time, but I…I love you."

Uncertain if his father heard him or not, Brian fell to his knees and buried his face in his hands. He sobbed, occasionally straining to suck in a breath of air once his nose clogged, choking and sputtering on the copious amount of mucus draining in the back of his throat. Someone grabbed his shoulder, tried to encourage him to come inside, but Brian didn't want to.

He wanted the cold to numb the pain.

Chapter Two: Escape

GRANTVILLE, KANSAS

Jameson Sr. Residence

1/15

I've been here two weeks now. Even though Nana's food isn't bad, I miss helping Mom cook dinner. I miss helping Becks with her art projects. I miss Dad coming home after work, cracking open a beer, and settling down in his recliner to watch TV. I miss the things I used to take for granted, the comfortable things. Our routines.

I miss them most of all.

Most of the time, I stay in my room—it used to be Dad's. I flip through photos on my tablet of Becks goofing off, of Mom sitting in her pajamas with her laptop, of Dad doing yard work or fixing the truck. Even though they're my family, it's almost like I'm looking at someone else's photos. The therapist says I'm trying to detach myself from reality to avoid grief. He might be right. When I remember that these are people I lost, that I'll never see them doing the things in those photos again, I want to curl up into a ball and sleep forever. I keep reliving the night of the attack, that week with Mom, the moment she pulled Becky's hand from mine and the door I couldn't break down to save her—who'd want to live with those memories? That sense of loss, of helplessness?

It makes sense why Dad did it now. Sometimes I want to give up too, go wherever Mom and Becks went. But Dad's still around, even if it won't be for long.

The last time they let me visit him, he was in some kind of white-walled chamber with a bed and a plexiglass window for observation. That was about a week ago. He was already showing the same symptoms as Mom: pale skin, thinning hair, lack of energy and appetite. The smile and laughter weren't there yet, but they will be soon.

A few times, Poppa answered the door to reporters who wanted to ask us questions—he yelled curses at them and slammed the door in their face. What do they want me to tell them? That my mom's and sister's bodies are still being held because of the "contamination" inside them? That even if they released them, I wouldn't be able to go to their funeral because of all the media attention? That when my dad dies, they'll keep his contaminated body too?

I couldn't even say goodbye to them. I should've spent more time with them, spent less of it with my eyes glued to a screen. Instead, they're gone, and I'm here with all these memories and regrets and not a goddamn thing I can do about them.

A WEEK LATER, Nana and Poppa's corded phone rang during supper. Poppa left to answer, but Brian only heard half of the conversation. Poppa kept nodding and saying "mm-hm" while Nana watched, her fork gripped in her trembling hand. Bits of pot roast flaked off.

"I'll be right there." Poppa placed the phone in the receiver. His calm tone didn't match the expression on his drained face.

Nana set the fork on her plate. "Do you need me to go too?"

"Stay here with Brian." He leaned in and whispered something to her, but Brian couldn't catch it. Nana gasped and nearly knocked her milk over.

"Is it Dad?"

Poppa placed a liver-spotted hand on Brian's shoulder. "I'll be right back. Ruby'll be here with you." He kissed his wife before he grabbed his keys and his worn tan coat and stepped through the front door into the blustering winter dusk.

Nana lifted her half-full plate and scraped the remnants of the roast into Rocky's food dish. He lapped at it eagerly while she placed the plate in the sink. She smoothed her hands over her skirt and gave Brian a feeble smile. "Why don't you watch the television for a bit, Brian? I need to run to the restroom."

Once she left, Brian shoveled a final forkful of tasteless green beans into his mouth. He retreated to the living room and plopped into Poppa's recliner, reaching for the remote. He cringed, disgusted by the layer of grime left by food-stained fingers pressing the buttons. Not in the mood for Poppa's favorite show, *The Beverly Hillbillies,* Brian flipped the channels for something else to distract him. He settled on *Family Feud.* Not a vast improvement.

When Nana returned, she hobbled over to her easy chair and sank into it with a sigh. Rocky hopped onto her lap, oblivious to the worries outside his home. Laughter echoed in layers as game show sound effects *zing*ed and *ding*ed all over the place.

Brian drummed his fingers on the worn arm of the recliner. "Nana, who called and what did they want?"

She scratched her permed white hair but kept watching the answers for "foods you eat in bed" as they flipped over. "The hospital asked Poppa to come in. They didn't want to discuss it over the phone."

Brian's voice rose with anticipation. "It *had* to be about Dad. But if he died, you'd go too. He hurt someone, didn't he?" Nana didn't say anything, but she stopped stroking Rocky's fur and dug her fingers into it instead. "If he did, he's going to infect other people. The only reason that Jim Sullivan guy didn't spread it first is because he killed everyone he attacked. Mom was the only one who survived."

"They don't know much about what made your parents sick. About what that man was ill with." Nana sighed and swallowed, the folds of her neck resembling a turkey's wattle. "Poppa once worked with some cows that got sick. But it was hard to tell until it was too late. People ate the contaminated meat and caught ill too. That 'Mad Cow' thing. They don't know how early this disease is contagious. They'll have to quarantine people and test them all. They're going to panic like the cows Poppa had to herd because people don't want to be herded either."

She took the remote from the table and raised the volume, an implicit signal their conversation was over.

POPPA RETURNED IN a disgruntled mood. Typically stoic and steadfast, his behavior concerned Brian: now, Poppa always seemed to slouch in his chair and watch the news or doze off. He barely ate. He sometimes cried himself to sleep late in the evening when he thought Brian and Nana had gone to bed.

Poppa didn't tell Brian what he'd been summoned to the hospital for, so Brian turned to the internet. His father had broken free of his restraints and ambushed a nurse at the hospital. When the nurse didn't report back to her superior, they sent a containment crew in to check on her. They found Brian's father gnawing on an ear clutched in his hand, pearl earring and all. He slipped past them and darted through the open door, down the hall, out of the hospital, and into the woods. Brian's passive father was gone; in his place, a vicious predator roamed.

But where did he go?

When the news cut in with an emergency bulletin at the end of *Wheel of Fortune*, Brian found out.

"This is an emergency broadcast from KSNT. The man who went missing from Topeka State Hospital, Joel Jameson, has been found after fleeing the scene of an attack on an unidentified motorist. Mr. Jameson was hiding in the trunk of the victim's car. When the victim stopped for gas, Mr. Jameson crawled through the back seat and bit the victim. Customers at the gas station witnessed the attack and were able to chase and subdue Mr. Jameson. The victim is hospitalized in critical condition. In related news, several other reports of bizarre, cannibalistic attacks have been reported not only in Topeka but in other Midwestern states. It's not yet clear how far these incidents have spread. Stay tuned for the latest information courtesy of KSNT, your source for local news."

Poppa shut the TV off and stood. He plodded outside with Rocky at his heels. Brian sat in silence, letting the news sink in while his ice cream melted in a scratched plastic bowl.

He met Nana's forlorn gaze as the front door swung shut. "Will Poppa be okay?"

Nana lifted her taped glasses from her gleaming eyes and rubbed them. "I don't know. I don't know if anything will ever be okay again. I think I'll go to bed." She stood and shuffled down the hall to her bedroom as if she was sleepwalking.

Brian followed Poppa out onto the porch. He sat smoking a pipe in a rickety rocking chair. When the tobacco sizzled, it lit the deep crevices of Poppa's face with ashen radiance.

"Poppa, can I sit with you?"

"Go 'head."

Brian sat in another rocking chair, inhaling Poppa's pipe smoke. The sweet scent made him want to sneeze. Rocky hopped up on his lap, looking at him for pets. Brian obliged.

Poppa blew out a cloud of smoke along with a prolonged sigh. "Your daddy's dead."

"I know."

A lone bird chirped as it flitted within the shadowed trees at the edge of the property.

Poppa tapped the pipe against a cracked gray ashtray. "You've been in our storm cellar, right? Remember where it is?"

Brian nodded, scratching behind Rocky's ear. It surprised him how little he felt at the news of his father's death, but in a way, he'd come to terms with its inevitability long ago.

"Good. I've got some things down there, but you'll need to help me fetch more. We might be able to wait it out a few weeks once things get bad."

"Poppa—" Brian curled his fingers against Rocky's fur. "How bad is it going to *get*?"

Poppa's blue gaze pierced Brian's, bright with vigor despite the effects of age apparent on the rest of his face. "I won't sugarcoat it for you: the world's gonna go to shit real soon. We're okay out here on the farm for a bit. I got me a .308 sniper and food to last. But eventually, either the sick ones or the folks that are left will find this place. Once this thing overwhelms the police and the military, it'll be each man for themselves. Before that happens, I'm gonna teach you how to take care of yourself and defend yourself. I'm not a book-smart man, but I'm smart in the way that matters. These urban people with their phones and computers aren't smart in the way that'll save their lives. It's the men who get their hands dirty who'll survive."

Brian thought of his mother. She'd succumbed to the illness, not the man attacking her. "And women."

"Them too. World can't go on without 'em. Ruby kept me goin' through a lot. Maybe you'll meet someone who keeps you goin' too." Poppa lifted the pipe to his lips and took a long, slow drag. "Rest up tonight. Tomorrow I'm gonna start teachin' you all I know. Write it in that journal of yours so you 'member."

Poppa blew smoke rings into the dark. They drifted away, floating up into the night sky until they disintegrated. There one second, gone the next, vanishing into the ether.

2/18

My first day of training coincided with my 19th birthday. Kind of annoying but appropriate, I guess. Poppa set up a range for target practice and let me try out his guns. The shotgun kicks too much, but I did pretty well with the handguns. Poppa has a rifle that was used to kill elephants in Africa, but I won't use it.

The reason elephants are scared of mice is because they don't want to step on them and kill them. Elephants understand that killing means taking life from something else. I think it's cruel to kill anything capable of that awareness—especially anything that's not trying to kill you.

3/9

The weather is going to get better soon. Nana spends a lot of time cooking and pickling food in jars. We have all this dry army ration stuff and even freeze-dried food that astronauts eat. But before we start going out and learning about hunting and gathering, Poppa wants me to help him inventory his survival kit. Nana helped me because he has so much shit. She says he was paranoid about getting nuked ever since he got back from the war, so he started stockpiling.

House/attic:
    Gallons of water, 10
    Cans of salmon, 5
    Dried beans, 5 bags
    Unsalted nuts, bulk cans, 3
    Trail mix, 5 bags
    Peanut butter jars, 10
    Beef/turkey jerky, 3 bags
    Instant coffee, 3 cans
    Granola bar boxes, 5
    Powdered milk, 3 cans
    Toilet paper, 3 cases
    Flashlight, 2
    Batteries, D cell, 6 cases

Backpacks, 2
First aid case, 1
Lighters, 4
Waterproof matches, 12 cases
Bowie knife, 1
Chapstick, 5
Candles, 5 boxes of 12
Aspirin, 3 bottles
Water tablets, 5
Cooking stove, 1
Spoons, 4
Forks, 4
Plastic bowls, 4
Compass, 2
Can opener, 1
Tent, 1
Sleeping bags, 4
Remington pump action shotgun, 1
Shell cases, 5 boxes of 10 (50)
Scoped .308 hunting rifle, 1
Rifle rounds, 6 boxes of 12 (72)
.45 Semi-auto Glock Pistol, 1
.45 clips, 10

Shelter:
Backpack, 1
1-liter jugs of water, 4
Food bars, 4
Blankets, 4
Ponchos, 4
Moist towels, 12
Tissues, 4
Glow-sticks, 10
First aid kit, 1 (98 pieces)
Multi-function pocket tool, 1
Solar-powered flashlight/radio/phone charger station, 1

He even has this creepy old medical dummy. He made me practice first aid stuff on it like making a tourniquet and stitching up wounds. Tomorrow he'll let me practice with a bow and arrows he made himself. He's going to show me how to make them too.

I wish I could say I'm enjoying this stuff, but it's only something to pass the time, to keep my mind off things. I still haven't forgotten what happened. I never will.

4/12

I had to kill a deer. I feel sick even writing this. While I tracked it, I knew something it didn't: that death was coming, and I was the one doing the honors. At first, I missed on purpose and the deer ran away. Poppa lectured me and made me track it all night. I decided I had to get it over with. The deer made this awful honking noise. Its ribcage swelled, fast and shallow, and it stared at me like it was asking why I'd done this to it.

I never want to kill anything again.

4/18

We heard a news report on the radio today. The man Dad infected hurt other people at the hospital. They were keeping him for observation, but he broke out and attacked a patient in the next room. Two nurses got injured trying to restrain him. Sedatives weren't working, obviously.

Since the report said the CDC was getting involved, I went to their website. Too many people are starting to catch this disease, so they're trying to identify and contain it. They were still calling it isolated but said things were happening in pockets. Their map showed Kansas with lots of threads going out from it.

People are still working, but they shut down the airport. Police barricades are set up at the state borders. I wonder if I'll ever leave this place.

Kansas might've been home for Dorothy, but it's hell for me.

5/21

Poppa set up an obstacle course for me. Sometimes I stop and do push-ups and sit-ups or use a punching bag. I think back to being unable to break down that bedroom door and pound the shit out of it until my fists hurt.

The CDC confirmed the disease spreads from person to person. Cuts from the infected get bacteria from their fingernails into the bloodstream. The bacteria destroy the part of the brain that regulates empathy: the anterior insular cortex.

What's scary is sick people can still plan. The articles I read said the man in the hospital learned where the cameras were. He hid behind the door or under the bed so they'd go looking for him. When the guards opened the door, he ambushed them, but they were armored and didn't get infected.

According to KSNT, people are being screened at hospitals and special centers now. The incubation period is one to two weeks. The CDC is working with samples to engineer a vaccine but haven't had any success yet. If only those fucking doctors had taken us seriously. I'll bet they're regretting it too.

They're calling it "The Stalker Disease" because of how the infected hunt: they hone in on their prey, watch and wait, then strike from a hidden location. They could be anywhere: under beds and tables, behind curtains, in closets, the dark corners of buildings, hidden in woods, caves—anywhere. Everywhere. I'd be just like that deer I hunted, blissfully unaware that something was watching my every move and waiting to kill me—or worse.

Poppa started working on barricading the doors and windows today. Next, we're going to get rid of furniture people can hide in or under and move everything else against the walls. He already pulled the doors off the closets and emptied them. Nana thought he was crazy at first, but they had a long talk and she helped us. Poor Rocky can't make up his mind between barking or hiding.

7/4

Happy Fourth of July (you can't see me rolling my eyes). Nana made a bunch of food and Poppa is grilling. Rocky won't leave him alone because he begs for scraps of meat and gets them.

The CDC still has us blocked in. Crime rates have gone up and there's a lot of looting and rioting. People are quitting their jobs because it's getting too dangerous. Luckily for Nana and Poppa, they've been retired for a while.

Tomorrow, we have to go out and get tested.

8/21

Our tests came back clean, but we're still under quarantine. They want to force everyone into shelters, but a lot of people like Poppa refuse to go and now the police and civilians are fighting. The military is coming in.

The news reported a case in Colorado today. Poppa won't leave the property. He sits in front of the TV all day and keeps a radio next to him in bed at night. Nana says she can't sleep with the blasted thing blaring at her, so she knits and does crossword puzzles in the living room. Most of the time, she falls asleep out there, so I throw a blanket over her.

We started working on fortifying the fence around the house today. We made an air horn alarm with a trip wire attached and an explosive one out of matches to create a flash. That way we can sleep and not have to worry constantly about keeping an eye out for intruders.

9/23

More traps today. Poppa says no one is going to visit the property anymore, so we might as well be on the offensive. He got out his chainsaw and cut down a bunch of trees, and we made a swinging log trap. We dug pits and set up a bunch of sharp sticks and rusty railroad spikes in them. Nasty stuff.

10/11

Today we got back from making traps and found Nana in front of the TV holding on to Rocky for dear life. The screen looked distorted and the anchors kept stumbling on their words. Their hands shook while they read from their papers.

There was an attack in Idaho and several in Nebraska. The containment failed: it's an epidemic.

The president cut into Our Regular Programming™ to declare a state of emergency because the riots got so bad the police went home to protect their families. The military is going to start setting up checkpoints. The streets are filled with looters. Stores are closed. The news station was shutting down and said the only future updates would be on the radio and the internet—while they lasted.

Then the TV buzzed, and the screen went fuzzy with static.

10/31

Happy Halloween, I guess.

Stalkers have spread to California and Florida. Poppa's the only one who goes outside. He takes his shotgun everywhere, even into the bathroom. Radio reports say people have formed gangs to ransack and loot stores. They even try breaking into houses.

No one has tried here yet. The power is still on and the internet still works.

11/30

Now all that works is the radio. The power went out three days ago when the last employees stopped going to work at the power plants. Kansas is a ghost state. Everything in a five-hundred-mile radius is reaching peak frenzy. Seventy-five percent of the population has turned or been killed.

Because I've been stuck here on the farm, it didn't really hit me how bad things were. Radios, TVs, and computer screens filter everything, make it seem fake. But Poppa took me out so I could see something in the real world: a Stalker trapped in one of our spike pits.

It looked worse than Mom. The skin was raw and torn, like someone with bad rashes who'd been scratching a lot. The stench of rotten eggs mixed with a Porta-Potty at a summer fair filled the air around it. The eyes staring up at us were milky white. Its scalp was bald and bloody. As always, it smiled.

Poppa made me take it out with an arrow. It stopped laughing, but a strange sound trickled out of it—a hiss mixed with a moan. Probably only its last breath, but what if it wasn't? What if it was trying to say something? If there's still a consciousness trapped in there, the same memories and thoughts of the person they once were?

When I heard those gunshots eleven months ago, I had no idea my life would change forever, let alone that I'd be at Ground Zero for some pandemic. Now everyone's lives have changed—if they're lucky enough to have one.

This might be the end of the world.

Chapter Three: Below/Above

12/4, GRANTVILLE, KANSAS

Jameson Sr. Residence
Just past midnight

The horrid screech of an air horn and strobe-like flashes of light woke Brian. He scrambled for the pistol he kept on his bedside table and peered through the boards covering his window, struggling to identify vague shapes in the erratic bursts of brightness.

The hair on the back of his neck stood on end when several figures slipped out from the edge of the moonlit woods and scurried toward the house.

"Brian!"

He spun around, heart thumping so fast and hard it hurt.

Poppa clutched his shotgun in both hands. "Grab what you need—you and Ruby are goin' into the cellar."

"But Poppa, I can help—"

Poppa jerked Brian away from the window. "No time, boy. Hurry up!"

Brian grabbed his backpack and ran after Poppa into the living room. Nana stood with a fleece coat on, covering her face with trembling hands. Rocky leaped against the boarded windows and barked until Poppa yelled at him to stop.

Poppa approached Nana and handed her something. "Ruby, take Brian to the shelter. I'll distract 'em, join you when I can."

"Buh-but Max—"

"I got to make sure you two are safe first." Poppa grabbed Nana's shoulders and pecked her cheek. She flung her arms around him and sobbed, afraid to let go. Adrenaline amplified Brian's confusion—he wanted to go, to *move*.

"No time for cryin'." Poppa pried himself from Nana's arms. "Go on, now. Don't worry about me."

"I love you, honey!" Nana cried as she shuffled away from him.

"Love you too, sweetheart." Poppa ran to the living room windows and swapped his shotgun for the rifle he kept nearby. "Stay low, in the shadows—I'm gonna fire a few shots to distract 'em. Look out for your nana, Brian."

Brian guided his grandmother toward the back door by her sweaty palm. He opened the door and ushered Nana through, shutting it behind him. His other hand clung to his pistol as he crouched against the side of the house in the crisp night air.

A shot shattered the silence: Poppa's rifle.

An excited flurry of voices followed. Not Stalkers.

People.

Brian and Nana slunk through the moonlit snow. He swept their footprints away to hide their path from the invaders. Another shot cracked the air. Brian moved faster, jerking Nana along with him as she muffled an anguished cry. Shadows slunk behind the barn about fifty feet away. One slumped into the snow after another shot discharged—a benefit of Poppa's night-vision scope and keen eyesight.

When they made it to the hatch, Nana's shaking hand struggled with the key. Brian snatched it from her and took over. He fumbled for the keyhole until the key slid in and turned with a *click*. Brian exhaled and lifted the hatch door.

"Hurry, Nana!" he whispered. He pressed his hand to her back and shoved her a little harder than he meant to.

Once she was down, he followed and lowered the lid until it blocked the luminous moon and shimmering stars overhead. It clicked shut, bolts interlocking with a reassuring *clink*. He felt for the rungs of the ladder until his feet grazed the ground.

A horrifying sea of darkness surrounded them, seemingly infinite.

12/6

We've been down here for two days.

There are two rooms: one for supplies and another with two small beds for sleeping. The floors are dirt and the walls are concrete. There's an electrical outlet (powered by Poppa's generator), but my phone has no service. My solar charger still had juice, so I hooked up my tablet and used that to pass the time. But it ran out, so here I am.

Nana sleeps most of the time. I keep wondering what's going on above and if Poppa is okay. Just like Mom, he's the glue that holds us together.

Bathed in the flickering glow of a lantern, Brian continued to write, tapping his foot to a song from his playlist. Something brushed his arm. His hand jerked, snapping the lead tip of his pencil. He yanked his earbuds out and swapped the pencil for the grip of a handgun.

"What is that, Brian?" The sound of Nana's weary voice calmed him. The rustling noises coming from the hatch had the opposite effect. "You think that's Max?"

"Shh." Brian held a finger to his mouth and lowered his legs over the edge of his bed. Faint voices echoed through the door. He approached it to listen but couldn't decipher any of the dialogue. *More than one. Not him.*

Bolt cutters wouldn't work on the industrial deadbolts. The only way in was with a key taken from Poppa's cold dead hands. Brian's gut knotted.

The noise stopped.

He sat on Nana's bed beside her, the pistol trapped between his knees as he tried to halt all the "what-if" scenarios circling in his mind.

When Nana spoke, he met her forlorn gaze. "Brian, we've lost him. The whole *world's* lost it."

A rigid smile strained Brian's lips. "Nana, don't give up. Poppa's probably hiding somewhere."

She curled up in bed with her fuzzy blue blanket. "I'm going to sleep for a little bit."

Brian let her be, rummaging for the multi-tool to sharpen his pencil. It created a swirl of wood as if he was peeling an apple. The sharpened tip hovered over the bare space of his journal page, but it remained as blank as his mind had gone.

SINCE HE WAS unable to write, Brian had fallen asleep. When he woke, Nana was still out cold. He turned on a lantern and carried it over to her bed. "Nana?"

She didn't answer. He reached out to shake her, his hand trembling in the milky-white glow. "Nana, you okay?"

Nothing. He swallowed as a wave of nausea traveled from his gut to the insides of his cheeks, filling them with bitter fluid.

He gripped her shoulder and turned her over. Glassy eyes stared back at him from above an open mouth with a stream of foam and half-dissolved capsules dried around it. Her frail hand clutched an empty orange container.

Brian collapsed to the ground, gasping for air, screwing his eyes shut in a bid to force away past and present. Tears fought their way past his eyelids and he wept until he couldn't breathe, shuddering violently, gasping for air. He hugged his knees to his body, rocking back and forth, burying his face in them.

I'm alone. I'm alone I'm alone I'm—

He snatched the multi-tool and pressed the tip of a small knife into his left wrist. A drop of blood escaped, trickling down the vein.

But he couldn't force himself to finish it.

He tossed it and reached for the pistol. The cold, bitter barrel entered his mouth. His finger trembled on the trigger.

Will someone find me down here with a gun in my hand and my brains on the wall? Find Nana bloated and starting to rot?

Or no one will find us at all.

The pain won't last. I won't feel anything ever again. The world will go on without me.

Fear gripped him deep inside, a black hole that spread outward until he hyperventilated. The concept of not existing, of not knowing what that *meant*, frightened him more than anything else ever could.

"Don't give up like I did, Bri."

He yanked the gun from his mouth.

I shouldn't be thinking like this. Poppa didn't spend all that time training me just so I could kill myself. He might be alive—I need to go out there and look for him.

But he couldn't leave his grandmother. Pictures in the family photo albums showed her holding him in her lap, his chubby baby fingers straining for her glasses. He used to sit in the living room with her, butt planted in that dented brown chair, and talk about his favorite cartoons even though she didn't watch them. When he and Becky begged her to take them to McDonald's for the latest Happy Meal toys, she obliged without protest. Every Christmas, she baked them a tin of cookies to take home.

She was gone in body but lived on in spirit, in *him*, and she deserved better than this.

Brian took the camping shovel from Poppa's stash and plunged it into the earth. The moist scent seeped into his nostrils. He inhaled heartily and dug for hours without pausing; despite his aching arms, he found the act cathartic.

He forced himself to rise and face Nana. He'd never forget this moment, the first time he'd ever been confronted with a dead body. A shell whose essence had been reduced to memories as intangible as air.

It wasn't disgust that rose in his throat or curdled his stomach. It was the ache of loss, of permanence, another stolen goodbye.

He wrapped Nana's already stiffening body in her pale blue blanket and struggled to lift her, surprised by how heavy she was despite her fragile bones and skin. Sobs choked him as he placed her in the hole and swept clumps of dirt over a beloved face warped by death.

Once he'd filled her grave, he packed the dirt and smoothed it over. He spelled "Ruby" above it with waterproof matches, then crawled into bed covered in dirt and sweat. Hot tears continued to trickle from the corners of his eyes right up to the moment he passed out.

ONCE BRIAN RECOVERED, he jotted an entry in his journal:

12/7

I'm leaving the cellar today. Wish me luck.

He grabbed the camping backpack Poppa kept stored in the cellar and squeezed as much of their supplies as he could into the various compartments. He slung it over his shoulders along with his bow and quiver. The overstuffed backpack might as well have been the weight of the world bearing down on him like Atlas.

Brian tugged on a sturdy pair of hiking boots and climbed the ladder with the pistol clutched in one hand. He paused, listening for noise before he pulled the lever to unlock the hatch. It slid with a resonant *thunk* that made him swallow.

Here goes nothing.

He pushed the cover up, squinting as his eyes adjusted to the brilliant midday sun. The sunshine was a sharp contrast to the weak flashlights and lanterns they'd used in the dim shelter.

A twittering bird created a misleading sense of calm. Brian poked his head through the open hatch to survey the driveway and yard: the barn doors were still shut, but the pig pen was open. A loose pig frolicked in the snow nearby. The chicken coop appeared to be undisturbed. Several dark objects lay in the distance, half-covered by white blankets. Clumps of snow coated the fringe of skeletal trees beyond the yard.

Brian emerged from the hatch, shut it, and beelined for the cover of Nana's dead azalea bushes along the side of the house. He clung to the bow in case something emerged from the milky mist of falling snow. The occasional tinkle of wind chimes from the porch disrupted the eerie silence surrounding the farm.

Something had shattered the door to the porch into jagged chunks of wood. A trail of bloody swirls and streaks led into the house, left by a foot which had become intimately acquainted with Poppa's homemade nail spikes.

Brian upended a patio couch and blocked the busted doorway with it. The front door hung open, revealing shadow-covered shapes within the kitchen. This was the point of no return: his grandparents' comfortable home had been warped into a haven for Stalkers and survivors alike.

Brian opted for courage and silence, swapping the pistol for the bow and keeping the bowstring taut. Balancing the arrow over his fingers and maintaining the tension made his muscles ache. He stepped through the front door and entered the house.

The lights flickered on when he elbowed the switch. Poppa's generator still had juice. But this didn't mean he was still around; if the intruders had overcome him, they wouldn't sabotage something as useful as a generator.

The state of the kitchen displayed a frightening picture. Cabinet doors hung open, stripped of all contents, and a dim sliver of light cracked through the refrigerator door. Plates, utensils, opened boxes, and jugs were scattered along the counter and dining room table. Near the sink, a gloved hand with a milk-caked spoon stretched across the floor. Brian inched toward it.

He let out a shaky breath. Not Poppa. Judging by the dark hole seared into the temple, it was one of Poppa's victims. He'd taught Brian to aim for the temple, a clear trajectory through the brain.

Brian moved into the living room, tracking the smudged trail of blood left by the injured foot. A gigantic hole shattered the tube TV into a square of reflective shards. Someone's body was draped over Poppa's recliner, but another temple shot injected a surge of relief into Brian. The shot Poppa fired into this intruder had also destroyed the TV screen.

He followed the dried blood up the hallway. It detoured into the guest bathroom before continuing to the master bedroom. *I have to check every room. Poppa could be in there. If not, I still need to take down anything that could take* me *down.*

Using his foot, Brian nudged the cracked door all the way open. Bloody handprints smeared the shower's tiled wall and the torn yellow curtain. The tub was empty. Someone had opened the medicine cabinet and scattered pills and capsules in the sink. Brian moved on.

Next, the spare bedroom where Brian had been staying. The rest of his belongings were still piled in a corner, untouched: clothes, toiletries, and shoes. Whoever'd made it this far hadn't been interested in rummaging. They'd been in a hurry, in pain, on a different mission.

Only the master bedroom and the attic remained.

Droplets of dried blood led Brian to the master bedroom. His feet sank soundlessly into the thin, aged carpet. When he reached the doorframe, he pressed his side to it and poked his head around to peer into the room.

Poppa's ancient computer sat near the window, surrounded by dusty books, a joystick, and boxes of PC games. Stacks of old magazines and yellowing sewing patterns were piled on a couch across from the window. Sunlight streamed through the sheer white window shade, illuminating Nana's sewing machine.

She'll never sew any of those patterns. Poppa will never play those games again.

Brian swallowed back his sentiments and rushed into the room. He swept into the blush-pink bathroom, arrow aimed, immediately scrunching his nose at a foul stench. A bullet casing lay at the bottom of the cloudy red toilet bowl. Bloodied tweezers and spools of Nana's sewing thread were in the sink. The wound had been cleaned here—but where had the injured person gone next?

The shower curtain remained, imposing and as Pepto-Bismol pink as the rest of the bathroom. Brian pulled the bowstring taut, ready to sink an arrow into whatever hid behind the curtain.

But what if it's Poppa?

Shouting his name would give Brian's presence away. But how else could he be sure he wasn't going to sink an arrow into his own grandfather?

If someone's there, I need to trigger them to come out from behind the curtain.

He grabbed the clean end of the tweezers, backed away, and hefted them through the crack of the curtain into the tub. They clattered but quickly quieted. Nothing moved.

He reached for the curtain, his hand shaking.

Something clicked behind his head. He froze.

A man behind Brian said, "I'll take that," and the curtain ripped free of the shower rod with a metallic clatter. Brian ducked, but a suffocating weight trapped him in the vinyl. Someone yelled, something exploded—maniacal laughter followed. *Fuck fuck fuck, one of them—*

Brian stopped wriggling within the confines of the curtain. He stared up at vague shapes through the opaque vinyl, the rancid stench from earlier now clouded by gunpowder. The shadows shifted as the horrible laughter and shrieking moved away from the bathroom. Brian covered his mouth, staring up at hazy pink as he listened to the struggle.

Two ear-splitting explosions preceded a chilling scream. More screams, devolving into desperate pleas that abruptly cut off. Wet gurgling faded in and out. A groan followed, then a faint but constant squelching.

Brian tried to calm his rapid breaths. He'd heard those sounds before from behind his parents' bedroom door. They haunted his nightmares. His sister's pleas for him to save her—

I can't go back. I'm here, now, trapped in a house with one of those things. Trapped underneath a fucking shower curtain.

If he waited, it might find him. He had to kill it while it was distracted.

If I move the curtain, it'll hear me. Can it smell me? Does it know I'm here?

He hadn't even *seen* it, only a blur of the curtain covering him. It hadn't grazed him, he was sure of that—the tacky pink curtain protected him like it once protected Nana and Poppa's vulnerable bathing bodies.

Brian tested the waters by moving the curtain. The wet sounds continued. He turned onto his stomach, still underneath the curtain. The munching paused. He held his breath. Immeasurable time passed before the noises resumed. He exhaled.

He lifted the curtain and poked his head out. The door to the master bedroom was open, revealing a pair of twitching feet on the floor.

Is...is that guy still alive?

Brian covered his mouth. The thought of being eaten *alive* filled him with a dread that chilled his bones and curdled his empty stomach. He prayed Becky had already bled out before she felt much more.

Stop thinking about things you can't change. Don't fuck this up.

Brian opted for the pistol over the bow, which would make too much vinyl-crinkling noise in his efforts to set the shot up. He steadied his right hand with his left and aimed down the pistol sights at the figure hunched over the man's twitching legs. It seemed to be pulling something apart with its arms, like elevator doors that wouldn't open. Both bodies were dressed in camouflaged hunting gear.

Once he edged over enough to see the thing's head, Brian squeezed the trigger. The jerking motion of the slide startled him, but he followed through, not taking his finger off the trigger. The loud *pop* rattled the insides of his ears as he fired again, watching the bloodied head jerk back and fall forward. It collapsed onto its hapless victim, unmoving.

Brian flung the curtain from himself and entered the master bedroom. A strange hybrid of croaking and a persisting snicker kept him on the razor's edge. He fired two more rounds, and everything fell silent.

The Stalker's face rested in the torn chest of the man who'd held a gun to Brian's back. The man's glassy eyes stared at the ceiling and blood dribbled from the corners of his mouth. Unable to bear the image, Brian jerked the comforter from the bed—hand-knit by Nana—and tossed it over the forever-entwined bodies of victim and assailant.

He slumped onto the bed, making the box-spring squeal in protest. His breath caught in his throat when he saw someone staring back at him—but it was only his own reflection in the bedroom mirror. Still, he barely recognized himself.

The gloss of youth seemed to have disappeared. He was taller, thinner, leaner. His hair poked out from underneath his beanie in tarnished golden curls. A thin layer of dirt coated his tan skin, once-clear blue eyes now watery and reddened. The dimple that showed when he smiled hid behind a tired grimace. When he tried, he couldn't even force himself *to* smile.

He aimed the pistol at his reflection, mock-firing.

"Bang. Rest in pieces, Brian Jameson."

Chapter Four: The Barn

12/7, GRANTVILLE, KANSAS

Jameson Sr. Residence
Early evening

Brian allowed himself a few moments of reflection, but he couldn't suppress the greasy scent of exposed innards penetrating Nana's knit comforter. He left to investigate the attic, shutting the door behind him and sealing that tomb forever.

After tossing a few glowsticks into the attic for light, Brian discovered Poppa's survival stash remained untouched. Brian experienced a joy that was new to him—the joy of ownership, of discovery, and in this case, a joy that seemed to promise him longer odds of survival. The only thing missing was Poppa himself.

The barn. That's the last place he'd go.

Brian descended from the attic and headed for the front door. Memories of holidays spent in the house took on a nostalgic haze as if his mind saw them through a photo-editing filter: the tree at Christmas with his family gathered around and the pleased smile Poppa always had when he got his annual gift of new socks; the kitchen table set with dishes filled with food, and Poppa's stern warnings to keep elbows off the table; Easter egg hunts in the yard with Becky giggling in a sunny yellow dress while the adults watched the children with reverent smiles.

Only echoes remained. A dead body slumped over Poppa's recliner where he used to watch *Matlock* and *M*A*S*H* reruns. The body on the kitchen floor occupied the spot where Becky stood on a step stool helping Nana with dishes. The eviscerated man and the Stalker entangled with him stole Poppa and Nana's places in their shared bedroom.

A surreal feeling overwhelmed Brian, a sense of disconnection. *Was it all a dream? Did any of it ever happen? Am I just now waking up?*

When he stepped through the front door, freezing cold air slapped him in the face and jolted him back to reality.

Brian crept along the house until he reached Poppa's battered truck. The door was open, and the wires of the ignition were loose. Brian didn't think driving was a great idea: he'd heard all the roads were closed and it would be a risky endeavor to undertake in the snow.

Poppa's crinkled McDonald's cup and Skoal tobacco filled Brian with a swell of fondness he'd never thought he'd feel for such things. It wasn't the objects themselves but how they reminded him of Poppa's routines. One of Nana's murder mysteries, *Murder Comes Knocking*, lay on the floor of the passenger side. It still had a bookmark in it, page sixty-eight. He tucked it into his backpack, taking care not to crease the pages so he could honor Nana's habit of keeping her books in pristine condition.

Brian dashed over to the side of the barn. A dog barked from inside it. *Rocky? He might've followed Poppa in there.*

For the first time in a while, Brian felt hopeful.

He circled to the front and opened the doors, cringing as they creaked. Alert barks blended with inquisitive moos as the setting sun cast a beam of light through a window high along the rear wall. Curious pairs of dark eyes watched him while he hefted the bow and strung an arrow over his fingers. Atop the loft, a small dog barked, leaping up and down in enthusiastic circles.

Beside it, a rifle scope glinted—and lowered. "Bri?"

Brian's knees nearly buckled. He released the arrow and wiped his eyes with his elbow. "Poppa! Are you okay?"

"Brian, shut that door and climb up here. Don't be gettin' sentimental. It'll get you killed."

Poppa's characteristic coarseness relieved Brian. He shut the door and hurried past the rows of befuddled cows. After he scrambled up the ladder, he flung himself onto his grandfather, not giving a shit if Poppa found hugs awkward or not. "Poppa, I was so worried when...when you didn't come for us—but I knew you wouldn't go without a fight. I saw those bodies a-and I knew I had to keep looking."

Poppa patted Brian's back before he withdrew from him. "You okay?"

Brian nodded.

Poppa's thin lips shifted from a slight smile into a frown. "Your Nana...somethin' happened to her, didn't it?"

Brian couldn't bring himself to answer. Poppa's wrinkled face sagged in defeat, his small eyes red and watery. "Knew this world would be too much for her one day. I was scared to let her go down there with those meds but thought havin' you around might keep her strong. I'm sorry, son. Ain't somethin' you should've had to deal with, 'specially not after what happened with your daddy."

Brian kneeled and pulled Rocky to him, trying to silence the excited dog. He looked up at Poppa. "Why didn't you come for us? What happened?"

Poppa sat atop a bale of hay, rifle between his knees. "After I sent you and Ruby down, I set a few more traps and holed up in the house. Took me some ammo and my sniper and set to shootin'. Traps got a few of 'em. Shot three more in the driveway when the idiots stepped on the rakes I buried, but two more snuck around the house and broke in. One of 'em got a foot full of nails, hauled ass down the hall. But a couple more came in after him, so I had to take 'em out and make a break for the barn. Saw one of 'em come out the woods on the way and popped him—another followed not long after. I've been waitin' here so I could finish 'em off and go check on you, but the buggers ain't left the house."

"Someone tried to get into the cellar," Brian said. "Nana and I thought it might've been you, but they gave up and left. After that, Nana... She went to sleep and never woke up."

"Did you bury her?"

Brian nodded, looking away. He pressed his face into Rocky's fur.

A long silence preceded Poppa's response. "She still down there?"

Brian nodded again, looking up in a bid to suppress tears threatening to surface.

Poppa sniffed, fighting a battle of his own. "So you went into the house lookin' for me? Or you come straight here to the barn?"

"The house. Those men were there. They're dead now." Brian let go of Rocky and sat on the bale of hay across from his grandfather.

"You kill 'em?"

Brian met Poppa's glassy eyes. "I think the guy you shot might've been infected. He took the bullet out somehow and hid in the bathtub. The other guy with the messed-up foot caught me while I was trying to see what was behind the curtain. I guess the Stalker heard him because he jumped out of the shower and pulled the whole curtain down on top of me. He started— he started eating the other guy. I shot them both."

"Did you get hurt?"

Brian shook his head.

"Good." Poppa exhaled. "Mental scars are bad enough. Don't need no others." He scratched his whisker-speckled chin. "One of them Stalkers took a bullet outta itself? I knew they could plan an ambush an' all, but I ain't never heard of 'em doin' nothin' like *that*."

"When Mom took Becky, she ran into the bedroom with her, locked the door—I think she even *barricaded* it." Brian shuddered. "Maybe she wasn't all the way gone yet. This guy either. He stank and looked messed up, but he was still dressed and..." Brian didn't want to think back to either memory anymore, so he trailed off and stared at his dirty boots.

Poppa reached over and patted his knee. "You're a smart kid. That's why I spent all that time teachin' you. Glad we're together, Bri."

Brian managed a shaky smile. "Me too, Poppa." He set his belongings beside him, his shoulders aching from the weight. "Everything's still in the attic. Should we go back to the house?"

Poppa shook his head. "More of 'em will come around, Stalkers and looters both. All the noise these fools made'll draw 'em in, and it's too risky to waste time settin' up more traps. Best to get some rest, then start movin'." Poppa patted Rocky as he hopped up alongside him. "We'll feed these animals first, let 'em loose so they can go where they please. Grab up whatever we can carry: food, water, weapons. Make sure we got good boots for hiking in case we can't get a couple of these old girls to carry us."

A weak chortle slipped out of Brian. "We're riding *cows*?"

Poppa managed a small smile. "Cows're better than a car—easier to fuel them up and make less noise. Roads'll be cluttered, barricaded, and cows can make it through where a car can't. Next best thing'd be a bicycle, but you can't tote much on that. If we stick to the open, we should be safe from Stalkers. They like hidin'. Even if we're exposed to other people, we can take a wound so long as they ain't infected. It's a sure shot we get infected if a Stalker bites or scratches us." Poppa sighed deeply. "You 'member Earl, right? My old army pal...had those twin grandkids you were friends with. I'll call him on the HAM radio and make sure they're okay."

Anxiety and anticipation dueled within Brian. Memories of a log cabin and a farm outside a big city returned to him. A pair of dark-haired, tawny-skinned children, Louis and Eva. His best friends—birthday parties, Trick-or-Treating, sleepovers—until his father overdosed and Brian's mother started homeschooling him to save him from the cruel taunts of children who knew too much and too little.

But their friendship hadn't ended with the usual whimper of children who simply grew apart—it ended with a physical altercation between Brian and Louis that caused both their parents to keep them from hanging out ever again. Frightened any other friends he made would be torn from him, Brian never let himself get close to any of the people he met during his summer jobs (YMCA lifeguard, mowing lawns, movie theater attendant).

The thought of seeing the twins again, of seeing who they'd become over the years, excited him. But he feared their memories of him weren't viewed through such rose-colored lenses—especially Louis, who Brian had left with a physical scar he feared might also be mental.

While Brian played tug-of-war with his feelings, Poppa put in the call to Earl. "Just me and my grandson. My wife didn't make it." Pause. "Thanks, Earl. Glad to hear the twins are holdin' up." Longer pause. "Good to know I still got a friend—everyone's out for themselves now. Mm-hm. I'm more scared of people than those things too. You and I know what they're capable of." Tiny pause. "Yep. See you soon. Thanks, buddy."

"So we're going to Earl's for sure?" Brian's fatigue kicked him in the face from out of nowhere—like the time he'd walked in front of Becky on her swing-set and she'd sent him sprawling onto his ass in the grass.

Poppa scratched Rocky's head. "We'll leave soon as the sun rises. Leaves us enough time to get some rest."

Brian rolled out a sleeping bag and curled up in it. "Why're you more scared of people than Stalkers, Poppa? I mean, Stalkers can hide anywhere, they're smart, and they wait for us, watch us."

Poppa remained on the haystack with Rocky in his lap. He frowned, the light catching him just right and displaying patches of hair that stuck out from his nose and ears. "Stalkers are animals. Sure, they're clever enough to hide, to hunt, but they ain't out there to *hurt*. Lions'll eat a gazelle alive if they can't kill it, but at least they *try* first. Most of the time, people hurt each other without intent to kill. Only the cleverest and cruelest of creatures enjoy makin' others suffer."

"How can you be sure they aren't out there to hurt? They smile. They *laugh*." Brian shivered as he thought of the body sprawled over the eviscerated man in Nana and Poppa's bedroom.

"I don't think they got any control over it. I've seen people laugh at the pain they cause. I know the look they get in their eyes." Poppa's Adam's apple bobbed as he gulped. After a deep sigh, he cleared his throat. "You hear about the My Lai massacre in school?"

Brian shook his head. "Most of the homeschool curriculums were pretty religious. Mom said they kept a lot of real history out of the books. She taught around it, but I don't think she ever mentioned that."

"My Lai was a hamlet, part of a village in South Vietnam called Son My. They thought it was a base for the Viet Cong, so Charlie Company went in there to clean it up. It was just a bunch of old men, women, and children. They tried to convince us the children were strapped with grenades, that the women had knives under their dresses and the old men had 'em in their walkin' canes. Not a one of 'em had a weapon as far as I know. Just village people tryin' to live their lives. When I tried to fight it, they told me they'd put me to a wall and execute me with the villagers. I stopped fightin' it.

"About five hundred were slaughtered. Piles of 'em on the roadside, down wells, burned in their village. Even shot the animals. Dead babies clutched in their mothers' arms. One time a bunch of women threw themselves over the children and got shot up. The kids survived, but as soon as they walked out, they got shot too. Women were mutilated and tortured. Pack mentality, they call it. War was an excuse for these barbarians to go unpunished for being murderers and rapists.

"Not all of us were like that, but we were outnumbered. The slaughter didn't stop until air support came by, noticed things wasn't right. They were killin' people with grenade launchers, machine guns, throwin' them alive into wells with a grenade chaser. Fella by the name of Thompson reported it all and the order was called in to stop. A few kids survived, I think. They tried to cover it up for a long time, but a man was there takin' pictures, documentin' it all. One of those pictures shows a coupla women with babies, one's screamin'. Lady on the right with her baby, she's buttonin' up her shirt 'cause a man just got finished with her. After that picture got took, they were filled with machine gun bullets. I learned then how savage people can be."

The wind continued to whistle outside as the lantern illuminated Poppa's glassy blue eyes. "Sometimes I wish I'd let them shoot me and throw me in one of those piles. When I was in those bloody marshlands, bugs buzzin' around me and the stench of death and gunpowder in the air, I used to think about puttin' the barrel of my gun to my temple and pullin' the trigger. But I got a letter from Ruby, said she'd given birth to your dad. I didn't even know she was pregnant. She didn't want to worry me, knew I'd want to rush home to be with her. Thought I owed it to your dad to be there for him since I took so many babies and their mothers from the world."

Brian wiped his moist eyes. "Sometimes…sometimes it seems easier to give up, but I'm scared if I die, there'll be nothing."

"Well, ol' Teddy Roosevelt once said, 'Nothin' in the world is worth havin' or doin' unless it means effort, pain, and difficulty. I've never in my life envied a human being who led an easy life. I've envied a great many people who led difficult lives and led them well.'"

Brian considered the former president's words. He doubted he'd make much sense of them this instant, or even in the next week. Perhaps he'd find some meaning in them weeks or months down the road.

As he closed his eyes and tried to drift away, a montage of scenes haunted him: the hybrid screams of his sister and the man who'd held the gun to his back; the guttural growls and manic laughter of the Stalkers; the bodies of babies and the elderly being blown to smithereens inside a well; crying women on their backs, pinned by soldiers with senseless smiles and emptiness in their eyes.

Despite the horror of the things he'd experienced, he feared the worst was yet to come.

Chapter Five: The Trip

12/8, GRANTVILLE, KANSAS

Jameson Sr. Barn
Sunrise

Light streamed through the window in a radiant haze, illuminating dust that swirled in the air and never seemed to fall. Time to go.

Brian and Poppa gathered their belongings and left to feed the animals, leaving their pens and coops open so they had a chance at survival. When they finished, they headed for the house with Rocky hopping at their heels. The sheen of snow coating the silent landscape made it seem like things had started fresh—like they were the only humans left in the world.

Poppa stopped to examine the bodies of the men he'd shot. He flipped them over without hesitation. They turned rigidly, locked in rigor mortis and frozen by the winter air.

Poppa turned their pockets inside out and tossed the contents to Brian. Brian examined them while Poppa grabbed their weapons. Coins clanked in his hands along with pieces of jewelry and a clip of pistol ammo. A tarnished pocket watch bore an inscription: *"To H—Time is infinite and so is my love for you—L."*

This tiny snippet of humanity made Brian question who "H" had been before he'd been reduced to a bloated body with a hole in his head.

Once Poppa finished sorting through their loot, Brian followed him toward the house. Poppa pushed the couch out of the doorframe while Brian glanced at the animals starting to wander outside their homes. It surprised him how few there were. Perhaps they sensed the change in the air, frightened of the new world.

They rushed to the attic in swift but careful bursts of movement. Rocky remained downstairs to alert them of intruders while they retrieved anything they could shove in their backpacks. They had one each for personal belongings and two loaded with supplies. When these bulged, pushed to the limit of their capacity, Brian and Poppa hurried out of the house.

Poppa stopped and looked back at it. Brian stood beside him, thinking of all the nights he'd spent there, all the meals they'd shared, all those moments of communal laughter and joy. Death had defiled their sanctuary.

Poppa's eyes squinted in the light of the ascending sun. His furrowed brow and deepening grimace made him look resolute but miserable; he resembled the salty sea captain in *Jaws* more than ever. "I never thought I'd be leavin' my house. My land, my farm." Poppa squeezed his shining eyes shut. "My *wife...*"

Brian yearned to comfort his grandfather, who seldom exposed his vulnerability, but they were both physically exposed standing out in the open. "Best to keep moving, Poppa. What's done is done."

Poppa nodded and wiped his eyes with his arm, staining the fleece coat sleeve. "You're right, son." He patted Brian on the shoulder, reaching down since he stood a good five inches taller than Brian—and, unlike Nana, his back didn't hunch. "I'll say goodbye to Ruby real quick. You don't need to go down there no more. Stay up here with Rocky and holler down if you need me."

Brian followed him to the hatch, more than happy to avoid the descent into the desolate shelter. While Poppa climbed down to bid his wife a final farewell, Brian cradled Rocky and kept watch. *I can't imagine what it must be like for him to lose the person he shared his life with. What it was like for Dad. I hope I never know.*

After a few minutes, Poppa climbed the ladder, his sun-seared cheeks flushed bright red. He locked the hatch, finding the strength to mutter, "It was nice what you done with the matches, Brian." He tightened his hunting cap over salt and pepper waves before soldiering on.

They powered through several inches of snow as the wind gusted over branches, making a grating squeak as they rubbed together. A cow's low bray drifted into earshot along with the delighted squeal of a loose pig and the frightened cluck of a lost chicken. They scattered amongst the yard, stragglers lingering near the truck and house. Two of Poppa's favorite cows remained in their stalls: Agnes, a stout Holstein, and Hildy, a thick, shiny Hereford.

Poppa patted them each on the nose as they stared at him with long-lashed eyes. "I trained Hildy and Agnes from calves. They took best out of all the ones I tried. Horses are too expensive to keep up with and I didn't have no reason for 'em. Too smart for their own good—not that a cow's stupid. Hildy and Agnes here know how to turn left and right and how to trot. Just not real comfortable to ride for long."

Agnes blinked at Brian, probably as excited to carry him as he was to ride her. Butterflies fluttered in his stomach as he conjured thoughts of the twins. "How long will it take to get to Earl's?"

"Should be about five, six hours, give or take. We'll follow Kansas River east once we're out of town. Make a southbound turn at Perry, stop at Clinton Lake and keep on until Ottawa."

Brian groaned, not looking forward to sitting on a cow for that long.

"Eat up, girls. Gonna be a long ride." Poppa slapped them each on the neck with an affectionate smile. They blinked in reply.

Poppa said cows were too bulky for saddles and they slipped around too much, but he fitted them with halters and reins. He helped Brian onto Hildy and hopped on to Agnes. Brian had ridden horses in Colorado with his family, but it felt strange not to have stirrups to put his feet into and a saddle horn to hold on to.

They traveled down the driveway armed with weapons and layered in coats, gloves, hats, and snow pants. Brian wore a scarf his mother knit for him. The cows had little blankets for warmth that were as slippery as Brian imagined the saddle would've been.

The silence of the snow-white landscape and Hildy's steady cadence created a deceptive calm, but Brian remained vigilant. His eyes swept around him, inspecting the woods for movement or shapes that didn't fit in. Although the cows plodded through the snow without a sound, Brian still feared the slightest motion or noise might draw something to them.

The solace of Poppa's land, a solid ten acres of farm and forest, misled Brian into thinking the world hadn't changed all that much. But when they abandoned the desolate country roads, the landscape painted a picture of the trauma it had witnessed. Derelict vehicles sat in the road, coated in sleet and sludge. A few doors hung open, left in their passengers' haste to abandon ship. Most were empty, suggesting people had either gotten blocked off or ran out of gas and fled on foot. Some were metal coffins for decaying bodies. Brian had no idea what was underneath the snow, which was up to the cows' knees, but he was thankful for it.

Hildy and Agnes squeezed through the packed cars. Every time they inched closer to one, Brian held his breath and aimed the pistol, waiting for something to grab him—but nothing did. Any lingering Stalkers must have followed the survivors elsewhere.

They probably freeze like regular people. I guess they're smart enough to stay out of the snow, find shelter.

Not long after passing a billboard for the lone restaurant in town, Almost Home Café, they reached the humble town of Grantville. There were other buildings—a gas station, a fire station, the post office and a few mom-and-pop businesses—but the shattered barricades nailed over the entrances also shattered the illusion of serenity cloaking the silent town.

They headed out of Grantville toward Muddy Creek. Frozen fields of corn stretched out to the sky, covering the vast expanse of land before them. Once the humidity and rain of spring returned, the pitiful brown stalks would transform into rows of lush green. As a child, Brian had been terrified of the movie *The Children of the Corn*. Although he'd since come to find it silly, the thought of the towering stalks—and what they might hide—once again filled him with dread.

Alongside the highway, a billboard for Newman University loomed high and proud. In truth, Brian had never decided on a college or a major: he'd been leaning toward Creative or Technical Writing. Brian faintly pitied himself for the loss of a choice, of a *future*.

All these empty structures without people to fill them, abandoned vehicles without passengers, and roads that would never be traveled again... It was starting to sink in that he wasn't the only person who'd been stripped of the future promised to them.

The entire world had.

BY THE TIME they reached Perry, the descending sun colored the sky with pale blue and pink swirls like cotton candy. They stopped at a small observation area for the Delaware River to let the cows drink.

"Should we clear out a building or find a car to sleep in?" Brian rubbed his arms; the needle-sharp cold air pricked his exposed skin.

Poppa climbed down from Agnes. When Brian slid off Hildy, he almost yanked her blanket down with him. She gave him a look he thought of as disapproving.

"Car'll get too cold and we'd be trapped. We should find a building to keep warm in. Air's moist, so it'll snow once the sun goes down. This shit weather's a damned catch-22: keeps all the other folks and Stalkers inside but makes travelin' hard for us."

While the cows drank from the river, Brian and Poppa stood in front of a lone Porta Potty.

"It's *freezing*—" Brian shuffled his feet "—and I don't want to go out in the open—"

"I'll check it out. Cover me." Poppa lifted the handle while Brian withdrew his bow and nocked an arrow, tugging the string back.

The door flew open. Poppa leaped behind it as a blur of white and brown lunged for Brian. The bowstring snapped against his arm and the arrow sailed into his pouncing assailant. His rapid pulse and the Stalker's gleeful laughter blended into a jarring rhythm of *ha thump ha thump ha.*

Brian stumbled and fell. He scrambled back while Hildy and Agnes lowed behind him. Poppa swung around the door and fired a shot point-blank into the Stalker's temple. It slumped to the ground in front of Brian, staring at him as its brains and blood pooled around its head. Dying chortles trickled out until the light glinting in those bloodshot eyes flickered out.

Poppa offered a hand to Brian. "Did we scare the shit outta him, you think?"

Brian accepted his grandfather's hand and stood, struggling to control his erratic breathing. His arrow jutted out of the Stalker's throat, surrounded by a mixture of caked blood and what looked like excrement from the Porta Potty. "I-I think he nearly scared the shit out of *me.*"

Poppa patted his shoulder. "You'll be all right, son. But it might be best if we get a move on and stop later to finish our business."

Brian nodded and climbed back onto Hildy, glancing down at the Stalker. Even though it was dead, it seemed to mock him with its enduring grin—a pleased "gotcha!" smile like someone jumping out from around a corner to scare a friend.

If Poppa hadn't been there, it might've really *gotten me. I missed its head and fell on my ass. It just...it just happened so* suddenly. *But that's all it takes: one moment, one scratch, one bite.*

While they rode, Brian vowed to keep a better handle on his nerves. When he had an opportunity to plan, he could manage—but when things surprised him, he didn't react in time. If he wanted to survive, he *had* to fix this. He had to anticipate possibilities and prepare for them, like they taught him in the driver's ed classes his parents made him attend: *Identify. Predict. Decide. Execute.*

A white sign with black silhouettes of dogs distracted him. The cutesy name evoked a chortle despite his still-recovering nerves: "Pawliday Inn Pet Resort."

"We should set up here," Poppa said. "Don't want to get too far into town where more of those things might be holed up. We'll turn south and follow the river soon as the sun rises."

The last of the sun's rays bathed the parking lot in a warm golden-red glow. The door to a black SUV sat ajar, but the SUV didn't beep to assert this fact to its absent owner. Discarded fast food wrappers, cups, and strewn papers were inside—along with a child's bloody car seat. The seatbelt was still buckled as if the child had been torn out of it.

Brian's breath caught in his throat as memories of his sister drifted into his mind. He swallowed back burning tears, the dark brown stains blurring into the mottled gray seat. He forced himself to look away and focused on a red Honda instead. Its driver's side door was missing entirely. Brian didn't see it anywhere. He pictured someone using it as a shield.

Poppa investigated the vehicles, retrieving anything of value. Once he was satisfied, he tied Agnes to a tree near the sunny yellow building. "Stay out here with the girls while I secure the place, son. Don't want nothin' poppin' out at you again."

Panic surged through Brian, the image of the shitty Jack-in-the-box Stalker still vivid in his mind. "I should watch your back! What if someone— or something—finds me out *here*?"

"I'll be fine and so'll you. If someone comes and takes the girls or somethin' spooks 'em, we're gonna have a helluva time gettin' to Earl's." Poppa jerked his head. "Keep that bow handy. You can handle yourself, just got startled back there. So did I. Don't beat yourself up over it."

Poppa pushed open the cracked front door of the pet hotel and disappeared inside it with Rocky at his heels. Brian hitched Hildy to the tree next to Agnes, patting her before he withdrew the bow.

Poppa will be fine. He survived the Vietnam War. He's a "Bad Motherfucker" straight out of a Tarantino flick.

A twig snapped behind Brian. He whipped his head toward the sound and lofted the bow. A bedraggled woman emerged from the wriggling bushes. Despite the arrow aimed at her head, her expression was euphoric. "Oh, thank God! You're the first person I've seen who—"

Brian launched the arrow into the ground inches from her dirty bare foot. He plucked another from his quiver and drew it back with the bowstring. "Don't take another step."

Her expression shifted from confusion into panic. "But I'm all alone! I'm unarmed—I won't hurt you!"

"I don't know that. Get out of here and I'll let you live." His voice trembled, not carrying the weight of his harsh words.

She clutched her chest, fingers grazing a torn plaid blouse that was too large for her. "I just want someone to help me find my baby! They took him, a-and—"

"Are you talking about that car? The SUV?"

She nodded.

He shook his head, trying to keep his breathing steady. "I don't believe you. I think you checked out the parking lot and you're making up a story so I'll sympathize with you."

"You're so young!" She ran a hand through matted dark hair. "How can you be this *cynical*?"

Keeping the bowstring taut made Brian's muscles twitch. His hands started to shake. "If you don't leave now, I'll sink an arrow into you. I won't kill you—I'll cripple you so it's easier for one of those things to get you."

The words coming out of his mouth were an amalgamation of things he'd absorbed from TV and movies. He felt guilty even saying them and not sure if he could follow through with his threats. He was trying to play a role exactly like she was.

"Look, I'm not crazy—"

"Exactly. Wouldn't a woman whose child was taken be out of her mind? I won't say it again: leave."

"Where's the other guy? Maybe he's more reasonable than you." Her eyes flitted to Agnes and Hildy.

She knows there's two of us. But if she was armed, wouldn't she have charged me by now?

Or I caught her trying to sneak up on me like the guy in the bathroom did. I can't let my guard down again.

"He'll be back soon," Brian said, "and he's *less* reasonable than me. You'd better go. That car's been here longer than you have. The blood's dry, and you'd have to be crazy to stay in the woods during winter when there's shelter nearby."

She took a step forward. He let go. The arrow sailed in a downward arc and clipped her thigh, making her wail like a jungle cat. "*Why did you do that? You son of a bitch!*"

He withdrew another arrow, but his hand shook and his pulse pumped through his ears. "I-I told you if you took a single step I would. You did. Now go on—get out of here!"

The woman clutched her injured thigh and sank to her knees. She buried her face in her hands as she cried—or faked it well. "My leg...my fucking *leg*. The only reason I'm still alive is because I ran..."

A pang of sympathy slowed Brian's racing heartbeat. She could have lost someone, even if it *wasn't* the baby from the SUV.

Of course, she could've taken it too.

Brian caught movement out of the corner of his eye. Poppa emerged from the front door of the building, summoned by the woman's howling. He held a finger to his lips as he slunk around the side of the building where the woman wouldn't see him. Brian lost sight of him.

The woman looked up, wiping her eyes as she nursed her bleeding leg. "I really did lose my baby. But I know I'll never get him back. I'm not crazy. But being on your own, you start to *feel* a little crazy, you know? Everyone's out to kill you or worse, and you just want someone to talk to..."

Poppa reappeared in the woods behind the despondent woman. *He's going to grab her and tie her up or something. Check her for weapons.*

Brian finally allowed himself a deep breath, relaxing his taut muscles. "Being alone must be scary. I lost people too." He tried to talk to her, to keep her distracted. "My parents and my sister. My grandmother too."

"That's horrible..." She wiped her nose with her sleeve. "How old are you? Did you graduate high school? College?"

"Nineteen. I didn't pick a college yet. Guess that's out of the cards now."

"Yeah. Well, I'm thirty-one, and I can tell you my degree did nothing for me *before* all this shit happened." She glanced to the side, fingering a broken branch trapped by half-melted sludge that had fallen from the branches above her. "I was in the car with my husband and my baby, Sam. Um, we were stuck in traffic, trying to leave town, but the military had already set up a blockade. All of a sudden, there were these loud bangs. Shots fired. People started trying to drive away, crashed into each other's cars. Some got shot. Others got out and tried to run, but they got shot too. Some crazy guy started attacking the military, so I got out of the car and ran. I freaked out so much I forgot all about my husband and my son. I ran until my feet were bloody, until I could hardly breathe. I, uh, God, it's hard to talk about ..." She forced a shaky smile. "My name's Heather, by the way—"

Poppa muffled her mouth with one hand and jerked the other in front of her neck. Red streamed from her throat in dark ribbons. She clutched at it, gurgling as she tried to talk. Her eyes glassed over, and she slumped forward, the upper half of her body sinking into the snow. A puddle of red soaked into it, spreading like paint on blotting paper.

Brian pressed his parted lips together, but his wide eyes remained glued to her body. Poppa pawed her corpse in search of valuables. He jerked something out of her jeans and held it up, the light catching it: a pocketknife.

So much for "unarmed."

Poppa flung the silver utility knife at Brian. It sank into the snow about a foot in front of him. Brian snapped out of his daze and kneeled to collect it, glancing at the dead woman. She stared back at him, blood still trickling out from the gaping hole in her throat.

Poppa stood next to the body as if it was nothing more than a tree stump. He looked into Brian's stunned eyes, his own softening. "Son, I know you hate killin'. But you mighta ended up with your throat slit instead of her. I couldn't take a chance—I had to protect my kin." He approached Brian and held out a gloved hand. "We gotta go in. It's gettin' darker—colder too. We'll block the doors as best as we can. Windows are already boarded."

Brian clutched the woman's pocketknife in one hand and grabbed Poppa's with the other. He stood and gestured to the dead woman. "What do we...what do we do about her?"

She said her name was Heather.

Poppa cast a casual glance in her direction. "Leave her out here. If they get hungry, they can have her."

This callous response startled Brian. "But..."

"Ain't a person no more. Just a body. Better her than us." Poppa patted Brian's back and headed over to free the cows. Brian cradled the knife in his hands.

Poppa barked out orders for Brian to start blockading the doors while he led the cows in. The distinct scent of animals assaulted Brian when he marched into the building. Open pet crates sat on the waiting room floor amidst torn magazines. The phone dangled from the counter, still attached to the receiver by an old-fashioned circular cord. Posters hung on the walls portraying eager dogs and cats with judgmental eyes.

Brian set his backpack down, glancing at the folded pocketknife. It warmed in his hand as it conducted his body heat. When he flicked the blade out from the black handle, he saw something brown along the edge and tip of the blade. *Old blood?* He noticed something else: an inscription on the back of the knife. *"To Christina—I owe you one."*

His eyes lifted to watch Poppa as he led Hildy and Agnes into the back of the building. *No one is who they seem on the surface. We all act, wear different faces. Even someone I've known my whole life.*

I guess I never really knew him until now.

Chapter Six: The Twins

12/9, PERRY, KANSAS

Pawliday Inn Pet Resort

The still-ticking pocket watch told Brian it was twelve in the afternoon when Poppa woke. He was grumpy about having such a short amount of time to get to Earl's, and their rushed, makeshift "bath" with moist towelettes left him feeling less than civilized. They had a long day ahead of them.

They headed south from the Pawliday Inn with Rocky squirming in Poppa's lap. The woman's body was gone—but she hadn't undergone a magical resurrection. Something had dragged her into the woods, into the darkness. Not knowing what was more of a blessing than a curse.

It took them about two hours to make it through Lecompton to Clinton Lake. Brian had been there before with his parents and Becky. He had memories of hiking the trails with them and drifting on the glassy lake in canoes. When Brian saw the campground, the phantom scents of bug spray and roasting marshmallows sent a wistful sense of nostalgia fluttering through him.

While Brian brushed snow from a picnic table, revealing abandoned utensils and Tupperware with a moldy ecosystem trapped inside, Poppa tapped his shoulder. "Look," he whispered, handing Brian his rifle.

Brian took it, his throat dry. "What is it?"

"Just look."

Brian lifted the rifle, finger on the trigger and eye against the scope. "Where am I looking?"

Poppa pulled the barrel to the right, pointing. "Up there, in the trees. On the other side of the lake." Excitement colored his smoke-damaged voice—unusual for him.

Brian zoomed in. A blur of tan darted behind the trees. He followed it, glimpsing low, rolling shoulders and a large head with rounded ears. Its golden eyes focused ahead of it as the tip of its long tail flicked.

"Woah. Is that—?"

"A cougar. Don't see those often here. No mountains for 'em. But they survive wherever and however they can."

Brian lowered the rifle, keeping his eye on the animal. "Do you think it'll come after us?"

Poppa shook his head. "Too far away. It's focused on somethin' else." He grabbed the rifle from Brian, aiming once more at the prowling feline.

For a moment, Brian feared the inevitable bullet piercing the air—but Poppa lowered the rifle and shook his head with an awed look on his face. "I'll be damned." He slung the rifle onto his shoulder and grabbed Rocky, who'd been playing at the water's edge while the cows drank.

Brian followed Poppa's lead. He grabbed his backpack and climbed atop Hildy. But he couldn't silence the questions churning in his mind. "Why didn't you kill it, Poppa?"

A gust of wind made the treetops sway as the cows plodded away from the lakeshore.

"Because I respect it. It's a survivor."

Resentment cursed Brian with boldness. "So was that woman."

"Couldn't take that chance. You're all I got left, so I gotta protect you."

"I think you would've killed her even if I wasn't around."

Poppa's head whipped to face Brian. "Don't fool yourself into thinkin' the world's different than it was—it's always been this way. Killin' is as much a part of life as eatin' and sleepin'. You're young and you got me to protect you, but when you were alone, you had to kill because you wanted to *live*. You don't feel guilty for that, do you?"

"No. But I killed a dying man and something that was already half dead."

"If the Stalker hadn't gotten to him first, you would've killed him."

Brian's lips tightened. He couldn't deny that possibility, though entertaining it made him feel guilty.

As if reading his mind, Poppa said, "The less guilt you feel, the longer you'll survive."

He respects the cougar because he relates to it. He thinks he kills to survive, like he killed those villagers in My Lai. But he's justifying it to avoid the guilt.

Silence accompanied their trek through the back roads. A few cars hugged the sides, parked in snow up to their tire rims. White palms pressed against the inside of a frosted window, framing a cherry-red smile. A lump tightened Brian's dry throat.

"Poppa," he exhaled, voice cracking, "look—"

But the face had vanished. The car containing it rocked, dislodging some of the snow clinging to it.

It's eating.

Poppa met Brian's frantic gaze and shook his head, kicking Agnes's sides. Quickening their pace, they hurried away amidst the still air. The eerie silence enveloping them made Brian feel as if he'd been swallowed up in another bubble, some sort of void where time didn't exist.

After a long stretch of sludge-coated roads and frozen cornfields, Poppa stopped. "That's their road. I'll sneak through the fields in case we aren't the first to show up. You stay here with the animals. If Earl's there, I'll come get you."

Poppa dismounted from Agnes as they approached the intersection marked with the green sign for Sand Creek Road. He looped her reins around a large Bur oak. Brian did the same with Hildy and hopped down.

"Why do you want to leave me alone again? That didn't exactly go well last time."

"Girls need lookin' after. If somethin' or someone shows up, you can either haul off on one of 'em or shoot. Stop doubtin' yourself—there'll come a day when I'm not around. Might as well prepare for it."

Brian scooped Rocky up as Poppa headed for a field of dried cornhusks. "Okay. But if I hear anything weird, I'm coming to help you—not running away."

Poppa looked over his shoulder and flashed Brian a crooked smile. "Be thankful you got some of your mother's spirit. I used to not think too kindly of her, but I realized she kept your daddy goin'. 'Course, part of the problem was he never thought he was good enough for her. Love cuts both ways like that sometimes." He sniffed, no doubt thinking of Nana, but said no more.

Poppa turned, angling his rifle in front of him as he pushed into the rows of brown stalks. Rocky squirmed out of Brian's arms and hauled after him, yipping as if saying 'Hey, wait for me!' An odd little knot twisted in Brian's gut, but he returned to the cows and soothed himself by petting them.

Brian drifted in the timeless void until distant barks pierced the veil. A lone crow cawed and soared into the sky. *Is he really chasing birds? That dumb dog.*

His smile shrank when a gunshot made Hildy's skin shiver underneath his hands. He scrambled for his pistol and withdrew it from his waistband, rushing into the frozen fields. Stalks snapped underneath his feet, cracking as he ran through the narrow aisles of dead corn. He collided with someone, something, nearly pulled the trigger—but it was only a gnarled scarecrow with a pointy hat covering its face. A tattered black coat draped over gnarled roots resembling the disemboweled man in Poppa's house.

Muffled voices floated over from afar. Brian pushed on, but common sense edged out boldness. He lowered himself to his knees and crawled toward the edge of the field until a roof and silo loomed in the distance. The sun descended beyond them, bathing the buildings in a bright orange glow. Smoke trailing from the chimney diffused into the pastel horizon.

"Your granddaddy said you knew we was comin'!" Poppa's voice soothed Brian's spiked nerves—to a point. His raspy voice seemed haggard, like he was struggling to control himself.

"I expected an old guy and a college kid—not a damn dog!" *Young, not Poppa's age. Not Earl. Louis?* His thickly accented, husky voice resembled Gambit's from the *X-Men* cartoons. Brian remembered this fascinating him as a kid. "Where is Brian, anyway? Somethin' happen to him?"

Brian pressed himself to the ground and lingered behind the stalks. He held the gun in front of him in unsteady hands. *He remembers me. Is that a good or a bad thing?*

"I ain't sayin' shit 'til I see Earl. Where is he?"

Someone else spoke: Eva. "Max, Tala started actin' strange, barkin' all the time and snappin' at us, so we had to put her down. Lou couldn't take a chance with your dog—it ran up before we saw you. I'm so sorry..." Tears choked her honey-smooth voice. "*P-Papère*'s gone, too. Stalker got him last night. Must've been...must've been the same one that got Tala."

Brian swept the stalks away from his face so he could see. A striking mirror image greeted him: lustrous hair the color of a raven's feathers and smooth tawny skin. Louis stood several inches taller than his sister, but both had a slender build and elegant features. Lush lips, straight noses, high cheekbones—but a lengthy scar streaked Louis's left cheek, and his eyes were dark compared to the warm brown of his sister's. Pitch-black like a shark's. His left hand aimed a handgun at Poppa.

Brian realized he'd been holding his breath. He released it through his nose, his chapped lips sticking together as moisture clouded above them. Poppa kneeled on the ground, his rifle lying next to a dark object on a coat—

Rocky. His little body heaved with shallow, nearly imperceptible movements. A growing pool of blood spread into the tan coat underneath him, leaking from a dark hole in his side. He strained for breath in rasping wheezes. An image of the dying deer flashed in Brian's mind.

Brian stood and burst through the dry stems, aiming his pistol at Louis. "Put the gun down, Louis." He cupped his shaking right hand with his left to steady it. "My grandfather's upset because you shot his dog. Can you blame him?"

Louis lowered his gun, his eyebrows and lips quirking as if he was impressed. "I was wonderin' where you were, Brian. Look at you, all grown up. Last time I saw you, you were still a *pischouette*."

Brian didn't know what a "pischouette" was, but he didn't care to inquire. He skirted Louis's obsidian eyes, which seemed to possess the gravity of a supermassive black hole. Instead, he glanced at Poppa as he caressed his dying dog. "You're a lot different than I remember too. I wish I could say I was glad to see you, but this isn't exactly a happy reunion."

Louis ran his hand through his parted bangs, which were cut in a swooping style straight out of a '90s boy band. "Brian, it was an accident, okay? We've been a little jumpy lately after what happened to our Papère and dog. Let's calm down, start over."

Eva approached Brian. She curled her trembling hand around his arm, coercing him to lower his pistol from Louis. "I'm sorry about your dog. Please, sit with him."

Brian kneeled beside his grandfather. Rocky's tail lifted at his presence, trying for one last wag.

Poppa gripped Brian's shoulder. "He lived a good life, Bri. Ruby saw him curled up in a Petco, thought he looked lonely and wanted to take him home. I tried pretty hard to pretend I didn't love him as much as I did—thought it made me seem weak or somethin'—but I loved him like he was a member of my family. He gave all that love right back." He screwed his eyes shut. Tears streamed down his rosy cheeks, pooling in the crannies of his thin, cracked lips. "Goddamn... Earl's gone, too."

Eva gripped Poppa's shaking shoulders. Rocky's chest no longer swelled beneath his hand. "I'm so sorry, Max. Let's go inside—there's a fire burnin' and I was gonna try to dredge up somethin' to eat."

Brian caught her eyes and offered her a terse smile as she helped Max to his feet. He ran a hand along Rocky's fur, remembering all the times he'd stroked it while Rocky curled up in bed with him. Those had been some of the worst nights of his life, and Rocky had been there with him as if he'd known. As if he'd *cared*.

Another thing loved, another thing lost.

Louis stretched his free hand out to Brian. "Look, I'm sorry I've been an asshole. We were friends once. We can be friends again, right?"

Brian contemplated the leather glove lingering in front of his face and the body attached to it. He couldn't tell what other weapons Louis might be hiding underneath his bomber jacket, or what he might have wedged in his jean pockets. Not much—they looked uncomfortably tight.

He scanned up to Louis's face and tried to search the depths of his eyes for a show of emotion, any indication of what he might be feeling. Remorse, grief, even sympathy. *Something* swirled in there, an intriguing glimmer like light rippling on a lake, but Brian couldn't identify what.

"We'll see." Brian accepted Louis's hand and was lifted to his feet with surprising ease. He strolled alongside him, following Eva and Poppa into the log cabin ahead of them—but the thought of leaving Rocky's body out there for the elements or scavengers to ravage drowned him in a tidal wave of guilt.

They entered the house, immediately surrounded by the warmth of the crackling fire. The scent of leather and something floral swirled in the air, the most pleasant things Brian had smelled in a long time. Poppa asked Eva to show him to the bathroom. Brian sat on the couch in front of the fireplace, watching his grandfather march up the dim hall with his shoulders slumped and head hung.

Louis sat in a wooden rocking chair next to the couch, stretching his lean legs out and resting his clasped hands in his lap. "This was Papère's chair. Used to sit here and smoke his pipe. Drove *Mamère* nuts. She'd whack him on the head with a rolled-up magazine. He never stopped smokin' and she never stopped whackin' him." He paused. "Until she died, of course."

Brian leaned forward and tucked his hands between his knees. "Did she die recently too?"

"Nah, she passed about three years ago. Cancer." Louis's eyes flitted to Brian's from the fireplace. "I was never really close to either one of 'em. Family's family, what can I say?" He shrugged and shook his head, glancing back at the fire. "She cooked our food and washed our clothes, and he put a roof over our heads and a bed under our backs. Slapped my ass raw when I was a kid too. He might've been a friend to your granddaddy, but I'm not exactly sore to see him go."

Brian's memory of Earl was more vague than his memories of the twins. "Um, I'm sorry to hear that. It was nice of him to wait for us, though."

"I'm gonna tell you somethin' but don't tell Eva or your granddaddy—I'll tell 'em once they've calmed down." Louis leaned forward, resting his arms on his knees. Brian stretched toward him, straining to hear Louis as he lowered his voice to a whisper. "Papère wanted to leave. But first, he was gonna take you and your granddaddy's stuff, tie you up and leave you here. Truth is, he didn't have as many supplies as he let on: the three of us burned through it pretty quick." When Louis caught Brian's shocked expression, he didn't say anything. He stared into the fire, the flames flickering in his eyes.

Before Brian could probe Louis for more information, Eva returned to the living room. Louis sprang back into the rocking chair, flashing her a charming grin. "*Ma chère sœur*—the kitchen calls, no?"

"So, go answer it." Eva sank into the couch at Brian's right side. Now that her face was close to his, he glimpsed a charming splash of freckles across the bridge of her nose. "Your granddaddy wants to go take care of Rocky and get your cows after he finishes in there. You're more than welcome to stay with us while he does. I think he wants to do it on his own."

Brian glanced at her fingers as they wrapped around his forearm. Her short nails were painted black, but the polish was chipping away. Although Louis's hair seemed to be evenly trimmed, hers had been shorn into jagged layers. The contrast intrigued him.

"Thanks." Brian cursed his momentary lack of eloquence.

Eva smiled, but it tightened into a frown when she glanced past Brian at her brother. "You apologized, right? You owe Max one too."

"Since when did you turn into *Mère*, Eva?" Louis scoffed. "Of course, I did. I'm not some damn savage, despite what all the assholes at school used to say. I'll get around to it with Max, don't you worry."

Eva clapped her hands to her legs. "Good." She sighed, her modest chest swelling and falling. "I still can't believe we cremated Papère this mornin'. Just yesterday, I was cookin' dinner for three of us. I thought it'd be two tonight, but I'm glad it's four." A strained smile failed to mask her shimmering eyes.

Poppa emerged at the end of the hallway. He looked at Brian, eyes red-rimmed and puffy. "Gonna go out, take care of Rocky and the girls. You okay in here with them?"

Brian nodded. Poppa stamped past the couch, opened the door and stepped out into the cooling air. A brisk draft billowed into the room as he shut the door. It made their hair flutter and shifted the dancing flames.

"You probably wanna clean up too." Louis's gaze lingered on Brian but didn't meet his eyes. Brian assumed he was lost in reminiscence. When his eyes darted up to meet Brian's, his lips quirked into a tentative smile. "Papère hooked us up to a generator. Got some gas left. If we leave soon, might as well be usin' it anyway."

Brian glanced away from Louis's captivating onyx eyes, starting to feel the heat of the fire. He unzipped his jacket, pulled off his beanie, and ruffled his hair. "Sure. Thanks."

Louis stood and stretched. The rocking chair creaked from the residual force. "The faucet's kinda funny. I'll show you how to work it while Eva starts cookin'."

"Or *you* can cook while *I* show him." Eva stood and folded her arms, head tilted.

A sharp eye tooth clipped Louis's lower lip when he smirked. "I only cook when I'm tryin' to get laid. But if you ask real nice, I'll come help you when I'm done."

Eva muttered something under her breath as she stomped off to the kitchen. Louis's smile faded, his finger trailing along the fireplace mantel. "I've been comin' here since me and Eva were babies. I always enjoyed seein' the animals more than our grandparents." He glanced at Brian and narrowed his eyes. "Your granddaddy said somethin' about cows, didn't he?"

Brian scratched his head, a little embarrassed. "We rode them here. They're pretty uncomfortable, but they're sweet." His eyes flashed to the deer heads mounted on the wall, an unpleasant dissonance stirring within him as he thought of Agnes and Hildy's innocent faces.

Instead, he cleared his throat and joined Louis in front of the fireplace. Louis lifted a framed photo of a pair of young children at the beach, obviously himself and Eva. "Hard to believe it's been nine years since I last saw you. You remember us much?"

Brian squinted as he scoured the image, searching for a spark to ignite his childhood memories. "Of course I do. You guys were my best friends. We hung out almost every weekend, ate lunch together at school..." He wanted to avoid discussing the scar on Louis's cheek, the reason for their estrangement, so he cleared his throat and blurted out the next thing on his mind: "I guess you really like that haircut since it hasn't changed in over nine years."

Louis set the frame down and ran a hand through his bangs. "If it ain't broke, don't fix it." He shook his head and wandered toward the hall. "Your hair got darker. You still look like a California surfer boy, though. I always found that funny since you were a bookworm and all." He sauntered ahead of Brian with a cock-of-the-walk strut: self-assured and a little jaunty, like a cowboy with his thumbs in his belt.

Photos adorned the walls of the hallway, displaying pictures of people Brian didn't recognize and the twins at various ages. Eva's photos were casual, capturing her in the moment with a bashful smile, but her eyes always met the camera. Louis's looked more rehearsed—such as the Abercrombie-esque shot of him posing in a swimsuit in front of a beach—but his gaze always focused elsewhere.

A picture of a Native-American woman in a traditional headdress intrigued Brian enough to make him stop in his tracks. "That's your grandmother, right? I think I remember her a little."

Louis took a quick look at it and kept walking. "Yeah, that's her. She met my Papère in Louisiana. He was Cajun and she was Choctaw. They got on like oil and water, but somethin' about that worked for 'em and my *père* and his brother were born there. They moved up here when he was in high school, and that's where he met my *mère*. She was from the Kickapoo tribe, full-blooded. Makes me and Eva about three-quarters Native. The rest is Cajun. Eva likes to say I took all of it, bless her heart."

Brian knew "bless your heart" was the Southern equivalent of saying "fuck you." It struck him as an odd thing for Louis to say about his sister, but for all Brian knew, they didn't get along. They'd gotten into the occasional childhood argument. Louis also seemed indifferent to his grandmother and certainly didn't seem to be mourning his grandfather.

"Louis," Brian whispered as Louis stopped in front of a door he assumed led to the bathroom, "are you going to finish telling me about your grandfather?"

"What about him?" Louis leaned back against the wall and folded his arms. "He was a piece of shit who used to beat me when I was a kid, wanted to screw his own friend over. I was gonna wait it out, deal with him once you got here, but that Stalker solved my problems for me."

Brian scanned Louis's eyes, unsettled by his indifference. No, not indifference—there *was* passion in his voice. Bitterness. He couldn't put his finger on what bothered him about Louis, but it might've been because there were too many things going on to narrow it down to one.

"Why did you tell me first?" Brian asked.

"I'm worried about how your granddaddy's gonna handle it since they were friends and all. Not to mention, he's gonna be salty at me over the thing with the dog." Louis exhaled and glanced at the ground, shifting his feet. "He and Eva have been through a lot. I wanted to wait for the right time, tell 'em both." His eyes fixed on Brian's. "If your granddaddy doesn't take it well, can you try your best to help him see reason?"

Louis possessed a strange charisma that overwhelmed Brian. When he realized his mouth was hanging open, he cleared his throat and hemmed and hawed over an answer. "Well, uh, I can try. He's kind of edgy right now. Like you with Rocky—our dog."

Louis reached out and grabbed Brian's shoulders, sending a shiver down his spine. "I remember you tellin' me how excited you were about your grandparents' new puppy. We never got to see it 'cause we switched schools, lost touch. I'd take it back if I could, shootin' your granddaddy's dog. I wanted to tell you I was sorry about that. I mean it."

Brian nodded and forced a smile, wondering when the tight grip Louis had on his shoulders would loosen. "Thanks." He wanted to apologize for leaving the scar on Louis's cheek, for the fight that ripped them apart, but he didn't remember why or how he'd done it. Seeing Louis and Eva now brought a lot of memories back, but this traumatic separation remained one of those muddled memories easily confused with a dream.

Louis's hands fell from Brian. He reached past Brian to twist the doorknob behind him. "If you want that bath, I'd better hurry up and show you how to work it. You don't wanna miss supper, do you?" He arched his eyebrows and opened the door, sweeping a hand out. "After you, *mon bell ami.*"

From what little Brian knew of French, Louis had called him something like "my good friend." Whatever memories Louis had of Brian seemed to be fond despite their falling out. *Better than him hating me, I guess, or I might be dead instead of messing with a water faucet.*

Brian watched and listened as Louis gave him instructions and demonstrated how to get the water temperature just right. Apparently, if someone turned the hot water valve first, an awful screech would hiss from the pipes. It was one of those idiosyncratic issues that seemed to plague every bathroom.

When Louis left Brian in peace, he stripped his backpack off and locked the door. He undressed and tried to enjoy a bath—the first he'd had in five days—but his mind kept circling back to Rocky's bloodied body and that final attempt to wag his tail. Tears started trickling down his cheeks into the warm water. He sank underneath it, letting the water transform his cries into bubbles of air. Not long after this cathartic release of anguish, someone knocked on the door and called for him: Poppa.

Brian rushed to towel off and dress. He shrugged on a button-down shirt and tugged on a pair of jeans. He unlocked the door and opened it to his grandfather. Without his layers of coats on, it seemed as though a strong gust of wind might blow him over.

Poppa closed the door and leaned his back against it. He clasped his weathered, freckled hands, thumbs stroking his paper-thin skin. "I buried Rocky. Rotten way to go, shot in the gut like that. I remember hearin' that animals can get sick too, but to lose Earl and Rocky within a day..." He sighed and tucked his chin against his chest. "We've got some shit luck, don't we?"

Brian toyed with the idea of revealing what Louis had said about Earl—but he worried Poppa would overreact and accuse Louis of something, possibly even Eva, and sacrifice their hospitality for more death. From what Brian remembered, Louis was a bold personality, always the one who had to be in charge and have his way. It would be wiser for Brian to try to renew the childhood bonds they'd shared.

He leaned against the counter and finished toweling off his hair. "Do you know how I left that scar on Louis's face, Poppa? I remember when it happened, but I don't remember *why*."

"I don't know much about it." Poppa's eyes evaded Brian's. "Your daddy said you were pretty shook up, that your mother didn't want you to spend time with the twins no more."

Brian's eyes widened as one of his hazier memories sharpened into focus. "I remember my first day back to school after Dad overdosed. Some asshole—I think it was Billy Butler—said something like: "Your dad took a buncha pills and tried to kill himself. I bet it's 'cause he hated you and your mom." Louis was there. When I started crying, he slugged that kid in the mouth. Mom decided to homeschool me after that. I was mad because I didn't get to see Louis and Eva at school anymore, and I blamed Dad."

Poppa lowered his gaze to the tiled floor. "That was a rough time for all of us. You were in a sensitive phase, tryin' to deal with what your daddy did and how it affected you and your mother. Mighta had somethin' to do with what happened with Louis later on."

"It seems weird that we'd fall out after he stood up for me. We were close, even if he *was* bossy..." Brian sighed. "It's so weird how you can remember things but not completely, like a picture with blobs of color but you don't know what they represent. I don't remember being mad enough to hurt him—I just remember being sad that I didn't see him or Eva again. I should try to talk to them about it."

Poppa's eyes sharpened over his hawkish nose. "I'd be careful around him. He got the drop on me and he ain't ever been in no war. But you be careful around her too. She's a pretty girl, and you're that age where—"

"*Jesus,* Poppa!" Brian grimaced and flung the towel over a rack mounted to the wall. "I'm not exactly thinking about that stuff right now."

"Your daddy said you were shy. Guess it's for the best, though—might rub her brother the wrong way if you put the moves on her."

Brian frowned, not prepared to dive into that discussion with his conservative grandfather. "I'm not going to put the moves on anyone. Do people even still *say* that? Besides, I don't want to get too attached to anyone. It's hard to trust people these days and easy to lose them."

Poppa offered Brian a placid smile. "I understand. Eva's a good girl, always has been. Louis...well, might be he's rattled. Might be he shot the dog because he wanted to, though." He sighed and shut his eyes, rubbing them. "I can't believe one of those things got Earl. He was careful. Eva or Louis musta been in trouble. That's the only way he'd let his guard down."

"You don't think...?" Brian wasn't sure how to word what was on his mind or how much to reveal. "Did Louis jump the gun with him too?"

Poppa's eyes locked onto Brian's, glinting. "That did occur to me. But I can't make sense of why, unless it was nerves. Earl never mentioned anythin' strange about Louis, only that he was a handful, always gettin' into trouble and lookin' for attention—liked to sneak into his liquor cabinet too. Could be he was feelin' overprotective of his sister or himself and—"

A knock at the door startled them into silence. "Supper's ready. Figured you'd be starvin'."

Poppa opened the door. A draft of air coasted in, cooling Brian's moist skin. He shivered as a drop of water rolled down the back of his neck.

Louis stood in the doorway brandishing a knife. He smiled and lowered it when he saw the wary looks Brian and Poppa gave him. "Sorry—she has me cuttin' the meat. C'mon, *garçons.*"

Brian trudged alongside his grandfather, following Louis down the hall into the cozy kitchen. The delectable aroma of cooked meat greeted them.

Eva spun toward them with a broad smile on her face, an apron strapped to her slender waist. "Soup's on!"

The last time Brian ate a proper meal, he'd been with Poppa and Nana. Rocky sat underneath the table, begging for scraps from anyone who'd dish them out. Now Nana and Rocky were gone, and in their place, a pair of twins he'd grown up with but scarcely remembered.

Eva's glowing gaze nearly made him melt into his seat, but Louis's charcoal eyes chilled him. An ember flickered within them, threatening to ignite into a firestorm.

Chapter Seven: Invasion

12/9, OTTAWA, KANSAS

Lavellé Residence
Evening

The pleasant atmosphere diffused into uncomfortable silence as they ate.

This must be as weird for them as it is for us. I never knew what to say during dinner with my family—I sure as hell don't know what to say to them. *"I'm glad to see you after all of this time even though you shot my dog. Oh, and I don't remember exactly why we got into a fight, to begin with, especially one so bad that our parents kept us from seeing each other again. By the way, I'm sorry I scarred your face even though I don't remember* how."

Louis drove his fork into a hunk of flaking meat. "Me and my family went to a few hoity-toity restaurants in the Quarter—in Louisiana, you know? They got all these forks, even teeny tiny ones for pickles. Why can't you use a regular fork to grab a pickle? Or your fingers?"

Eva's eyebrows lifted as if to question Louis's choice of topic. Brian offered both twins a polite smile before sipping from a glass of water.

"I hate to ask—" Poppa dabbed his mouth with his cloth napkin "—but how'd it happen?"

Eva's face fell. Louis sat back and inhaled, dropping his napkin on the table. "I got no idea how it got in. They're smart as shit—probably slithered down the chimney like fuckin' Santa Claus. But nothin' seemed off: we played a board game, had supper, and settled in for some sleep. All of a sudden, Eva lets out this wildcat scream—"

"Let me tell it." Eva sighed and ran her hands through her jagged bangs. "I went into the kitchen to get a drink of water. I thought we left some food out 'cause it stunk like rotten eggs, so I flipped a light on to look for it. That awful Stalker was hidin' under this here table. As soon as I saw it, it grabbed me by the leg—thank goodness I had long pajamas and slippers on. I screamed and kicked it in the face, but it grabbed my braid and yanked me down. I guess the racket woke Papère and Lou. All I know from that point on is that it kept laughin' like some freaky circus clown, and I heard a buncha yellin' and gunshots. Then nothin'—just silence."

Louis hung his elbow over the back of his chair. "Once Eva was all settled down and the damn thing was dead, Papère pulled up his sleeve, showed me four long gashes on his right arm. He asked me to take care of it, to finish it after he fell asleep so he wouldn't know it was comin'."

Poppa pushed his plate forward and clasped his hands, resting them on the table in the spot where the plate had been. "So he got scratched on the arm wrestlin' this thing away from Eva? And he took you aside later and asked you to shoot him?"

Louis nodded, clasping his hands to mirror Poppa's. "That same night. Didn't want to chance it. He was all shook up, worried about gettin' me and Eva sick. I took a gun and a pillow and pressed 'em both to his head while he was sleepin'. A better fate than some." Louis's calm gaze flitted to Brian's before he looked back at Poppa. "I know you and Papère were war buddies, but it's probably for the best that it happened this way."

Poppa stayed silent for a moment, screwing his paper-thin lips together. A speck of crumbs clung to them. "Come again?"

"Papère didn't wanna leave. All his memories were here, he said. We stuck it out for a while 'cause we were safe, had enough resources. If any Stalkers or looters showed up, Papère and I managed to scare 'em away or kill 'em. But we kept usin' things up and weren't goin' out to get more. Once he got that call from you, he said he planned to take your things and make a break for it with me and Eva. Didn't want Eva to know 'cause she'd never go for it. He didn't want to kill you, just wanted to tie you up in the middle of the night and haul ass with your stuff. I didn't wanna put Eva through that, so I planned to stop him...except that Stalker stopped him first."

Eva tossed her napkin to the table and hissed, "*What*?" while Poppa stared at Louis, trying to examine his expression for any hint of deceit.

"Louis—" Eva leaned onto the table and twisted his chin so he faced her "—why was I out of the loop for *so much* of this stuff? And why would he steal from his own friend?"

"Because you were Papère's favorite grandchild. He wanted to protect you from the big, bad world." Louis shoved his plate away as if he'd suddenly lost his appetite. "Who would he wanna protect more, huh? You or some army buddy he drank beers with every other Fourth of July?"

The twins stared at one another without flinching. Poppa's hand slipped underneath the table. He kept a holster strapped around his thigh—Brian feared he'd withdraw the handgun from it.

"How exactly were you gonna stop him, huh?" Eva's hand tightened into a fist against the tabletop. "Would you have killed him anyway?"

"I was gonna expose him, leave it up to Max to decide what to do." Louis exhaled through his lips. "I already told Brian. I just wanted you and Max to have some time to process the shit from earlier—"

"No wonder you didn't seem upset when he died." Eva leaned back in her seat and folded her arms. "You hated him, didn't you?"

Louis leaned forward onto the table, the motion of his arms making the dishes clatter. "He never took a belt to *your* ass, did he?" He scoffed at Eva's stunned reaction. "That's what I thought. The real world is ugly, Eva. Better get used to it now."

A subtle sound cut the silence: tapping against the kitchen window.

Poppa rushed to grab his rifle from the living room. Brian fumbled for his pistol while Eva slid a handgun from her holster. He noticed a flash of tan stomach as her shirt lifted, but he didn't let his eyes linger.

Eva's frantic eyes darted between Louis and Brian's. "Do you think it's another Stalker?"

"They're supposed to be less active once it gets dark," Brian said. "But I read some reports that they attacked in the middle of the night. I don't know when—or if—they sleep."

"Adaptation." Louis spun the cylinder of a revolver with an impressive barrel. "Predators follow their prey, watch it, adjust their schedule to it."

Eva bit her rosy lip. "If somethin's tryin' to get in, they might try other doors and windows. We should check them."

"Hold on a minute." Louis held up a finger before darting out of the kitchen. Eva's eyes followed him until he disappeared, her brow knit. She clutched the pistol in both hands and kept it in front of her heaving chest.

Poppa returned to the kitchen. "Livin' room's clear. I pushed a couch in front of the door, checked the barricades on the windows. Where'd your fool brother run off to, Eva?"

"Uh, Papère's room, probably. He never let us go in there. Lou said he kept his war stuff underneath a floorboard. Maybe he wants somethin' from that?"

Poppa tapped Brian's shoulder and handed him a flashlight. "We need to kill the lights."

Eva looked at Poppa like he was crazy. "What? *Why?*"

"I can hear pretty good, and I'd rather they not see us. Plus, I got a night-vision sniper."

Eva tapped the toes of a dirty leather boot. "Can those things see in the dark too? They might be able to smell us. I mean, I don't know how they hunt, exactly. All I *do* know is that I don't want to get that close to one again if I can help it."

Louis jogged back into the kitchen with an assortment of dark objects gathered to his chest. He approached the others as they leaned in to inspect it. "Two walkies and a pair of night-vision goggles. Figured they'd come in handy."

"You keep the goggles, I got my rifle." Poppa held his hand out. "I'll take one of them walkies, though. I was just tellin' your sister we need to hit the lights. You know where the generator is?"

Louis nodded. "I'll take care of it, check the other rooms on the way. Eva, come with me."

She managed a drawn smile as she looked at Brian and Poppa. "Good luck. It might be an animal—at least, I sure hope it is."

The twins disappeared down the hall. Poppa connected the walkie to his belt. Brian clung to the heavy Maglite and his pistol. He glanced at the dishes still cluttered on the table and thought back to the picnic table at the park. *Everyone was in the middle of something when they abandoned their homes or fled from wherever they were. These interrupted scenes are spread all over the world now, frozen in time like photographs.*

"Make sure the barricades on that window are sturdy." Poppa gestured to it with his rifle. "I got you covered."

Brian sighed and dug his fingers underneath the wooden planks, horrified a hand would burst through and grab him. When none gave way, he exhaled and moved on to the door.

Static erupted from the walkie. Brian's heart raced as he struggled to reach for it, trapping the flashlight between his arm and side. "—master bedroom and bathroom are secure. We're about to go into the basement to turn off the generator. Over."

Brian hit the button to reply to Eva. "Copy that. Kitchen is clear. Moving into the living room now. Over and out." He clipped it back onto his belt and returned the flashlight to his left hand.

Brian and Poppa headed into the living room. The fire still flickered, crackling as it struggled to consume what remained of the wood trapped within it.

Brian examined the couch stacked on its side against the front door. "Will this hold?"

Poppa moved to the window beside the door, slipping the tip of his rifle between two boards. "Against a Stalker, it should. A person might get it open. Not too quietly, though."

The lights cut out. Aside from the glowing fire, darkness concealed the contents of the room. The immense and all-consuming silence of the house made Brian's breathing sound as loud as a jet engine.

Brian lifted the walkie to his lips. "Eva, you guys cut the power, right? Over."

A shrill ring pierced the air. Brian cursed and nearly dropped the walkie. Eva's garbled reply came through the speaker, but Poppa hissed, "Turn it off—*now*." Brian obeyed.

The *briiiiiiing* persisted: a doorbell. Poppa strained to see who rang it from his position behind the window. *Who the hell would* do *that? Stalkers can barricade doors and lock them, maybe even pick the locks—is it really so bizarre that they might try to trick people into coming outside?*

A strange echo came from behind him; something ricocheting against metal. His nose crinkled, filled with a pungent scent—

Smoke.

Before Brian could move, Poppa jerked him to his knees and dragged him into the kitchen. He shoved Brian underneath the table and flattened himself to the ground, one arm over Brian's back. "Grenade!"

A deafening explosion sent sparks into the air like fireworks. Brian covered his head with his hands, his rapid heartbeat pounding with the ringing in his ears. Dying embers scattered across the living room floor, briefly illuminating shattered bricks and wood from the fireplace. Smoke clung to the inside of his nose and he struggled to keep himself from coughing.

No Stalker would've climbed on top of a roof to lob a grenade into a fireplace. People did this—but *why?*

How many are there? What kind of weapons do they have? Will they draw Stalkers in?

The ground shuddered beneath him when another explosion erupted right next to him. His shoulders jerked as he struggled to suppress a gasp. Gunpowder commingled with the smoke, acrid and sour.

Poppa remained next to him, a reassuring warmth in the darkness. He elbowed Brian and crawled out from underneath the table toward the living room. Brian clung to his grandfather's sleeve, banging into smoldering debris. He tried to picture where they were going.

We came from the kitchen, went into the living room. Now we're close to the front door—

He gasped when his hand ran over something warm.

A body. Poppa shot someone. Something.

Poppa kept crawling. Brian moved with him. He wiped his hand along his side, the flashlight still gripped in it. His stiff hands were practically glued to the metal wrapped within them.

Now we're in the hall. Poppa stopped and nudged Brian, urging him to go in a different direction. *Where does he want me to go?*

Brian still couldn't see, but he knew he was between a door to the right and a guest bedroom catty-corner from it. His instincts compelled him to head for the bedroom. Once inside, he kicked the door shut behind him.

The period of silence and darkness before he clicked on the flashlight felt like an eternity. A bright sphere illuminated a bed pressed against the wall, a wooden dresser, a cracked closet door, and the dark circle of a gun barrel. He lifted his, started to squeeze the trigger—but he recognized Eva's panicked gaze behind the gun.

Relieved, he lowered his pistol. She did the same with a shaky smile. After double-checking the boards on the bedroom window, he clicked the light off and scooted into the closet with her, feeling the reassuring heat of her body radiate against him. "Where's Louis?"

"He shot one," she whispered. "He left me in here and went lookin' for more."

"He left you?"

"He said I'd be safer. He doesn't want me holdin' him up." She sighed. "What about your granddaddy?"

"He left me too. Wanted me to hide somewhere. We were in the living room when someone threw a grenade down the chimney."

Eva gasped, quickly cupping her hand over her mouth. "So they *are* regular people."

"You saw one?"

"I turned my light on to make sure the one Louis shot was dead. Didn't look long—I was half-scared he'd wake up—but his face was all funny, like a mask or-or makeup. I assumed it was a Stalker."

"Did he have a weapon?"

"I don't know. Everythin' was kind of a jumble." She grabbed his arm with her left hand, still gripping her pistol in the right. "Should we wait here?"

"They wanted us to. Guess we're the dead weight. If we hear the door open, shine your light and I'll aim my gun."

"I can shoot too, you know." The intimidating edge to her voice reminded Brian of her brother. He didn't want to piss her off.

It only takes one hand to hold a flashlight. I can still shoot if I have to.

"Fine. You aim, and *I'll* shine the light."

Eva shifted against Brian, resting the pistol against the tops of her knees. A faint but distinct sound echoed: a gunshot. Eva's fingertips dug into his arm. Wood groaned under the weight of footsteps outside the bedroom door.

The door creaked open. Eva moved her hand so both supported the pistol.

She elbowed Brian, letting him know she was ready. He turned the flashlight on. Her shriek and the pistol firing next to him made Brian flinch as he tried to absorb the sight before him: a person with a chalk-white face and a raised arm, swinging something that reflected in the beam of the flashlight.

Their attacker's body jerked back as Brian's bullet sank into it. He couldn't see where. He tried to fire again, but the pistol clicked.

How? It was a full clip!

He shouted Eva's name. She fired again, grazing the intruder's shoulder. They spun back without falling to the ground.

Someone else entered the room. Eva shifted her gun but didn't shoot.

"This Purge shit is played out, motherfucker!" Louis's shot knocked the invader into the wall. As their body slid to the floor, he put another bullet in it for good measure. Blood spattered the eggshell-white wall, dripping down in gruesome streaks. Chunks of gore clung alongside it in sporadic patterns.

Louis kneeled to inspect the body, night-vision goggles strapped to his face. Brian crawled out of the closet and joined him, aiming his flashlight at the bullet-riddled body. Louis angled his head toward Brian. "You could pour water outta this asshole like a waterin' can."

Brian reached for Louis. "There might be more out there. Let's go back to the closet, wait for Poppa—"

"Are you kiddin' me? These assholes invaded *my* house. I'm not gonna play Seven Minutes in Heaven with you—I'm gonna hunt 'em down."

Louis's persevering boldness impressed Brian. Part of him wanted to listen to his grandfather and stay safe, but another part of him wanted to follow Louis and take the invaders out. He was tired of waiting, of being surprised.

Eva crawled over to inspect the body. "It looks like one of those things, but it isn't smilin'."

"It's a mask," Louis said, "painted up to look like one. Probably think they're scarin' people, but they're gonna end up gettin' shot. Darwinism hard at work." He pulled the mask back, revealing the face of an ordinary man. His lifeless eyes stared at them as blood trickled from his mouth.

"Fucking asshole," Brian muttered. "What the fuck is *wrong* with people?"

Louis put a hand on his shoulder. "Listen, he's dead. Let's worry about the livin' and go look for your granddaddy. Where'd you last see him?"

"The door across from here." Brian fiddled with his gun but couldn't figure out why it had stopped firing.

Louis snatched it from him and tapped the base of the magazine with the palm of his hand. "You didn't have it in all the way."

Brian's cheeks heated, flustered by how easily Louis solved a problem he wasn't even aware of. "Thanks. My grandfather taught me a lot of things, but I guess I forgot that lesson."

"You're just rattled. Sometimes we forget things when we're distracted." Louis stood and offered his hand to his sister. "You okay, Eva?"

She nodded and took it, letting him pull her to her feet. Brian stood and followed them, passing the dead body with a ridiculous fear that it might lunge for him. It didn't. Even if it had been a Stalker, they didn't rise from the dead. *Thank God for small favors.*

Louis took point, so Brian turned his flashlight off and followed the twins out into the hallway. He kept the gun in his right hand and the flashlight in his left, but Eva curled her hand around his left wrist so they wouldn't lose each other in the dark.

"Careful—feel the steps out with your toes." They descended the basement steps behind Louis. "I don't see anythin' yet. Brian, close that door behind you."

Now that his blood flow had slowed, Brian realized how cold it was. He shuddered, pressing closer to Eva's back. A pleasant scent like baby powder made his nostrils flare to absorb it.

After about ten steps, Louis halted. "Ah, shit."

Brian and Eva tripped over each other, nearly knocking Louis to his knees as they fought to gain their composure. Once they righted themselves, a wet cough drifted up from the basement.

Brian tried to lift the pistol, but Louis lowered his arm. "Put that down. Just turn your flashlight on."

He aimed the bright cone of light into the basement, scanning over a washer and dryer, the generator, and stacks of knickknacks and junk lining the brick walls. Dust swirled in the air. The concrete ground was bare, save for a few scuffs and cracks—and a crimson stain. Brian followed it to a pair of shabby boots and faded blue jeans.

He ran to Poppa and kneeled to inspect the dark wound in his gut. The stained swell heaved shallowly. But Poppa's eyes were open, and he managed to shove Brian's flashlight away. "Get that light outta my eyes, son."

When he coughed, blood spattered onto his lips. Brian stood. "Eva, I need my first aid—"

Poppa snatched Brian's hand. "Don't bother. I'm losin' too much blood. Hurts like a sonuvabitch." He lowered the back of his head onto the concrete pillar he was propped against.

"What happened?" Eva asked quietly, approaching them while Louis kept his distance.

"I heard somethin' movin' down here." Poppa coughed again, winced. "Told Brian to hide. Went down and felt the burn, knew I been shot. Heard but didn't see the fucker scramblin' up the steps."

Brian's eyes stung, but he managed to keep his voice even. "We killed one upstairs. It might've been him."

"Glad you're okay, son." Poppa wrapped his hand in Brian's coat sleeve as Brian kneeled at his side. "You did good."

Louis cleared his throat. "I'll go check the rest of the house. Come on, Eva."

She stood and squeezed Brian's shoulder before disappearing up the stairs behind her brother.

Poppa coughed again, but it sounded thicker this time—*wet*. "I don't know how the fucker got me. I made it through a war and part of the gotdamned apocalypse only to have some coward plug me in the dark. He was up and out before I could get a good look at him. Hell, mighta been a her, even."

Brian's nose stung from the effort of keeping his eyes from welling up. "Are you sure I can't do anything?"

"I don't wanna leave you." Poppa's glassy eyes were starting to water. "I know I'm all you got. I won't lie—I'm scared. For both of us."

Poppa blinked. Tears streamed down his cheeks, crushing Brian's attempts to restrain his own. They poured until his grandfather's face was a fading blur of bloodstained fabric and ashen skin.

"What I done in the war, I wrestled with my whole life. Murderin' all those people. I told myself they made me do it. I was okay with snuffin' out all those lives because they weren't *mine*. I wanted to live." Poppa squeezed his eyes shut. "When it came down to it, I was a coward. I could kill all those innocent people but couldn't take my own life." His eyes opened and looked into Brian's. "But now I know why I lived: so I could prepare you for all this. You're the only Jameson left now, Brian."

If Brian spoke, he knew the dam would break. He kept his trembling lips shut tight.

Poppa let out a moan, either of grief or pain. "I can't barely see your face now—" he reached up to Brian's face with a shaky hand "—but it's the most beautiful thing in this ugly world. Reminds me of your daddy—I loved him so much, but I don't know if he...if he ever knew." When Poppa coughed again, bloody spittle dribbled from his chin.

Brian flung his arms around his grandfather's neck and buried his nose in the fuzzy collar of his moth-eaten jacket. It still smelled like Old Spice and cigarette smoke. "Poppa, I-I don't know how I'm going...how I'm going to keep going—"

"You got to," Poppa said in a small voice, "so you can be the light in someone else's darkness like...like Ruby was for me."

Brian retreated from Poppa and lifted his gun with shaky hands. He steadied himself as best as he could and tried to wipe his blurry eyes. He had to see where he was aiming so his shot would be true, so he could put his grandfather out of his misery instead of making the pain worse.

"I got to go to my sweetheart." Poppa sputtered. "Help me get to her quick, son."

Brian blinked back tears. His shaking hands leveled the pistol.

A shot rang out, resounding and momentous. Poppa's head slumped against the collar of his worn coat. Flecks of blood stained the creamy wool collar. A trickle dripped from the entrance wound in his left temple, slow and steady.

The gun clattered onto the hard floor. Brian dragged his trembling fingers down the hot liquid clinging to his cheeks, sickened by the coppery smell, unable to look away from the shell of Poppa's body.

I couldn't do it. I didn't. I...

He lifted the flashlight and angled it toward the basement steps. Louis lowered his revolver, smoke still swirling out of the barrel.

Eva shoved past her brother and jogged down to Brian's side. She wrapped her arms around him, but all the heat in the world couldn't warm him. He stared at Louis, his gut fluttering like a million moths buzzing around a porch light. A sudden onset of painful nausea overtook him. Eva made soothing sounds against his ear, stroking his hair, mothering him.

Louis descended the stairs and shoved the revolver into a holster at his hip. He lifted his goggles, the whites surrounding his pitch-black eyes accentuated by halogen light. "House is clear. Do what you need to."

Brian's lips parted to demand if Louis had killed the one who'd had the gun, the one who'd shot his grandfather, but a pained sigh took the place of his question.

Louis approached Brian and patted his head as if he was a dog who'd obediently finished a trick. He meant to offer consolation, but it reminded Brian of Rocky, of the strange business with the twins' grandfather, of the smoke swirling out of the revolver and the flames flickering in those coal-black eyes.

As he stared into them, the tendrils of darkness inside him spread and took hold.

Chapter Eight: Moving On

12/10, OTTAWA, KANSAS

Lavellé Residence
Morning

Brian sat with his grandfather's body, lost in the void where time existed only as an abstract creation. Eva stayed by his side, sometimes rubbing his back and shoulder, but Louis turned the generator back on for light and left to examine the rest of the house.

When he finished, he returned to Brian and Eva. "Looks like they busted in through the bathroom skylight. Found one dead in the living room, then the two I took care of. Guy in the spare bedroom had this." He held a revolver by the grip and popped the chamber loose, spinning it. "No bullets. Musta used the last one on Max, switched it out for the machete."

"He mighta followed you in," Eva said to Brian. "After…" Her eyes drifted to Poppa before lowering to the ground.

Brian looked from the wrinkled hands curled at his grandfather's sides to Louis's searching eyes. "Why did you do it, Louis?"

Louis kneeled at Brian's side, his fingers picking at frayed threads on his jean pockets. "I came down to check on you, but I didn't want to intrude… I overheard your conversation, didn't think it was a memory you oughta have. I already put one grandfather outta his misery—better me than you."

"It's just weird that you shot Rocky and both our grandfathers." Brian pressed his dry lips together, skirting Louis's gaze. "I mean, you wouldn't shoot *me*, would you?"

"Brian, look at me." Louis held his hand to his chest. "Scout's Honor, I didn't know the dog belonged to you and that he wasn't infected. And I meant to do you a favor with your granddaddy. As for shootin' you? Not gonna happen unless you shoot at me or Eva or a Stalker gets you. And I'll make sure no Stalker even touches a golden hair on your head."

Eva squeezed Brian's shoulder and stroked it with her thumb. "We're your family now and you're ours. We'll look out for each other."

The resentment and suspicion Brian felt toward Louis withdrew—for now. In its place, he felt begrudging gratitude because he didn't have to shoot his grandfather. Not only that, but Louis had saved him when his panicked oversight about the pistol clip left him in the lurch.

"First things first, we gotta pack up," Louis said. "We can't stay here. Brian, your cows are a little shook up but good to go. We'll take them, see if they take to pullin' a cart so we can carry as much as possible." Louis sighed. "I hate to ask, but what you want to do about your granddaddy?"

Brian didn't want to leave Poppa on a cold basement floor propped up against a concrete pillar with his brains splattered on it. "You said you cremated your grandfather, right? Let's do the same for mine."

Louis nodded. "I can handle that. But we need to be ready to leave right after in case the assholes who took our horses see or smell the smoke, decide to double back for us or send a few of their buddies."

"Where are we goin', Lou?" Eva asked. "Everyone we got is gone."

"We don't know that for sure." After a moment of silence, Louis's eyes lit up. "Papère wanted to head down to New Orleans, see if *Tante* and *Nonc* were still there. But he was only hopin' their *boat* was. I say we travel down, see if they're still there. If not, we might find the boat key at their condo."

Eva furrowed her thin eyebrows. "Where would we sail? With what gas?"

"You remember that island we went to with 'em across the Gulf?"

She nodded. "It was real nice. Isolated. Quiet."

"If the weather's good, we'd get there in...hmm..." Louis stuck his thumb between his lips. "I think it was about six hundred miles, give or take. Even if we only went ten per hour, that's sixty hours. We could make it there in three days. If we can't find their key, there'll be dozens of other boats docked in New Orleans. Some might have gas still in 'em, and we still got what's left from Papère's generator."

Eva's crossed legs bounced. "But what if people already sailed them somewhere? Or they drifted out to sea?"

"Not every boat is gonna be gone, I guarantee you. Lotsa boats down there for personal and commercial use. And *I* learned how to sail, unlike you."

"Stop talkin' down to me, asshole!" Eva socked her brother in the shoulder. "Why do you want to go to some island, anyway?"

"An island is contained, right? It has its own ecosystem: rivers, fish, animals. This one happens to have a resort on it—sure, might mean clearin' out some Stalkers, maybe some survivors, but there's already shelter there."

"Wouldn't it be better to find an island with no people?" Eva glanced at Brian, checking to see if he was buying into Louis's tentative plan.

The truth was, Brian had no plan of his own. He still hovered somewhere between past and present, numb to what was going on around him.

"Every island's gonna have somethin' or someone on it," Louis said, "but they mighta already evacuated the resort when shit went down. Besides, it's close to the mainland if we need to leave. We can head for Cuba or Florida."

Eva sighed. "*Or* they closed it off and everyone is trapped there. Brian, you gotta have an input on this too. What do you think?"

Brian snapped to life, glancing between the expectant twins. "Um, what's it like there?"

"It's fuckin' gorgeous." Louis's eyebrows quirked over expanding pupils. "White sugar sand, clear blue sea, palm trees swayin' in the breeze, all these little bungalows on the beach with hammocks on the porches. Imagine layin' out in a hammock, driftin' in the sea breeze or sunnin' on the beach. We might even get lucky and find some booze in the kitchen."

Brian's mind conjured idyllic and appealing images. Louis had practically sold him a timeshare.

"Don't let him sucker you." Eva arched her eyebrows. "My brother has a way of gettin' what he wants."

"Well, shit, Eva." Louis clicked his tongue. "You got somethin' better planned?"

"Not really... It just seems like a long trip to make." She sighed. "I guess Tante and Nonc's place is better than nothin'. But I bet they left."

"They're too stubborn to leave. They probably stuck it out." Louis's eyes skimmed from Eva's to Brian's. "You okay? You don't have to go with if you're not up to it. We could stay here a night or two, but I wouldn't suggest it—more of 'em might come back."

Brian shook his head. "No, you're right. Let's do it. You know how to get there?"

Louis nodded. "Got a crappy paper map, but it'll do. I'll mark a route once we got some time, but we should get packin'."

Brian gathered his and Poppa's belongings while the twins packed theirs. As Brian rummaged in the living room, Eva stepped in. She leaned against the smoke-singed wall. "Lou's gonna take care of your granddaddy for you. Why don't we go work with your cows, see if we can get 'em to pull the cart?"

Brian nodded and marched outside with her. A brilliant sunrise suffused the snow with an ethereal golden glow. They kept a vigilant eye on their surroundings, but the peaceful landscape held no surprises for them. A crow darted into the fields, settling atop the scarecrow's outstretched arm to preen itself.

Eva and Brian entered the barn. After making sure it was clear, she led him to the cart and took the lead. "Lou was never interested in this kinda stuff." Eva fiddled with the yokes. "He'd go huntin' and fishin', but I think he felt like he was above all the grunt work. We used to have animals, but after Mamère died, Papère didn't have any interest in workin' the farm anymore."

"Do you buy all that stuff about your grandfather?" Brian stroked Hildy's side. "I can't tell if Louis is efficient or impulsive."

Eva laughed and clipped a chain to the yokes. "Both, probably. Papère *did* have a bad temper, but I guess I was spared most of it. Lou's attitude always ends up gettin' him into trouble, and they did bicker sometimes. I guess I believe it. After Mamère died, Papère got mean again. He made your granddaddy seem downright cuddly." She frowned. "Oh, I'm sorry. I shouldn't—"

Brian shook his head. "You don't have to walk on eggshells. I'm used to losing people. The virus took my parents and sister, and my grandma killed herself. And you might remember what happened with my dad, so…"

Eva dropped the yoke and chain and moved to his side. Her small but strong hands gripped his shoulders. "I'm sorry I made you remember all that again. I'm sorry it even happened." She wrapped her arms around his neck and leaned in for a quick, tight hug. He inhaled a whiff of something sweet like honeysuckle in her hair. When she withdrew, she dragged her fingers through it. "Mère and Père died in a fire. Lou and I had to move here with our grandparents. That all happened after we grew apart, so I guess you never heard."

"I'm sorry, Eva." Her expression conveyed the grief he tried to suppress. He wanted to let the building tears go, but he knew plenty more would fight their way free when he said goodbye to his grandfather.

Instead, he sniffed and swallowed them back. "It all feels like a long nightmare, like I'm expecting my mom to wake me up for breakfast. I'll do my schoolwork, my dad will come home, and we'll eat dinner. Then we'll watch some stupid movie and I'll stay up way longer than I should dicking around on my tablet."

Eva's deep brown eyes glimmered. "We took it all for granted, didn't we? We had no idea how easily we could lose it. I still miss my parents. I cry about them sometimes..." She bit her lip, debating whether she wanted to reveal more. She decided against it and smiled instead. "Well, we'd better get on with it. Lou'll want to get out of here sooner than later."

They finished working with Hildy and Agnes, who, true to Poppa's assurances, were clever enough to take to their new duties. Brian swore Agnes gave them a disdainful look, but he might've been attaching personality to her so he didn't feel such an aching sense of loneliness.

Louis joined them before long, depositing an assortment of bags and containers onto the cart. He tied it all down with twine and a couple of tow straps after covering it with a tarp. They left their transportation and belongings locked in the barn while they journeyed into the backyard to take care of Poppa's remains. A charred pyre towered into the horizon, topped with a red-and-white striped blanket. The silhouette of a body shaped it into peaks and valleys like a mountain range.

Louis strode over to the pyre and grabbed a small box of matches from it. "I know you wanna say a proper goodbye and all, but we gotta make this quick." He slid the box open and withdrew a match. "Let me know when you're ready."

Brian approached the pyre. "Got it." He pressed a hand atop a stiff lump he assumed was Poppa's shoulder, struggling to find the words for something he was still having trouble coming to terms with. "We have to go, Poppa, so I can't say much. And I don't even know if you can hear it, if you're here in some way, or anywhere anymore." He exhaled and shut his eyes. "I appreciate everything you did for me—not just after, but before this...this *thing* happened. All the holidays we spent at your house, the meals we shared, the smile and wave you gave us every time we came and went. Even though you're gone, I'll remember the things you taught me for as long as I live." Brian looked up at the clear blue sky, struggling to keep the tears from rolling over the brims of his eyes. "I hope you're with Nana and Rocky. And Dad, Mom, and Becky. If you are, tell them I miss them."

He stepped back and looked at his grandfather's body one last time. Before his tears could overwhelm him, Brian nodded at Louis. Louis struck the match and tossed it atop the pyre. It rippled with flame, smoke drifting into the crisp winter air as the wood crackled and split.

Louis approached Brian and nudged his arm. "Better get a move on, *boug*."

Brian's mental exhaustion prevented him from questioning whether this was an insult or an endearment. The twins marched him back to the barn, one at each side as if they were his bodyguards. Their sympathy agitated him in a strange way. He wanted them to see him as an equal, not someone they needed to look after.

But who else did he have? Without them, he was alone.

Brian shook these thoughts out of his mind, distracted by the plumes of smoke ascending from behind the house and the sickening scent of roasting flesh. He tried not to think of Poppa's body disintegrating into ash and bone, to tell himself Poppa was at peace now, that memories of My Lai and the loss of his loved ones would no longer plague him—but Brian would suffer in his stead.

The dead never suffer, only the living who mourn them.

DURING THEIR TRAVELS, the silence stretched into agonizing gaps that encouraged Brian's mind to work overtime. He flashed back to the night before, thinking of ways he could've saved his grandfather—and resolving, with regret, that there was nothing he could've done. Thinking of ways to change the past was a torturous, fruitless endeavor.

Once the sun started to set, Louis slowed Agnes so she strolled alongside Brian and Hildy. "We should find somewhere to stop off, settle in for the night." Louis adjusted the map with a crisp crackle. "We're near some place called Lakeside Park. It's a bit far from 69, but it's good to camp near water."

Eva shrugged from behind her brother. "I have no problem with that. I *do* have a problem with my butt, though—these cows are so damn uncomfortable!"

Brian smiled at her as she cringed and wriggled. "Sorry. Imagine what it's like for me and your brother." He looked at Louis. "I haven't been down this way much. As long as you know how to get there, let's go."

Instead of looking to Poppa for leadership, he now looked to Louis. If Brian tried to make a go of it on his own, he didn't know where he'd even head for—and he didn't want to be alone. He liked Eva, and...well, sometimes it was easier to do what Louis wanted and avoid pissing him off.

Louis didn't lead them astray: they made it to Lakeside Park within the hour. A snow-covered dock had frozen in the middle of the spacious lake, which reflected the fleeting colors of a dusky sky. A stretch of sidewalk curved alongside the lake and an empty parking lot behind several picnic benches and two green Porta Potties. Brian relayed his experience with the Porta Potty Stalker to the twins—and his reticence to linger near what he now perceived to be putrid death traps.

"I'm sure there's a cabin nearby for the park ranger or whoever looked after the park." Brian tugged on his hood as a sudden chill whipped across his face. "Let's go look at that park map. It'll probably show us where."

"Good thinkin'," Louis said. "Might be supplies too. Flare guns and such."

They led the cows into the parking lot and searched the sun-faded map for the ranger's cabin, fingers trailing along scratched plexiglass. After locating the cabin and memorizing the trail, they followed it to a vast clearing. A lone hut sat enclosed in a field of snow, firewood piled on the porch. Bare tree limbs squeaked in the breeze, casting crepuscular shadows along the snow.

Louis hopped down and gestured for his sister to stay put. Brian slipped off to follow him, resting his hand against his pistol as his bow and quiver swung against his back. He couldn't remember what it felt like to wear a single layer of clothes or go without a weapon anymore.

When they approached the corner of the quaint cabin, Louis froze. He signaled for Brian to get behind him and leaned in to whisper against his ear, "There's a shed back there. Door's open—I think someone's in there."

"We should leave—" But Louis scurried away before Brian could finish talking. Louis pressed his back to the side of the shed, holding his revolver in front of his chest. Aggravated, Brian debated whether to follow him or to slink around the other side of the cabin and get a different view. He figured Louis could handle himself and opted for the latter option.

Despite the frigid air, Brian swore he was sweating. He hid against the cabin wall closest to the shed. Rustling noises came from inside the diminutive building. When Brian leaned around the corner, he glimpsed a man with a metal instrument in his hand chopping into some sort of meat.

Not a Stalker. Maybe someone trying to survive out here.

"Mister," Brian called out. The weapon froze in mid-air: a butcher's cleaver covered in dripping ichor. "I have a gun aimed at you, so don't make any sudden movements. I need shelter for the night. I don't want to hurt you or steal anything from you."

The man turned slowly, lowering the cleaver. His bundled clothes obscured his bulk or lack thereof, but he wasn't much taller than Brian. His eyes widened above a crooked nose and cracked lips. "I-I'm coming out. Don't shoot me, please. Just getting dinner ready."

"Put the cleaver down," Brian ordered, jutting his chin.

The man obeyed. A bowl sat atop a table with pieces of some sort of animal scattered around it. "Y-you're the first person I've seen in a couple of months. What're you doing out here?"

Louis crept around the side of the shed, gun aimed. Remembering Poppa's impromptu murder of the woman with the pocketknife, Brian stepped forward. "Don't shoot him, Louis—he's unarmed."

Louis flashed Brian an aggravated glare—if looks could kill, Brian would've dropped dead then and there. He joined Brian and kept his revolver trained on the strange man trapped in the shed. "Make any sudden moves and you're as dead as that deer you're cuttin' up."

"Oh, my—two of you!" The man smiled. "I'd certainly enjoy the company."

Louis arched his eyebrows and glanced at Brian as if to say, "Don't mention Eva, you idiot." Brian read him loud and clear.

"My name's Henry." The man tugged on the brim of a tan Stetson hat. "I'm the park ranger—well, I used to be. What're your names?"

"I'm Brian." Brian managed a tight smile. "Funny enough, Henry's actually my middle name. I always hated it. Um, this is—"

"Louis. I wouldn't have told you, but Blondie woulda blabbed it anyway." Louis rolled his eyes. "Henry, is that cabin safe? You been sleepin' in it?"

"Yes—and I have canned food, wood for the fire, and plenty of blankets!" Nervous energy spiked Henry's meek voice. "We could all sit and have dinner together—"

"Or I could kill you now and take it all." Louis cocked the revolver's hammer.

"*Louis.*" Eva appeared from the corner of the cabin, leading Hildy and Agnes by their reins. "Who're you tryin' to impress with this macho bullshit? You both got guns aimed at the man—clearly, we have the upper hand. Why don't we go inside and make sure he's unarmed? One of us can stay up with him while the other two sleep. Then we can leave him be."

Louis looked between Brian and Eva, his eyes narrowed. "You two are gonna get us killed, you know that?"

"You just want to stay for the night?" The energy in Henry's voice faded. "Where are you headed, if I might ask?"

"You're only a stop on a long path to nowhere," Louis said. "Now take us into your cabin. If you try anythin' funny, I won't let either of them stop me from blowin' that hat right off your head, Ranger Rick." He gave Eva a downright dirty look and didn't bother with Brian.

Henry stepped out of the shed. Louis pressed the muzzle of the revolver against Henry's back and marched him around to the front of the cabin. Brian and Eva followed, sharing an uneasy glance.

Henry climbed the steps and reached for the doorknob. "You'll have to excuse the mess." When the door creaked open, a rancid malodor wafted out and flooded their noses. Eva bent over, gagging, while Brian covered his nose with one arm. It reminded him of his mother's repugnant odor during her final days.

Louis jerked Henry back by the hood of his parka. "You gone crazy, *fonchock*? What the hell is this nasty shit?"

Brian approached the open door, keeping his arm pressed against his nose. A dissonance of hushed giggles greeted him. His gaze drifted from a round table set with coffee cups and bare plates to the four chairs surrounding it—and the figures seated in them.

The Stalkers fixed their clouded eyes on him, utterly still. Their arms were chained behind them to the rails of the chairs, their feet handcuffed to the legs. Cracks threaded through their skin like aged porcelain dolls, and a few pathetic wisps of hair clung to their heads. Their strained smiles were mockingly cheerful.

When Eva strolled up behind Brian, she retched and quickly ran off the porch. She fell to her knees and clutched her gut while Hildy and Agnes nosed at the snow, oblivious to the scent—or perhaps trying to block it out.

"What the hell were you thinkin' chainin' those freaks up?" Louis shook Henry by the fur collar of his jacket. "Were they your family or somethin'? *Mon Dieu!*"

"N-no." Henry lifted his hands in front of him, speaking in a small voice. "I found them."

"And you brought them *here*, with you?" Louis shook his head and stammered, at a rare loss for words.

"It got so lonely, especially when the radio went quiet..."

Brian lowered his arm from his face so he could speak. "The smell doesn't bother you?" He coughed, the rotten fetor clinging to the inside of his nose and mouth.

"At first it did. But I got used to it. They won't hurt you. Sometimes they get a little excited and knock the chairs over, but I've gotten used to having them around."

"So what, you have tea parties with your fucked-up little dolls?" A bemused chortle slipped out of Louis. "I hope this is the tip of your crazy little iceberg."

Eva joined Brian, struggling to speak and hold her breath at the same time. "Henry, right? I don't think I introduced myself: I'm Eva, Louis's sister." She approached Henry, maintaining a valiant front. "Henry, this isn't safe. We can't stay with you if they're here. And wouldn't you rather have real, live people for company?"

Henry glanced to the side, clearly thinking of the four Stalkers clanking around behind him. "But you'll leave tomorrow. They'll be here for a long time."

"But what if one of them breaks free?" Brian asked. "How can you sleep with that possibility? If you're lonely, it might be better to come with us."

"Brian," Louis sighed, "you can't adopt him. He ain't a kitten or a puppy for us to feed and clean up after. Me and Eva are already stuck with *you*."

Brian glared at Louis, not appreciating his contrary attitude and condescension. Eva kicked her brother's foot while Henry wasn't looking.

"You think I'm crazy, I know—" Henry lowered his head and gazed at the porch "—but this is all I have. I don't have the families coming out to the park anymore, no kids playing, no lovers embracing. Even the geese have gone away. Now all I have is my routine: I wake up, have coffee, go hunt, and feed my family. I talk, and they listen. They *need* me."

The sun descended beyond the dense rows of skeletal trees. A tiny orb glowed in the sky, but the hazy light provided no warmth. They had cows to look after and belongings to store, and they needed sleep and shelter themselves.

"I ain't gonna stand in this doorway all night." Louis tapped a steel-toed boot and gestured with his gun. "Take them outside."

Henry balled his fists at his sides. "But they'll freeze!"

"Either you take 'em out or I shoot 'em. Your choice."

"Fine—" Henry relaxed his hands. "—but this is murder."

"You think I care? They'd murder you before you could even fuckin' *blink*." Louis shoved Henry inside, warily eyeing his dining companions. They stared at Louis, giggling like they knew a secret they'd never tell him.

Brian and Eva kept their distance as Henry pushed the first chair through the doorway. Louis kept his gun trained on the forlorn man. "Don't set them free, either. Leave 'em tied to those chairs like you have 'em."

Henry didn't respond. He trudged over to the edge of the woods with his delicate cargo and set it down. The Stalker's eyes followed him, teeth exposed in a permanent smile by its shrunken lips. It didn't writhe or attempt to escape its shackles, or even exhibit any signs of aggression toward Henry. Brian puzzled over this, concluding it had gone into some sort of dormant state because Henry kept it fed.

After Henry lined the other Stalkers in a row next to the first, he headed into the shed. He emerged with blankets in his arms, but Louis yelled at him before he could drape them over his exposed companions. "Are you fuckin' kiddin' me, Henry? Our cows need those more than those gigglin' assholes do!"

Henry's normally passive gaze hardened when he directed it at Louis. Concerned Henry's resentment might eventually erupt into violence, Brian tried to mollify him. "We have to protect them—we have a long way to go and they're our only transportation. Is there anywhere they'll be safe?"

"I'd keep them on the porch." Henry stared at the four Stalkers with a blank expression. "They'll settle down once the blankets warm them. You can peek at them from inside the window."

Eva grasped the blankets from Henry with a soft smile. While she took care of Agnes and Hildy, Louis eyed the shed. "Why's that shed got no door? We need to store our stuff somewhere."

"A buck smashed into it trying to run from something, so I took it down and chopped it up for firewood." Henry coughed and rubbed his arms. "No one comes around anymore. Your things should be safe overnight."

Louis clicked his tongue and looked at Brian. "Make yourself useful, boug. You got to have some muscles underneath all those layers of clothes, right?"

Brian shoved past Louis, more concerned by his *own* escalating temper than Henry's. Aside from the backpacks containing their clothes and toiletries, he shifted their belongings from the cart to the shed. A dismembered deer head stared at him from the table, its tongue drooping out. His stomach soured when he flashed back to the deer he'd killed and the light fading in its dark eyes, revealing his reflection. Grimacing, he piled as much as he could on the ground and left the yoke and cart next to the shed.

When Brian returned to the cabin, Henry was on his knees washing the floor with gloves, a bucket, and a car sponge.

"Got to get the smell out to sleep here," Louis explained when he saw the puzzled expression on Brian's face. "Eva, you think you can manage on your own for a moment?"

"Uh, sure." She withdrew her pistol, keeping it aimed at the floor while Henry scrubbed.

Louis snagged Brian by the hood of his jacket and pulled him outside. Brian stumbled down the stairs before jerking free and shoving Louis, too agitated to think straight. "What the hell do you think you're doing? You can't pull me around like some dog on a leash!"

Brian backed away until he bumped into something firm and knotted: the cabin wall. Louis closed in on Brian, their breath puffing out of them in mingling clouds of moisture. "Yeah? Well, I don't wanna be jerked around, either. What kinda shit were you pullin' back there? If you'd let me take this nut out, we wouldn't be holdin' his hand through this just to get a night's sleep."

Brian tried to edge away from Louis, but he had him pinned. "Your sister had a hand in that too—why the hell am *I* the one dealing with your shitty attitude? Are you pissed because you're stuck with me now?" The words still stung as Brian recalled them. "What happened to trying to be friends again, huh?"

Louis pressed his palms against the wall, head dangling in front of Brian. Their erratic, heavy breaths created a strange symphony. Brian considered reaching for his pistol, but Louis looked up with a sympathetic gaze that stayed Brian's hand. "Look, I'm sorry. When we were kids, you and Eva used to go along with whatever I said—I'm not used to this, and I was pissed. But you have to understand, I'm tryin' to look out for us."

"You don't have to look out for me." Brian's voice lost its edge as his stiff muscles relaxed. "Just treat me like an equal, not someone who's beneath you. I can look out for myself."

Louis backed away and grazed his scar with his fingertips. "I'm aware of that."

Brian wanted to grill him about that damned scar, but a chuffed titter drifted over and reminded him that they weren't alone. They were exposed, vulnerable to the elements and predators—animals, humans, former humans...

Time and place. Not now.

Their eyes met, searching for answers to questions they couldn't yet ask. Brian swallowed the lump in his throat and peeled his back from the wall, able to step forward now that Louis had retreated. "Look, we should go in—but before we do, I want to let you know that I want us to trust each other. I don't want us to butt heads, try to boss each other around—we need to work together. Not just for ourselves, but for Eva. My grandfather killed a woman right in front of me and I didn't even know he was going to do it. What he did made me question everything he taught me. I was worried you'd do the same thing to Henry, and I couldn't stand by and watch again. I want to make it to this island, but I don't want to lose myself on the way. Does that make sense?"

Louis pressed his dry lips together. He wet them, but his response didn't come to him with his usual rapid-fire speed. A thoughtful expression replaced the cynicism Brian was used to. "You get to this island, maybe you'll find yourself."

Brian scoffed and rolled his eyes. "Yeah? Well, I don't think this is the time for an existential crisis."

"*Au contraire, mon ami*: an apocalypse is the *perfect* time for an existential crisis." Louis patted Brian's shoulder before he headed for the porch. "Our lives are in a constant state of crisis."

Surprised by the depth of Louis's observation, Brian mulled it over while he followed him into the cabin. Eva and Henry were in the middle of their own somber conversation. Henry's bucket sat on its rim with the sponge drying on top of it. The cabin still smelled faintly unpleasant, but a crackling fire helped mask the lingering stench.

"Your sister's sweet." Henry sat cross-legged on the ground across from Eva, who was perched on the edge of the bed.

"*Too* sweet." Louis unzipped his bomber jacket to reveal a black turtleneck. "And you'd better not get any ideas."

"Oh, you don't have to worry about that." Henry wrung his hands and glanced at Brian.

Louis's eyes narrowed. "Don't get any ideas about him, either."

"Is he related to you too?"

"Hardly. We're about as different as sunshine and shadow." Louis sat next to his sister and pulled off his gloves, rubbing his hands in front of the fire.

"Childhood friends." Brian stripped his parka off. Snow plopped onto the ground, already beginning to melt. "More or less."

Louis flopped back on the bed, hands linked underneath a splay of silken ebony. "I'm beat. You and your little family wore my ass out, Henry." He shut his eyes, long lashes fluttering against tan skin. Before long, his chest swelled in a deep, steady rhythm that complemented the heavy breaths escaping his aquiline nose.

"I can barely keep my eyes open." Eva yawned and stretched, her shirt lifting to reveal a slight swell of stomach hanging over her jeans. "I can try to stay up with you though, Brian."

Brian glanced at Henry. He kneeled in front of the fire, gazing into the dancing flames. Bags puffed underneath his heavy eyes and his thin lips curled into a slight grimace. Somehow, this beanpole of a man had corralled four Stalkers without getting injured. Sheer determination? Desperation?

But Brian didn't fear him. He pitied him.

"I'll be fine, Eva. Get some sleep. I'll wake one of you up when I get tired."

"You're a sweetheart." She pulled her legs onto the bed and curled up beside Louis. Within minutes, her snores overtook her brother's.

Brian sat beside Henry. Although he wasn't scared of him, he still debated whether he wanted to start a conversation with some nut who'd kept a collection of Stalkers.

"I know what you're thinking," Henry murmured, "but I'm not crazy."

"Maybe not, but you look tired."

Henry turned his head to look at Brian. "I can't sleep. I'm too worried about them."

"Well, that's fine. We can talk." Brian bundled his legs against his chest and wrapped his arms around them. "So, tell me what your life was like before the pandemic."

Henry's close-cropped red hair gleamed in the rippling orange light cast by the fire. "I worked here for ten years, straight out of college. I lived here—it *was* my life. I had more freedom here than in town. Even with all the changes in society, Kansas never changed—Bible Belt through and through. So, I wasn't ever popular."

Brian had no trouble connecting the dots, but he didn't understand what the big deal was. "Why didn't you move?"

Henry sighed. "Because I was never good with change. Ironic, isn't it, that I'm still alive?"

"You were probably used to living a hard life."

"Maybe." Henry managed a small smile, but there was no happiness behind it. "And you?"

"My family's dead." Brian shut his eyes and inhaled. "The twins are childhood friends of mine. My grandfather took me to their place because he was friends with their grandfather, but they're both dead now. Stalkers and raiders, take your pick."

"I'm sorry to hear that." Henry reached out to comfort Brian. When Brian didn't flinch, Henry curled his fingers around Brian's shoulder. "I didn't lose anyone. Well, I didn't have anyone to lose. But I know...I know it hurts."

"I'm sorry we did this. It's a desperate time, I guess. Desperate times, desperate measures. It still seems like the longest, most horrible dream I could ever think up."

"I know the feeling." Henry returned his hand to his knee, digging his fingers into the fabric of his snow pants. "I know you think I'm disgusting for keeping them here, the Stalkers. I'm used to people thinking I'm disgusting, so I don't care. But that doesn't mean it hurts any less."

Brian returned the gesture of comfort Henry had offered. "I don't think you're disgusting. My mom explained to me that you're born a certain way—no one can choose the way you feel, or who you feel it for."

"Your mom sounds like a smart woman. A lot smarter than my parents. They kicked me out when I told them. Not that I was ever close to them, but still...being hated by your own family is the worst feeling in the world. Being hated for *existing*. They expect you to change, but how can you? And they lash out because it's easier to hate something than to try and understand it."

"People suck. But there's not many left of them, I guess."

Henry snickered. "That's the irony of it. I miss people. I miss lazy fast food workers and stuck-up rich people, shitty drivers, corrupt politicians...I miss watching other people live their lives. Even if I wasn't a part of them."

Brian almost offered to let him come along, but he remembered his intense discussion with Louis and didn't want to upset the delicate trust they'd established.

"I know you were gonna offer, but I'm fine here. Plus, I don't think *he'd* like it." Henry leaned closer to Brian so he could whisper, "Eva already asked, but I don't want to get her into trouble. You guys should ditch him."

Brian withdrew from Henry and shot him a disapproving glare. "I'd never do that! Besides, he's smart, decisive, good with guns…"

"You're making excuses for him." Henry's smug smile irritated Brian. It reminded him of the Stalkers and their secret-keeping grins.

"No, I'm not. I'm listing reasons to keep him around."

"You're forgetting the most important one." Henry cupped his hand over his mouth. "You like him. Or you did before, at least."

Brian narrowed his eyes but didn't blurt out the swift denial that came to mind. Instead, he tried to quantify exactly what he felt and how to label it. "I wouldn't say that. I *like* Eva. Louis intrigues me."

"How long have you been friends?"

"Well, our grandfathers knew each other before we were even born… So, I guess our entire lives up until I was about ten. Louis and I got in a fight; that's how he got the scar on his cheek. Our parents stopped letting us hang out after that."

Henry frowned and furrowed his brow. "Was it an accident or did you mean to hurt him?"

"I remember being angry at him for some reason…" Brian held a hand to his forehead, trying to will the memories out, to adjust the focus. "I wanted to hurt him. He had a habit of being bossy… I'm sure you can still see that. I guess I got tired of it."

"I would too." Henry tapped his fingers on his knee. "But even if you *did* get mad enough to hurt him, it's only because you cared about him. People say hate and love are opposites, but really, they're just two different forms of passion. The opposite of that would be feeling nothing for them at all."

One of the logs popped in the fire. The scent of burning wood drifted into the room, making one of the twins groan in their sleep. At least Brian *hoped* they were both sleeping so they didn't overhear his conversation.

Brian leaned back on his arms and stretched his legs out to the fire to warm his toes. "Eva hasn't changed much. When I'm around her, it's like we're picking up where we left off—it's *comfortable.* But there's this weird thing with Louis…I *want* to like him, but I'm scared to for some reason."

Henry scooted forward, fixing his alert gaze on Brian. "Life's short, especially now—you shouldn't be scared to open up. Trust me: you don't want to be some crazy guy living in a cabin with Stalkers for company."

Someone stirred on the bed. Brian looked over and saw Louis perched over the edge, attempting to detangle his hair with his fingers. When their gazes locked, a ripple of anxiety shuddered through Brian. *How much of that did he hear? We were pretty quiet...right?*

Louis squinted, covering a yawn as he struggled to transition from exhaustion to alertness. "Hey, boug. You wanna get some shut-eye?"

Brian relaxed. If Louis *had* heard any of that, it didn't seem to be bothering him.

Henry didn't look enthused about swapping conversation partners, but the fog of fatigue clung to Brian. He stood and stretched, groaning as his limbs cracked. "You sure? You weren't asleep long."

Louis stood, rubbing his face. "I can get by with a cat-nap or two. Get some rest." He tapped Brian on the arm with his fist as they passed one another. "Just keep your hands off my sister."

Brian's attempts to read Louis's expression proved to be a frustrating venture. In this case, the best response was none. He crawled into bed, taking great pains to avoid brushing any part of Eva's slumbering body.

SHOUTS FROM OUTSIDE woke Brian and Eva. They took one look at each other before bounding out of bed with guns in their hands and shivers rippling down their bodies. The fire had gone out and neither of them had shoes on.

Brian opened the door. Hildy and Agnes stood on the porch with their ears pricked forward. He followed their gaze and saw four toppled, shattered chairs with bloodstains underneath them and the bodies of the Stalkers strewn about in pieces like a tornado had mowed through them. Henry kneeled in front of them, sobbing hysterically with a gun in his hands. He kept it aimed at Louis, who was obviously failing in his attempts to talk Henry down. It didn't help matters any that Louis pointed his own gun right back at Henry.

"Louis! Henry!" Eva rushed to her brother's side, but she hesitated to aim her gun at Henry. Brian followed her, regretting his lack of boots; his socks were already soaked through.

"What happened?" Brian asked whoever would answer him first.

"We came out here to check on his pets when he woke up." Louis kept his eyes glued to Henry. "Somethin' got 'em in the night, and he flipped his lid when he saw 'em. Scurried over to the shed before I could peg him, grabbed the revolver I snatched from the robber. I thought it was empty, but I guess this crazy fucker carries a quick loader on him."

"They're dead because you made me do this!" Henry sobbed. "For all I know, *you* did it—they were fine when I went to sleep!"

"Don't blame me, you delusional motherfucker! You think I kneeled down and took chunks outta 'em with my teeth? Look at that shit—somethin' was *eatin'* 'em. Maybe they were eatin' each other!"

The idea of Stalkers cannibalizing one another disturbed Brian but didn't surprise him. Their undying grins troubled him more—especially because one beamed at him from a detached head.

Henry cocked the hammer of his stolen revolver. "You don't know how lucky you are!" Tears streamed down his beet red cheeks. "You don't deserve your sister, your friend—you don't deserve anything you have! Why is it everyone loves people like you and people like me die alone?"

Louis opened his mouth to reply—but an earsplitting explosion cut him off. Louis lowered his gun. Eva slumped to her knees in front of Henry as a puddle of blood and brain matter pooled around his head.

Brian jogged over to Henry, but he recoiled when he saw his face: it had frozen in the moment of death, eyes and cheeks reddened with tears still streaking them. Snot and blood clogged his nose and a trail of saliva dribbled from his gaping mouth.

"We gotta go." Louis grabbed Eva's arm, helping her to her feet. "Gunshot'll draw 'em in."

Brian looked over his shoulder at Louis. "Can't we do something with his body?"

"Put him in the damn cabin if you want." Louis disappeared into the shed, voice muffled as he spoke from inside it. "Leave the door open so he can feed his little friends. I'm gonna load our things onto the cart and get the cows ready."

Brian couldn't tell if Louis was upset or angry—probably both. But Eva was on the verge of tears, so he met her on the porch and wrapped her in a tight hug. She didn't cry for long. They parted, heading inside to dress in weather-appropriate gear before they took care of Henry's corpse.

Brian and Eva carried him into the cabin and laid him on the bed, smoothing the blanket over his body. Aside from Eva's occasional sniff, they packed their things in silence. The last thing Brian grabbed was a photo of Henry kneeling in front of the lake, smiling as he pointed to a deer drinking from it. He seemed so awed by something he'd resorted to killing.

Brian slipped the photo into his journal. He bent over Henry's tiny work desk and shut his eyes, breathing low and slow through his lips to keep himself together.

Louis didn't shoot him. He could have. But even if Louis did go out and hack those Stalkers to pieces while we were sleeping, it wasn't wrong: if they'd broken free, they could've come in here and attacked us.

Regardless of whether Louis pushed him or not, Henry's problem was one they couldn't solve—so he'd solved it the only way he'd known how.

After all, the dead are never lonely.

Chapter Nine: Shadows

12/11, FORT SCOTT, KANSAS

Afternoon

No one wanted to talk about Henry. Even Louis was atypically silent—at least until he stopped near a bright green sign declaring "Fort Scott–10 miles." He stared into a field off to the side of the sludge-covered road they'd been traveling down. "What the fuck is *that*?"

Eva and Brian peered around Louis, straining to see the "that" in question. A white entity gleamed in the hazy sunlight with blinding brightness. They advanced into the fields, encountering melted lumps of metal and plastic half-covered by the melting snow. Once they got closer, the mysterious object revealed itself as the torn tail of a wrecked jumbo jet. It stuck up into the air at a diagonal angle, ripped in half at the middle. Judging by how far the nose of the plane was buried in the ground, it had plunged down at a violent speed.

Louis hopped down from Agnes and pulled Poppa's sniper rifle from his back. He aimed it at the plane and peered through the scope.

"What are you doin', Lou?" Eva patted Agnes as she stayed seated on the cow, her eyes darting to survey the otherwise derelict field.

"There's heaps of luggage in there," Louis said. "Think of all the stuff we could find. People bring snacks on planes all the time. Bottles of water too. And clothes, toiletries—who knows what else?" Louis lowered the rifle and looked back at Brian and Eva. "We haven't had the opportunity to add to our supply, which we've steadily been eatin' through. We have plenty of space here—those things don't swarm, so it'll be easy enough to kill one or two if they pop out."

"But what if it's a trap?" Brian asked. "Isn't it weird that no one else has looted the wreckage yet? Or they already did, and all that luggage is empty."

"Brian's right," Eva said. "It seems too good to be true. We're not runnin' out of anythin'."

"Yet." Louis narrowed his eyes. "Three people go through an awful lot of food and water. Not to mention toiletries. You want to be stuck without toothpaste and soap? Wipes too? We'll be one step away from primitive society."

Brian slid down from Hildy and strolled up to Louis. "I guess it wouldn't make sense to wreck a plane as a diversion—it might've been there for a while. And looters would take everything, not waste time and effort laying out a trap." He sighed, thinking of all the things he'd never had a chance to do. "I've never been on a plane before."

Louis clapped a hand to Brian's back, startling him. "Never? Man, you really *were* sheltered. Let's go change that. Eva, you can hang back if you're scared—"

"Stop babyin' me, Lou! Last time I hung back, you two got into a mess with poor Henry."

Louis let out a defeated sigh. "Fine. We all go together. But watch yourself, Eva—I won't always be able to cover you."

Eva nodded and hopped down from Agnes, leaving the cows to indulge their meager wanderlust. A blustering wind whipped through the field as they approached the tilted tail of the plane. Louis climbed up through an open emergency door and helped his sister and Brian in after him.

A roof remained over the cabin, protecting its contents from the elements. The walls kept the wind at bay for the most part, but an awful howl hammered against the dense layers of plastic. Each step they took made the fiberglass floor creak—and they had to pick their steps carefully to avoid the body parts scattered around. Most were skeletal, wrapped in torn clothing. Others still had mummified strips of dried skin wrapped around the bones.

Although Eva and Brian shared a troubled glance, Louis's eyes were alight like a kid at Christmas. "Damn. Look at all this stuff. Hell, there's bottles of water still sittin' in cupholders. Funny that a little tube of plastic can keep together while a human body explodes."

"I wonder what brought it down?" Eva murmured. Because of the angle, they had to hold onto the seats as they climbed up. Some of these were more precarious to touch than others due to the bodies still strapped in them.

A bottle rolled past Brian's foot, tumbling into the bottom of the cabin. "Someone on board could've been sick."

The closed restroom doors made his muscles tighten with apprehension. The rest of the wreckage seemed relatively safe: luggage ejected from the overhead compartments littered the aisles alongside a food cart with plastic cups and bags of nuts and pretzels. Oxygen masks dangled from overhead, some still strapped to bleached skulls.

Eva's dazed voice hauled Brian out of his visual explorations. "My God…" She stared at two skeletons trapped in a window seat. A child perched on an adult's lap. Their skulls were pressed together, turned toward the window.

Brian stood locked in place beside Eva. Her trembling hand reached for his. He threaded his fingers through hers and squeezed.

"What are you two doin'? Stop starin' at all these dead bodies—you're gonna see a lot more sooner than later. Help me look through this stuff before our luck runs out."

Brian met Louis's irritated glare and frowned, releasing Eva's hand. They worked their way up from the tail end of the plane until they reached the edge. Ever the intrepid explorer, Louis jumped over onto the front half of the plane. Snow fell in clumps to the exposed field below, but it didn't rattle Louis in the least. He held out his hand for Brian or Eva. "Hurry up. It's not as far as it looks."

Eva gave her brother a skeptical look, but she didn't hesitate for long before she leaped across. The floor shook a little under her added weight, but the plane maintained its position. Both twins looked at Brian, Eva's expression more concerned while Louis's was impatient and a little amused.

Louis curled the fingers of his outstretched hand. "Boug, just pretend it's a video game or somethin'."

"You don't die for real in those!" Brian hissed, contemplating the distance to the ground beneath him. If he fell, he'd be taking at least a hundred-foot plunge into a few precarious inches of snow below him. "Fuck me, that's *far*."

"Come on—you're a brave boy, aren't you?"

Louis's goading tone and wriggling eyebrows agitated Brian. Whether he'd intended to pressure Brian into jumping to prove a point or not, it worked: Brian went for it. He tumbled onto his knees in one piece, both twins fumbling to get a hold of him and keep him from rolling down into the flight deck.

While Brian caught his breath, safely sandwiched between his twin saviors, he glanced across at the tail section of the plane. *Jesus—I really jumped over from that?* Perspective was a treacherous thing.

Once he recovered, they stood and resumed searching the plane for supplies, banging and brushing against each other in the cramped aisles. Brian suppressed his guilt as he rummaged through suitcases and duffel bags, discovering a whimsical Hawaiian shirt, a book on how to talk to your cat (and get it to talk to *you*), a 3DS with a cracked screen, a gold necklace with a charm of an Egyptian god on it, and retro cat-eye glasses still in their case.

A silver wedding band was clutched in his hand when something clattered in one of the lavatories near the cockpit. All three of their heads turned in unison. Louis dropped a quart bag back into a suitcase and withdrew his gun. Eva and Brian did the same.

They backed away from the lavatories as quietly as they could, struggling with the precarious upward angle. Every footstep Brian made sounded as loud as a bottle falling in the shower.

One of the doors shook.

Louis aimed his revolver and backed away, nearest to the two doors. Eva remained between Brian and Louis, scrambling to keep from falling as they retreated toward the torn edge of the plane. Brian glanced at the gaping maw they'd have to jump back over if they wanted to escape into the tail section.

An unmistakable pounding erupted from within the locked lavatory: somebody trying to get out. The red "occupied" signs glinted in the sunlight streaming through the cabin windows. As Brian watched, one of the reds switched to green. The door swung open with a blur of motion and something popped out into the aisle. Louis fired a shot and slunk behind a food cart, kicking it so it slid down the tilted aisle and trapped the figure against the cockpit door. Brian grabbed Eva's arm and pulled her back with him, trying to make room for Louis. No one spoke. The only sounds were their haggard breaths and the cart rolling over squeaking fiberglass.

A barely audible snicker swelled into feverish laughter. Beyond the handcart, a head rose into view, decrepit hands with jagged talons clinging to the edge.

The explosion of Louis's gun made Brian's ears ring as it blasted a gruesome hole into the Stalker's forehead. The cackling ceased.

"One of these emergency exits is open," Louis called. "Get over here, Eva—I'll help you through."

Eva clambered down to her brother. He grabbed her arm to steady her and helped her settle onto something. When he placed a hand against her back and pushed, she disappeared. Since Brian hadn't been on a plane before, he wasn't familiar with how the emergency exits worked. It might as well have been a magic trick.

He scrambled down to the open door, sputtering when he saw the inflatable slide stretching to the ground. "A *slide*?"

"Yeah, when kids act up on the plane, you open the door and shove 'em out on it. They think they're at some magical sky playground. Then *splat*."

Brian's nerves eased as he snickered at Louis's snarky joke. Louis smiled, obviously pleased with himself.

Brian plopped down onto the air-filled rubber. Because of the direction of the impact, it hovered at an awkward angle. He worried he'd start sliding down, then roll and go *splat* face-first into the snow like Louis's imaginary children. "I'm not gonna lie—this is a little freaky."

"It's not gonna be graceful, but it *could* be fun." Louis dangled his head out of the window in search of his sister. She stood near the cows, about twenty feet down from the window. "Go on, boug—I'll be right behind you."

Brian sighed and scooted forward, feeling absurd for fearing this pseudo-childish activity. He squeaked down along the vinyl. When it curved left, he kept going straight and wound up sinking into several feet of cushioning snow. While he lay there staring at the sky above him, several objects flew into the air and sank around him: suitcases and bags filled with their prizes from the plane.

Brian angled his head to look at Hildy and Agnes, who stared up at the plane with dead grass hanging out of their mouths. Eva ran over to check on him but stopped in her tracks when her brother completed his equally awkward descent, plummeting into the snow about three feet from Brian. When Brian rolled his head to look at Louis, the ludicrousness of the situation struck him. He laughed for the first time in a long while.

Louis's head flopped back into the snow, an incredulous expression on his face. But he started to snicker while Eva loomed over them, staring at them like they were a couple of nuts. Hildy and Agnes joined her, nosing at Brian and Louis.

Brian had no idea how such a stressful situation had evolved into this absurd scene—maybe their accumulated tension needed some sort of release.

Even though the air and snow were freezing, the sun was shining, and he was laughing.

JUST AFTER SUNSET, they passed into Missouri. They stopped for the night at Prairie State Park, a picturesque area filled with fields of dead tallgrass. The images Brian conjured of colorful wildflowers and a sweeping sea of green made him eagerly anticipate spring; he was tired of wearing layers upon layers of clothes and waddling around like a penguin.

They selected the Nature Center for shelter. Although they had camping gear, they reserved it for instances when they might not make it to lodging in time for sunset. Entering buildings remained an unnerving task, but they'd developed a routine: Brian went in first with the bow with Eva and Louis behind him. Both twins were armed, but Eva was the designated torchbearer and Louis picked off whatever Brian didn't take down.

A lone Stalker crawled out to greet them inside the Nature Center, but Brian sank an arrow into its face. They still disturbed Brian and Eva, but Louis treated them as a non-event.

After tossing the body out, they blocked the doors with a sturdy wooden table and a curio shelf displaying arrowheads and animal bones. Freed of the yoke and cart, the cows meandered around the lobby while Brian and the twins entertained themselves with a variety of interactive displays, including a vast diorama of the prairie in varying seasons. Louis climbed atop a taxidermy bison and pretended it was a bucking bronco, cracking his sister and Brian up.

They moved on and read some of the informational displays, which covered aspects of the park like wildlife, flora and fauna, and artifacts found within it. The indigenous relics fascinated Eva, but Louis seemed scornful of them and passed them by altogether. Instead, he snatched a map from a pile scattered on a table and flopped into a cushioned armchair. "This place is huge: four-*thousand* acres. There's a ton of hikin' trails too—pfft! Gay Feather? What a name!"

"That's your tribal name, isn't it?" Eva asked with a smug smirk, sinking into the chair next to him. Foam protruded from a long gash in the rear cushion.

While Louis flashed his sister the bird, Brian settled on the floor across from them, content to sit anywhere other than a cow's back. He stretched onto his back and looked up at the ceiling, studying the vaulted wooden beams.

Eva turned to peer through a gap between two boards covering the window. "It's so quiet now. There's no background noise—no car engines, no train tracks, no people chatterin'." She sighed, her chin sinking into the top of the chair. "It's kinda sad."

"I'd rather hear crickets chirpin' and leaves rustlin' than any engines or whatnot, anyway." Louis gazed off into the distance at nothing in particular. "I was never a big fan of people, to begin with. They were never big fans of me, either."

"Yet you always had girlfriends." Eva turned back to face Louis. "Did you ever love any of 'em? I can't remember one lastin' longer than a month."

Louis's eyes narrowed. "Quit nosin' into it, Eva. How would you like it if I asked *you* about love and shit?"

"I've never been in love, but I wish I had." She curled her knees against her chest and leaned her chin onto them. "What about you, Brian? Has that bug ever stung you?"

Her phrasing made him laugh. He sat up and looked between both twins as they anticipated his answer. "No, but I'm kinda okay with that. I've already lost everyone I loved. If I'd lost someone I was *in* love with, I don't know if I could handle it."

"You haven't lost everyone, silly—you have us." Eva's lips quirked into a smile, but the aloofness in Louis's gaze quickly chilled the warmth of her assurance.

He stood and patted his sister's shoulder. "I'm pretty shot. I think I'll set up my sleepin' bag and call it a night." He headed for the back of the building, ruffling Brian's hair as he passed him.

Brian smoothed his hair. "You think he's okay?" he asked once Louis was out of earshot.

"He's fine. He's just off his meds, so he gets a little cranky."

"Meds?" *That might explain a few things.* "Are they important? Should we check a pharmacy or something?"

"Oh, they had him takin' a few. It'd be pretty hard to find 'em all." She looked away and sighed like there was more she wanted to say but wasn't sure she should.

"Eva." Brian stood and sank into Louis's still-warm seat next to her. "He's not...dangerous, is he?"

She blew air through her lips like this was a ridiculous question. "Not to us. To other people?" She scoffed. "You've seen him in action, right? Honestly, I'm amazed he's taken to you like he has. I guess that childhood bond goes a long way."

Now or never: I have to ask. "Eva, do you remember why we got in that fight? The one where I scarred his face?"

Eva sank back in her chair, folding her arms. For a moment, Brian worried she wouldn't tell him. But she leaned in close to him and spoke in a hushed voice, "It happened durin' our eleventh birthday party. It was the first one after the thing with your dad. You were a little withdrawn and your fuse was a lot shorter..." She sighed, hesitating.

Brian reached out and grabbed her arm. "It's okay. I won't get angry."

Her eyes lowered from his, but she looked up at him and took a breath to prepare herself. "I'd gotten a toy Lou wanted—some kinda Nerf gun. I said we could share, but he snatched it away from me and started chasin' me all around the yard, shootin' me with it. I started cryin', but our parents were inside gettin' the cake ready. The rest of it's kinda mixed up. I think you punched him, made him drop the toy. He got mad and pushed you down. You grabbed one of Père's knives from his fish-scalin' stump, tore into Lou's face with it. He didn't make a big deal about it, even tried to cover up for you, said it was an accident. But I blurted out that you did it, and that was that. Your mama and daddy practically had to drag you into their truck. I got shooed inside with Lou, but I could still hear you yellin' up until they drove you away. Louis kept strokin' his bandage and fussin' at me for blabbin'. It didn't make much sense to me how he wasn't mad at you for cuttin' him, but he was *pissed* at me for sayin' you did it."

Brian massaged his temples with his fingers, attempting to draw the memories from his mind. Faint flashes came to him, but they never developed into full scenes. He remembered the ride home more than the party. Sitting in the back seat of that same old truck, looking down at his hands and seeing blood underneath his nails. He dug into them but couldn't get it out.

Jesus. Why would I have gotten so angry over something like that? I might've been angry about the thing with Dad still, took it out on Louis.

All these years, he's had to live with that scar. Why was he never angry at me?

Eva curled her soft hand around his forearm and shook it. "Hey, you okay? You're zonin' out."

He blinked and focused on her, lips quirking into an uneasy smile. "Oh, sorry. I...uh, I was remembering a little. Do you think I should say something to him? Apologize?"

Eva rolled her eyes. "He was bein' an ass anyway. And I'll tell you somethin': he only got worse, so it's not like he learned anythin' from it. He kept holdin' it over my head, remindin' me that the reason we never saw you was because I didn't know when to keep my big mouth shut. Bless his heart, my brother isn't one to let things go."

There it was again: the Southern version of "fuck you," this time from sister to brother. Their contentious relationship didn't resemble his own bond with Becky in the least, but it might've been because he and Becky had a twelve-year age gap between them.

"I'm sorry I told them, though," Eva said. "I missed you. Did you miss us?"

Brian nodded, coerced by her anxious expression. He didn't want her to feel like she should punish herself when he and Louis were the ones to blame. "Yeah, for sure. But are you sure Louis is cool with me? I mean, since he holds grudges and all..."

"Don't worry about him so much. If he didn't want you with us, you wouldn't be." She shoved his arm, a playful smile flattering her winsome face. "Even if he makes a fuss over it, I'll stick up for you. I liked you then and I like you now." She bit her lip and tucked her hands between her knees. Brian studied her face, recognizing a slight flush when it colored her tan cheeks.

His stomach tightened into a knot. Whether it was because her interest flattered him or frightened him, he didn't know yet.

Instead of pursuing the conversation, Brian made a quick excuse about how tired he was and asked if she'd be okay on her own for a bit. Eva nodded with a disappointed pout. When Brian curled up in his sleeping bag, he only pretended to sleep.

AFTER A BREAKFAST of oatmeal and instant coffee, they headed out. The second they stepped through the front door, Louis threw his arms in front of Eva and Brian. "Hold still. Do you see them?"

Brian froze, fearing Louis had seen Stalkers—or worse, a group of people. He squinted, trying to see through the haze of falling snow. After a few moments, several brown blurs sharpened into something he recognized.

"Are those buffalo?" He'd never seen one in the wild before, let alone an entire herd of them.

Louis whacked him on the back of the head. "Those are bison, *bête!* Buffalo have a hump and bigger horns." He lifted his rifle from his shoulder. "Either way, one of those would turn out a lotta meat."

"Louis!" Eva pushed the barrel of the rifle down. Although they were covered head-to-toe because of the harsh weather and the threat of infection, her exposed eyes narrowed into an obvious glare. "Haven't you had enough violence for a while?"

Louis's dusky eyes narrowed right back at her. "Fine. But you can't spare everythin' forever. When you get hungry enough, you'll be more than happy to plug one in the head."

"Don't we have enough to lug around as it is?" Brian rubbed his head, more embarrassed about his misidentification than annoyed by Louis's blunt correction. "We shouldn't expose ourselves just so we can skin and butcher a buf—a bison."

"Give you an inch and you take the whole damn foot," Louis muttered, but he slung the rifle back onto his shoulder.

Once Agnes and Hildy meandered outside, they worked on hooking up the yoke and cart to Agnes. The majesty of the bison roaming in the field about a hundred feet away lifted Brian's spirits.

Some things haven't changed. Maybe some things have even gotten better.

Louis sulked on the ride, but Eva and Brian sat together and chatted back and forth. They were in a better mood from sleep, the prior night's fulfilling conversation, and the uplifting sight of the bison herd. Brian suspected part of Louis's grouchiness could be attributed to his growing closeness to Eva. Wary of Louis's missing meds, Brian dialed back his chattiness and focused on keeping an eye out while they rode.

After several silent hours of riding, they approached a sign numbered "290" and left the backroads for asphalt covered in scattered mounds of snow and ice. The scenery blended together into one long panorama of bleached ground and cerulean sky with the occasional stretch of gnarled trees and dilapidated buildings. Most of the buildings were farmhouses, but a few were gas stations and churches. They were stereotypically prevalent throughout the Midwest.

"Hey, Louis," Brian said as the buildings started cluttering together, "isn't going into town a bad idea?"

"Our supplies won't last forever. Water's runnin' low, and I'm tired of what food we got. I'm tired of snow, mud, and dead trees too. I need a change of scenery."

"Yeah, but there might be people here," Brian said. "Or Stalkers."

"It's a hick town," Louis said. "Doubt there's much traffic through here anymore. If there *were* any stragglers, they've moved on by now."

Brian sighed. Louis's eyebrows and lips were fixed into a determined expression. For whatever reason, he was in a surly mood and wouldn't be easily swayed. "If you think we're equipped to handle whatever we might encounter, then I'm fine with it. But don't be stubborn about it for the sake of being stubborn."

Louis whipped his head to look at Brian. "Well, tell me your grand plan then, genius: where should we go instead?"

Louis's sharp gaze cut through Brian, making his voice falter. "I-I haven't been to Missouri before—I wouldn't know where to go. I just want you to think of all the angles, Louis. Once you're set on a certain path, it's hard to steer you in a different direction."

"If you try to steer me, you'll be in for one wild ride." Louis snickered and looked ahead of him. "Try not to worry so much, *mon ami*—I don't make these decisions on a whim. With all this silence, I've had a lot of time to think." He gave Brian a sidelong glance. "There's gotta be a little give and take, here—we do it your way, then we do it mine."

Brian knew Louis was referring to the episode with the bison where Brian and Eva had stayed his hand, which had no doubt left a sour taste in Louis's mouth and tipped the balance of power out of his hands. Brian decided to let it drop.

Aside from a crow cawing on occasion, the town—Carl Junction, according to a sign they passed—was devoid of any signs of life. A few cars still lined the sidewalks, but it seemed most people had fled to larger towns. Their search for supplies landed them an ax from the fire station and some Big Red from a gas station, but little else.

"Look!" Eva pointed to a large building: Spinning Wheels SK8 Center. "We haven't been to one of these since we were eight or nine." She elbowed Brian. "You were with us, Brian."

A vivid recollection of tables with children, cake, and presents came to Brian. Eva blew out candles while Louis smiled and tore into presents. Cheesy songs played in the background, soon joined by clapping and cheering. A disco ball spun in the dark, casting glowing squares on the shadowed objects within the room. The smell of greasy food and popcorn permeated the air—the smell of childhood.

"Ooh, look." Louis's lips slid into a broad grin as he read from the marquee. "We can rent a bouncy house!"

Eva groaned, but Brian couldn't hold back a snicker. She tugged on Louis's sleeve. "Don't be an ass, Lou. Why don't we take a break and see if we can go in?"

Louis's smile faded when he looked at his sister. "Eva, you really wanna waste time in there?"

"Lou—" her arms brushed Brian's back as she crossed them "—what's all this talk about give and take if you don't let us have a say? There might be food in there. We didn't find a lot before, so we might as well try. Heck, we might even find skates!"

Louis sighed and glanced at Brian. "Brian, what do you think?"

Brian shrugged. "I don't see why not. It's boarded from the outside and the barricades are intact, so I doubt there's anyone inside. I bet it's a lot nicer in there than most of the buildings we've been in. Let's do it."

Eva pressed her hands to her mouth, suppressing a giddy squeal. They headed into the empty parking lot, climbed down from the cows, and approached the front of the building. A large piece of plywood nailed to the door blocked their entry. People trying to get into the building had left several cracks in it but were obviously unsuccessful.

The ax made short work of the damaged wood. Darkness obscured the contents of the building beyond the glass door. Louis aimed his revolver while Brian tried to open it—but it wouldn't budge.

Brian slid the pocketknife from his jean pocket and kneeled in front of the keyhole. He stuck the tip in and wiggled until he heard a *click*. After he withdrew the knife, he slid it between the door and the striker plate, searching for the latch. Once he maneuvered the latch out of the jamb, the door swung open under the palm of his hand.

Eva kissed his cheek. "My hero!"

Louis didn't look as enthused. He swept by them, nudging Eva with his elbow. "Take care of the light, Eva. Grab your bow, boy wonder."

After a quick sweep of the ticket counter and lobby, they ushered the cows and cart in and pushed a dining table against the door. They kept their backs to it while Eva scanned the room with her flashlight, highlighting an air hockey table, a pool table, and a row of ancient arcade games. The dining area dipped down to a square rollerboard surrounded on three sides by fabric-padded walls.

Eva wandered around, her face alight with wonder. Louis and Brian followed with their weapons aimed. It was like going back in a time machine—except they'd arrived in a weird, alternate universe where the rink had been abandoned. A wall of cubbies held skates in assorted sizes, worn and returned by numerous skaters over time.

Long gone, probably dead.

The orb of Eva's flashlight reflected from a glass display case containing prizes forever unclaimed. She bent down to examine the cheap plastic toys and sugary junk lined in their glass prison. "They must have closed down when they heard the reports on the radio. Boarded it up and left it like a kinda time capsule..."

Louis kneeled next to their cart and withdrew something from a duffel bag: a lantern. He set it on the edge of the pool table and tugged his scarf from his face. As he grabbed one of the cue sticks, he caught Brian's wandering gaze and quirked his eyebrows. "Wanna give it a go?"

Brian approached the table and rubbed his palms along the soft felt surface. He slid a finger over one of the racked balls, glancing up at Louis. Light glinted in his eyes, the strong contours of his face gleaming as his grin shifted in the shadows.

"Don't tease me." Louis ground the chalk cube onto the tip of his cue stick. "If you've already got a finger on the thing, you're committed. Let's do this."

Brian lifted the other stick from the table. "What about Eva?"

Louis's eyes shifted to his sister, who was entertaining herself with the different prizes and occasionally sucking on a ring pop. Brian contemplated joining her to rummage through the candy, but Louis's voice snatched his attention. "We'll be here all day if she plays. She takes too long, overthinks every shot. It's just you and me, boug. Now hurry up and break those balls."

Brian sputtered and looked at Louis, attempting to decipher whether he was trying to be funny or not. His snaggle-toothed smirk indicated he was. Brian lifted the rack and set it aside, chalked his cue stick, and set the cue ball in front of the others. Determined to show Louis up, he stepped back and calculated his shot, trying to focus as he angled the tip of the stick underneath his curled fingers.

The cue ball struck the rest and sent them clattering across the table. Several rolled into the pockets: Brian counted four. He credited his dad for teaching him at their old house in the suburbs—the one they'd lived at before he lost his job.

Louis circled around the table, brushing by Brian as he surveyed the pool table. "Impressive. So, what else are you good at besides archery, lockpickin', and pool?"

Brian smoothed his bangs from his forehead. "Not identifying animals, apparently."

"Nobody's perfect. Now, I'm gonna go for seven here, I think." Louis lifted the cue stick and sat on the edge of the table, lining a shot behind his back. His eyes flitted up to meet Brian's as he hit the cue ball into the solid red one, knocking it into the far corner pocket.

Brian shook his head, idle hands toying with the cue stick. "Is there *anything* you suck at?"

Louis smiled and shrugged. "There's plenty of stuff I haven't tried—I'm bound to suck at some of it, right?"

They carried on like this for a while, too caught up in their game to notice Eva until she finally wandered up. She watched them for a bit, interested at first, but Brian noticed her gradual loss of interest and the restless way she tapped her feet.

At one point, she groaned and rolled her eyes. "Ugh—when are you two gonna end this? You've been goin' at it *forever*! Let's skate or somethin'."

Louis set his cue stick onto the table and quirked an eyebrow at Eva. "There's no music, *bête*. We should get out of here, keep lookin' while we still got daylight."

"Oh, so you get to have fun and do what you want, but what *I* want doesn't matter?" Both twins' body language indicated an imminent volcanic eruption of sibling rivalry, so Brian felt compelled to neutralize it.

He abandoned his cue stick and dug around in his backpack until he found his tablet and powered it on. "It's not the same, but we could use this. It won't be loud enough for anyone to hear outside. Besides, I think the walls here are pretty thick."

"Awesome! Let's do it!" Eva smiled at him and unzipped her puffy gold jacket. She pulled it off and set it on a table alongside a red plastic cup before bounding over to find a pair of skates her size. Her pale pink sweater and fitted jeans hugged her slender curves as she stood on tiptoe, straining to reach one of the cubbies.

Louis caught Brian's eyes when they detached from Eva's physique, sending a guilty little shudder through Brian. He approached Brian and reached to guide the tablet between them. His head brushed against Brian's, the aroma of cinnamon gum drifting from Louis's lips to Brian's nose.

Every nerve in Brian's body seemed to tingle. His breaths shortened and sharpened. Something swirled in his stomach, making him nauseous instead of ravenous. He thought he was on the verge of having a panic attack.

"What've you got on here?" Louis asked. "I doubt you've got much I know. No Nine Inch Nails or Disturbed, right?"

Brian exhaled. He'd been worried Louis was about to threaten him for looking at Eva. Now he worried Louis would judge his taste in music. "I listen to everything except rap and country, pretty much. I'm sure I've got "Closer" and "Down with the Sickness" somewhere in there."

Louis scrolled through Brian's song library, bangs draped over his eyes. Brian struggled to read them as they scanned and skimmed the song titles. He breathed in a light scent of soap or cologne, something like tobacco and leather. *One of those "manly" Old Spice scents?*

"Some of it's okay—" Louis withdrew from Brian's side "—but I can tell you're a little hipster."

Anxiety transformed into incredulity. "Am not!" Brian immediately regretted his childish reaction and attempted to save face. "I mean, no, I'm not. I like to try different things, is all."

Louis arched his eyebrows and smirked, stripping his bomber jacket off. He tossed it onto the pool table and went to join his sister, who promptly put her hands on her hips and complained about something. Louis snagged a pair of skates which had been unreachable for her. Now that he could directly compare, Brian decided Louis's jeans were tighter than hers.

Why am I thinking about dumb shit like that? Brian shook his head and cued a playlist. He raised the volume to full before he ran over to find himself a pair of skates. Eva and Louis passed by him and strolled onto the rollerboard, disappearing into the shadows.

Brian strapped on his skates and joined them, reliving a sensation he hadn't experienced in over a decade. It wasn't the same as a 5.1 stereo system blaring the trendiest tunes and a disco light spinning overhead, but the glow of their lanterns and the music from his tablet provided a comforting echo of the past.

The air cooled his skin as he glided through dim light, making it ripple like a strobe. All three of them drifted in their own bubbles, afforded safety and privacy they hadn't been allowed for a long time.

A subdued song with a staccato, synth-based beat began playing. Lyrics about shadows and dreams lulled Brian into a transcendental headspace. The spark of nostalgia was a tempting black hole to jump into, but it was only a dream he'd have to awaken from eventually.

He shut his eyes and coasted through the cool breeze, focusing on the sounds and sensations surrounding him. *I don't want to leave this building. I don't want to leave this moment.*

A hand gripped his. He opened his eyes to see Louis looking at him with an expression somewhere between concerned and thoughtful—an unfamiliar look for him. "You fallin' asleep? You were about to skate right into a wall."

Before Brian could reply, Eva glided up to them. She reached out for Brian's other hand and squeezed it tightly in hers. "We all needed this. It might be silly, but I don't see why we can't remember the good times and forget what's outside for a little bit."

Brian shut his eyes again. Louis and Eva's warm hands transported him to a more innocent time, a time when they were children discovering the world together. Memories of past experiences in the rink alternated with the present until nothing existed but the moment they were in. Their shadows flickered along the wall, doomed to follow them out of the building.

Louis broke the silence. "Time to grab what we can and head out."

Brian had to let go.

They removed their skates and replaced their coats and boots before foraging for more supplies. Hildy and Agnes had settled down for a nap, obviously not enthralled by Brian's music. When it shut off, they awoke and meandered around trying to discover what was edible. Brian and Eva corralled them and hooked the cart onto Hildy. He led the cows to the front door while Louis shoved the table out of the way.

Brian looked back at the empty rink; it was as if they'd never been there.

Like we were just ghosts drifting by.

A strange sound snapped him out of his reverie: a shotgun pumping.

"No sudden movements. Hands in the air."

Two people stood in front of the open door: a man with a sawed-off shotgun and a woman with some sort of old-fashioned machine gun.

"*Shit,*" Louis hissed through clenched teeth. He lifted his hands. Eva and Brian followed.

"You're lucky we're friendly or you'd all have holes in your heads," the woman said. "You're the first people we've seen come through town since we arrived." A knit beret tilted over her jet-black bob, the trim edges brushing a sequined crimson scarf. Round glasses concealed her eyes and a huge fur coat swallowed her body. The tips of maroon high-heeled boots stuck out from beneath an ankle-length black skirt.

A fedora tipped over the man's dark hair, which swooped in waves above a pair of Ray-Bans. He puffed on a cigar like some mobster from a movie, ash falling onto a tan scarf and a fur-lined coat. The cuffs of his dress pants hung over shining Oxfords. Considering the circumstances, the youthful pair looked remarkably attractive and clean. But because of the impractical nature of their outdated attire, Brian found them more frustrating than threatening.

"What do you want?" Louis asked through gritted teeth. "It's cold out. If you wanna talk, let's go somewhere warmer like back in the buildin'."

"I got someplace better." The man lowered his gun a hair. "I don't wanna aim this gun at you, but I'm scared you might shoot me. Don't take it personal, friend—you got the fire in those coal black eyes."

"Positively smoldering." The woman spoke with a sultry Texas drawl. "Now, be a peach and give us your weapons so we can move on. We killed most of the nasties that stuck around here but more could pop out any minute."

The duo disarmed Brian and the twins. They escorted them along the road with the man leading and the woman taking up the rear. Hildy and Agnes trudged alongside Brian, towing the cart. They weren't the least bit intrigued by their new companions.

"I think you'll get a kick outta our digs." The man also spoke with a drawl, but his voice was gravelly—probably from all those cigars. "We've got a setup in Joplin. Used to be a real swanky juice joint but it closed down. Back when it was open, you had to go in the phone booth out front and dial 999, ask for Donnie's Taxi. Nifty, right?"

Louis directed a resentful glare toward the stolen sniper rifle and bow the man had strapped to his back. "You got names I can call you besides "Asshole" and "Bitch"?"

"Well, all right, firecracker!" The man chortled. "You can call me Spike Dexter; my partner-in-crime is Parker Valentine."

"Are those even real names?" Louis asked with a frustrated groan.

"You can go by whatever you want now." Parker shrugged as they strolled through town toward an unknown destination. "I, for one, am quite happy to abandon my identity from before."

"Ditto," Spike said. "No need to go back to something you can't go back to. And what can I call you? Or are you okay with "Dick"?"

"His name's Louis," Eva said before Louis could insult Spike again. "I'm his sister, Eva."

Parker trailed a silken finger along Brian's cheek. "What about this little sugar cookie?"

"Leave him alone," Louis said. "You better not be cannibals or some shit."

"Don't worry." Parker swung a bag zipped tight with the rest of Brian and the twins' stolen weapons. "We won't eat *you*. All that heat would give us indigestion."

Spike led them into the parking lot of a Dollar General beside two cars with their doors ajar. Parker leaned against one, keeping her machine gun aimed in the trio's direction. Spike placed a gloved hand on her slender arm. "Wait here with our new friends, baby, and I'll go get Scooter." Brian hoped this "Scooter" wasn't another wannabe mobster.

While Spike strolled around the building, Eva watched Parker withdraw a cigarette from her coat and press it between her cherry red lips. She cleared her throat to get Parker's attention. "Miss Parker, how did you end up in Joplin?"

Parker took in a puff of smoke, the tip of the cigarette crumbling into ash. The smoke blended with the hazy air when she exhaled. "Spike and I were looking for my sister and her family in Shoal Creek Estates, south Joplin. The place was a wash except for a couple of holdouts. They told us they'd escaped a raid on the Estates, that everyone else had been murdered or kidnapped by some gang. They killed themselves the next morning." Parker tapped the cigarette. Ash fell to the ground and melted into the snow. "Survivor's guilt, I guess. Nasty business."

Eva bit her lip and glanced at Louis. "Our house in Kansas got broken into by these weird guys in masks. Think they're from the same group?"

Parker's gaudy sunglasses flashed in the sun when it managed to break through the clouds. "Well, I certainly hope there isn't more than one gang in the Midwest. This one popped up real quick. They were more than happy to take advantage of the chaos those creatures caused. What did they call them on the radio? *Stalkers*." She shrugged her shoulders and shuddered. "Nasty pieces of work. Those grins, that *laughter*—ugh!"

Spike strolled out from behind the derelict Dollar General rolling a scooter alongside him. *Guess they're not as creative when it comes to naming their transportation.*

Parker strapped her duffel bag to the scooter, then hiked up her skirt and climbed atop it. Spike settled in ahead of her and revved the engine. Brian shuddered, fearing the noise had awoken some slumbering evil.

"Here are your options," Spike said, "either we zip away and add your guns to our arsenal or you come hear us out, have a drink, and take a shot at getting your guns back."

Brian glanced between Eva and Louis, wondering if he looked as dumbfounded as they did. "Isn't that blackmail?"

"Not really, sugar." Parker strapped her machine gun to her back and wrapped her arms around Spike's torso. "Blackmail would be threatening to plug you if you didn't agree to come."

"We're just trying to nudge you a little." Spike tossed his blunted cigar into a pile of snow, where it fizzled out with a hiss. "So? Guns or no guns?"

Eva threw up her hand. "I vote go. They could've killed us and taken our guns if that's all they wanted, but they didn't."

"You ever stop to think *they* might be part of that gang?" Louis asked. "That this is all some kinda con to lead us into a trap? If they don't want us dead, why would they want us alive?"

Parker dug into her coat and tossed something in the trio's direction. Brian kneeled to retrieve it while Louis and Eva peered over his shoulder.

It was a photograph of a family: a smiling man and woman and a little girl hugging a fluffy golden retriever. They all wore cheesy Christmas sweaters, even the dog. A note scribbled on the back in Sharpie said: *To "Parker" and "Spike"—Don't get big heads when you go all Hollywood! Merry Christmas from the Tuckers (and Sparky)!*

Louis folded his arms and grumbled. "That could be anyone's photo. Hell, you coulda killed them and taken it off them yourselves. Picked up your *noms de plume* too."

"If you want your guns, you'll find us at Caldone's: the brick building with the red telephone booth out front. If not, it's your funeral." Spike smacked Parker's leg and hit the gas. "Let's blouse, baby."

With that, they zipped away onto the road, kicking up a pile of sludge and leaving a dirty trail of tire tracks behind them. Brian and the twins shared an incredulous look before they scrambled onto the cows and hurried after the bootleg Bonnie and Clyde.

Chapter Ten: Fireworks

12/12, JOPLIN, MISSOURI

Early afternoon

Within the hour, they arrived at Caldone's, a brick building with boarded glass fronts crammed between a consignment shop and a computer repair store. A telephone box with peeling red paint and frosted windows sat outside the speakeasy. Overturned metal garbage cans, bent lampposts, and thick-trunked trees with skeletal limbs lined the derelict sidewalk in front of the buildings.

They dismounted the cows and approached the building, trying to figure out how to enter it. All they had for defense was Brian's pocketknife; Parker and Spike hadn't found it because they didn't pat him down. Maybe looking like a sugar cookie paid off.

"Should we throw a rock or somethin'?" Eva rubbed her folded arms. "Get their attention?"

"Theirs and who else's?" Louis tapped the side of his head. "Think, girl: sound draws those things out."

"They said something about dialing a number in the phone booth," Brian said. "Not that the power works anymore."

He and Eva stepped toward the phone booth while Louis stayed back with the cows. "Don't get too close to it. You know those things like to pop outta shit—"

The door jerked open, a blur of mottled corpse white blending with the snow. For a split-second, the Stalker froze, deciding whether to go for Eva or Brian—the cows lowed and Brian felt pressure around his stomach pulling him to the ground. A series of ear-shattering explosions synchronized with red gushes spurting into the snow at Eva's feet. She stumbled back as the Stalker slumped forward, clutching a handful of slush in its clawed hand.

Brian looked down at the arm wrapped around his stomach and recognized the tan leather of Louis's coat. His head drooped back against Louis's as he exhaled and glanced up, following his cloud of breath to a second-floor window in Caldone's. Parker leaned over the sill with her smoking tommy-gun, a rouged smile brightening her face.

"You kids okay? Thought we got most of those things, but I guess they're still the champions of Hide-and-Seek."

Brian pulled Louis's arm from him so he could stand and wipe the snow off his rear. He went to extend a hand to Eva. She took it, her fingers trembling against his. She gave Louis a withering look as she stood. "You let go of the cows, Lou. You should go get them." Her tone was strained and bitter.

"What's up your ass, Eva?" Louis glared at her as the wayward cows peered at them from an alleyway across the street.

"You saved *him*—" her eyes flitted to Brian "—not me. That's fucked up."

Louis folded his arms. "He was closer to me, and the thing was about to jump. I didn't have time to think—I acted."

Spike squeezed in next to Parker behind the window. "No time to stand out there arguing, either. Get the heifers settled and hurry in—door's around back."

While Louis wrangled the cows, Brian peered up at Spike and Parker. They whispered something to each other, but all he could make out was the word "kids" before they replaced the particle board in the window. Brian pushed it to the back of his mind and circled to the back of the building with the others.

Parker held the back door open. She'd removed most of her winter gear and now wore a posh sweater with beading stitched around a V-shaped neckline and a knee-length pleated skirt. Strings of yellowed pearls swirled around her neck and dipped into the neckline of her shirt. All of it could've come straight from one of the thrift shops Brian's mom used to drag him to.

Parker eyed the cows and stepped out. She closed the door behind her. Brian expected her to smell like mothballs, but she left a sweet aroma like jasmine in her wake. "The heifers won't fit in here, I'm afraid. You know what they say: bulls in a china shop. Let's stash them in this parking garage over here."

"Um, how do we know you aren't leadin' us into a trap?" Eva asked.

Parker grinned at her, one hand wrapped around the tommy-gun's grip and the other on her hip. "Sweetheart, I didn't mow that Stalker down so I could kill you later. That would've been a waste of valuable bullets." She lifted the muzzle of the tommy-gun and nudged Brian with her elbow. "Quick, sugar—march your cute little patootie over there before mine freezes off."

Parker followed Brian to the parking garage while he led Hildy and Agnes. She retrieved a tiny silver key and handed it to him, watching (out for?) him while he unlocked the padlock and opened the shutter. A gust of icy air billowed out from the sinister interior, but Parker assured him she and Spike had already investigated the garage and found more dead bodies than living. In other words, "Your heifers'll be *fine*, sugar."

The protesting sounds Agnes and Hildy made as he pulled the shutter down implied they weren't as sure of this as Parker was. Brian locked them in with their cart and belongings, hoping Parker and Spike weren't scheming to keep everything now stored in the parking garage.

Parker marched Brian and the twins back to the speakeasy and herded them in ahead of her. The door swung shut behind them with a weighty *thud.*

People don't want to be herded, either.

The inside of the cramped building was pristine. Brick walls supported vaulted, gold-paneled ceilings and surrounded a plethora of mahogany tables and crimson chairs. Metal lanterns hung above two rows of maroon booths, and fake vines curled and clung to the walls. An upstairs balcony hovered above them, complete with tables and chairs. The ambiance evoked memories of endless soup and breadsticks from days past.

Spike sat downstairs in the right rear corner, puffing on another cigar within the sanctuary of a booth. His hat was on the table instead of his head, revealing a luxurious swell of dark waves tapering down below his ears. High cheekbones and tan skin complemented his electric blue eyes, which had an almond slant to them. Stubble coated his square jaw and lined his lips. They quirked into a crooked smile as he waved them over. "Come have a seat, kids." His other hand rested on a sawed-off shotgun gleaming ominously from the tabletop.

The stuffy air compelled them to slide their winter gear off before they joined Spike. Louis sat first. Eva lingered with her arms folded like she didn't want to sit next to him. Brian scooted in instead, finally followed by Eva. The tension simmering between the twins swirled around Brian like a heat wave.

Parker glided in alongside Spike. She hung an arm over his shoulder, long eyelashes fluttering over bright green eyes. Her relaxed body language contradicted the intimidating machine gun tilting over the edge of the table.

Brian studied Spike's jaunty gold-striped dress shirt and the cinched black vest he wore over it. A silver chain draped into the vest pocket. He couldn't see Spike's pants, but he assumed they matched the vest. His curiosity got the best of him, so he asked, "Why do you wear those old-fashioned clothes? They're not exactly practical."

"We were both actors—" Spike tapped ash into an ornate gold ashtray "—so we're used to escaping the real world. What better time to escape, right?"

Parker smoothed her hands along the contours of her blouse, curving them over her bosom. "These clothes transport us into another world, into other lives..." She sighed, her façade slipping for an instant before she perked up again. "Why, I'm being an awful host—I should get you kids some giggle water!"

Parker slid out of the booth and strolled past a tall wine shelf devoid of bottles. The bar's glass cases had been destroyed and depleted, but she retrieved a bottle from below the counter and lined three glasses alongside it.

After she poured the drinks, Parker brought them to the table and returned to her seat. She swirled her pearls with a slim hand, regarding Louis from underneath the shade of her blunt bangs. "Have a drink and loosen up, firecracker. I don't know what's plugging you up, but you need to flush it out."

"Why would I do that?" Louis asked. "For all I know, you spiked it with somethin'. No pun intended."

Spike snatched a glass and pressed it to his lips, his Adam's apple bobbing as he swallowed. He wiped his mouth and shoved the drink back over to Louis. "There—nothing to worry about except for my cooties. Drink up; it'll put some hair on your chests." He winked at Eva. "We can always get you something with less kick, dollface."

Eva smiled and glanced down at the table. She slid a glass to herself. Brian reached for his and wrapped a hand around the stem. He tipped the drink between his lips. The burn nearly numbed his throat, but he forced it down while he scanned between Spike's ice-blue eyes and Parker's glittering green gaze. They probably considered this some rite of passage in their weird world.

A pillared candle cast flickering light as Spike blew a steady stream of smoke at Louis. He crushed his cigar into the ashtray. "All right: time to stop bumping gums. You remember that gang Parker was telling you about? They have her sister and niece, the dames from the photo."

Louis narrowed his eyes and waved the smoke away. "I thought this gang was a buncha thieves and murderers. Why're these chicks alive?"

Parker laced her gloved fingers in front of her face. Light and shadow danced along her delicate contours, fighting for dominance. "Because they're women in a man's world."

Brian and Eva shared a concerned glance. If this was true, it was a dismal fate for a woman—let alone a child.

Louis took a swig of his drink and tapped his fingers on the varnished surface of the table. "What does this have to do with us—and our weapons?"

Parker's lips curved into a frown that didn't flatter her otherwise immaculate face. "We know where they are, but we don't have enough firepower to take them on. We need help."

"There's no way I'm lettin' you drag us into some raid on a group of armed bandits." Louis downed his drink and slumped back in the booth. "Even if you gave us our weapons, we might die anyway."

"I know it's a lot to ask," Parker said, "but we could make a deal. There's a fireworks shop nearby, but it's awful big and close to their hideout. If you help us clear the place out and grab some fireworks, we could draw those thugs somewhere with a bunch of explosions and get in to free my sister and niece. Say we give you half your weapons back—will you at least help us with that?"

"Searchin' a fireworks shop isn't much different than lootin' other stores," Eva said. "I say we help them. At least give them a chance to get Parker's family back. Imagine how awful it must be—"

Louis slapped his palm against the table, jostling everything on it. "I don't want to put my ass out there for people I don't even *know*. The only people I care about are sittin' in this booth next to me."

"Then get your weapons back so you can protect them." Spike's hand twitched against his shotgun. "You're lucky we're offering to compromise. We could make you go all in."

"I've never been a gamblin' man." Louis dragged his hands down his face. "Fuck it. Of *course* Eva wants to help. What about you, boug?"

While the candle flickered and sizzled, Brian looked from Eva's hopeful gaze to Spike and Parker's pensive faces. He met Louis's narrowed eyes with a sigh. "Without our weapons, we'll never get where we want to go. We'd have to search for new weapons or stuff to jury-rig them with."

"Fine—since I'm outvoted, we'll help find your fuckin' fireworks." Louis pointed a finger between the two actors, moving it from side to side like a Cobra on the edge of striking. "But as soon as we're done, you give us our shit and send us on our merry way."

"Deal." Spike held out his hand for Louis to shake, but Louis ignored it. Brian took it instead, surprised by how firm and dry Spike's handshake was. The scent of aftershave clung to Brian's hand when he withdrew it.

Eva downed the rest of her drink. "I'm sorry: the only excuse my brother has for bein' such a dick is how small his must be." She glared at Louis, lips curling into a spiteful smirk.

Louis balled his hand into a fist next to his empty martini glass. "You keep runnin' your mouth and I'll slap you like Père used to slap Mère."

Both actors kept their expressions neutral and their mouths shut while the twins stared each other down. The storm clouds brewing in their eyes gave the air an ionic charge.

"You're tryin' to puff up your feathers," Eva said. "You'd never hit me—"

Louis slammed his glass onto the table, cracking it from stem to rim. "Keep talkin' if you want me to fix that."

Eva's eyes widened when she realized she'd pushed Louis too far. Brian took advantage of her stunned silence and twisted to face Louis, blocking the twins' view of each other. "Louis, calm down. It's just the alcohol talking, right?"

Louis bit his lower lip until blood welled. "It might be sayin' a thing or two."

I have to distract him, snap him out of this. Brian grabbed Louis's shoulders. His tensed muscles relaxed underneath Brian's hands and his eyes focused on Brian's, pupils dilating until only a thin rim of iris remained.

Now that he held Louis's attention, Brian didn't know what to do with it. If he let go or looked away, he might shatter the spell keeping the beast at bay. Instead, he maintained their eye contact. Those dangerous eyes seared into Brian's until his hands tingled like he'd slapped them onto a cactus. Heavy breaths swelled in the sweltering air, but he didn't know if he was hearing his own or someone else's.

"Whew!" Parker stood and fanned her face with her hand. "It's getting a bit hot over here. I'm gonna go cool off at the bar."

Spike followed her out, rapping the table with his fist. "Any of you want more, you're welcome to join. Long day ahead of us tomorrow. A long night too, by the looks of things."

Brian felt trapped, not only by the situation with Parker and Spike, but by the strain dividing the siblings. He released Louis and lowered his eyes from him, light-headed from the alcohol or something else entirely.

A shiver rippled through him as Eva's hand glided down his back. "Brian, why don't you get some air? You look a little pale." She slid out to let him escape the suffocating heat of the booth.

He scooted out after her and swept his bangs from his sticky forehead. "Are you two gonna be okay?"

Eva nodded. "We argue all the time. It's just a little worse than usual because of the way things are, you know?" Her eyebrows quirked like she was trying to remind Brian of the missing meds. "We'll be fine. Trust me."

Relieved to have a break from the tension, Brian approached the bar and settled onto a cushioned stool beside Parker. Spike poured himself a glass of gin and knocked it back dry. He set it down with a deep sigh and a shake of his head. "So, kid, is your pal usually that much of a prick, a dick, and an asshole, or did I catch him on a good day?"

Brian leaned his elbows against the counter, pressing his fingers to his temples as the throb of a headache emerged. "I don't know. Sometimes I like him, and other times he scares me. He's so goddamn *intense*."

"Well, I'd keep him on a short leash: that dog likes to bark, and I sure wouldn't want him to bite." Spike poured a drink from the nearly empty bottle and pushed it over to Brian, expertly performing the role of Swanky Bartender. "How'd you meet up with those two anyway?"

Brian inhaled and explained the series of events leading up to their encounter outside the skating rink. Spike slid around the counter to sit at Brian's other side. "Geez—I'm sorry to hear all that. A kid your age shouldn't have to go through this bullshit. But I'm impressed you've made it this far. You're the bee's knees."

Brian would never get used to that old-fashioned slang. "Thanks. What about you guys? I can't tell if you're really from Texas or if you're trying to sound like you are."

"We met in Tennessee during a production of *The Great Gatsby* seven years ago," Parker said. "I still have the flyer."

Spike spun the empty glass in front of him. "We were living in Texas when the pandemic blew up. We read about it online, thought it was all hooey until we saw a report on TV. When it was all over Pandora, Sirius XM—every form of broadcasting you could think of—we knew it was serious. We didn't have much time to prepare, but one of our friends was a prepper. We managed to bribe our way into his shelter. That friend of ours got infected. Wanna know how? His own damn kid. Kid got bit at school the week before, they didn't think anything of it—'oh, the kid's withdrawn, psychological trauma, blah blah'—and the kid took a chunk out of his arm down in the shelter. I shot them both without another thought. We all have our triggers where the mask comes off. Mine is Parker."

Parker lightened the somber atmosphere by nudging Brian with her elbow. "What's yours? You making it with the dame?"

Brian's cheeks burned, but he assumed it was mostly from the alcohol. "We're just friends."

Parker's crimson lips curved into a Cheshire grin. "What about her brother? You two had me clutching my marbles with that hot little exchange. You know about the Six Second Stare, right? Means they either want to bump you off or barneymug you."

Brian's forehead crinkled. "Huh? I have *no* idea what you just said. Does someone want to hit me with a mug that has a purple dinosaur on it?"

"Now *I'm* the one who has no idea what you're talking about. How much did you drink?" Parker shot him a playful grin and gave his shoulder a light shove. "You want it straight, daisy? He either wants to screw you silly or murder you. Possibly both if he's *really* crackers."

Brian groaned and dragged his hands down his face, the dim light making his eyes strain and exacerbating his growing headache. The room swam around him in streaks of mahogany wood and golden trim. "I was the one who cut his face, you know. Nine years ago. I'm scared he's held a grudge this whole time. If he gets that pissed at his own sister, I can't imagine what he'd do to *me*. I really hope he doesn't wanna kill me."

Parker tucked a stray tendril of hair behind Brian's ear. "I wouldn't worry about it. As soon as you grabbed him, he switched over like a traffic light. His sister looked positively flabbergasted. I'd bet *my* bundle on the purple dinosaur."

"I dunno why I'm talking to you guys about this stuff." Brian's head flopped onto his outstretched arms. "I just met you and you stole our weapons. And you talk all weird, dress funny. I can't take you seriously."

"We're just likable, easy-to-talk-to folks," Spike said. "And you're ossified. Before you ask, it means drunk."

"So say 'drunk' then." Brian swiveled his head to look at Spike. "Do you ever feel like you're dreaming? This whole thing's felt like a dream ever since I heard those gunshots in my room. I wanna wake up. I wanna see my mom and dad. I wanna see Becks."

"I want to see my family too." Parker swirled a hand against Brian's heaving back as he started to cry. "That's why we need your help."

Spike's face blurred into a blotchy swirl of beige and chestnut. "Trust me, kid—we want to wake up too. Parker and I think of this as another play, one last show before we go. Once that curtain falls, we take our final bow together and the lights go out forever."

Brian imagined shadow-cloaked rows of barren seats and an empty stage draped in velvet curtains, the silence of the auditorium amplified by the roaring applause preceding it. A permanent darkness that suffocated the senses, the absence of existence. Nothingness. Death.

It finally made sense to him why Spike and Parker acted the way they did, why they wanted to pretend. Why his father tried to escape all those years ago.

Accepting the inevitability of death made life seem as pointless as performing to an empty theater.

BRIAN AND THE twins woke with varying degrees of hangovers. Eva's was mild, and although Louis had drunk more than her, he tolerated the pain (un)surprisingly well. Any time a merciless light shone into Brian's eyes, he swore his brain was fighting its way out of his skull.

When they rode out to retrieve the fireworks, Brian was still battling a raging headache, an overwhelming sense of vertigo, and the regret of a loosened tongue. He recalled swirling galaxies penetrating his eyes and the sensation of needles in his fingertips but little else after it.

Spike and Parker led the way, pulling Scooter into a field within walking distance of Black Market Fireworks. The wide beige building—decorated with at least three signs for "Black Cat"—loomed behind a dilapidated smoke and liquor shack, a few shattered planks hanging from the front doors. Two cars stripped of tires and doors remained in the parking lot, buried in about three inches of packed snow.

Since Louis argued against only Parker and Spike going in armed, they relented and returned Brian's bow to him. They either suspected he didn't have the skill or cunning to sink an arrow into both their heads.

Agnes and Hildy roamed in search of food while Spike and Parker pushed the doors open into endless darkness. Eva reclaimed her role of torchbearer, joined by her brother while the actors led the way. Brian stayed crammed in the middle where he always seemed to be.

Their flashlights swept over rows of empty shelves with the occasional box of fireworks. All the large varieties had been claimed; most of what remained were the smaller, less impressive types like sparklers and snakes. Brian suspected scavengers had snatched up the fireworks for their components, not to set them off in their driveways.

"It stinks in here." Eva's voice echoed amidst the empty aisles. Brian knew she couldn't mean Spike's pleasant aftershave. Within seconds, the foul stench of what could've been week-old garbage with spoiled milk and rotten meat in it assailed him.

Louis swept his sister behind him, sticking next to Brian with the flashlight while Brian kept an arrow pulled taut with the bowstring. Parker and Spike held up the rear, armed with their Typewriter and Shorty, as they called them.

The farther back into the store they went, the worse it stank. Brian wanted to gag at the pungent, sickly sweet scent invading his nose. He *tasted* the spoiled milk and rotten meat. But he couldn't cover his nose, so he had to hold his breath and release it in sharp gasps before swiftly inhaling and holding it again. The others suffered in silence around him.

A torn banner above the back room advertised "EXPLOSIVE DEALS!" When they entered, the cone of Louis's flashlight highlighted a large shape on the ground. It wasn't a box—it was a body. A Stalker curled into a fetal position on its side.

Brian drew the arrow back, but Louis put a hand on his arm. "Wait—it's dead."

Eva pinched her nose. "The robbers, maybe?"

Because Louis boldly ventured near it, Brian joined him. The others moved up behind them to investigate the body. The reason for the intense stench became apparent when they saw its intestines stretching out of its stomach like links of sausage. Chunks of muscle were missing from its limbs down to the bone. Although the telltale smile remained, the eyes were gone, probably plucked out and eaten like grapes.

"Oh, sick!" Parker muttered from behind them, briefly dropping her affected Texas drawl.

"Well, now we know they eat each other." The inflection of Spike's voice straddled the line between awed and deadpan. "It hasn't been dead long. They mighta both been infected and got trapped in here."

"So where's the other one now?" Brian asked under his breath, retreating from the mutilated body. They rushed to put their backs into a corner, gathered into a tight cluster while the twins lit both sides of the room with their flashlights.

Eva gasped and pointed. "Up there!"

Brian followed her finger to the top of one of the shelves in the far-right corner of the room. A pale figure balanced on all fours, frozen in the act of crawling.

For a second, Brian thought it might've been someone who'd climbed up to hide from the Stalker in the room—but when his eyes moved to the torn flesh of its smile, he knew exactly what he was looking at. He held his breath, lifted the bow toward it, and pulled the arrow back with the string. It vibrated like a plucked rubber band.

The Stalker's clouded eyes fixated on him. It scuttled along the top of the shelves toward him, a human body warped by inhuman movements. Brian's skin grew clammy, somehow cold and hot at the same time. *It couldn't see us, still doesn't, but it hears* me—

Gentle pressure cupped his trembling right elbow and left hand. Breath tickled Brian's ear. "You got this, boug. Take it down—quick."

When Louis's hands retreated, Brian steadied himself and released the string. The arrow whipped over his index finger and soared through the air. It sunk into the scrambling Stalker's neck and sent it hurtling to the floor.

Brian fumbled for another arrow, sweaty hands clinging to the insides of his gloves. The Stalker rose to its knees first, its upper torso springing up afterward with its arms dangling at its sides. It tilted its head onto its shoulder, making gurgling noises as it tried to laugh. Its jerky movements reminded Brian of a marionette.

Another arrow through the temple cut the strings.

Brian's shoulders slumped as he lowered the bow. His head and arms ached, and his vision swam in wavy lines of dull color. "Ugh. I feel sick." The potent stench wafting from both corpses didn't help matters any.

"You need some fresh air." Spike patted the top of Brian's head. "I think the rest of us could do with some too. The rest of the place looked clear. Let's gather up what we can find and start setting things up."

They made a swift exit out of the back room and returned to the main floor, scouring the shelves for anything they could get their hands on. Brian tried to assure the others he was fine and that he needed some space, so they split up and searched on their own. He took the opportunity to lean against one of the shelves and catch his breath, withdrawing a bottle of water and chugging what little remained in it along with a handful of pain pills.

Someone put a gentle hand on his back, startling him. "You sure you're okay?"

Brian spun and put his back to the shelf, offering Eva a wan smile. "Yeah. Still trying to get that smell out of my nose and throat."

"Ugh, me too." She rolled her eyes. The delicate curves of her face gleamed in the radiant light of his lantern. "Hey, I came to ask you for a favor. I think there's somethin' good on top of one of these shelves, but I can't reach it."

Brian smirked. "You didn't want to ask Louis for help, huh?"

"He always teases me about bein' vertically-challenged." Her agitated expression shifted into something more playful. She socked Brian in the shoulder. "C'mon. Help a girl out."

Brian followed her to a shelf in the rear corner of the main floor. She pointed out the box and stood on tiptoe, demonstrating how high she could reach. Brian brushed the box with his fingertips, but it was too far back to get a hold of. He used his bow to hook it instead and dragged it down into Eva's waiting hands.

"You're so clever." She smiled and gazed down at the box in her hands, gloved fingers stroking the dusty laminate. She glanced up at Brian. "Do you remember spendin' the Fourth of July with us?"

Brian's brow creased. "We used to grill at your house, right? Not your grandparents'—the one by the lake. We'd try to catch fireflies out there."

"That's right. Père and Lou would set up the big stuff while you, me, and Mère ran around with sparklers. I was scared they'd burn me, but you showed me what happened when yours died out. That it didn't hurt at all." She set the box down and reached for his hand. "I always thought you were brave, especially after you stood up to Lou like you did. I wanted to thank you for doin' it again in that restaurant. When he drinks, it makes him nastier than usual—I don't know what I woulda done if you hadn't stopped him."

"Oh, no problem." When he glanced down at their joined hands and thought about what Louis might do if he saw this, his palm started to itch. "Um, you guys are twenty, right? How did he drink?"

"Bein' underage didn't stop him. He would just steal Papère's beers. Papère'd get so drunk he didn't even know he was missin' any." Her fingers tightened around his as her eyes angled up to the ceiling. "Papère could be a nice man at times, but I guess it was only to me and when he wasn't drunk. Lou takes after him and Père, and I think he hates it." Her moist eyes looked back into Brian's as she released his hand. "But let's stop talkin' about my brother."

Eva stood on her toes and snatched Brian's scarf, forcing his head down to meet hers. Her soft lips caressed his, but he didn't reciprocate. He clenched his hands at his sides, not sure what to do with them—not sure what he even *wanted* to do.

She rocked back onto the flats of her feet before he could decide. Her eyebrows furrowed as she looked around the room. "I guess this isn't the most romantic settin', is it? Especially not with everyone rootin' around for fireworks. Your mind probably went straight to my brother, worryin' over whether he saw that or not."

She wasn't wrong.

"I'm still feeling a little sick, is all." Brian relaxed his fists. "And there's this weird situation with Spike and Parker. I mean, they even admitted they're acting. I don't know what to expect. This plan with the fireworks, her missing family... It could all be lies or only some of it. I could try to sneak up on them, take them out with the bow—"

"You just wanna do that because you think it's what Louis would do. But we don't have to do things his way—he's not always right." She grabbed the box from the shelf. "Besides, I don't wanna kill two people who love each other. Love is one of the only beautiful things left in this world."

"That could be a lie too," Brian said. Eva hugged the box against her chest, but her heavy sigh still carried in the hushed air.

When Louis showed up to let them know Spike and Parker were ready, Eva shoved the box into his arms and stalked off without a word. Louis sputtered, the beam of his flashlight shining in erratic angles as he struggled to keep the cumbersome box from falling.

"The hell? I told her I was sorry last night—why the fuck is she still mad at me?" He pried open the box with one hand and scoffed. "Why'd she shove an empty box at me? *Gros bête.*" Louis tossed it to the ground. Brian suspected Eva's request for help had been a ploy to set him up for that kiss. He'd underestimated her by attributing all the craftiness to Louis.

"It's not you," Brian said. "She's mad because I suggested trying to take out Parker and Spike." And because he didn't react to her advance in the way she wanted him to, but he wasn't going to tell Louis that.

"Figures." Louis propped his elbow against the shelf, eyes flashing to the side to make sure the others were out of earshot. "We don't have much time, but we could work somethin' out. If you get the drop on Spike, I can take Parker down, get her in a chokehold. If he really loves her, he'll do whatever we ask—like give us our goddamn guns back."

Brian folded his arms and leaned his shoulder against the same shelf. "They're armed. We'd have to time it right. We can't stroll out there with an arrow in their faces and tackle Parker like a quarterback." Brian sighed. "I don't know. Eva said she didn't want to kill them because they're in love. I mean, it could all be a lie, but what if it isn't?"

Louis arched his eyebrows and lowered his flashlight onto the shelf. "I never took you for such a sap. You believe in fate, soulmates, all that kinda shit?"

"Not really." Brian blurted out the question on the tip of his tongue. "But why do *you* keep going? Why do you put up with this shitty weather, with Stalkers jumping out of airplane bathrooms and phone booths, with scavenging for supplies and living out of bags? We just live day to day, and for what? We'll die eventually. Why draw it out?"

Louis took a step closer to Brian and clapped a hand onto his bicep. "Don't you dare turn into your daddy. He was an idiot for tryin' to leave you and your family, and you'd be an idiot to leave us. Eva and I are your family now. That's what you live for." His hand slid down Brian's arm until it caressed his elbow. Goose bumps rippled underneath Brian's sleeve. "I keep goin' because I'm not the kinda person who gives up. You have that in you too—that's why you stand up to me. You stood up to me before, left an impression on me in more ways than one."

The sickness in Brian intensified. His already sour stomach fluttered. He swallowed but his throat had gone dry and a lump stuck in it. The needles that usually only stabbed the tips of his fingers spread throughout his body, making him feel like he was someone's voodoo doll.

"Louis, I—" A rapid burst of fireworks cut off the apology on the tip of his tongue. They both shuddered as Louis released Brian's arm, realizing they'd been lost in the timeless void together this time.

"Fuck. They already set 'em off." Louis snatched his flashlight and met Brian's startled gaze. "We can still go for it, try to get their weapons from 'em. If you see Spike, aim an arrow at his face. I'll take care of Parker."

Brian and Louis dashed to the entrance of the store amidst the crackles and hisses of erupting fireworks. They shoved through the doors together and burst into the parking lot. Exploding sparks of color and glittering silver showers rained from the sky above them, thunderous blasts alternating with whizzing whistles and shrill pops. Smoke swirled in the air, obscuring the actors and Eva from view.

Brian searched for Spike and found him kneeling in front of a box with a macabre jester's face on it. He drew an arrow back as Spike continued to light the fireworks with a gold-plated flip lighter—but Parker stood next to Spike, aiming her tommy-gun at Eva. "Put the bow down, sugar."

Kaleidoscopic colors filled the twilight sky until they faded, leaving Brian staring at Parker through the cloud of smoke. The last of the fireworks sizzled out with a pathetic little whistle and a final *pop*.

"Why are you aiming your gun at Eva?" Brian kept the arrow pointed at Spike as he stood, slipping his lighter into his vest pocket. He'd lost Louis somewhere in the smoke, but he knew he was around, trying to weigh his options and work up a plan.

Spike withdrew the sawed-off shotgun from his overcoat and hefted it toward Brian. "Isn't it obvious, kid? Because you're aiming an arrow at *me*. Where's your buddy? You have a nice little pow-wow in the warehouse?" His eyes darted from Brian's for an instant, but Brian didn't want to release the bowstring in case Parker pulled the trigger on Eva. "Louis, you don't have much time—better make your move. I've got two barrels aimed at the boy you're stuck on, and my moll's got her gun trained on the sister you're stuck *with*. You go for Parker, I shoot Brian. You go for me, Parker shoots Eva. Now, I wonder who you're more worried about saving?"

Silence answered him. But Brian felt a tingle of energy like static electricity and knew Louis wasn't far away.

"Don't make us burn powder," Spike seethed through clenched teeth. "Show yourself or we shoot them both and leave you with no one. Brian, you lower that bow—I know it's gotta be hurting you. If you don't, you're gonna be hurting a lot worse soon."

Brian lowered his bow, but something about the way Spike spoke reminded him of his own faux aggression toward the woman outside the Pawliday Inn. *He's still acting. But why?*

While Spike was earning his Oscar, Parker broke character. Her wide eyes darted to Spike, her lips parting as her thin eyebrows knit together. "Honey, are you sure about this?" It was the one thing she'd ever said Brian knew wasn't part of the act. *Her voice is breaking. She thinks he's taking it too far.*

Distant echoes of barking dogs filled the silent air. Spike cracked his neck and exhaled. "On the count of three. One... Two..."

"Fuck you." Louis stepped into the parking lot from behind one of the abandoned cars, his hands in the air. His furious eyes swept from Spike's to Eva's. "If you hadn't stormed off, you wouldn't have given them a chance to pull a gun on you. Your little temper tantrum ruined it for us."

Despite the gun aimed at Eva this entire time, she'd kept her composure—until now. She collapsed to her knees and wailed, beating her fist into the snow. Her voice constricted into a pitiful whine as she tried to speak through her cries. "Why're you blamin' me? Wh-why do you *always* bl-blame me?" She stammered and sucked in a hearty gasp of air. "You were in there with Brian—you didn't care about me bein' out here alone with them! She held a gun to my head, Lou! She coulda *killed* me!"

"Dollface," Parker sighed and kneeled next to Eva, "we didn't want to do it this way, but we had to. We couldn't bring you to them—it would've given it away, given you a chance to run. So we had to bring them to you." She reached over to smooth Eva's tear-streaked cheeks with a gloved hand, but Eva brushed it away. "Every lie has a bit of truth to it, and sometimes you get the best performances out of people when they don't know they're performing."

Parker stood as a group of men wearing black approached through lingering tendrils of smoke. Painted masks covered their faces. They had no identity, no emotion, nothing to mark them as "human" anymore. Nothing except the desire for self-preservation, to hurt others so they could persevere. So they could prosper.

One man marched ahead of the others, brandishing a machete over his shoulder. He towered over the rest of the group by at least a foot. When he spoke, the dogs whining and straining at their leashes quieted and stopped moving all at once. "Spike, Parker. Well done. Did you enjoy celebrating the Fourth of July this December?" A hint of humor colored his gruff voice, but his expression was unreadable behind his eerie flesh-toned mask. Unlike the bizarre expressions painted onto his minions' masks, their leader's lacked any affectation whatsoever.

"I don't know how anyone can enjoy this." The bravado in Spike's voice vanished. "Let's head back before we draw more Stalkers in. Last batch was a bitch to take out."

Various pairs of eyes flitted from face to face, trying to feel out the dynamics at play. Spike and Parker seemed to be trying to keep their expressions neutral. The masked men gave away no emotion at all, even with their body language.

"Come with us." The tall man tilted his head. He turned and walked ahead of them, his men swarming around Brian and the others like piranhas devouring fresh prey.

They marched through the last of the smoke and sun toward an uncertain but inevitable fate.

Chapter Eleven: Dimmer and Dimmer

12/13, JOPLIN, MISSOURI

Night

As night descended upon them, they arrived at an amusement park that reminded Brian more of a county fair than Disney World. A chain-link fence with barbed wire lining the top guarded a multitude of run-down rides not worth protecting even *before* the pandemic.

Once they marched through the gate, the rides glowed with neon lights. Upbeat calliope music played as a carousel swirled to life, riderless plastic horses bobbing up and down. The Ferris wheel rotated as a gleeful voice cackled over a loudspeaker: "BUMPER CARS! GO-KARTS! COTTON CANDY! TRY YOUR HAND AT OUR ARCADE! EEEEEVERYONE'S A WINNER WHEN YOU'RE HAVING FUN! GET YOUR KICKS AT ROUTE 66!"

A low growl rumbled in Brian's throat. Dread replaced his childhood sense of wonder.

What do they want us for?

Spike and Parker told us that story about her sister and niece to throw us off, lower our guards and rope us in—but why not take our weapons and turn us in?

Something isn't adding up here.

They continued deeper into the park, traipsing over crushed candy wrappers and tickets half-buried by the snow. The gang escorted Brian, Eva, and Louis to a building filled with pens and hay—a petting zoo.

Except people were in the pens instead of animals.

The masked men shoved them into cells and locked them up without a word. Eva curled into a fetal position in the corner and cried into her knees while Louis examined his for structural weaknesses. Brian's eyes swept over the other prisoners, who looked back at him with forlorn expressions. His heart ached for them as he imagined the suffering and loneliness they must be enduring.

Wait—that's them. The mother and daughter from Parker's photo. Dirt and desolation warped the woman's once vibrant face, and her scant clothes were in tatters. The little girl kneeled in the cell next to her, her tiny hands curled around the bars of the pen as she peered at her new neighbors.

Brian tapped one of the iron shafts. "Hey, kiddo. Do you have an aunt? An actress who goes by 'Parker'?"

The woman's dull eyes brightened. She spoke over the little girl before she could answer Brian. "Don't talk too much in here. They'll silence you." Her eyes shifted to the door. When she was certain the guards weren't coming in, she looked back at Brian and nodded.

I'm not going to get anything more out of her. Maybe they are Parker's family. Or Parker stole her name from that photo, took her identity from this woman's real sister.

Spike and Parker had a plan to free them, but it was only a ruse to get us here. They must work for these masked creeps.

But why work for them if they have Parker's family?

Louis's eyes darted from the woman to Brian, narrowing slightly.

It's not adding up for him, either.

They could only wait and wonder.

SEVERAL DAYS PASSED. More and more prisoners were led away from the building until only a few remained. They endured primitive living conditions, using a bucket for waste and eating dry bread and drinking mud-flavored water. Brian craved a bath more than anything—anything except answers. He hadn't seen Spike, Parker, or the man who led this bizarre masked gang.

The woman and her daughter were still caged, though the woman was sometimes led out and back in. Her disheveled hair and clothes made it obvious what was happening in those gaps. Eva tried to put on a brave face, but the slight crease in her forehead implied she was worried about enduring the same fate.

All three of them had been searched before they were locked up. Brian and Louis endured this indignity in silence, but Louis yelled at the bandits when their wandering hands lingered on Eva. He took a hard punch to the gut for his attempts to defend his sister. Because of this distraction, they'd forgotten to search Brian's boots and hadn't found the pocketknife he'd hidden under one of the insoles. Brian had been trying to pick the lock on his cage, but the angle proved to be too awkward and the bars were too sturdy to cut.

Brian contemplated digging out the knife to try again—but the door clicked open, letting in a stream of blinding light that made him wince.

The tall man entered. His impassive face and hulking figure reminded Brian of the serial killer from *Halloween*. The machete strapped to his belt didn't dissuade Brian from this impression.

"Sorry to keep you waiting so long." He gestured for the two men who flanked him to leave. His bright but bloodshot eyes peered at them through the mask. "As you may have gathered, I'm the leader of this operation. They call me the King. A bit trite, but it stuck." His voice was low and raspy. He'd either shaved or lost his hair, and an odor clung to him like clothes left in the washer for too long.

"What happened to the other prisoners?" Brian asked.

"They were tested." The King approached Brian's pen and gripped the bars with large hands. His nails were trimmed but filthy, and his skin was pale. The sores and scratches reminded Brian of his mother's descent into madness. "The ones who passed either decided to join me or they were sold to someone who might have more use for them than I would."

Boldness went hand in hand with dread as Brian continued his discourse with the King. "One of those things made you sick, didn't they?"

The King didn't react. Brian swallowed. Finally, the King's hands moved up to his mask. Without a word, he lifted it over the top of his head like he was peeling away a thin layer of adhesive. Eva gasped.

His face was warped and twisted: his shrunken lips ripped at the corners, exposing his molars in a horrible, skeletal smile, and his nose crumbled into a clay-like mass. His eyes weren't as cloudy as most Stalkers', but they still opened into the same seemingly unblinking stare. Reddish-brown streaks stained his pasty cheeks.

"My reaction was similar to yours when I saw this," the King said. "Disbelief, shock. Eventually, resignation. At first, I was relieved—but then I realized I'd be like this for the rest of what life I might have left. It's not much different than being trapped in the cells you now sit in."

Louis peered out at the King's bared face, obscured by his iron bars. "Did anythin' change besides your body? Like your mind? How you think? Feel?"

"My memories are intact. My self-awareness, unfortunately. My desires, thoughts."

Louis's eyes narrowed. "What about your appetite?"

"I'm not keeping you to eat. You're too valuable for that." The stretched smile seemed to tighten. "Your cows were delicious, though."

Shock and grief pierced Brian's aching gut. Tears stung his eyes as he thought of Agnes and Hildy's gentle natures. They'd lost everything—except what they'd left at Caldone's. And that was only if Parker and Spike hadn't taken that too.

"Why do you need to take everything?" Brian bit back his anger as the King's impassive eyes regarded him, paired with that infuriating grin. "Why do you send people out to rob and murder?"

"We only kill the ones who fight back." The King's tone bordered on offended. "People are more valuable alive."

"That's bullshit!" Brian beat a fist against his cell bars. "Your people shot my grandfather—we have the gun! Talk to Spike and Parker if you wanna check for yourself, because they took it!"

Louis gave him a sharp look, surprised by his outburst. Eva's eyes gleamed with moisture, upset by Agnes and Hildy's cruel fates.

"I used to buy junk no one wanted," the King said. "I would fix it up to resell, put ads out until the right person saw it. One man's junk is another man's treasure, and I know how to convince someone I have just the thing they need. Now, more than ever, people need things: things to survive, to make them *want* to survive. Most of all, they need other people. Some want a toy to entertain them, some want companions, pleasures of the flesh. Others hunger for flesh in a more...literal manner. Now I have to evaluate you and see what *your* worth is. Put some ads out for you, see who bites."

The King's choice of the word "bites" chilled Brian to the bone.

"You said you test them first," Louis said. "Is that what you're gonna do to us?"

"I had no idea you were the ones who killed my men. That...intrigues me. I think you have a high chance of passing. However—" he moved over to Eva. "—I have a proposition for you."

Eva looked up, her cheeks red and tear-streaked. She wiped her eyes and shook her head swiftly. "I'm not interested. I know what you do to that poor woman over there—I'd sooner die!"

The King retreated from Eva's pen. "My condition prohibits me from certain activities that might damage my goods, but my men have to let off steam now and again. But you're a diamond—a beauty with spirit and tenacity. If you don't want to take the test, you can come with me now. You could be the thing *I* need."

Eva couldn't bring herself to look at the twisted man. Louis displayed rare restraint. He didn't seem intimidated by the King, but he might've been considering his sister's safety. His temper and impulses had an unpredictable ebb and flow.

"I'll take your test." Eva matched the King's forceful stare. "I don't care if I die or if you sell me off to someone else—I'll never belong to you. And don't think it's because I'm disgusted by your face; it's your personality that disgusts me."

A low, deep laugh rumbled from the King's throat. It was guttural, like the bellow of an alligator. Once it died out, he tugged the mask back over his mangled face. "So be it. I'll return for you shortly."

As soon as he closed the door and the bolt clicked shut, Eva's resolve crumbled. She buried her face in her knees and sobbed. The woman across from her watched, no hint of emotion on her drained face.

Brian wanted to reach out to Eva, but he couldn't even *reach* her.

THE KING RETURNED with several of his masked lackeys the next day.

"It's time."

Nerves and nausea overtook Brian as they were released from their cages. He exchanged a brief, panicked look with Eva before they were led away, but the handcuffs keeping Louis's hands restrained behind his back preoccupied him.

"How are you testin' us, exactly?" Louis kicked a rock as they emerged into the clear night air. Brian inhaled, his eyelids fluttering shut. The clean air was a refreshing change from the animal stench of the pens, and he was enjoying the freedom of moving his legs again.

"I'm going to test your resourcefulness and abilities. See what your selling points are."

Brian's eyes opened. "And if we fail?"

The King said nothing. He slid a finger across his throat, the smile etched in his face hidden behind the indifferent façade of his mask.

They paused in front of the building, still cuffed. The King circled in front of them while his men surrounded them. "I'll be observing safely from outside along with my crew. They will be armed and you will not, so the odds are *not* in your favor. The lights and rides are all on; use them to your advantage. The buildings are unlocked, so feel free to dart in if you're feeling in need of some cover—maybe you'll find a friend, maybe not. All three of you will participate at the same time, but you will start in different locations. Better say your goodbyes now. Even if you survive, you'll still be torn apart."

"Oh, God," Eva said breathlessly. Louis didn't say anything—he just stared into the distance with a remoteness that sometimes overtook him.

The King's men kept their guns aimed at the trio but uncuffed them and let them go. Eva flung her arms around her brother's neck and muttered things Brian couldn't hear—he suspected they were apologizing to each other for the recent animosity between them. While they spoke, Brian gripped the pocketknife he'd hidden inside his sleeve.

When Eva let go of Louis, Brian reached for her hands and slipped the knife into them. He wrapped his arms around her, sighing as she tucked her chin into his shoulder. "Good luck, Eva. I'm really glad we got to see each other again." He wanted to apologize to her for not reciprocating the feelings she'd developed for him, for making her feel like she wasn't desirable, for not understanding why he felt—or didn't feel—the way he did. He wanted to tell her he cared for her, that she was kind and strong, and that maybe, just maybe, the reason he didn't kiss her back was because she reminded him of the mother he still desperately missed.

But the words caught in his throat and would stay there forever.

Eva kept her hands linked behind his neck when they parted. She stood on tiptoe, her eyes shining, and kissed him lightly on the lips. "No matter what, don't forget me. You only die when no one remembers you even existed." She kept the knife hidden in her sleeve and offered him a smile as if to say, 'I have it. Thanks.'

Brian returned her smile before Louis stepped into view. He gripped Brian's face and forced it toward him. "You'll be fine, boug. You're a quick learner and have sharp instincts—go with your gut and don't hesitate. I'll see you on the other side." He slid one hand to the back of Brian's neck, his fingers digging into it as his anxious eyes searched Brian's.

It occurred to Brian this was the first time he'd ever seen Louis this worried, which made his own raw nerves sting worse than they already were.

He tried to think of what to say to Louis, but the words didn't form as easily as they had for Eva. His thoughts jumbled into something like, *You make me nervous and I feel guilty for cutting your face even though you shot my grandfather and his dog, but I still sort of like you and I definitely admire you, so please don't die and I hope I'll see you again.*

The guards gripped their arms and wrenched them apart before he could get a single word out. Brian lost sight of the twins, but he knew if he had any shot at seeing them again, he needed to keep it together and listen to Louis's advice.

An assortment of chaotic lights flashed to the tune of cheery fairground organs, mocking Brian's pleasant carnival memories. But the experience wasn't complete without the smell of fried food, and there was no crowd to create the comforting backdrop of delighted cheers and thrilled screams. Long-frozen snow coated everything in a majestic sheen aside from the rotating rides. The air chilled him through his thin hoodie and jeans, but at least his socks were dry and it wasn't snowing.

The two guards gripping his arms stopped outside the Ferris wheel. Their faces were fully covered by volto-style masquerade masks painted with elaborate gold swirls. "Line starts here. Keep your arms and legs inside at all times. This ride is not meant for pregnant women or anyone with pre-existing medical conditions. Your goal is to find all six tokens; you find them all, find *us* outside the fence. The King sends the dogs in after three hours. Haven't seen many people survive those."

They released Brian's arms. He jumped as a hand patted his rear. "Good luck, kiddo."

That voice... That aftershave.

The guards marched away and left Brian alone. When he stepped forward, he felt pressure in his rear jean pocket. He dug his hand into it and touched a cold, jagged mass: a small ring of keys. A thick piece of folded paper was wedged behind it.

Spike. He slid this stuff into my pocket. But I can't read this note yet—not until I have better light and privacy.

Brian approached the rotating cabs, which squeaked like they needed a good oiling. The cold numbed his exposed skin while he counted them. When something finally caught his eye, his heart raced: a Stalker huddled in one of the cabs, its hunched shoulders shuddering.

The cab ascended. The Stalker seemed blind; it probably hadn't heard him over the squealing cabs. The way it shivered affirmed to him that cold *did* affect them. It was freezing to death and couldn't move. When it was a safe distance away, he picked up his count.

A glint on the floor of another cab caught his eye. He clambered in and picked up the dirty token, which had "66" imprinted on one side. The cab ascended with frustrating sluggishness, metal grinding on metal. The dilapidated state of the park made Brian think it had been closed *before* everything went to shit.

The lights still work, though. And that awful music.

While he waited for the Ferris wheel to descend, he flipped through the ring of keys to see if any were labeled. Nothing clear, but one had a smudged "P" on it. Another had been used so much the brass coating was chipping away. He'd try those first. The King said the buildings were all unlocked, but Spike had given Brian the keys for a reason—obviously, the King wanted to keep something locked up.

Next, he snatched the letter from his pocket, struggling to unfold it so he could put his speed reading to use. The LED lights shining from the Ferris wheel provided him with just enough brightness to read.

Kid,

Sorry for the subterfuge—if we'd straight up asked you to hand yourselves over, you never would've agreed to it. Like Parker told Eva, sometimes you get a better performance out of someone when they don't know they're performing.

When we went to the Estates and learned Parker's sister and niece were kidnapped, we knew we had to track this gang down and find a way inside, learn their routine. We were performing for them, for you, for ourselves, trying to make what we had to do easier. We had to prove our "loyalty" to the King, and I had to work doubly hard to keep Parker out of his clutches, convince him our acting was more valuable to him than our bodies were to someone else.

We needed to time it right. To find the right people. We watched the three of you while you rooted around in Carl Junction. You're capable—especially for your age—and the younger the prey, the more the King could charge. You'd be a good haul, get us in good with him, make him lower his guard. I'm sorry you had to sit around and suffer, about what he did to your animals, but we couldn't talk to you. I'm not going to ask for you to forgive us, but please try to understand why we're doing this.

What I want you to do now is cause some confusion. The keys I gave you unlock the building next to the carousel where the breakers and generators are. Cut the power. The King's men'll run around like they're trying to put Humpty back together again.

They also unlock the storage area where some of your weapons are. Go northwest from the power room to the big brick building. The King has the only keys to the lockers, but you're resourceful enough to find something to work with. I'll keep him distracted—work your way to that storage building and get outta here. If I were you, I'd head for the fence opposite the ticket booth—the buildings and rides block most of the moonlight. Parker's going to free her family and we're gonna escape all this. She'll try to help Eva too. Your buddy Louis doesn't need any help except the psychiatric kind.

Best of luck,
Spike AKA Craig

Brian rushed to read the note and barely had time to process what it said. All he knew was Spike had no reason to pull one over on him now—he might as well keep going.

He climbed out of the cab and booked it for the nearest building—and crashed right into someone or something that hadn't been there a moment ago. He struggled to get his balance and looked up, hoping to see Eva or Louis.

Instead, he made a garbled sound of shock. A strange mascot suit stood in front of him, impassively staring at him through plastic eyes: a pink Easter bunny out of someone's nightmare.

The situation was so bizarre he almost laughed.

Did some sick person put a Stalker in the costume?

When it raised its arms straight in front of it and lunged for him, he didn't find it so amusing. He jumped back and bobbed around it, running until he could put his back to a wall. He had to pause to catch his breath—his chest hurt. His stomach grumbled with hunger, he had a headache, and his legs burned from the strain of running.

When he finally caught his breath, he peered around the corner of the building and looked back at where the mascot had been. His eyebrows quirked. It had toppled over and was flailing in the snow as if it was trying to make a snow angel. The carousel beyond it whirled while the mascot continued to writhe. One of the rotating horses had a figure seated on it. Brian couldn't tell who or what it was—but even if it *was* Eva or Louis, he wasn't about to go inspect it unarmed.

Brian rushed over to the adjacent building and tried the door. It didn't budge. He fumbled for the keys to try them in the locks. The "P" worked where the worn key failed. After he stumbled into the building, he put his back to the door and locked it.

The lights were on, illuminating walls filled with breakers and humming generators. A heavy-duty flashlight lay on the ground, no doubt placed there by Spike. Brian grabbed it and approached breakers labeled with acronyms such as "CRS" and "MLT." He couldn't waste time deciphering them, so he flipped the main breaker and shut the generators off. All sounds died down to complete silence as the lights cut to darkness.

They know someone's in here now—time to move.

Brian gripped the door handle and turned the flashlight off so the beam wouldn't give his position away. He opened the door and slipped the key into the lock, and then bashed down the bow with the flashlight until it snapped off.

Good luck getting back in to turn the power on, assholes.

He felt his way along the rough brick wall, using the dim starlight to navigate the faint outlines of the park. Even though he couldn't see his own breath, the beams of the bandits' flashlights and the halos of their lanterns gave their location away. Brian kept out of their line of sight and hurried over to the next building. He tried the knob. It turned, so he avoided it.

He moved on until he found a knob that didn't twist completely. Fortunately, the door faced away from the confused bandits as they scurried through the night. He felt for the lock with shaking hands and jabbed at the brass plating surrounding it.

Just like that night with Nana.

When the key slid in, he exhaled and twisted. He locked and shut the door behind him, then clicked the flashlight on with his thumb.

A vast room loomed beyond him. Piles of stolen belongings were separated by type: clothes, medicine, food, and junk. The weapons were stowed in secured lockers, so Brian focused his attention on the piles out in the open. He left the flashlight on the ground and sifted through the tools, searching for something to pry the lockers open with.

The doorknob rattled.

Shit—someone with a key?

Brian snatched the flashlight and squeezed into a tiny crevice between the wall and lockers. He turned off the light and waited.

Moonlight flooded in as the door opened. A shadow hovered in the open doorway. When the door shut, it left Brian in a void of silence and darkness. He waited for his vision to adjust, but he couldn't make much out. Whoever was inside moved stealthily, not using any source of light to search the room.

Would a bandit do that? Or is someone trying to trick me out of hiding? It's not Spike, is it? Or Parker—?

The energy of the room shifted as if the person was closing in on him. He held his breath, scared to swallow. An abrupt tickle in his throat made him want to clear it or cough.

Of course.

The air in front of him warmed. Muffled breathing approached him.

Something grazed him and instinct kicked in. He swung the flashlight—but a force stopped his wrist. A hand covered his mouth and pressed him back into the corner. "Who the fuck are you? Answer me before I choke the life outta you!"

When Brian recognized the accent, his knees nearly buckled. "Louis, it's—"

"Brian?" The hand around his neck relaxed. Brian clicked the flashlight on. Louis squinted and grimaced. "Ah! Get that outta my eyes, boug!"

"Sorry!" When Louis released Brian's wrist, Brian lowered the flashlight, trying to think of a way to condense Spike's letter for Louis. "I don't really know how to say this: Spike gave me a set of keys and a letter. He told me to cut the power, to find the lockers and grab our weapons, but the King's the only one with the keys—"

Someone fumbled with the door lock. Louis tugged Brian's sleeve and dragged him underneath the pile of unsorted clothes. Brian clicked the flashlight off. Louis wrapped an arm around Brian's back to keep him pinned as if he suspected Brian might spring up like a cat from an unwanted lap.

The door opened. Two beams of light shone into the expansive room with masked men behind them.

"The door was locked. Whoever got in to cut the power might not have made it here yet."

"Or they locked it behind them, asshat."

"Rude. How do you think they got to the breakers?"

"A key or ace lockpicking skills."

"And how would they get a key?"

"Ace pickpocketing skills."

The other bandit sighed from behind his doll-like mask. "Man, I miss the old days when the only people good at that shit were nerds who did it in video games."

"Like you?"

Their banter made them seem like actual people instead of faceless enemies. Still, they were desperate and dangerous—and capable of cruelty beyond that of the Stalkers.

A shaft of light swept over the pile of clothes Louis and Brian hid beneath. Louis tightened his fingers into the fabric of Brian's jacket. Brian held his breath.

"I don't see jack shit in here. Maybe they didn't make it in yet."

"Ah, the other guys will find them—" His voice cut off. "Wait a minute. Look at this."

Louis's nose dug into Brian's hair as he whispered, "I'll take one, you take the other."

Louis crawled out and lunged at one of the bandits. Brian followed, bringing the flashlight down on the other's skull with a sickening crack. The man wobbled and slumped to the ground, moaning. Brian didn't hear a sound from Louis or the guard he'd grabbed. He angled the flashlight in their direction, revealing the guard on the ground with a puddle of blood underneath him. A thin red line leaked blood from his throat.

Images of Poppa and the woman at the Pawliday Inn flashed through his mind as his eyes moved up to the dripping blade in Louis's hand.

When Louis caught Brian's confused gaze, his eyes moved down to the knife. "I killed him. I know. I'm sorry, but—"

"That's my knife. I gave it to Eva."

Louis skirted his gaze, his shoulders slumping. "I know. I found it on her."

"You—you found it on her?" Brian tried to connect pieces of a puzzle that didn't yet fit. "Parker was supposed to help her—"

"You think it's a coincidence Spike told you to go here and two bandits showed up lookin' for you?" Louis wiped the blade on his jeans and slid it into his pocket. He approached Brian, a scowl warping his attractive features. "They tested us, all right. Eva failed."

Brian stared through Louis as he spoke, his voice distant like an echo. The pieces were connecting and forming a picture Brian didn't want to see finished.

Louis placed his hands on Brian's shoulders and stroked them with his thumbs. "Brian? Are you hearin' me?"

Brian dug the nails of his free hand into his palm and looked up at Louis. The warm glow of the bandits' abandoned flashlights lit the crevices of his face: the shallow skin underneath his eyes, the parallel lines of his straight nose, the curves of his lips.

Warm hands continued to grip his shoulders, squeezing and shaking.

"Eva's gone. All we've got is each other now." Louis sighed as he continued to look into Brian's dazed eyes. "We gotta grab our shit and get outta here. They'll be on us in no time. We can cry on each other's shoulders later."

He pulled Brian in for a quick embrace. Brian's arms remained stiff at his sides like he was a robot or some strange clone of himself—a body with no soul.

She's...gone? What does that mean*? Dead? How?* Why?

He knew Louis had found her; the knife was proof. But he couldn't believe—didn't *want* to believe—that Parker would've harmed Eva. That Spike would've led him into a trap. None of it made sense. His mind looped in circles, trying to work out what was happening.

Louis's fingers dug into Brian's cheeks. "Are you with me, Brian? I can try to pick those lockers open with the knife, but we need to hurry."

Brian focused on Louis's determined gaze. It helped him escape the quicksand of despair he'd started sinking into. He nodded.

Louis patted his cheek with a tight smile. "Good. Shine the flashlight for me."

"Wait—I can do it." Brian stepped back and offered Louis the flashlight in exchange for the knife. "Hold this for me."

Louis followed him over to the lockers. "You sure you got this?"

Brian inserted the tip of the pocketknife into the padlock of the first locker. He jimmied it for a bit until the door fell open to reveal a large Magnum revolver, a pistol, and a few clips of ammo. He tossed these to Louis after inspecting the guns to see if they were loaded.

"Nice—a Walther PPK with a silencer," Louis murmured. "And a .357."

Brian moved on to the next locker. *Don't hesitate.* He repeated his success and was rewarded with his grandfather's self-made bow. A warm surge of emotion reminded him of the promise he'd made to Poppa. He grabbed the bow, along with the quiver of arrows and one final weapon wedged behind it: an AK-47.

Aside from some boxes of ammo and a lone grenade—all of which he took and handed to Louis—the rest of the lockers were empty. Louis stuffed everything into a duffel bag he'd rummaged from the junk pile. When Brian approached him, Louis handed him a pair of gloves and a thicker coat.

"Can't have you goin' out in that. There's a pair of boots too. Slide those on while I get ready."

Brian shrugged into the coat and tugged the gloves on. "Spike said to go to the fence opposite from the ticket booth, but I'm not sure what to do. What you said about Eva—"

"If he said to go there, let's go. They're expectin' you, not me. If they're waitin' for us, they'll be the ones gettin' a surprise." Louis strapped the AK to himself and tucked the Walther PPK into his jeans. He'd snagged a new coat and gloves too, and a pair of combat boots. He laced these up while Brian tugged his on. "I found a pair of bolt cutters in that junk pile. Thought we'd use 'em anyway. You cut, I'll cover."

I guess some people run off adrenaline and anger, delay their grief. I can't dwell on it either.

Louis caught Brian's eyes on him and quirked his dark eyebrows. "Ready?"

Brian nodded. Even if he wasn't prepared to abandon Eva—or accept that she was gone forever—he was ready to leave this hellish fairground behind.

Louis aimed the silenced pistol and opened the door. Brian's bow and quiver hung around him, but the bolt cutters and flashlight occupied both of his hands. They crept through the moonlit snow amidst a backdrop of barking dogs and men yelling to one another.

Brian felt for the chain-link fence. When he found it, he handed Louis the flashlight and cut through the links. Every snip of the metal sounded as loud as a gunshot, but he powered through, trying to make a line tall enough for them to crouch through.

Snip, snip, snip.

The barking grew louder, the voices clearer.

"Hurry!" Louis hissed.

"Almost there." Brian rushed through the next few loops of metal. He pried it apart as much as he could and managed to squeeze through, clothes catching on the shorn metal.

Louis hurried through behind him, shoving Brian's back. "Go, go! They'll see us soon if we don't move!" He lobbed something into the air before grabbing Brian by the elbow and hauling ass.

Something shook the ground. A bright light flashed behind them, followed by a percussive blast like someone firing a cannon. Streaks of fire soared into the air above the park, shooting stars stippling the night sky. *He threw the grenade—*

Louis pulled Brian with him. When they passed a green street sign, they stumbled behind the modest cover of a few trees to catch their breath. Brian wheezed while he stared up at the bright halo of the moon. Clouds obscured flickering stars as a light flurry of snow drifted down, melting as soon as it reached him.

A muffled voice cut the night air. "So, you made it out. And with quite a bang."

Louis whipped around, pistol aimed. "We're gettin' outta here—you ain't stoppin' us." He barely had enough breath to speak.

The trees concealed two bandits. They stepped out and lowered their guns before peeling back their masks. Brian's heart pounded in his ears as he aimed the flashlight at them, too out of breath to talk.

A familiar pair of bright blue eyes looked back at him. The cupid's bow lips beside them slid into a hesitant smile. "You got the note. Good."

Brian's mouth opened, but he could only spare enough breath for one word. "Eva—"

"I should shoot you now for what you did to her," Louis said. "For what you did to *us*."

Spike moved to block Parker, holding his shotgun in front of him but keeping the barrel tilted toward the ground. "Listen, we—"

"Remember how you threatened to shoot my sister? To shoot Brian?" Louis stepped forward, pressing the muzzle of his pistol to Spike's forehead. "I should put a bullet through your head, splatter your brains on *ton amour*. Want her to watch you die?"

Parker lifted the typewriter in Louis's direction. "If you shoot him, I swear to God or whatever you believe in that you're going down next."

Brian reached for an arrow and strung it. He aimed it at Parker, his breath clouding in front of him. "I don't want to do this, but I don't understand what's going on. What happened to Eva?"

Spike swallowed as Louis shoved the gun barrel deeper into his forehead. "Parker went to get her sister and niece. By the time she got to Eva, she was gone. I-it was bad timing. We never meant for it to happen."

"Louis, please." Desperation colored Parker's trembling voice. "You know how much it hurts to lose someone you love, right? It's the worst kind of pain you could ever experience, the sort of pain that never goes away. We only did what we did because I love my family, and Spike loves me. I know Eva's gone, but you still have Brian—he means a lot to you, doesn't he?"

Two shapes moved behind Spike and Parker—a woman and a child peering out from behind one of the skeletal oak trees looming over them. "A-aunt Billie," the little girl called, but her mother snatched her back and clapped a hand over her mouth. Parker pressed herself to Spike's side and whimpered.

The urge to seek vengeance for what Spike and Parker had or hadn't done dissipated. No matter what lies the actors told, they'd been telling the truth about wanting to free the woman and her daughter—and about their loyalty to each other. Brian had to honor Eva's belief that love was the only beautiful thing left in the world.

He lowered his bow and reached for Louis's arm; his muscles were taut underneath the coarse fabric of his sleeve. "Louis, Eva wouldn't want this. Let's leave them be and go before that asshole and his men find us."

Louis's muscles eased underneath the gentle pressure of Brian's hand. He lowered the gun from Spike's forehead. "I don't ever want to see any of you again. Whether you had anythin' to do with what happened to my sister or not, you're still the reason we ended up in this situation." He reached out and gripped Brian's hand, squeezing it tight. "If you follow us, you don't get a second chance."

Spike backed away with Parker toward the woman and child, his bright eyes gleaming. "Brian, I'm sorry. Your stuff's still in the parking garage. The key is underneath the bar in a tip jar. Our real names are Craig and Billie. Her sister is Cassandra, and her niece is Bailey. Thanks to you—"

Louis tugged Brian's hand, forcing him to move. Spike's words drifted into the night as Brian ran farther and farther away. The breeze whipping against his face numbed him into a dreamlike state, nearly convincing him that none of this was real—"Parker" and "Spike," the fairground, Eva's death—that he *had* fallen asleep in the skating rink and when he woke, he'd be right back there with Louis and Eva.

But Louis was next to him, holding his hand, their fingers threaded together like fibers braided into a single rope. Louis's grip kept him rooted to reality, gave him something to cling to.

If he let go—

Chapter Twelve: Picking Up the Pieces

THE NEXT THING Brian knew, it was daytime, and he was looking at the top of a tent. He reached out and felt empty space next to him—he was alone.

The tent flap unzipped. Brian scrambled for a weapon, but the only thing next to him was his backpack. His journal and tablet stuck out from the front pocket. *How did that get there? Those were at Caldone's—*

Louis thrust his head in. "I saw you sit up—" His eyebrows lifted when he saw Brian's frantic expression. "Sorry, I didn't mean to scare you. I just wanted to make sure you were okay."

When Louis climbed into the tent, Brian noticed a fire outside with a makeshift spit overhead. The scent of smoke swirled in the air, acrid yet aromatic. "Where are we?"

Louis sat next to Brian. "We went southeast to a place called Beaver Lake. When I woke up, you were still asleep, so I fished a little. Don't worry—I kept an eye on the tent."

Brian scratched his head, trying to pick apart the tangled waves. "How long was I asleep?"

"Sixteen hours, more or less." Louis combed his fingers through his own jet-black hair, which was immaculately straight and smooth. He seemed to have washed while Brian was sleeping. "I got bored and tried to use your tablet, but I didn't know your passcode. I read your journal instead. Sorry. That book you had in there was too borin'—buncha old ladies drinkin' tea and stuff. You're a way better writer."

He offered Brian a sheepish smile. Brian should have been outraged by this invasion of privacy, but after all he'd been through, he didn't have it in him to care. Thankfully, he hadn't had the time to write any personal thoughts about the twins—the last thing he'd written was his entry about leaving the cellar.

"How did you get it back?"

"You don't remember?" Louis shook his head. "Okay, well, we ran all night, went back to Caldone's to get our stuff. Everythin' was there except for our weapons and ammo, but we couldn't pull the cart. We snatched what we could, kept movin', made it here. Took a few days and we didn't sleep, so I guess it makes sense how you don't remember all of it."

Brian watched Louis's gloved hand as it curled into the fabric of Brian's sleeping bag. He remembered holding onto that hand for a long, long time. So long his own grew sticky with sweat, even numb.

He reached for Louis's hand and gripped it to reassure himself that he was awake, that losing Eva hadn't been a dream, that *this* wasn't a dream. "The last thing I remember is running away from Spike and Parker. Is...is Eva really gone?"

Louis glanced at the hand covering his own. For a moment, Brian feared Louis would withdraw his hand, withdraw from Brian—but he flipped his hand over and linked their fingers, squeezing until the beige of Brian's fingers turned white. "It's just us now."

Brian pinched the bridge of his nose and looked up in a bid to repress his tears. "I-I can't believe it. I'm still not even sure what happened."

"Parker didn't kill her." Louis's thumb stroked the back of Brian's bare hand. "She abandoned her and went right for her own sister—I guess she didn't care about mine. I found Eva in the arcade with the knife in her hand, took it from her so it wouldn't go to waste. Picked her body up and locked her in an electrical closet so nothin' would get to her. She'd already been through enough."

Brian couldn't tell if Louis was suppressing his feelings about his sister's death for his sake or if he hadn't processed them yet. He seemed to be holding up remarkably well—but Louis always seemed to handle everything that way.

"It might've been a coincidence, those other guys showing up when we were getting our things back." Brian wanted it to be true, for Louis to agree. "Spike and Parker lowered their guns when they saw us. That wasn't a trap."

"I coulda been jumpin' to conclusions 'cause I was pissed." Louis glanced away from Brian. "Do you regret not killin' 'em?"

"No. Eva wouldn't have wanted us to. Besides, we don't know for sure what they did or didn't do. All I know is Parker really cared about that woman and girl, and she and Spike really did love each other. They used us, but wouldn't we have gone to similar lengths to rescue Eva or each other?"

Louis's brow furrowed over steely eyes as they swept back to Brian. "If we see them again, I won't hesitate to pull the trigger. They had their chance; if they're smart, they won't waste it."

Brian didn't doubt him, but he hoped the opportunity never presented itself. He was ready to wipe his hands of Spike and Parker—or Craig and Billie—and to try to accept Eva's death and move on. Dwelling on things only made them more painful.

Louis released Brian's hand, his eyes softening. "You okay?"

"Yeah. Just hungry."

Louis patted his knee. "Let's go eat, then."

Brian followed him outside. What else was there to do besides keep going?

The view outside their tent would have been magnificent in the spring. A frozen lake stretched beneath a radiant sunrise, reflecting warm streaks of pink, orange, and red. Majestic trees surrounded the shore, dark limbs home to twittering morning birds and skittering squirrels. The scent of smoked fish wafted from the firepit, so Brian snapped a twig into a skewer and jabbed it into one of the roasting fish. He joined Louis on a log and tore into the charred fish with a satisfied moan.

Louis spread his map across his lap and pointed to it while his other hand held a skewered fish. "We're about here, southeast of Bentonville, Arkansas. Factorin' in sleep, it'd be about a week and a half before we got to New Orleans. You still wanna go?"

Brian shrugged and poked the tip of his already empty stick into the ground. "What's the point?"

"You wanna go back?"

Brian looked up at Louis. "Back to what?"

"Exactly."

Wary of the distant woods surrounding them, Brian glanced around. "If you still want to go, I'll go with you. It doesn't matter where, I guess."

Louis stood and placed his hands on his hips, looking out at the lake like an explorer surveying the land. "We'll stick to the original plan. I want out of this country, away from this miserable weather. I want the sun and sand, the sea breeze, and a fresh start." He looked over his shoulder at Brian. "You're the only thing I don't wanna leave behind."

The tingle Brian was growing accustomed to rippled through him again. He wasn't sure why Louis said this—maybe to reassure him—but it warmed him from the inside out and made him smile despite the pain he was still trying to suppress. "I'll stay with you until the bitter end."

A smirk spread across Louis's face as he turned and returned to the fire pit. He was dressed in a trench coat, turtleneck, and those tight jeans that looked so uncomfortable. The AK-47 was strapped to his back and the pistol would be tucked somewhere in his jeans. He crossed his arms. "I'm good to go, but you need to get dressed. You wanna wash up first? I'll keep watch."

Brian shuddered at the thought of splashing himself with cold water in the freezing air. "It's way too cold."

Louis rejoined Brian on the log. He faced the opposite direction so they could keep an eye on their surroundings. "You remember goin' with us to Joyland, that Podunk park?"

Brian nodded. "I think so. How old were we?"

"I think we went for your eighth birthday. Me and Eva turned nine the November before. It was February, so it was still cold out but not snowin'. There were no lines, so we decided we were goin' to go on all the rides—but you couldn't pay Eva *nothin'* to get her to ride the log flume." Louis sighed. Her name filled Brian with a stinging swell of melancholy. "We decided to show her up, so we sat our asses in the log and laughed about how stupid Eva was and how much fun we were gonna have. Two minutes later, we came off that ride so cold we were shakin' all over. We went into the bathroom to try and dry off under a hand dryer. When I tried to unzip my jeans, my hands were so numb I couldn't get a grip on the damn zipper. Some attendant in there was cleanin' and felt bad for me, gave me a pair of rubber gloves. When we came outta that bathroom, both of us shiverin' and shakin' and half numb, me with these rubber gloves on, Eva and our parents bust up laughin'. It's not one of my favorite memories, but it's still so vivid."

Brief images flashed in Brian's mind. More than anything, he recalled that feeling of incredible numbness, the tingling and the shivering, and the embarrassment of being laughed at by a group of people who were enviably dry.

Brian grinned and elbowed Louis. "I do remember that. We felt so *stupid* afterwards, and Eva kept rubbing it in our face that she was dry. It really pissed you off."

"She had a habit of doin' that." Louis's smile shrank. "I used to be jealous of her. Everyone always doted on her, called me the 'bad' child. Most of the time, I got into trouble even when she was the one to blame."

Brian carefully considered what to say, unaccustomed to Louis opening up. "Brothers and sisters sometimes fight because they think they're not getting enough attention from their parents. It's normal."

Louis's shoulder brushed against Brian's. "I know you lost a sister too, and your parents, like me. I came home from school to a buncha police, fire trucks, and the house still smolderin'. I saw a buncha grown-ups whisperin' to each other, lookin' at me but not talkin' to me. My grandparents had to tell me my parents were dead. At first, I didn't believe it, thought I was havin' a nightmare. Eva wailed and carried on, but I just sat there starin'. I felt nothin', like there was a void inside me. I think it's easier to feel nothin' than to let emotion overwhelm you. I used to bum my Papère's cigarettes, steal from his liquor cabinet—smoke weed, whatever. Anythin' to escape."

"I stuck my nose in my tablet, or in a book. TV, video games... A lot less—"

"Destructive? Yeah. I probably fucked myself up worse. You and I couldn't be more different." Louis sighed and dragged his hands down his cheeks, his eyes blank and distant. His fingers lingered on the scar Brian had left.

"I actually think we're pretty similar."

Louis's hands fell from his face and he clasped them under his chin as he looked at Brian. "Hm?"

"The scar I left. On your cheek." Brian cleared his throat. "I think we both realized it's easier to be angry than let ourselves suffer. When my dad tried to kill himself, I was angry at him instead of letting myself cry over it every night. Because I was angry at him, I was angry at *everything*—everyone. Including you. I'm sorry I cut you."

Louis scratched the side of his nose and sniffed. "I was bein' an ass anyway and I knew it. I forgave you, but I never forgot. How could I? Any time I looked in a mirror, there it was. So many girls asked me about it, tried to tell me it was sexy or whatever... But I'd lie and tell every single one of 'em a different story. It wasn't that I was ashamed... I just didn't wanna keep relivin' it."

Brian fought the urge to reach out and stroke a finger along that scar, to feel the memory he'd etched into Louis's cheek. "I'd undo it if I could. I mean, you were the one who punched that asshole at school giving me shit about my dad."

"He deserved it." Louis skirted Brian's gaze. "I got detention, but it was worth it. I wasn't gonna stand there and let you take it."

Brian's lips parted, but too many things were going through his mind to pick which one he should say. A warm swell fluttered through his chest that was unfamiliar to him.

He settled on a simple, earnest, "Thank you."

Louis searched Brian's eyes for a while, but he seemed to be at a similar loss for words. He stood and offered a hand to Brian instead. "Enough of this bondin' shit; we're a hair away from bein' in some indie comin'-of-age flick. Let's pack up. We gotta head through the Ozarks."

Brian accepted Louis's hand, welcoming the warmth and strength that had guided him. He followed Louis to the tent. "I've never been."

Louis bent down to pull up a spike. "Man, you really *are* a city boy."

"Ever since my mom pulled me out of school, I've been about as sheltered as you can get. I lived in my own little world until my mom was attacked."

Louis moved to the third tent spike. "I can't stand it inside my head. I need somethin' to keep me occupied. I hated bein' around a buncha snot-nosed boys, but Boy Scouts was fun because of all the time we spent outdoors and what we learned. Survival shit, you know? Came in handy for all this."

Brian managed a grin. "I can't picture you in that cheesy uniform."

"Oh, I hated it. It woulda suited you better." Louis jerked up the last spike and tossed it into the bag Brian held open for him. "Let's finish this up and get goin', Boy Scout."

They drifted into an easy rapport, perhaps because of the void Eva left behind. Their light-hearted chatter didn't fill it, but it was better than silence.

THEY TRUDGED ON past decaying farmhouses and barren fields, bogged down by their backpacks and steady snowfall. Once the sun started to set, they stopped in a small town called Kingston. A post office sat to the west and a bed and breakfast was two blocks east of a grocery store called "Grandpa's." The town was so sparse and quaint it seemed like Brian was in another time, a time before he'd existed. The thought of all the things that had happened before he'd entered the world made him feel insignificant.

"A bed and breakfast, huh?" Louis stared up at the compact two-story building, adjusting the backpack he wore and the second one he had at his feet. "Just what we need. Let's see if we can find somethin' to eat and a bed to sleep in."

Louis approached the building and peered into the window past a crooked neon "OPEN" sign. Brian squeezed in next to him, inspecting the contents of the building. The interior resembled a small-town restaurant, though Brian could only see one table and four chairs set at it, one of which lay on its side. A sugar container had spilled across the table, knocked over in a struggle or by someone leaving in a hurry. Dead plants lined the wall beneath weathered picture frames. A ceiling fan collected dust, and a birdhouse with "Welcome" carved above it offered hospitality no longer available.

"They didn't have time to board this place up." Louis moved to the side of the building. "Easy access but not just for us. Let's check the back."

They moved to the rear of the faded brick building. One of the two windows above them had an AC unit wedged between crumbling bricks. A reassuring spray-painted message covered the door: *"There are no ghosts in the land of the dead."*

Brian reached for the doorknob. "Probably locked, but here goes."

He twisted. It swung open freely, surprising him. Louis aimed the Walther PPK while Brian stepped inside, his foot kicking something that clattered away.

Louis turned his flashlight on and pulled the door shut behind him. A metal lid settled on the floor by Brian's foot as the flashlight highlighted glinting pots and pans and a three-compartment sink. The musty air smelled far more pleasant than most buildings they'd encountered.

Brian knew the routine: look first, scavenge later. But the prospect of finding food was mouthwatering. A warm meal and a bed, something he'd once taken for granted, were now the peak of luxury.

They explored in silence, peering into corners and crevices and underneath furniture. After they'd cleared the ground floor, they moved upstairs. The stairs creaked underneath their feet no matter how carefully they moved. Framed photos of rural landscapes and animals ascended the walls with them.

Two doorways sat at the top of the stairs, one open, one closed. A table placed between them was topped with a cracked vase enshrining desiccated flowers and a pillared candle that had melted over like the leaning tower of Pisa. Dust and cobwebs clung to everything. Brian muffled a sneeze as he followed Louis through the open door.

A small square of light shining through the window illuminated a bed with a tacky jungle-themed bedspread and a suitcase with clothes tumbling out of it. A tube TV sat on a dinged-up dresser to the left. The bathroom door hung open, displaying tiny travel-size soaps and shampoos from varying hotel chains lined on the counter.

While Brian swept these up and deposited them in his backpack, Louis gestured to the closet door in the rightmost corner of the room. Brian gripped the knob with one hand and tugged the accordion-style door to the left. "Gah! Shit!"

Louis pushed him back with one arm and peered around him. "Aw, fuck. That's messed up."

A skeleton dressed in loose clothes kneeled and faced the wall, held up by a belt looped around its neck. Louis reached in to retrieve a crumpled note from the side of the body.

This is the end, my only friend...

Brian slid the door shut, leaving the skeleton in its chosen resting place. They returned to the bathroom he'd poked his head into. The spilled pill bottles in the sink and the shower curtain blocking the tub didn't reassure him. He swallowed, the uneasy feeling in his gut intensifying.

Louis looked at him, nodding toward the curtain with his gun and flashlight aimed. Brian sighed and gripped the moldy vinyl with unsteady hands. He jerked it to the right, startled but not surprised by the body sitting in the tub. It had decomposed into a skeleton for the most part, devoid of clothing and lying atop a pile of rancid goo. A notepad was propped on its lap. The pen underneath the skeletal right hand had the name of the B&B printed on it: "Fool's Cove."

Brian reached for the pad, trying to avoid contact with the body. Its skull tilted to the left, watching them desecrate its grave.

Brad couldn't take it. They wouldn't let us leave this shitty bed and breakfast. What kinda name is "Fool's Cove" anyway? All the reports on TV said it was spreading worldwide. It's a shitshow. Brad took the easy way out and left me to find him. I took a bunch of pills, and now I'm going to pamper myself with a hot bath. I deserve it. To whoever reads this, take what you want but at least have the decency to pull the curtain back. I'm modest. Thanks.

Louis pulled the curtain shut after they replaced the note on the skeleton's lap. "One more room." He nudged Brian's arm.

They proceeded to the remaining door. Brian feared he'd open this to some other horrible scene, but Louis's flashlight illuminated a pristine room with no personal effects. The bed was even made.

After a quick sweep of the room, Louis exhaled and tucked his pistol in his jeans. "All clear. Let's go try to find something to eat and settle in for the night."

It was a far cry from the usual excitement of entering a hotel room and anticipating a stay with room service, vending machines, shitty cable TV, and chlorine-scented pools. Brian set his backpack on the floor alongside Louis's before clambering down the stairs after him.

Brian and Louis locked and blocked the doors to the best of their abilities before scavenging the kitchen for food. They lucked out on some canned food, opening it with a can opener and heating it with the flames of drugstore lighters. The beans and vegetables inside were microwave hot—cold in the middle, scalding everywhere else—but they filled their stomachs. They also managed to mix some instant potatoes and found a gallon of water under the sink, the seal still on it. It was like finding Aztec gold.

Satisfied, they headed back upstairs with their modest haul.

Louis sat on the bed and pulled his shoes off. "We should both sleep. We're gonna need to be alert tomorrow. Besides, it's dead quiet out here and I'm a light enough sleeper that I'll hear if anythin' tries to come in."

"You can have the bed. I'll set my sleeping bag up on the floor." Brian unzipped his jacket and folded it by his backpack. Since it was still cold, he left his jeans and sweater on. Louis did the same, pulling the covers free from the bed before climbing in.

He glanced down at Brian and patted the empty space beside him. "I don't mind if you don't. Besides, it's fuckin' freezin' in here."

Brian balked at Louis's offer. He scurried into the bathroom with his backpack and slathered some of the travel-size lotion on his skin, soothing the dryness and freshening his scent. Before they left their campsite, he'd caved and spot-washed with the freezing lake water, but he remained self-conscious about his cleanliness. Although he felt dirtier than he was comfortable with, he decided he was passable enough to sleep next to Louis.

When he emerged into the bedroom, his flashlight illuminated Louis's perplexed expression as he sat up against the headboard. "You okay? You hauled ass in there. Half thought the food got to you."

Brian set his pistol and flashlight on the bedside table. He cleared his throat and climbed under the covers next to Louis, turning off the light. "I only wanted to freshen up since you offered to let me sleep with you."

Brian felt Louis slink down beside him and pull the cover over himself. "That's awful considerate of you, but I didn't notice anythin'. I mean, we *all* got a little funky when we were in those damn pens."

A prolonged sigh slipped from Brian as he thought of Eva. "Are you okay, Louis?"

"As okay as I can be. You?"

Brian folded his arms over his chest and stared up into the darkness. "You don't think we'll end up like those people in the other room, do you?"

"What, killin' ourselves?" Louis turned to face Brian, his breath tickling Brian's ear. "You're thinkin' about your dad, aren't you?"

Brian wriggled closer to Louis so he could absorb the heat radiating from his body. He caught a light scent of something, possibly the La Quinta lotion. "Yeah."

"Okay, listen to me." Louis's drowsy tone sharpened. "Next time you think about that, I want you to think about somethin' else instead."

"Like what?"

"Whatever makes you happiest."

Brian thought about what had given him those little sugar rushes of pleasure. "Crisp fall air. The smell of cinnamon. Bundling up in a warm blanket when it's cold. Discovering a new song and listening to it on repeat for an hour."

Louis's hand found his arm and squeezed it. When it retreated, Brian missed it. "You can still do a lot of that. You're all bundled up in a warm blanket now, right? Does that make you happy?"

Warmth rippled through Brian. "I guess so. What about you? What makes you happy?"

Louis wasn't as quick to answer as Brian expected. A noise rumbled low in Louis's throat as he contemplated his reply. "Roastin' marshmallows and hot dogs in front of a fire. Hot sun on my skin while I chug a cold drink. Skin-slappin', sweat-drippin' sex." The warmth flickered out of Brian, replaced by a flutter in his gut he mistook for digestion. "Sorry—was that too blunt?"

"It's okay." Brian cleared his throat. "Did you have a girlfriend when this happened?"

"I don't think I ever had a *real* girlfriend. I hated goin' out on dates, all the awkward small-talk, 'gettin' to know you' shit. I got bored. I'd fast-track it by sayin' shit to 'em in French—even if I insulted 'em, they didn't know any better. I'd tell 'em I said some bullshit like 'you're so beautiful' and they'd melt at my feet."

Brian thought of the mysterious missing meds and some of Eva's more cryptic comments about her brother. "So, you never connected with anyone?"

Louis didn't answer this question so readily. He sighed in the silence that preceded his answer. "It was physical stuff, not mental. They wanted me 'cause they thought I was 'exotic' or a 'bad boy,' and I wanted them because I wanted to get off with somethin' besides my hand." Louis wriggled, his foot kicking Brian's under the blankets. "What about you? I bet the girls all loved you since you're all sensitive and you got those bedroom eyes and pouty lips."

Brian scoffed, surprised to hear Louis of all people describe him that way. "I, uh, wasn't around too many people since I didn't go to public school. I mean, I had summer jobs and there were people I liked, but it never went any further than kissing and some awkward fumbling in a car or movie theater."

It took a few moments for Louis to reply. "People, eh?"

Brian's stomach knotted with fright that Louis would panic and force him out of bed—or worse. "Please don't read into that. I only meant—"

"Chill out. Labels are outdated anyway, right? You gotta find whoever does it for you, I guess." Louis sat up and stretched, his bones cracking. "Sometimes you gotta do it for yourself. I'm gonna go to the bathroom—try to get some sleep, boug."

The mattress squeaked as Louis's feet settled onto the floor. The wood creaked underneath the weight of his steps while he slunk to the bathroom. Brian closed his eyes, attempting to shut off his senses—but in the dead silence of the room, he heard every sound Louis made. He tried in vain to ignore it.

The now undeniable attraction he felt toward Louis made him feel guilty for not feeling the same pull toward Eva. He couldn't imagine how much he'd ache from her loss if he had; he'd only had time to consider her a friend, albeit a good one, before he lost her.

If he lost Louis, not only would he be alone, he'd lose the one person who'd truly drawn him into their orbit. Louis fascinated him for some reason—maybe because of the childhood bond he'd sought to reclaim. Or because Louis suffered from some sort of illness like the depression Brian inherited from his father. Mostly because Louis acted with a confidence Brian admired. Obviously, the tight jeans and swarthy good looks had a great deal to do with it. So did the exotic accent and all the sensuous French language. Brian believed Louis when he said it made girls melt at his feet.

"Boug" … I have no idea why he calls me that or even what it means.

Brian curled onto his side and propped a pillow over his ear, trying to make Louis's inevitable return to bed less torturous. But when Louis flopped down with a satisfied sigh, the heat radiating from his body kept Brian wide awake.

Chapter Thirteen: The Ozarks

KINGSTON, ARKANSAS

Morning

After a meager breakfast of dry cereal, they left Brad and his companion behind. Unfortunately, Brian's liberated desires traveled with him out of the bed and breakfast. He tried to write it off as a manifestation of his loneliness triggered by Eva's loss, but he suspected his interest in Louis was directly responsible for his lack of interest in Eva. The awkward fumbling he'd mentioned to Louis had been with girls, but he'd developed mild attractions to both genders. This, however, was more than a mild attraction, and it preoccupied him whenever they weren't scavenging derelict buildings for supplies or dispatching the Stalkers hiding within them.

Brian found it ridiculous that he'd survived a pandemic only to be plagued by this wishy-washy relationship crap.

After an indeterminable amount of time, they made it to a small brown sign along AR-21 announcing they were entering the Ozark National Forest. Louis dug into his backpack and pulled out his phone, which he occasionally charged with Brian's solar charger.

Louis fiddled with it and shoved the screen in front of Brian's face. "Boom. Saved the PDF ages ago." Brian squinted as he read a map of the park gleaming behind the glass. Louis had zoomed in on an area with "*Upper Buffalo Wilderness*" written above it.

"Guess my bad habit of not deletin' things came in handy." Louis moved next to Brian and hooked an arm around his neck. He swiped the screen with his left thumb and pointed to a road that went west of Buffalo River and curved under it. "We'll take 16 south to 21, which runs south through the Ozarks. We can hit up the river and the rec area along the way."

Yet again, Louis's competency impressed Brian. "How long will it take us to make it through the woods?"

Louis scrutinized the scale on the map. His lips moved as he counted in his mind. "It's about twenty miles away to the rec area, so it'll take seven hours to get there. We got about nine hours of daylight."

"Okay." Brian affected a deadpan tone. "Are there buffalo there? I need to learn how to tell them apart from bison, remember?"

Louis's arm slid from Brian's neck as he broke into a broad grin. "Did you try to make a joke? Aw, look at that: a smile! That's a good look on you, boug."

Brian winced as Louis slid his hand under Brian's hood and ruffled his hair. "What does that word mean and why do you keep calling me it?"

"It means 'boy.' Callin' you by your name seemed too formal, I guess. Why—do you want me to call you somethin' else?"

Brian sighed as he regarded the long road ahead of them. "Call me whatever you want. I was just curious." He wasn't looking forward to walking one bit. He'd thought riding Hildy and Agnes had been awkward, but he realized now it had spoiled him. He wasn't out of shape, but he couldn't imagine how he'd feel after seven hours of nonstop hiking. Not only that, but he was exhausted from the shitty night of sleep he'd struggled through.

"You may regret that offer later." Louis smiled and slapped Brian's arm. "Let's get goin'."

They abandoned the paved road to follow a trail cut through dead maple, oak, and dogwood trees. Snow that hadn't had a chance to melt coated the rocky landscape, so both Louis and Brian broke off branches to use as walking sticks in the treacherous terrain. An agitated squirrel scurried from branch to branch in the trees above them.

Poor thing must've lost its acorn stash. People and animals alike are losing things all over these days.

The trail led them back to AR-21. Aside from a few abandoned cars, the road was empty. The Ozarks were so remote the military hadn't even bothered with them. It seemed like the perfect spot for a survivalist to set up—someone like Poppa, or even Louis. But the isolation would drive Brian out of his mind like poor Henry...

Louis stopped dead in his tracks and stretched an arm in front of Brian. "Look." He gestured toward the edge of the woods with his pistol.

Brian's eyes squinted as he struggled to make out what Louis had seen, but it was too far away and too vague. They approached, weapons aimed. Upon closer inspection, Brian identified a naked, bald person with unblemished skin.

Not a person—a mannequin.

Louis kicked it down. "Who the hell would put this creepy shit out here? We got another Henry on our hands?"

Brian glanced back at the mannequin as they retreated from it. Its expressionless painted face stared after them as if silently pleading with them to return. This reminder of the King's masked men sent a shiver through Brian's already shivering spine.

"Maybe someone is trying to scare us into the woods," he whispered to Louis, "to get us off the road. They might be watching us from somewhere."

"Either they want to fuck with people because they're cowards who get off on stupid pranks, or they're tryin' to lure us like you said. But picturin' some sick fuck with an armful of mannequins hurryin' to set 'em up before we get there is ridiculous. They've been waitin' a while, not just for us. Keep movin' before the cold numbs us or some crazy asshole catches wind of us."

The hazy air resembled a low cloud sitting atop the trees. Because of the diminished visibility, they maintained a cautious pace. Every shape seemed to be something it wasn't, something hiding amidst the fog, waiting to strike.

The halo of Brian's flashlight illuminated several red smears along a desiccated tree trunk.

Louis narrowed his eyes. "The *fuck*?"

The erratic streaks spelled, "*HA HA HA!*"

Brian spun in a circle, distracted by a sudden sound. Louis looked around, his eyes wide and alert—he'd heard it too.

A giggle.

"This is startin' to feel like I'm in some high-school haunted house." The timbre of Louis's voice escalated. "More annoyin' than terrifyin', like someone's tryin' too damn hard."

Snow drifted into their faces, nearly blinding them. A branch broke somewhere in the distance. Brian suppressed a startled gasp and grabbed Louis's arm. Louis kept both hands on his pistol, but he didn't shake Brian off.

Brian hurried along with Louis as ambient noises alternated with silence, the fog varying in thickness. He aimed the flashlight ahead of them while Louis kept the silenced pistol ready.

Brian collided with something on the road. It tumbled into the snow as Louis snagged Brian's jacket and jerked him back. Louis kicked something away: a hand wrapped around a gun. A flag stuck out of it painted with "*BANG!*" in the same bright red staining the tree.

While Louis investigated the body, which was dressed as a cowboy, Brian leaned down to inspect the detached hand. He recoiled and flung it to the ground when he glimpsed bone and frozen muscle inside the stump.

Drawn by Brian's impulsive gasp, Louis approached him and put a hand on his shoulder. "You okay?"

"They're not mannequins..." Brian stood and stepped back.

Louis kneeled to inspect the detached hand, his brow creasing behind the curtains of his dark bangs. "Someone's got too much time on their hands." He stood and managed a wan smile. "Bad pun, right?"

Brian was too disturbed to be amused. He stared at the fallen cowboy and his toy gun until Louis grabbed his hand and dragged him away.

That airy giggle still reverberated within his mind.

They continued down the desolate road until they reached a dirt road that branched out from the highway, framed by power lines that disappeared into the woods. A cloud of mist obscured the property. Once it drifted by, Brian's breath froze in his chest: someone had decorated the yard with "mannequins" posed in positions ranging from mundane to obscene. Something was painted on the side of a decrepit barn.

"BYE BYE!"

Louis's flummoxed face would've made Brian laugh if he hadn't been so shocked. He only now realized his jaw had fallen, so he shut it and forced himself to swallow even though his throat was dry. He switched his attention to a dilapidated house. The curtains in a second-story window parted to reveal a face peering out at them.

When something else moved, he realized some of the bodies weren't lifeless.

Without saying anything to Louis, Brian snatched his wrist and pulled him into a mad dash. They ran until they encountered a rundown Buick, yanked open the nearest door, and hurtled inside.

Shut the door, lock it, inspect the back seat—empty.

Louis reached over Brian and grabbed something between the passenger seat and the door. Brian gasped as he swung back with the seat. Louis did the same to his. When Brian looked at him, Louis lifted a finger to his lips. His unusually wide eyes stayed locked on Brian's.

A face peered into the window above Louis, hands pressed against the frosted glass. The pale face of a smiling Stalker peered through a thin layer of ice. It tugged on the driver's side door handle, still staring.

Thank God he locked the door. Will it break the window? It has to know we're in here. Fuck fuck fuck!

The Stalker vanished from the window—but a metallic *thunk* came from above them. It was on the roof.

Louis aimed the silenced pistol above him. The slide jerked back and shells ejected, a series of holes appearing in the ceiling. A heavy weight slumped into it as a trickle of blood pooled along the rim of one hole. Louis jerked away before a plump drop splashed onto the gearshift.

Aside from their ragged breaths, all was silent. Nothing stirred outside the car.

Louis ran a hand through his bangs, exhaling. "I think I got it." He sat up and reached for the door handle, but Brian grabbed his shoulder.

"Are you sure?"

"Just cover me, would you?" Louis handed Brian the pistol. He aimed it while Louis pulled the door handle. Nothing moved, so Louis exited the car. Eventually, he knocked on the passenger side window where Brian sat.

Brian opened the door. Louis grabbed him by the shoulder and tugged him out, pulling him to his side. "Careful: don't want to catch what he's got."

Brian gazed up at the roof of the car: the Stalker sprawled over it, drizzling blood into the snow. A pool of it puddled beside the door Brian had exited. He lifted his foot, examining it. "Gross."

"Snow'll wash it off." Louis squeezed his shoulder. "Let's get."

Brian wasn't about to argue. He gave the sprawled body a final once-over before following Louis, who possessed a combination of impeccable aim and amazing luck.

The trek to the river was agonizing. Louis had shut the phone off to conserve power, but he seemed to know where he was going. Although Brian was sore, freezing, and tired, he was relieved to have a break from giggling Stalker hoarders.

Why did they do it? Because they were bored?

It doesn't make sense. It's creepy and weird, and I'm better off not thinking about it anymore.

"My feet are *killing* me." Brian was desperate for a distraction. "Are you sure we should still go to Louisiana? To this island?"

Louis stopped walking and unscrewed the cap from a bottle of water. He kneeled beside the river and punched a hole through the thin layer of ice coating it. "Birds fly south durin' winter for a reason: we're doin' the same. Warmer weather, easier prey, more water. Besides, we need *somewhere* to aim for."

The occasional rustle of dead leaves and the squeak of rubbing branches exacerbated Brian's fatigue. He flopped down onto the rocks beside Louis and reached into the river. He splashed ice-cold water onto his face to jolt himself back to a more alert state of mind.

"I'm exhausted," he muttered. "I've never even been to this island. I'm not sure if I want it—and if I *do* want it, is it even real? Is it even what I want it to be?"

Louis stood and tucked the bottle into his backpack. "What do you want it to be?"

Before Brian could answer, he spotted something large and brown across the river. For a second, he thought it was a bear, but he realized they were all hibernating and chastised himself for this panicked assumption. It had four legs, a brown coat, and antlers.

"That'll feed us for a while," Louis said. "You can take it out with an arrow or I can cap it with the PPK."

Brian watched the creature drink, still trying to pinpoint what it was. Killing it hadn't even crossed his mind. "No. It's a survivor."

Louis sighed. "Your granddaddy taught you to hunt, didn't he? Mine did. Taught me to skin and gut, too. So, what's the problem? We gotta eat, and I'm tired of junk food."

Brian licked his dry lips, thinking of a steaming, juicy steak with a peppery crust. Then he thought back to the soulful stare of the dying deer and the final flicker of light in its eyes when it breathed its last. "What is it? A moose?"

Louis gave Brian a condescending look. "It's an elk. You know what *anythin'* is besides dogs and cows?"

"I didn't think those were down here. I thought they were farther north."

"Pretty rare, I think. Got hunted to near extinction." Louis watched the elk, which had lifted its head to scan for predators. "Might be they feel safer with less humans around. Surprised a Stalker hasn't got it yet, but I suppose it's too cold for most of those things to make it out here."

"If it's endangered, I'd rather not kill it. We'll find something at the rec area."

"You're too soft-hearted, boug. We're endangered too, if you think about it." Louis withdrew his PPK and aimed it at the elk. "Better to die from a shot to the heart than get ripped open by some other animal."

Brian reached for Louis's arm and tried to push it down. "Louis, don't."

Louis resisted. "My stomach is grumblin' and my mouth is practically waterin' at the thought of fresh meat. Let go, Brian!"

Instinct kicked in: he gripped Louis's left wrist and twisted the gun away from them, putting pressure on Louis's elbow with his other hand. When Louis winced and relaxed his hand, Brian pried the gun away. Brian was too focused on what he was doing to notice the curses Louis yelled at him—he was on autopilot, his consciousness gone somewhere else.

When he snapped back to awareness, the PPK was in his hands, muzzle trained on Louis.

"Made it run away, *de'pouille*! What the fuck are you doin' aimin' a gun at me? All because of some damn animal! Fuck!" Louis's blurred face came into focus. He shook his head, his brow creased and his lips parted, teetering between incredulity and rage.

I could've killed him. What the hell was I doing?

Brian dropped the gun and collapsed to his knees. He held his hands to his face, trying to reconcile the mixture of exhaustion, distress, and remorse bubbling within him.

Snow crunched as Louis kneeled in front of him. Brian's shoulders flinched when Louis's hands fell on them and tightened. "Explain to me what just fuckin' happened."

"I...I had to kill a deer when I was training with my-my grandfather. I'd never killed anything before. I'll never forget the awful noise it made, the way the light went out of its eyes." Brian lowered his hands from his face, pressing his dry, trembling lips together. "I don't want to kill unless I have to. I'm tired, I'm cold, and I'm sore...and I just—I just snapped. I'm sorry, Lou—"

Louis reached out and tilted Brian's chin up, the gesture hovering between forceful and tender. "I forgive you, but don't you *ever* aim a gun at me again." He stood, offering his hand to Brian. "Let's move on. It's colder than a snowman's junk out here."

Louis trekked on like nothing had happened, but Brian kept thinking back to the incident. It bothered him that he didn't remember their escape from the fairground, and that he'd blanked out and turned a gun on Louis. He drove his already fragile mind on a looping track that threatened to veer wildly off course.

"Ah, there it is!" Louis called out. Brian swerved back onto the path.

Now that he wasn't lost in his thoughts, his body decided to remind him how much of a toll had been taken on it. The pain from his feet radiated up into every nerve of his body, into his fingertips and his throbbing head. It hurt so badly his body seemed to go numb, made him feel weightless like his feet weren't even touching the ground.

The dirt road in the distance blurred into a mirage of white and brown. His ears rang as everything spun sideways.

WHEN HIS EYES opened, he was in bed.

Did I pass out? What the fuck is wrong with me?

He didn't recognize the ceiling above him or the sheet pulled over him. When he peered over the edge of the bed, he realized he was on top of a bunk bed. Louis was on a couch below him, sprawled out reading a magazine. The lantern glowed from a table next to him. A counter with a sink lined the wall across from Louis. Short white curtains covered the windows above it, but no light came through them. It amazed him that Louis wasn't asleep.

"Louis, what time is it?"

Louis pulled the magazine to his chest and craned his head to look up at Brian. "I was beginnin' to think you'd decided to stay in la-la land. Who'd wanna come back to reality, right? It's been, I dunno, two, three hours?"

"Jesus. How did you get me here?"

"It wasn't far, so I carried you."

Brian knew Louis was strong both physically and mentally, but this impressed him beyond anything else Louis had done yet. "Really? You had to be exhausted from the cold and all the walking—and with my weight on top of it? I mean, *I* passed out!"

Louis shrugged. "You aren't that heavy. No wonder, with the diet we had lately. You hungry? There's still a few cans in the supply bag and half a box of instamash."

Brian's stomach grumbled, but he was hesitant to leave the warm, comfortable bed. "Thanks for taking care of me. Especially after what I did—"

"Don't worry about it." Louis looked back at his magazine. Naked women in lewd positions covered the pages. "When I got to the campground, there were a few campers still set up. Doors were open on some. I guess a few people left in a panic. No bodies or Stalkers, though.

Might be some in the others. Figured we'd check 'em for supplies come daylight."

Brian forced himself to climb down out of the bed. He instantly regretted this—his tender feet made it feel like he was stepping on knives instead of carpet.

A pained sound came out of him that made Louis drop the magazine again. "I got good news for you: the water tank isn't empty, they put anti-freeze in, the pump works, and the battery's got juice."

Brian had never been in a camper before. He stared at Louis, not sure what any of that meant.

Louis's eyebrows arched, his lips quirking into a crooked smirk. "A camper virgin too, huh? I'm sayin' you can take a hot shower. I already got one."

Brian's eyes widened; a hot shower sounded so heavenly he pinched himself to make sure he wasn't still asleep.

"Someone siphoned the fuel—" Louis tossed the magazine onto the table "—and the water's no good to drink. But thank goodness for small favors."

Brian pulled his shirt over his head, eager to get to it. Louis sat up. "Don't get excited yet. I gotta show you how it works, then go turn the pump and heater on."

Louis strolled ahead of Brian and opened the door to the bathroom. He pointed to the shower, which could barely hold one person. "Showerhead is detachable. See that lever? Turns the water off and on. Turn off the water while you're washin'. You can't sit and soak in the thing for long or it'll run out fast."

This disappointed Brian, but he was still eager to have an actual shower.

Louis backed out of the bathroom. He hovered in the doorway with his hands wrapped around the frame. "That's the second time now I've had to show you how to work a faucet. You're gonna have to start payin' me."

"That sounds like the set-up for a bad porn flick."

Louis backed out of the doorway and cracked his neck. "The plumber and the chick who needs her pipes cleaned, right?"

Brian rolled his eyes and gripped the door handle. "Why don't you go back to your magazine and fill me in when I get out?" Embarrassed by his unintentional double entendre, he shut the door before Louis could respond to it. He undressed and stepped into the shower, hoping Louis hadn't caught the grimace on Brian's face.

When the water turned on, it was ice-cold. He cursed and backed into the door, shivering. He didn't step in until the spray warmed up to a more inviting temperature. Hot water soaked into his hair and ran down his body, soothing his aching muscles.

He forced himself to shut it off and washed with a bar of soap already in the shower. Louis had used it, but Brian didn't care. He lathered it all over himself, into every nook and cranny. When the heavenly water returned, the layer of grime once coating him swirled into the drain below him.

Turning the water off and stepping out of the shower proved to be more difficult than such a simple act should've been. When he did, his skin chilled to ice. In his haste, he'd forgotten to carry a change of clothes in, so he tugged a towel from the rack and wrapped it around his waist. Teeth chattering and skin prickling, he opened the door to a cruel *whoosh* of air. "Fuck me, it's *cold* in here!"

Louis peered over his magazine at Brian. He lowered it to his lap, his lips twitching like he was trying to force back a smile. "You clean up nice. I thought you'd be a stick under all those layers, but you got a nice little swimmer's build goin' on. Explains how you disarmed me."

A rush of steam followed Brian out of the bathroom. "My grandfather made me work out, learn self-defense." His shoulders hunched as another shudder ran down him, making goose bumps erupt on his skin. He hurried over to his backpack and tugged out anything that remotely resembled clothing. "You read my journal; you should know these things."

He snatched a change of clothes and rushed into the steamy bathroom. When he emerged, Louis startled him by tossing a blanket into his face. "Why don't you sit down on the couch, *pauvre bête*? And share that blanket—I'm cold too."

Brian sat. He noticed a box of playing cards laid out on the table next to a wind-up radio. Louis settled beside him and pulled the corner of Brian's blanket over his shoulder until it draped over them like a cape. "Thought I'd try the radio, but it was nothin' but static. Cards'll pass the time, though. You know any games?"

"Not too many." Brian opened the box and inhaled the scent of the cards; he'd always enjoyed the aroma of fresh ink. "Twenty-one. Solitaire. Go Fish."

"Gin Rummy?" Louis didn't seem satisfied with such simple games.

Brian shook his head.

"Man, I have to teach you *everythin'*. You're rackin' up that debt."

Brian managed to smile now that his teeth weren't chattering. "Put it on my tab. I'll find a way to pay you back."

Louis smiled and shook his head. "Promises, promises."

He proved to be an efficient and thorough teacher, and soon they were playing Gin Rummy, huddled up for warmth. Brian didn't care that Louis seemed to win almost every match—he enjoyed the companionship and the effects of the shower on his sore body. Either his or Louis's skin retained the subtle scent of the soap, which reminded Brian of burnt wood.

As the night wore on, the inside of the camper plunged to excruciating depths. Brian pressed himself against Louis, too cold to feel self-conscious.

Louis didn't peel himself from Brian, but he did elbow him. "You're gonna have to pay me for the heat too."

Brian glared at Louis, his temper shortening as the temperature dipped. "Don't start with me—you're cold too. If the water heater worked, there's got to be a regular heater in here. How do we get it going?"

Louis rubbed his hands together, glancing at the fanned hand of cards he'd set face down on the table. "Takes propane, and it doesn't work when it's too cold out." His knee leaned into Brian's. "I can go try it, but I'm sure we can find another way to warm up."

Brian's stomach fluttered. Although he hadn't eaten yet, it wasn't hunger. Not the usual kind, anyway.

He stared straight ahead, brow creased as an awkward silence draped over them like the blanket. Louis's cool gaze and warm body made Brian experience a range of emotions he didn't have words for.

He could've been trying to feel me out back in the bed and breakfast—but he had girlfriends. I'm reading into it, right? I shouldn't say anything, just keep the game going.

Louis snatched Brian's hand. "Brian—"

Brian shuddered and swallowed. He definitely wasn't cold anymore.

Louis leaned around him. His breath tickled Brian's face as he spoke. "Do you hear that?"

The tension coiled within Brian's body shifted from a warm pulse into rigid tightness. He listened, examining Louis's focused gaze in the fluorescent light cast by the lantern.

Scratching. Branches scraping against a window.

The scratching faded. Louis lifted his pistol from the table. Brian glanced between Louis and his backpack, not sure if he should go for a weapon of his own.

The doorknob jiggled back and forth. Someone or something was trying to get in. Brian recalled the Stalker tugging on the car door.

Brian started to get up, but Louis waved a hand at him, indicating for him to stay seated.

The rattling stopped.

Something scraped against the walls. Scrambled—above them.

It's on the roof.

Louis and Brian looked up, following the sounds with their eyes. It pried at the plastic paneling covering the vent above the bed. Brian racked his brain for something he could use to block it. While Louis kept his gun trained on the vent, Brian dug into their supply bag and clambered up to it. He tore strips from a roll of duct tape and taped them over the horizontal slats. He wasn't sure it would hold, but it was better than nothing.

The tugging stopped.

"Louis," Brian whispered, "the windows?"

Louis rushed over to the windows—and chortled. He gestured for Brian to join him, a smirk on his face.

Puzzled, Brian moved beside him. Something black, gray, and furry bounded away in the snow outside.

"A raccoon?" Brian shook his head, bewildered. "But the vent—and the doorknob!"

"They got hands. Probably stood on his hind legs and went for it. Clever son-of-a-bitch. You ever seen 'em try to wash cotton candy, though? Shit disappears, and they look around like they're tryin' to figure out a magic trick." Louis's smile faded when he looked back through the window. Brian made out a shape following the raccoon in the dim luminescence—a much larger, taller shape.

A person.

His eyes widened as the raccoon scampered into the woods beyond the campground and scrambled up a gnarled tree. The figure followed, scaling the trunk in pursuit of the frightened animal.

Brian watched, pressed close to Louis as the raccoon leaped and climbed to higher branches, evading its pursuer with sheer speed and agility. The defeated predator jumped down to the ground and scurried away on all fours, disappearing into the night.

Louis and Brian backed away from the window and moved the table in front of the door, a few stray cards sliding to the ground. They didn't return to their game.

Chapter Fourteen: Giddy Up

OZONE RECREATION AREA

Afternoon

Louis woke Brian at noon. After they ate, they packed and layered on their winter clothes, in a hurry to make the most of the daylight they had left.

Brian rubbed his sore feet as he slid on his boots. "Lou, remind me again why we don't put our gas into this RV and drive it the rest of the way."

"The roads'll be blocked and the engine makes too much noise." Louis shrugged on his coat and tucked the PPK into the waistband of his snug jeans. "What we need is somethin' quiet that can make it through blockage."

"Like a bicycle?"

Louis snickered. "What're the odds of findin' one, let alone two?" He raised his foot onto the table and laced up his boots with quick, firm movements. "I got an idea. Eva had a friend in middle school, went to a ridin' academy not too far from here. We used to visit her. Why don't we try there?"

Brian ran his hands through his hair and sighed. "If you insist. My feet hurt like hell."

"Want me to carry you again?" Louis's lips quirked into a mocking grin. "Give you a piggyback ride?"

Brian rolled his eyes and tugged his beanie on. Whatever mood Louis woke up in dictated how he'd act throughout the day. Today he was mischievous, which was worse than when he was feeling imperious.

They checked a few of the RVs for resources before heading back onto the road. As they emerged from the isolated Ozarks, they passed the occasional wrecked car and battered building. Brian had gotten so used to them they nearly blended in with the landscape as if they were as organic as a tree or mountain. Destruction and dereliction were the new normal.

After a few hours, Louis stopped beside a nondescript white sign and wiped some of the half-melted snow from it. A broad grin creased his bronzed face. "I still got my photographic memory: this is it." Louis pointed to a wooden building in the distance. "Stables are over there. If there were any horses, they're dead or gone by this point. But no reason *not* to look."

Brian wasn't excited about sneaking into yet another dangerous building and seeing a dozen or so dead horses. The thought alone made him feel depressed. Horses were meant to be free, to run wild in fields together—not to die penned up alone.

They continued toward the stable, their feet crunching in the snow. Frosty snowflakes melted against the small window of skin exposed by their hoods. Brian searched for splashes of red in the bleached landscape—the raw wounds marking every Stalker he'd seen.

Louis stopped beside the corner of the stable, eyeing the western entrance. "Door's open. Careful in here, boug."

Brian nodded while Louis positioned himself on one side of the open door. When Brian moved across from him, Louis caught his gaze and mouthed, "flashlight."

Brian maneuvered around the cumbersome bow to remove the flashlight from his backpack. When he pressed the button, the light flickered and died out. The batteries were drained.

"Lantern?" he whispered to Louis.

Louis frowned and rummaged for the lantern while Brian stored the flashlight. "Can't see as far with this," he said under his breath as he held it out to Brian.

Brian took the lantern and returned his attention to the dark building. The halo of light didn't reach far and illuminated himself—making him a prime target for anyone inside. He darted in, set the lantern on the straw-coated ground, and withdrew the bow in its stead.

The scent of moist earth filled the building. In the rear, barrels of hay surrounded a collapsed loft. Parallel stalls lined both sides of the narrow walkway. The scuffed doors were shut and some of the troughs still had hay in them.

Brian moved down the aisle, peering through the metal grates on top of the stalls. Most were empty. Others had equine skeletons in them, curled up in the corner like they'd laid down to die. A disappointed sigh escaped him.

He slid the tip of his arrow between the metal grate of the next stall and leaned forward—a blur of motion popped into view and rattled the door. Brian cursed and released the arrow, stumbling backward.

Louis caught him around the middle as the gate crashed open, propelled by a lunging Stalker dressed in a tattered coat and trapper hat. Despite the arrow sticking through its neck, it cackled as if Brian had been the butt of a bad joke.

He dropped the bow and reached between himself and Louis to withdraw the pocketknife from his rear pocket. He slashed wildly in front of him, pushing against the Stalker with his feet as it reached for him, teeth gnashing and spittle flying.

The instant Brian managed to plunge the knife into the Stalker's eye, he and Louis tumbled back into a pile of scratchy hay on the floor. Louis stood and kicked the stall door shut. The Stalker's arms plunged through the narrow gaps in the gate, flesh scraping off as it reached for him. Jagged fingernails snagged the collar of Louis's jacket, but he was too close to shoot it without getting blood all over his face. He tried to wriggle out of the jacket while keeping the door shut.

Brian felt for the gun in the waistband of his jeans. He cocked the hammer and aimed at the Stalker's head between the rails of the gate. "Louis, get outta that jacket and get over here!"

Louis jerked out of his coat and staggered back. An acrid scent and sonic shockwave filled the air as Brian fired. The Stalker stumbled away from the stall. It stood in the hazy circle of lantern light, drifting back and forth. Blood poured from a gaping wound in its cheek.

How is it not dead?

Before either of them could try for another shot, an eruption of sound to their left startled them. Hooves clacked against the concrete floor, accompanied by the agitated whinny of a horse. It sped into the light and collided with the Stalker, sending it to the ground with a wet *crunch*. Several more followed.

The Stalker didn't stand. The horse eyed Brian and Louis warily, snorting and pawing the concrete floor. The moment was so surreal Brian had to pinch himself.

"*Mon Dieu...*" Louis muttered, picking up his stained jacket.

The horse backed away. Brian approached the door and reached through the grate. "Easy, there. It's okay." The horse held its ground. Its ears perked, so Brian kept talking. "You've been lonely, huh? Were these your friends?" He thought about the crashed loft and the hay strewn on the ground and in the troughs. "I can tell you're smart. You can come with us. We need you, and you want some company."

The horse's warm breath tickled his fingers when he reached for it. He stroked the velveteen fuzz of its nose, relieved when it made no attempt to bite or run. "Good boy. Or girl. I'm Brian, and this is Louis."

He withdrew his hand. The horse's bright eyes followed him as he moved to open the door. It backed away when the gate creaked but didn't run. When the two boys emerged, it took a step forward again.

Brian looked down at the Stalker's body and the pulpy mess its head had become. He leaned down and withdrew his arrow and the knife, intending to wash them when he got the chance.

When he stepped toward the chestnut brown horse, it held its ground. White socks covered its legs, matching a white diamond on its forehead. Ribs poked out from its swelling belly, but he couldn't see any other bones—thin, but not starving. He stroked its coarse forelocks. It nickered, perhaps pleased by his touch.

It isn't wild—it must have stayed here for some reason. Probably the other horses. Guess it was scared to be alone too.

"Gotta make sure it isn't infected." Louis eyed the horse's bloody front hoof. "It seems okay now, but if it had a cut, that infection's spreadin' as we speak."

"Okay." Brian scratched the horse's silky ear. "We have to go. Let's get out of here and take a look at you in the light."

Louis snagged the lantern while Brian grabbed his bow. Brian's heart swelled with pride as the horse followed him. It touched him to have broken through to such a frightened and isolated creature. He related to it like Poppa had related to the cougar.

They emerged into the light, revealing layers of mud and dirt coating the horse. The lack of a rather telltale organ revealed it was a female.

Louis regarded the horse with a scrunch of his nose. "She's a grimy ol' thing."

"Grimy, huh?" Brian looked into the inquisitive horse's long-lashed eyes. "We can call you 'Grimes.' Everyone needs a name, you know."

"There's a well over there." Louis pointed to it. "No good to drink, but good enough to rinse off poor ol' Grimes. I'll go see if I can rummage up any ridin' gear."

Brian scratched Grimes's chin, reaching out to tug Louis's sleeve with his other hand. "You sure you'll be okay? That was close back there."

Louis lifted the bloody jacket clutched in his hand. "It only grabbed my collar. Must've had blood on its hands. Fucked up my favorite coat, so I'm pissed. Other than that, I'm fine. You?"

"I feel okay." The discovery of the horse had distracted Brian. "I kicked it, but my leg and foot were covered. It didn't bite or scratch me."

Louis brushed Brian's arm with his hand. "I'll be back. Take care of the horse."

"Okay." Brian managed a weak smile. "Be careful."

While Louis headed in the opposite direction toward a riding pen, Brian led Grimes to the well beneath a delicate trickle of snow. Grimes shivered, tickled by the water when it melted on her coat.

Brian smiled, pleased to have an animal around again. Although Grimes allowed him to wash her, an agitated snort let him know she was not at all pleased with the temperature of the water. She had no open wounds: no bites, no scratches, not even a nick in her hoof.

While he cleaned his knife and arrow, he entertained Grimes with idle conversation. She had no idea what he was saying, of course, but her ears perked forward like she was trying to listen. When he strolled away from the well, she followed behind him, nosing through the snow in search of grass.

Louis met him midway, holding up a blanket and reins. Brian's knees weakened with relief.

"The horse good?" Louis slung the blanket over her back. She jerked away, but Brian patted her neck and she stayed put. He nodded while Louis handed him the reins. "Saddle's AWOL, but the blanket'll do. Know how to put these on? I'm gonna wash my coat."

Brian nodded, though he didn't remember all that well—he just didn't want Louis to know. He tried to finagle the halter and reins onto Grimes while Louis sauntered away. She snorted impatiently and shook her head.

When Louis returned and examined Brian's handiwork, he said in a deadpan tone: "You got no idea what you're doin', do you? You got it on upside-down."

Embarrassed, Brian slugged him in the shoulder and turned before Louis could catch the flush in his cheeks. "I didn't grow up on a farm like you, asshole."

Louis cupped Brian's cheek and spun it toward him, smirking. "Look at those pink cheeks! Don't be so embarrassed; you can't be good at somethin' until you practice. Let me hang my coat to dry and we'll work with her a bit—train you too, while we're at it."

Louis draped his coat over a tree branch bathed in sunlight. Without a saddle, Brian couldn't get on easily. Louis boosted him up and gave him a few pointers, helping him recall the basic commands. Grimes seemed hesitant at first, but she soon eased into it and seemed to enjoy herself.

When Brian helped Louis on behind him to test Grimes's endurance, she held up well—but Brian lost his balance and took Louis with him. They rolled into a pile of snow with Grimes nosing at them. Brian and Louis looked at each other and sputtered into laughter, reminded of their clumsy descent from the plane in Kansas.

Grimes lingered nearby while Brian stared up at the orb of light penetrating through the clouds in divine rays. His hand snaked over to Louis's. When Louis took it, Brian closed his eyes, bathed in warmth despite the wintry air surrounding them.

GRIMES MADE TRAVELING much easier. She carried their extra backpack and camping supplies, and since they no longer had to walk, they took turns napping. Louis slept behind Brian and used Brian's backpack as a pillow. His light, constant breaths reassured Brian.

Their supply of food and water was perilously low, however, so Brian slowed when he spotted a small grocery store. He pulled back on Grimes's reins and reached behind him to pat Louis's knee. "Lou, do you think it's a bad idea to look in here? We're running low on food."

Louis's head lifted from Brian's backpack. "Hm? What's that? A grocery store? Haven't had any luck so far—here's as good a bet as any."

They approached the front of the store and hitched Grimes to a bike rack. She watched them with interest, snorting when she realized she'd be stuck there instead of going in with them.

As they moved toward the doors, an open newspaper dispenser caught Brian's eye. A small stack of papers remained, so he reached in to retrieve one. He examined the front page.

BRUTAL SLAYINGS IN KANSAS MAY HAVE BEEN
CAUSED BY VIRUS

The attacks that devastated multiple families in Kansas and spread to neighboring states may finally have an origin.

It all started with Jim Sullivan and his vicious act of familicide. A friend of Mr. Sullivan's, who wished to remain anonymous, claimed that Mr. Sullivan began to exhibit strange behaviors after a trip to the South Pacific for work.

"He came back jet-lagged, still recovering from a bad case of food poisoning. He said he tried something new and exotic. He wouldn't tell me what it was, other than to say it was meat."

What kinds of exotic meats could Mr. Sullivan have eaten?

"Jim always had a 'try anything once' mantra. Bison, kangaroo, turtle soup... You name it, he's tried it. I can't say it with 100 percent certainty, but the attack on his family may not have been the first time he ate long pig."

A humble American businessman eating human flesh abroad? It sounds like the stuff of horror films. But the recent attacks— such as Ellen Jameson's butchery of her young daughter—seem just as horrifying and outlandish, and there's no question of their existence.

After being ambushed by Mr. Sullivan, Mrs. Jameson began exhibiting the same savage behaviors. She infected her husband during his futile attempt to save their daughter, and he is now being studied for traces of the virus. Supposedly, it spreads through the consumption of contaminated meat or the contact of bodily fluids. And now similar attacks are occurring in Colorado and Missouri.

What could be more terrifying? An incurable virus that turns people into cannibalistic savages or the possibility that there is no explanation for their behavior?

"My grandparents tried to shield me from what happened to my family," Brian murmured, still clutching the paper. "They even chased away journalists who tried to interview me. But I found articles online. They said horrible things about what my mom did to my sister, but I only heard her screams. She kept calling my name and begging me to help her, but I couldn't." He sniffed, trying to fight the tears welling in his eyes. "All these people all over the country read about the death of my family—they sensationalized it, made it into some cheap horror story to sell their papers...and people bought into it because it didn't happen to *them*."

Louis snatched the paper from Brian's trembling hands and tossed it to the ground. He crushed it with his boot heel. "That shit's in the past now. All the people who got their jollies readin' about your sufferin' are long gone. Probably got to experience it firsthand."

Louis rubbed Brian's back. Brian tore his eyes from the crumpled paper and moved on.

They entered the grocery store through busted sliding doors. The front of the building glowed in the sunlight but was as dark as a cave deeper inside. They looked at each other. Louis shrugged and shook his head, his "here goes nothing."

The shelves were bare. Most of what remained was scattered on the floor, some of it opened and the contents spilled. A pungent scent lingered, though Brian couldn't be sure if it was rotten food or something else.

Darkness surrounded the halo of light from Louis's lantern. The silence amplified any sound they made as if they were in a stadium, so they tiptoed and avoided the scattered boxes and cans.

Louis came up with a pack of batteries from one of the check-out lanes, but it was the wrong kind for their flashlights. He muttered a curse and moved on while Brian noticed a body slumped over a register, still wearing a green vest with the grocery store's name stitched on it.

Did a Stalker or a person get to them? Maybe someone who didn't want to pay for their doomsday stockpile.

Eventually, they found the batteries they were looking for. They also snagged a few more boxes of pasta, along with jars of sauce and some canned fruit. The three bottles of water they found rolled under a shelf made it worthwhile—and they lucked out on Milanos and Cheez-Its flattened in the aisle during some sort of stampede.

A light clink echoed from the rear of the store while they dug inside the bag of Milanos, possibly a tin can falling or rolling.

They stopped chewing, each looking down either end of the aisle. Brian aimed the flashlight, freshly loaded with new batteries. Something scuffled across the linoleum floor ahead of him. He took a step back. "Louis—"

"I know. Go for the exit. Keep watchin' my back."

Brian caught movement in the circle of his flashlight—something white, crawling on all fours. He lifted the revolver with his right hand. Another Stalker peered around the corner of the aisle, its mad smile gleaming crimson through the window of its torn flesh.

A third slunk into sight. It sat at the end of the aisle, its knees drawn up in front of it. Brian reached for Louis, whispering, "Two of them in front of me. I think they're blind like the one in the warehouse."

He froze, his hand still on Louis: three became four, then five. More were pouring out from the back of the store like insects emerging from a hive. He'd never seen them hunt together. Lone Stalkers were formidable enough—an entire swarm seemed inescapable.

Louis's arm jerked twice. When Brian dared to look behind him, he saw two bodies on the ground ahead of Louis. Louis grabbed Brian's arm. "We have two options," he whispered while Brian kept his eyes on the Stalkers in front of him. "Try to stay quiet and sneak out of here or unload on them and run for it. If we stay, more will come."

Brian backed up until he stood parallel to Louis, both facing in opposite directions. "Let's walk towards the front as quietly as we can—if they notice us, we'll make a run for it."

Louis angled the lantern in front of him and crept forward while Brian kept the flashlight aimed behind them. Something moved on top of the shelves—a Stalker climbing up from the adjacent aisle with catlike dexterity.

Brian swallowed, keeping a mental count of how many there were—*seven*. He didn't even want to know how many were in front of them, but he suspected most had been hiding in the rear of the store. They didn't favor the light.

At least these didn't seem to notice it. But they still sensed Brian and Louis's presence, possibly from the vibrations of their footsteps or their heavy breaths. The pale creatures continued to follow them, though some skittered away and disappeared into other aisles. The one on top of the shelf crawled along it, its jittery snickers layering atop the muted chortles of its companions.

They made it to the gap in the aisles, exposing them on all sides. Brian swept his light to the left. It highlighted the grinning face of a Stalker mere feet away from him. Every muscle in his body tightened to keep him from moving or making a sound.

Clouded eyes stared at him but didn't *see* him. The instant he moved, the instant the fabric of his jacket or jeans brushed together, it would be on him. Brian kept his flashlight in his left hand but lowered it underneath the gun to steady it. He pulled the hammer back with his thumb. The Stalker leaped for him but crashed back to the ground as Brian's gun exploded.

"Run for it!" Louis wrestled with the band of the assault rifle and bolted toward the square of light at the front of the store, Brian at his heels. The deafening rattle of the rifle startled Brian so much he nearly tripped over his own feet. The vibrations rippling through his body made his teeth ache. Bodies jerked in the erratic beam of his flashlight, some slumping to the ground, others undeterred. He fired on them with the revolver, thumb glued to the hammer.

When Louis's rifle clicked, a Stalker dashed up and swiped for him. He bashed it in the head with the butt of the gun and withdrew his silenced pistol, putting a bullet in its forehead for good measure.

Something crashed into the metal shelves. Louis went down, stumbling over a body on the floor. Brian doubled back for him and dragged him to his feet. He fired on a Stalker skittering around the corner in front of him. It flew back into a rack of magazines and toppled onto the ground. The light was so close now—just beyond the checkout lane ahead of them.

Brian ran as fast as he could, the ringing in his ears drowning out any other sounds. His wet soles slid on the linoleum and he stumbled into the lane, bashing his head against the plastic edge of the conveyor. The pain was dizzying, but he forced himself to stand up, feeling Louis pushing against him from behind.

He cried out when something popped up next to the cash register, reaching for him like an actor in a cheesy haunted house. He fired but a *click* informed him the chamber was empty. An explosion of gore splattered onto his arm and shoulder anyway. Brian saw Louis withdraw the PPK.

A shadow emerged from the light ahead of them: Grimes stood in the doorway, her torn reins dangling from her head. She pawed at the ground with an anxious whinny.

Brian dashed for her, stumbling and skidding onto his knees at her feet. Louis snatched the back of Brian's jacket and jerked him to his feet.

He shoved him onto Grimes by the seat of his pants. Once he was up, Brian reached to help Louis on behind him. A startling amount of white shapes clambered over the fallen bodies of their compatriots.

Brian kicked Grimes's sides, but she'd already started running. He lost his balance and nearly slid off, but he flung his arms around her neck and caught himself. She started to sweat against him. He caught her reins in his hands—they'd been chewed at the ends so they were no longer connected in a loop. Louis fired behind them, but Brian didn't dare look. He held onto Grimes for dear life, vowing to find apples, carrots, or something rare and delicious to reward her with later.

After Louis emptied his gun, his arms wrapped around Brian's torso so tightly it squeezed the air out of him. Brian wheezed and leaned forward, trying to pull free.

"Sorry," Louis muttered breathlessly, easing off.

Brian looked past Louis's flushed face. The horde scrambled back to their hideout, blending with the icy snow as they slipped into the parking lot.

"Easy, girl." Brian patted Grimes's sticky neck. She slowed to a trot, shaking her head. "We'll stop for water when we can."

Louis stayed silent for a while, shaken by their narrow escape. Eventually, he muttered, "I liked it better when they *hid*."

Brian's head fell back, gently nudging the front of Louis's. "God, can you believe we made it out of that?" His skin burned with the heat of the blood pumping beneath it—so much that his skin itched.

"By the skin of our teeth. I didn't know they fuckin' worked together. I can handle one or two, but that was like a Wild West posse or some shit."

Brian examined the dwindling buildings around them. They were heading out of town, but he had no idea where. He tried to figure it out by the position of the sun: it was directly ahead of them, high in the sky. *It's midday. We're still going south.*

Louis rustled around in their food-stuffed supply pack, mumbling while he struggled to find what he was looking for.

"Are you okay?" Brian asked. "You fell back there—"

"I saw you fall too. Hit your head." A hand squeezed Brian's clean arm and slid down it before retreating. "I'm okay. Are you?"

Brian glanced at his bloodied jacket with a sigh. "I'm fine. Tired, but fine."

Louis stopped messing with the bag and held something against Brian's back. "We should still check each other out later, clean or get rid of any clothes with blood on 'em. I gotta figure out where we're at." He'd collected himself quickly—or wanted it to seem like he had. Brian was still shaking all over even though he wasn't cold. No matter how much he tried, he couldn't stop it. "Good—we're not too far from the Arkansas River. We'll hoof it there and follow 89 east to 15. We'll find shelter after that and keep on south."

"How much longer, do you think? I'm tired of Arkansas."

"About eighteen hours, plus sleep. So about two days. I don't think you're gonna like Louisiana much better, though."

Brian groaned. "Anything's better than Arkansas."

Louis snorted. "They shoulda made that their state motto."

They made a brief stop along the river. While Grimes drank, they ditched their bloodied clothes and performed a cursory visual inspection of each other before they changed. Neither of them had any injuries from the scurry, aside from a few superficial bruises.

Three hours later, they wound up at a collection of buildings belonging to the Game and Fish Commission at the edge of the river. They managed to find one large enough to shelter Grimes and small enough for them to clear out without much hassle. After they ate, they settled down to sleep.

Brian fought the urge to curl up next to Louis for warmth and wriggled into his own sleeping bag instead.

Chapter Fifteen: So Close

LITTLE ROCK, ARKANSAS

Morning

Something tugged on Brian's hair. He yelled and sat up, staring breathlessly at Grimes. She blinked at him and snorted. He assumed she was hungry.

After a brief breakfast of cookies and crackers, and canned fruit for Grimes, they stopped by the lake to fetch water. Snow no longer fell. What remained on the ground was beginning to melt, making for a slightly less miserable journey. Brian was thankful for Grimes in numerous ways, mostly for sparing his feet—even if his ass wanted to remind him it was suffering in their place.

Once the sun started to set, they ate and headed onto a dirt road that took them down to 81. When they saw a sign for a place called "Drenco Oil and Gas, Inc.," they followed the road to a clearing with two buildings: a warehouse and a smaller office building. A lone pick-up truck parked outside contained the bountiful loot of a used spit cup and an empty beer bottle.

Grimes headed south to a nearby creek. She buried her face in it and drank long and deep. Crickets chirped as Brian and Louis filled their empty bottles with freezing water. A twig snapped. Grimes lifted her head, ears pricked forward.

Brian stood and screwed the cap back onto his bottle. As he turned, a searing pain tore through his body. He crashed face-first into the frigid water, making every nerve in his face sting. Something wrapped around his throat that kept him from swallowing the mucky water. He couldn't hear anything except a vacuum of silence. When he opened his eyes, the bitter cold forced them shut again. The pressure around his throat tightened. Brian clawed at it, his flailing legs kicking against something.

He fumbled for the knife in the pocket of his jeans. His fingers were already going numb like they had after the log flume. His breath gave out, and he inhaled a noseful of freezing water—but the pressure eased.

Brian shot out of the creek with a desperate gasp and fell onto the river bank, coughing up the water that had gone into his lungs. Burning pain seared his aching muscles and his nose tingled like soda had gone up into it. His vision was blurry, but his ringing ears cleared enough for him to hear a sickening *crunch* followed by a pulpy squishing.

Brian rubbed his eyes. One figure straddled another on the river's edge, arms up in the air, then down. Up, down, crashing into the ground. Something splattered into the air. The body below convulsed as if it was a motor response to some stimuli.

By the time Brian managed to stop coughing, the figure on top had rolled off the body with the twitching feet. Grimes squealed frantically, rearing upright at the edge of the woods. Brian struggled to make sense of everything, half propped by the muddy creek bank. Water dripped from his soaked body.

Louis.

He scrambled up the bank, propelling himself onto his feet. Nothing could've prepared him for the sight that followed: a body with no head, only a pulpy mass of bone and muscle with one cloudy eye. The feet no longer twitched.

Louis lay beside it on his back, a gore-stained rock and one of the King's masks next to his outstretched hand. His eyes were shut, and his normally dark complexion was sallow—but his chest moved.

The King didn't forget about us. Fuck. I can't leave Louis out here. We're exposed, and there might be more of them.

"Grimes," he whispered. She approached him with an apprehensive snort and lowered herself to her knees when he urged her to. A swell of appreciation warmed his cold body, but he didn't have time to reward her.

He dragged Louis over to her through the mud and snow, exhaling through his lips. Louis only had an inch and a bit more muscle on him than Brian, but he seemed to weigh five hundred pounds.

Once he'd managed to position Louis on top of Grimes, he noticed a dark stain in Louis's right shoulder. Brian's body seized with panic. *A gunshot wound. The blood loss knocked him out. Fuck—I have to hurry.*

Brian climbed onto Grimes and sat behind Louis to keep him from sliding off. Another body lay in the clearing, his brains pooling out of a nasty exit wound.

"Slowly, girl." Brian clutched the reins and fought to keep Louis from slipping. He eased Grimes to the office building with no choice but to secure it himself—it was almost night and they needed shelter, especially before Stalkers or more of the King's men showed up.

Brian hopped off Grimes, leaving Louis draped over her. He crept over to the angled deck and peered in through the open windows. The inside looked inconspicuous: abandoned desks, destroyed computers, an overturned chair. Another empty building—a skeleton without a beating heart.

Brian climbed in through the window, gripping the silenced pistol. The building smelled like mildew. No scents of rot or meat wafted into his nose, which he was still snorting water from. His wet clothes conducted the cool air and made him shudder.

He didn't want to take too long and leave Louis and Grimes alone in the cold, so he moved swiftly through the lobby into each office, making mental notes of furniture he could pile up to block the doors and windows.

A note was written on a whiteboard in a small boardroom:

Gary, we're not coming back. You should leave too. The key's in back, in your favorite little guy. We left you a few you-know-whats.

Brian didn't know what this cryptic message meant, but now wasn't the time to figure it out.

Once he'd determined the building was clear, he went outside and led Grimes in. By the time he finished barricading the entrance, his body was so tender he wanted to flop onto a sofa and pass out. But he couldn't leave Louis on the horse.

He wrapped his arms around Louis's waist and pulled. His weight set Brian off-balance. He tumbled onto the floor, banging his head on the leg of a table. Louis sprawled on top of him, light breaths tickling Brian's face. Brian dragged himself out from underneath Louis's dead weight and kneeled beside him, stripping the backpack from his back. He dug into it, hoping the waterproof claims were true. Fortunately, only the outside was soaked. The interior was untouched. He retrieved the first aid kit with shaking hands.

Okay, first of all, I need to see where the bullet went. If it hit a major artery, he'd be dead already.

Brian turned Louis over to remove his coat and backpack. He tugged his shirt off, revealing a torso in perfect shape. He'd been shot in the back with no exit wound; the bullet was embedded inside him.

I can dig it out if it's not in too deep.

He folded Louis's coat inside-out and propped his head on it, leaving him lying on his stomach. A dark hole singed the skin next to Louis's shoulder blade, surrounded by dried blood. With any luck, the bullet had lodged next to it, slowed by the backpack and halted by the bone.

The other guy must've shot Louis in the back while Mush-head tackled me. Louis turned, shot him dead, then pulled Mush-head off me and bashed his head in. Jesus—he must've had a lot of adrenaline going to block the pain from the gunshot.

Brian unfurled the contents from the first aid kit. He rolled up his sleeves and slid on the sterile vinyl gloves first, then dug out medical gauze, iodine, and disinfectant wipes. After he'd retrieved the flashlight from his backpack, he turned it on and aimed it into Louis's wound. Metal glinted about an inch and a half into the muscle, but Brian couldn't tell if there were any fragments.

He rubbed disinfectant wipes around the wound in gentle circles. When he'd finished, he dribbled iodine onto it and dabbed it with gauze. He grabbed the forceps—but it would be too cumbersome to try to dig with one hand while the other held a flashlight. He abandoned the flashlight and foraged for the lantern in Louis's backpack instead.

Once he set the lantern up, he had both hands free. He used tweezers to open the wound and hovered over the dark red circle with the forceps, playing real-life "Operation."

I hate that game.

Brian forced himself to take a deep breath and relax before he inserted the forceps. He held it and clenched his jaw, carefully digging around the bullet.

Not low enough. I can't get a grip. Is it stuck in something? Bone?

He dug a little deeper and squeezed again. Blood welled out of the wound. It made it hard for him to see, so he abandoned the tweezers to dab at it with gauze. Once he could see again, he returned the tweezers to the wound and parted the flesh. The forceps clicked together underneath the bullet. Brian slid them out and examined the bullet: a .22 round, not hollow point.

Good. No fragments.

Brian swapped the forceps for the flashlight. He aimed the light into the open wound. Blood pooled inside it, so he soaked it with gauze to see if any pieces had broken off. The bullet looked intact, but he had to be sure.

Nothing. He grabbed a gauze pad and held it to the wound to slow the bleeding. Louis kept breathing, shallow and slow. Brian checked the gauze and wound intermittently to gauge the amount of blood. When he decided the bleeding had slowed enough to close the wound, he prepared the suture kit.

He grasped the needle with the driver and held Louis's skin with the tweezers. Cringing, he drove the curved needle through Louis's skin. It took four stitches to close the wound. He knotted the last stitch and cut the suture. Satisfied with his work, he taped a piece of gauze over the wound and wrapped a cloth bandage around Louis's shoulder and chest.

Brian collapsed beside Louis on the floor. He stared at the jumble of medical supplies, the mound of bloody gauze, and the tiny bullet that had caused all this hassle. When he shut his eyes, he instantly fell asleep.

SOMETHING STROKED BRIAN'S cheek. His eyelids fluttered open, but everything looked blurry and bright—*daytime*. The room smelled of manure, which was to be expected since he'd locked Grimes in with them.

His vison focused. Louis looked at him through heavy-lidded eyes, his complexion still pallid. His dry lips lifted into a tender smile. "Welcome back to the land of the livin'. I wouldn't be here if it wasn't for you."

Brian had been so exhausted he didn't even remember passing out until now. He swallowed as the hand stroking his cheek retreated. "How do you feel?"

"Like a freight train slammed into my shoulder." Louis tried to sit up, but he winced and flopped back onto the ground. "Please tell me you got painkillers in that first aid kit."

Brian nodded and rolled over to his backpack. He dug into it for the pills and a bottle of water for Louis to swallow them with. He sat up, holding two paper packets in one hand. "Tylenol or Advil?"

"Both. *Merci.*"

Brian tore the packets open and cupped the pills in his hand. Louis propped himself up against the couch. He grabbed the pills from Brian's hand and popped them into his mouth, following them with the bottle of water Brian offered. Louis tilted his head back, Adam's apple bobbing as he chugged the water down in one go. Brian thought about wiping the water dribbling from Louis's chin, but he decided it would be inappropriate.

Why do I even care about dumb shit like that? He almost died, for one thing. For another, I woke up with his hand on my face. Who knows how long he was watching me sleep? We've crossed too many boundaries to worry about wiping away some goddamn water.

"Thanks. I was fuckin' thirsty." Louis winced. "Can you help me up?"

Brian stood and grabbed Louis's left hand with both of his. He pulled him up and helped him settle onto the edge of the bland waiting room couch. Before Brian could retreat, Louis's good hand reached for his neck. "Fuck me—he got your neck good. Must hurt like a bitch. You okay?"

Now that Brian wasn't focused on Louis's well-being, his neck ached to remind him of his neglect. "Yeah. I mean, it hurts everywhere. But I'll be okay. We should stay here a few days so we can both rest."

"Some other asshole shot me while that one tackled you. That King fuckwad must've ordered you taken alive—I can't imagine why and don't want to. But I took out the fucker who shot me with the last round in my clip, tossed the gun, grabbed a rock, and jerked the other guy offa you. Bashed his head in."

Louis's stormy eyes darkened beneath a creasing brow, reminding Brian of how intimidating he could be. After they lost Eva, he'd seemed to calm down a little—but flashes of menace sometimes emerged.

Brian shuddered as he recalled the cloudy eye peering at him. "I can't believe you did that with a rock—*while* you were bleeding from a gunshot wound."

"I wasn't gonna let him fuckin' drown you." Louis's furrowed brow relaxed. "I wasn't thinkin'. I panicked. When I got him off you, all I could think about was how bad I wanted to hurt him. The last thing I remember before I passed out was seein' you spring up outta the water. I guess once I knew you were okay, my brain finally let my body take a break."

Louis's concern touched Brian. He forced a smile back. "Well, thanks for getting him off of me."

"Thanks for takin' a bullet outta me and stitchin' me up." Louis brushed the bandages Brian had wrapped around him with his fingertips. "You surprise me sometimes. For every time you don't recognize an animal or don't know how to work a faucet, you do somethin' like this. It's like you don't know your own strength until somethin' pushes you to it."

Brian sank onto the couch next to Louis and flopped against the rear cushion. "I inherited my dad's depression and self-doubt and my mom's resourcefulness and tenacity. They're usually at odds, though."

"Don't beat yourself up. I'm fucked up too." Louis leaned back against the couch cushion. "Sometimes I get angry out of nowhere. Most of the time, I just feel empty. After my parents died, it got really bad—I had to go to a therapist. They prescribed me a buncha pills, took notes while I talked. But I never learned anythin' about myself and it never fixed the problem."

Brian angled his face to look at Louis. "The medication didn't help?"

"To a point. It kept my impulses in check, but that empty feelin' was still there." Louis looked back at Brian, his brow creasing. "I'm startin' to feel somethin', though. I don't know what—just somethin' in there that wasn't there before. I don't know if it means I'm gettin' worse or better."

Brian decided to press Louis while he was in a forthcoming mood. "Did they ever tell you what they thought was wrong? My therapist said I have Atypical Depression. It means I'm not depressed all of the time—but my dad wasn't either, and he still tried to kill himself."

"The therapist said I had somethin' called a Borderline personality. I still couldn't tell you what that means. My grandparents didn't believe it. They thought I was moody and wanted attention. Tried a bunch of tough love, but that sure as shit didn't help. Eva tried to look it up once, I think, but I wasn't interested when she tried talkin' to me about it." Louis sighed and swept his bangs back from his face. "I guess I shoulda listened to her. But no one wants to believe there's anythin' wrong with them."

Brian clasped his hands in his lap and twiddled his thumbs. "Well, honestly, you *can* be moody. But I don't think there's anything wrong with you. I mean, aren't we all a little fucked up? We can be fucked up together."

Louis pressed his lips together while he searched Brian's eyes. His brow knit, and he bit his lip; he obviously had something he wanted to say but didn't know how to. Since his left arm was next to Brian, he reached over with it and grabbed Brian's knee. "*Je suis à toi, et tu es à moi.*"

Brian's focus shifted from the hand gripping his knee to Louis's face. "Are you trying to fast-track this conversation?"

Louis's eyebrows arched. "*Oui.*" His hand retreated from Brian's knee. "It was startin' to get a little sappy."

The butterflies in Brian's stomach stopped flapping around. "What'd you say, anyway? I know '*toi*' and '*moi*' means 'you' and 'me.'"

"There you go, surprisin' me again." Louis leaned forward, his chest bare aside from the bandages wrapped around his right shoulder. "Guess I'd better be careful what I say to you, *boo.*"

The intimacy of this endearment surprised Brian, unless it meant something different to Louis—who could tell with him? "I've graduated from 'boug,' huh?"

"With flyin' colors." Louis stood and swiveled his torso, stretching to test the flexibility of his injured arm. His wince indicated it wasn't much. "I'm gonna head to the bathroom. You should feed Grimes—the whole time we were talkin', she was starin' at us. Kind of a mood killer."

Brian had been so enmeshed in his conversation with Louis he hadn't even noticed Grimes standing in an office watching them through the door. It startled him enough to make him sputter and move a hand to his chest.

He resisted the urge to follow Louis down the hall and fling his arms around him, babbling about how relieved he was that Louis was still alive and how much he cared about him. Instead, he mulled over Louis's enigmatic French phrases and attended to Grimes.

THEY STAYED AT the office building for several days to reconvene and let Louis heal. He kept his arm in a makeshift sling, but if it ached, he wasn't admitting it. Brian found the key mentioned in the whiteboard note: the "little guy" was a ceramic pig with a hollow opening. The key opened a locker in the warehouse with a few boxes of bullets. Poor Gary never got to them.

Since they were running low on food and worried about more people— or worse—popping up, they searched the warehouse and moved on with a full can of fuel. A chill still clung to the air, but most of the snow melted to sludge as they went farther south. Sickly yellows and greens crept into the dreary browns and grays of their usual scenery.

Louis let Brian do most of the navigating. He marked out their path in pen, so all Brian had to do was pay attention to this and use the compass. Louis drifted in and out of sleep while his body healed, trusting Brian to protect them both. Brian thought back to that uneasy conversation outside Henry's cabin and mulled over how far they'd come since then. Maybe Eva's absence united them.

Around four hours after they left, they approached a sign: *"Now leaving Arkansas—come back soon!"*

Brian reached back and shook Louis, glowing with enthusiasm he hadn't felt for weeks. "Hey, King Louis—we're almost in your state."

Louis came to with a surly groan. "I always hated that name because everyone said it wrong. I mean, why the fuck does it end with an 's' if you don't pronounce it? Besides, why would my parents name me after some French asshole who wore make-up, wigs and high heels?"

"Geez—didn't mean to hit a nerve. I thought you'd be excited. I mean, we're almost there. We just have to make it to New Orleans."

Louis sighed. "Sorry to rain on your parade. My shoulder's achin' and I feel useless, is all."

Grimes trotted past the sign. Brian exhaled, glad to *finally* leave Arkansas. Of course, Louisiana didn't look any different. State borders were only invisible, imaginary boundaries that meant nothing nowadays.

Louis patted Brian's side. "We're still in the South, boo. We haven't escaped the churches and Confederate flags until we get on that boat. Once we do, we can escape the whole damn country."

They'd made it so far that the distance between the Louisiana border and New Orleans seemed relatively negligible. Without Louis, Brian wasn't sure where he'd be—or if he'd even be *alive*. He gave Brian the motivation he needed, the drive to keep going. For so long, the island seemed like a dream, something abstract. Now that it was closer, more tangible, Brian wanted it more than ever, more than *anything*.

So close, yet so far.

Chapter Sixteen: Swampland

CHEMIN-A-HAUTE STATE PARK, LOUISIANA

Morning

They camped for the night at a lakeside park. The 60-degree highs and 40-degree lows provided a welcome respite from the cold weather they'd struggled through. In the morning, Brian admired the vista of cypress trees breaking through the bayou mist. Ducks coasted through the water, joined by stalking egrets along the water's edge. He searched for the eyes and snout of a prowling alligator but was disappointed not to see one.

After they'd washed and filled up on water, they headed back on the road until they entered a town called Log Cabin. A few quaint shops lined the barren roads. They ducked into one called "Southern Charm Flowers and Gifts" for lunch, thinking it would be an easy building to case because of its small size and undesirable contents. They were wrong.

A tall woman sprung up from behind the front counter with a shotgun aimed at them. Brian and Louis trained their weapons on her—but something brushed against Brian's leg. He stepped back and glanced down into an orange tabby cat's bright-green eyes.

"That's my Jonesy." The woman's deep voice startled Brian. "I saw you got a horse out there—keeps lookin' in here like it's worried 'bout you. She don't wander, either. Means you treat her good, aren't bad folks."

"Her name is Grimes," Brian said. "What're you doing in here?"

"Takin' a break. My fat ass can't handle too much ridin' in one go." She lowered the gun a hair. "I got a bike. Doubt you'd want it: it's purple and gots sparkly streamers and a little basket my cat rides in."

"Why'd you jump up and aim your shotgun at us?" Louis held the pistol in one hand but was unable to steady it with the other. "You coulda stayed outta sight, snuck out while we were lookin' around."

"'Cause you was gonna find me eventually and I didn't want you to get the drop on me first." The woman's tight curls bounced as she tilted her head. Her bright eyes connected with Brian's. "I'm Dionne Etienne, by the way. But everybody call me 'Lady D.'"

"Brian Jameson." Brian released the tension on his bowstring but kept the arrow aimed. "He's Louis Lavellé."

"Louis Lavellé... That the dude who writes the Westerns? Or maybe he a porn star. Matter of fact, you both too pretty for the 'pocalypse. How you make it this long?"

Brian resisted the temptation to glance at Louis's face—he imagined his expression was incredulous, at best. "Well, my grandfather was a Vietnam vet. He knew how bad this was going to get, so he trained me. And Louis was a Boy Scout." A slight grin cracked Brian's neutral expression.

D slid out from behind the counter and leaned against it, keeping her shotgun in front of her. The cat jogged over to her and circled around her leg, brushing against a knee-length boot covered in dirt and dried mud. "I'm from New Orleans. I used to live there with my brother, was a psychic in the Quarter—not no hoodoo voodoo shit. Just palm readin', numerology, that kinda thing. I got sent up north durin' the clean-up from Katrina, never managed to make it back down to my brother. I'm hopin' if he survived Katrina, he can survive this shit. We come from tough stock—too much pepper in the gumbo." D swatted at the cat when he nibbled at her coat. "Where y'all headed?"

"South," Brian said, "to find a way out of the country."

D reached up and primped her hair, sighing. "I don't got much: Jonesy, a bag of my clothes and lookin' good stuff. Some Slim-Jims, Pringles, greasy ol' gas station food. Flat soda. The only weapon I got is this shotgun. But I'll make you a deal: if Boy Scout holsters his pistol, I'll lay my shotgun on this here counter. You can even keep your arrow trained on me, Sunshine. Sound doable?"

"Why me?" Brian didn't want to keep straining his arms.

"I don't much like the look Boy Scout's got in his eyes. And I got a better chance of survivin' an arrow than a bullet."

"He's good with it." Louis glanced down as the cat trilled and trotted over to him. It rubbed its head along his foot. Louis shook his leg to shoo it away. "He'll hit you where he wants to hit you—so don't give him a reason to." He lowered his pistol by a hair. "On the count of three, we both put our guns down."

While Louis counted, Brian pulled the string back with the arrow balanced over his left hand. Once Louis reached "three," D set the shotgun on the counter and Louis slid his pistol into his holster. Brian let the string slacken some but not completely.

"I don't care if we hold hands and sing 'Kumbaya' as long as you don't try to kill me." D bent down to lift Jonesy and cuddled him to her robust bosom. "Since we all headed south, I got a proposition for you: help keep me and Jonesy alive and I'll do the same for you. You ain't got to share nothin' with me. Six pairs of hands and eyes are better than four, right?"

Louis tapped Brian's elbow and gestured for him to follow. He joined Louis a reasonable distance from D where they could speak privately but keep an eye—and arrow—on her. "Is she for real? A cat, a bicycle, and a shotgun—sounds like the set-up for a joke. How the hell can she help us?"

Brian watched D while he leaned his head into Louis's neck. "I kinda like her. She's got character."

Louis blew a raspberry that sounded like the horse. "I feel like I'm your daddy and you're beggin' me to let you keep some pet you found on the street. Two if you count the damn *chat*."

Brian groaned. "You'd make a terrible father."

"I never wanted kids—can't stand 'em. Never wanted a wife and the damned white picket fence, either." Louis scoffed while Jonesy squirmed to get out of D's arms. The shotgun remained behind her on the counter, but she didn't make a move for it. "I don't even want *her*, especially after the shit those actors pulled. Hell, for all we know, she's one of the King's flunkies. Another goddamn actor, even. I don't need anyone except you."

As much as this flattered Brian, it didn't deter him—which he suspected was Louis's intent. "Louis, your arm's a handicap. We could use the help. Why don't we give her a shot?"

"Let's not." Louis narrowed his eyes, but his features relaxed into a resigned expression. "I guess I'll have to meet you in the middle: if she wants to come with us, we'll take her gun. We'll see how it goes from there. Otherwise, it's so long and good riddance to Miss D."

"*Lady* D."

"Whatever." Louis's attention shifted from Brian to D. He approached her and held out his hand. "You can come with us on one condition: you give us your gun."

D parted from the counter. "Say what? How'm I gonna help you out with no gun?"

"We had a bad experience with a couple in Missouri," Brian said. "We don't want to repeat it. I understand how hard it is to trust people now—

I'm sure you do too. If you stay close to us, we can protect you until we decide to give you your gun back."

"Stay in front of us where we can keep an eye on you. You stop when we stop. Whatever you find, you keep; same goes for us. Make any funny moves and it's lights-out for you." Louis waggled his fingers. "Hand it over or we walk outta here and go our separate ways. No harm, no foul."

Jonesy leaped out of D's arms. She sighed, folding them over her chest. "I dunno. I've been awful lonely ever since I lost my man—sure would be nice to have more than a cat for company. He don't talk back. But like you said, it's hard to trust these days—how do I know you won't keep my gun, take everything else I got?"

Sympathy welled within Brian as soon as she mentioned losing someone she loved. The presence of the cat reassured him. He sensed the cat comforted D like Rocky once comforted him. "We've lost people too. I lost my entire family, and Louis lost his—except for an aunt and uncle, maybe. You don't have to believe me, but I want to avoid any violence I can. The only beautiful thing left in this world is love—and trust, by extension."

D's eyes scanned between Louis and Brian's, the tightened muscles of her face relaxing. Her arms fell from her chest, hands clasping in front of her stomach. "That's beautiful, Sunshine. You got a sensitive soul. But what about your friend here? Can I trust him not to put a bullet in my back?"

Brian glanced at Louis. He'd lowered his outstretched arm while D expressed her concerns. "He's helped keep me alive this long. If you don't give him a reason to shoot you, I'm sure he'll do the same for you."

D's eyes narrowed as they met Louis's. "I'm sure there's plenty of reasons he'd wanna shoot me. We strangers—the two of you ain't, is you? You known each other; got some intimacy between you. That's what keeps him from shootin' *you*."

"Lady, I ain't shot anyone who didn't have it comin'," Louis said. "Now stop flippin' and floppin' over it and make up your damn mind already."

D's thin eyebrows arched. "You get right to it, don't you? Shit. I guess I don't wanna be alone no more, and I don't wanna have to deal with those ugly-ass Stalkers on my own. Only reason I made it this far is 'cause Gus was with me—Jones too. Jones don't like Stalkers. He hisses and runs off soon as he smells one. Kept me outta a good bit of trouble. What people I seen, I tried to avoid—most of 'em looked ragged, got the crazy eyes. You two the first I seen who got themselves together. You mighta kept each other from goin' crazy."

D sighed and reached behind her for her shotgun. She grabbed it by the barrel and handed it to Louis. "Don't make me regret this, Boy Scout."

"Stop callin' me that." Louis took the shotgun. As soon as it was in his hands, Brian let the bowstring slacken. "If you don't, I'll start callin' you Crazy Cat Lady."

D flashed him a bright grin that bared her off-white teeth. "Ever since I can remember, I been callin' people nicknames. It's just my way. I can think of a couple other things to call you. I'll make sure to run 'em by you while we travelin'." She held up a gloved finger. "Lemme grab my bike from the back. You can pull your gun out if you scared—I won't blame you."

Louis didn't pull it out, but he kept his hand on his holster. His dark eyes flashed in the sunlight that broke through the front door, illuminating a floor cluttered with broken knickknacks and desiccated flowers. "Brian, I swear... You're too nice for your own damn good. And I'm a sucker when it comes to you."

Brian's brow crinkled as he searched Louis's eyes, trying to figure out why he'd said that and what he meant by it—but Louis had already looked away, keen eyes locked on D as she fiddled around in the rear of the store.

D returned with a purple and silver bicycle. Jonesy sat in the basket, swatting at the shiny streamers dangling from the handlebars. D now wore a deep purple backpack with a large rhinestone "D" keychain dangling from a zipper. Brian couldn't resist smiling at this eccentric image.

D grinned back at him. "You got a smile that lights up the room, Sunshine. It ain't hard to see why Louis-boy ain't never shot you. I hope we get to be good friends. I could use some light in these dark times." She maneuvered herself onto the bicycle seat, which sat a little low for her long legs. "Lead the way, boys—if Jones hisses, haul ass in the other direction."

With this uneasy truce established, they exited the store and returned to Grimes. She nickered and swished her tail when she saw Jonesy and D, clomping up to touch noses with the eager cat as he strained to meet her from his basket.

D beamed. "Aww, look at that! They already best friends." She stroked her chin with her thumb. "What's that line? Ah! 'Louis, I think this is the beginning of a beautiful friendship.'"

Louis took Brian's hand and settled onto Grimes behind him. "If you say so."

While Louis and Brian traveled, they kept their talking to a minimum. Most of their conversations happened once they were safely inside shelter for the evening. But D talked a *lot*. She had numerous questions and anecdotes which provided a welcome change from the silence of the landscape but added another layer of tension for Brian. He had to shush her several times, warning her about the Stalkers with amplified hearing. It bothered Brian a little, but he could *feel* Louis behind him trying to bite his tongue.

For a little while, D listened. But she'd always forget and start talking about something else. Her choice of topic was sometimes so random Brian wondered if she had ADD or something. *Another person to be crazy with.*

When D started complaining about her feet, they decided to find shelter for the night. About an hour of sunlight remained, so they entered a town called Baskin. They meandered through a small suburb, D's streamers fluttering as she rolled alongside them. Brian thought back to Louis's comment about the house with the white picket fence: the American ideal, impenetrable and everlasting. As he looked at the broken windows and dead lawns, he realized how illusory their security had been.

D rolled to a stop. Brian pulled back on Grimes's reins, following D's eyeline. A two-story house loomed in front of them, a bright yellow message painted on the exterior.

Supplies in here! Had to leave, couldn't take it all!

D folded her arms over the handlebars of her bike. "If it sound too good to be true, it probably is. I bet it's all been snatched up, anyway."

"We're runnin' low, though," Louis said. "What if we pass up food? Water? Ammo? Besides, we gotta sleep *somewhere.*"

Brian was more in line with D's suspicions. "Louis, your arm—"

"You don't have to baby me, boo." Louis's good hand dug into Brian's side. "I can still do plenty of things with *this* hand—like fire a gun."

D cleared her throat. "I'm sure you fire on all cylinders, Louis-boy, but we ain't sleepin' in some place painted with a 'Welcome! Come In!' sign. It's like they askin' for trouble and we answerin' the call."

Jonesy hopped out of the basket and dashed to the doorstep of the house before they could further debate entering it. He poked at the door with his paw, nudging it open, and darted inside. Grimes made a worried whinny and pawed the ground.

"Jonesy!" D tried to whisper and yell at the same time. She stamped a foot, much like the horse. "Shit! Jonesy, honey, come back!"

When the cat didn't return through the cracked door, D shrugged her shoulders back and pushed out the kickstand of the bike. She stood and looked up at Brian and Louis. "Guess I'm gonna have to go in the damn house anyway. You understand love, right, Sunshine? Well, I love that damn cat. Either let me have my shotgun or come in with me, cover my ass while I hunt Jones down."

Brian slid down from Grimes. She nickered and nosed his arm, but he wasn't sure if she was imploring him to stay or to help find the cat. He had the feeling the cat would find his way out without their help. "I guess we might as well clear the place out, stay for the night. I'll help you."

Louis took the hand Brian offered and slid down beside him, his breath clouding in the brisk air as the sun abandoned them. He withdrew the silenced pistol, though he only had one clip of ammo left for it. "Slow and silent—you got that, D? Don't go yellin' for that cat until we clear the place—"

She was already stalking forward in bold pursuit of her errant cat. Louis groaned and followed her alongside Brian, leaving Grimes free so she could run if she needed to. They approached the door with their weapons drawn.

When Brian crossed the threshold of the house, a body on the ground stopped him dead in his tracks. Thin skin still clung to the skeleton and a disgusting stain surrounded the body, left by fluids from decomposition. The top of the skull had been shattered.

D stood near the body with a crumpled note in her hand. Her face was nearly as crumpled as the note. Brian stepped next to her and read it.

Knock knock? Who's there? Above. Above who? Above you!

Louis jerked Brian back by the sleeve. They looked up at the ceiling— and a shotgun hovering above the door. "Don't shut the door. It was already open when the cat and D went in, so they didn't set it off."

D nodded. "Poor sucker was probably lookin' forward, not up. He closed the door outta habit before he saw the gun. *Boom*! Murder, she wrote."

Brian examined the shotgun. It was flush against the wall and wouldn't have jutted out far enough to see until someone stepped inside. "We should disarm it and leave. The rest of the house might have—"

A perfectly timed explosion cut him off, followed by a frightened yowl. Jonesy dashed down the stairs on silent, nimble paws, a blur of orange disappearing into the living room.

D opened her mouth to call for him, but she covered it when she caught Louis's death-glare. "I got to get him outta here," she whispered. "He ain't gonna budge now that he's scared out his damn skin."

"Are we really gonna stay in this place just for a cat?" Louis hissed as they stood frozen in front of the door. "I doubt the shotgun's the only thing in here rigged to kill us."

"You're the one who wanted to look for supplies," Brian said. "Besides, you said we needed somewhere to sleep."

Louis glared at him. "Yeah, like next door. I'm not jumpin' at the bit to find out what else they got set up in here. What if the King's gang did this? Lured people in, kept 'em from leavin'?"

D folded her arms, her lips set in a defiant grimace. "I ain't leavin' without my cat—" She blinked. "Wait—who this 'King' dude?"

"It's a long story." Brian sighed when his last memories of Eva returned to him. "Now really isn't the time to tell it."

"We'll go next door. You can stay here, wait for the cat," Louis said. "If you find any supplies, they're all yours."

D remained stubbornly fixed next to the couch. "You talk a big game, but now you pussyin' out."

"No." Louis's irritated glare flashed with something more menacing. "Your cat's the one who pussed out. I'm tryin' to save my own skin. Whatever's in here ain't worth it—your cat included."

It aggravated Brian that he was stuck in a situation he'd tried to circumvent. Louis wanted to go in, and now he wanted to leave. D wanted to avoid it, but now she wanted to stay.

D loves her cat. Jonesy is the only thing she has left.

"D, we just met you—" Brian glanced between her and Louis "—but I understand how much your cat means to you. Let's try to wait a bit and at least disarm this shotgun, take the ammo."

She surprised him by crushing him to her in a tight embrace and kissing his cheek. "Oh, baby boy, you too good for this world!" D released Brian, shaking her head at Louis when she saw the pistol aimed at her. "I know, I know—I touched your precious. He's still shiny, don't you worry."

Louis lowered his gun and gave her a dirty look. "I ain't fuckin' Gollum and he ain't the One Ring." He dipped his thumb into his mouth and smudged it on Brian's cheek, trying to wipe away D's lipstick. "You really gonna stick around to wait for the runaway cat of someone you just met? Even though you heard that explosion and saw the shotgun?"

Brian shoved Louis's hand away, jaw clenching before he spoke. "Listen, I want you to understand how important Jonesy is to D. Parker and Spike had each other, and you've got me. Or I've got you. Anyway, that King guy is lonely and miserable because he only values things, but things don't *really* make you happy—relationships do. Even ones with animals, like us with Grimes. Don't you care about her?"

Louis scanned Brian's eyes, exhaling. "Yeah, but she's not stupid enough to go runnin' off somewhere."

"Louis—" Brian arched his eyebrows, giving him the same pleading look Brian's mother used to give him "—do this for me. Please."

Louis's shoulders slumped as he rolled his eyes. "Fine. But next time I wanna do somethin' *you* don't wanna do, I'm gonna remind you of this."

D cleared her throat. "I'm super thankful to y'all, I really am, but let's take care of this boomstick so we can shut the door—it's makin' me anxious."

Brian moved to a worn leather couch mauled with claw marks from some errant pet. "We can push the door shut with this. The couch will absorb the shot and we can stand on it to dismantle the gun."

D helped him push it. Even though they knew it was coming, the deafening *boom* of the shotgun made them flinch. Stuffing poured out of the giant hole blown into the couch, reminding Brian of Louis's gunshot wound.

The closed door and boarded windows prevented any light from entering the house. Brian took his backpack off and rustled through it for the lantern. D held it for him while he climbed up and worked to deactivate the shotgun, recalling the time he'd spent setting up traps with Poppa.

Despite the chill air, sweat beaded on his brow by the time he'd finished. He ejected the remaining shells from the gun and handed them to Louis.

Louis glanced around the small foyer they had yet to branch out from. "While we're here, we should explore. Make sure we're alone."

"Aren't you worried about more traps?" Brian asked.

"If it was up to me, we'd already be gone, boo." Acidity seared the sweetness out of Louis's endearment.

They could've heard a pin drop in the silence. No footsteps creaked down the stairs. No Stalkers leaped out of alcoves with jarring laughter. No guns blasted or rattled, and the cat didn't yowl or meow.

Louis handed D the lantern and informed her she was on "light duty." She spun it in an arc, highlighting the stairwell to their left and the kitchen directly in front of them. The living room to their right contained a gigantic flat-screen TV that glinted in the light.

They approached the kitchen with slow, deliberate steps. When D's boots made a clacking sound on the tile, she bent to remove them. She tiptoed onward in her socks.

A full six-pack of beer sat on an island in the kitchen. On the counter, an open package of moldy bread accompanied a bowl of putrid sludge that might have been fruit. Typical kitchen décor surrounded these abandoned edibles: hanging utensils, oven mitts, and generic paintings of steaming coffee.

Magnets clung to the refrigerator, some over pictures and notes. Brian leaned in to examine photos of an inconspicuous family with a burly, white-haired patriarch, a tiny, timid wife, and two smiling girls barely in their teens. A memo posted below the photos read: *The beer's bangin'—take one.*

D leaned in to look at the beer. Brian hissed, "Don't touch it!" and pointed to the note. She jerked back with a startled expression like she'd been about to touch hot lava.

The cupboards were all shut. A notepad on the counter next to the bread said: *Help yourself!* They decided this meant the cupboards were rigged to maim or murder them in some way, and they weren't going to test this hypothesis.

The open pantry was stocked with a treasure trove of cans and boxes. Grocery bags were balled together on the floor. No wires or guns gleamed in the lantern light, but they avoided it for now. Better to loot in the daylight after they knew the house was empty.

They moved into the living room, strolling over a circular rug past a pair of dirty loafers and a coatrack with a tan coat still clinging to it. They didn't bother to lift it in case this covered another gun.

Framed paintings of countryscapes adorned the wall. A mounted deer's head stared at them, its blank black eyes another eerie echo of the deer Brian had been forced to kill. An expansive leather sofa blocked the back half of the room from view. Old gossip and hunting magazines littered the coffee table in front of it. It still had water rings on it from sweating glasses. A remote sat atop one of the magazines beside another note:

> *Check out the DVD collection. Shame we won't ever watch them again.*

"DVDs!" D exclaimed under her breath. "Oh, I miss movies! Wonder what they got?"

She moved toward the shelf, but Brian held her in place with his arm. Although she was a grown woman, he might as well have been babysitting Becky all over again. He retrieved a loafer from the hallway and tossed it into the living room, aiming toward the DVD shelf. It landed with a gentle thump—until something sailed through the air, shattering the TV screen and rocking the DVD shelf. Crossbow bolts stuck out of them.

"Idiot." Louis glared at D. "Haven't you learned not to do what those stupid notes say? Bolts probably came outta the deer head. You'd have been just as dead if Brian hadn't stopped your ass."

D's eyes narrowed to crinkled slits and she pursed her purple lips, but Jonesy darted out from beneath the couch and sailed past them into the foyer. They rushed after him, but he streaked up the stairs before they could reach him and disappeared into the hallway. A sign taped on the wall next to the stairway read: *WATCH YOUR STEP.*

"Watch out above you." Brian gazed up at the stairs. "Jonesy made it up—if something's there, it's not down low."

The best solution was to crawl up the stairs on all fours. Brian, who was in front, caught the trigger first and pointed it out: a single, faintly glinting wire about five feet up from the top step. It disappeared into the walls on either side.

"This is *fucked up*," D hissed as they crawled onto the second floor beneath the trip wire. "Who the fuck does all this? Crazy trip wires and deer heads hidin' crossbows and shit—it's some messed-up version of those room-escape things!"

Louis shushed her. She clicked her tongue but kept quiet.

Three doors awaited them upstairs, two on the left and one on the right. An attic door hovered above them with a string dangling down. Brian prodded the first door on the left with his gun. He held his breath as it creaked open.

The room obviously belonged to one of the young girls from the photos on the fridge. Pictures of attractive men were taped on the wall above an immaculately made bed with a heart-shaped pillow. Photos clung to the sides of a mirror hanging behind a makeup-lined desk.

"Jonesy," he whispered, "are you in there?"

A white blur flew at him. He pressed his back to the hallway wall and leveled the revolver. Rattling chains and high-pitched cackling formed an ear-splitting dissonance as hands with gnarled nails strained for him.

Before he could pull the trigger, the Stalker's head exploded into a mist of blood and chunks of brain matter. It sank onto the ground, still and silent. Louis crawled next to Brian, the barrel of his PPK smoking. "See? I can still make do with one arm."

Brian peered into the room. Chains circled the Stalker's wrists and ankles, connecting to the wall inside the closet below a rack of clothes. A note was pinned to its grungy pink dress.

GOTCHA!

Brian glanced up at the smiling girls in the photos pinned to the mirror. His stomach lurched. When he encountered Stalkers, he forgot they had been people once—people with lives and loved ones. Killing them was necessary for his survival, might have even been a mercy to the minds trapped in those twisted bodies.

He shook his head and gave Louis an appreciative pat before they moved to the lone door on the right. Brian poked it with his gun. He retreated as it squeaked open—but it was empty. A shower curtain pulled to the side revealed an empty tub. Spilled makeup filled the sink and a plunger stuck out of the toilet. A note was taped around it.

Rats are coming up through the pipes. I set traps for them at the end of the hall.

That left one last room and the attic. Brian doubted Jonesy had magically levitated into the attic and closed the door behind him.

Bullet holes had torn through the last door on the left. They were high enough to have gone through someone's head and torso but not low enough to pierce a cat streaking into or from the room.

"Jonesy," D called, her voice wavering, "come here, baby. Mommy's here with her friends."

Nothing happened. After a minute or two, a blur of orange shot past Brian's face and made him gasp. But Jonesy didn't go to D. Something in the corner of the hall distracted him: a rat trap with a small chunk of moldy cheese in it. He nosed at it, hovering mere inches from the spring-loaded trigger.

"Jonesy!" D swatted the carpet. "Come here, you stupid cat! Ain't no rat in there!"

Jonesy lifted his head to look at her. His whiskers twitched as he mewed in reply.

If he sets it off, what'll happen?

The intriguing device distracted Jonesy once again. He grazed the trap for the briefest of seconds, testing the device with a ginger paw.

"Damn it, cat!"

Something sailed through the air past Brian and collided with Jonesy. He caterwauled and jumped at least a foot into the air before sprinting past them and down the stairs.

Brian exhaled and let his head flop onto the dingy brown carpet.

D asked Brian to retrieve the hoop earring she'd flung at Jonesy. She took it and crawled back down the hall. "We gonna bother with the attic?"

"Somethin' is wedged up in there," Louis said from behind her. "Hold the lantern up, D."

She obliged. Louis's sleek hair gleamed in the light. "Looks like a toothpick. The tip's barely stickin' out. We pull that rope, the pick comes loose and sets off a bomb or some shit to level the whole place."

"I don't know if it's worth it." Brian scratched his head with his free hand. "I don't want to get my hand blown off—or worse."

"I agree with Sunshine," D said. "Might be nothin' up there—nothin' but trouble."

"The food in the pantry is plenty." Louis handed D the lantern. "I've been on my hands and knees so long I'm startin' to feel like I'm in that porno of yours. Let's move."

They crawled down to the foot of the staircase. While they stretched and cracked their joints, Jonesy strutted up and mewed as if nothing had happened. D cursed at him, but he rubbed against her leg and curled his tail around it, warping her anger into affection.

Well played, Jonesy.

The back door in the kitchen was boarded shut and the couch would hold the front door. The only remaining variable was the attic, so they decided they might as well try to get some sleep. Brian and Louis went to dig out their sleeping bags while D withdrew a fluffy sweater from her backpack.

"You don't have a sleeping bag?" Brian asked.

She shook her head. "Nope. I use this here sweater as a pillow and my coat for a blanket. I throw it over my legs so my feets stay warm."

Brian handed her his sleeping bag. "Here, take it."

D tilted her head, her eyebrows knitting. "You sure, baby?"

Brian nodded. "I'll stay up and keep watch while you guys sleep."

"You sure you don't wanna snuggle up with coonass over there?"

"What?"

"It's slang for Cajun. In other words, she means me. If you want—" Louis swatted at Jonesy as the cat tried to pounce at his zipper. "Get, cat! I don't want your fur all over my shit!"

D snickered and looked back at Brian, gently clasping her hand over his. "Thanks for stayin' to help with Jonesy. I know you think I'm dumb—and you sure as shit think *Jonesy* is—but it means a lot to have someone understand how much that furry asshole means to me. You got a friend for life now—ain't no gettin' rid of me even if you want to!" She snuggled into Brian's sleeping bag with a contented sigh. "*Bon nwi*, boys!"

"*Bonne nuit*," Louis replied with an exhausted sigh.

After they settled in, Brian pulled out his journal and stared at it in the dim glow of the lantern, reexamining the phrases Louis had started teaching him back in the Drenco office building. They didn't have much to do back in the days when Louis was recuperating.

I wonder if any of this is real or if he's just fucking with me.

Something moved out of the corner of his eye. It leaped onto his journal, tearing into the pages. He gasped and looked down into Jonesy's bright-green eyes.

"Mrow?"

Brian exhaled and dragged a hand along Jonesy's back. He rubbed his head against Brian's hand encouragingly and spun in circles before settling onto Brian's journal.

Brian set his pencil aside and sighed. *I forgot when cats want attention they don't let you pay attention to anything but them.*

Still, Jonesy's soft fur and gentle purr soothed him. It comforted him to feel a heart beating against his leg and the tip of a tail gently twitching on his arm. It conjured memories of Rocky curled up in bed against him as he cried himself to sleep.

"You were worth all the hassle," he murmured into Jonesy's twitching ear, "*doux chat*."

WHEN MORNING CAME, they decided not to push their luck and left the attic alone. They looted the pantry instead, tying bags of groceries onto either end of a broken table leg. Grimes came running when they called her, so they climbed onto her and balanced the wooden post between them. D gave her canned apple slices for her troubles.

They left the house behind and traveled south down 425. A gentle breeze blew, rustling a few stubborn leaves still clinging to branches. The sun loomed high in the clear sky. Since the air was warmer during the day, Brian was comfortable in a lighter jacket and no headgear. The breeze rustling his hair refreshed him.

He shut his eyes and tilted his head back, enjoying the warmth of the sun on his skin. When he opened them, D was ahead of them. Her streamers flapped on the handlebars of the bicycle, twinkling like precious stones. Jonesy peered over the top of the basket, ears twitching as he watched the scenery drift by him.

One thing Brian noticed about Louisiana was how *flat* everything seemed. Aside from the occasional tree, their only vistas were long stretches of brittle grass and shrubs. He imagined it wasn't pretty to look at even in the warmer months. Kansas, Missouri, and Arkansas hadn't been much to look at, either.

The island won't be like this.

He pictured the island as an oasis in the middle of the desert, something untouched by the devastation of the pandemic and cut off from the world, from Stalkers and marauders, from the traumatic memories of his past and the haunting specter of a life not yet lived. Louis would be with him, and maybe D and Jonesy. Getting Grimes onto a boat and across the Gulf of Mexico wasn't something he wanted to ponder, so he abandoned this train of thought.

They pressed on, keeping west of the river to avoid the center of Baton Rouge. The flat fields and sparse trees now surrounded trailer parks and churches. On occasion, they passed a bucolic lawn with an old-fashioned plantation-style house beyond it. Brian tried to imagine he was in the past, but he assumed it wasn't a past D found pleasant to revisit.

Soon they entered something resembling a town again. The melting snow revealed every lost detail: blood stains and dried gore on the asphalt, discarded personal belongings, and remnants of decaying bodies. Parking lots contained shopping carts filled with rotten mush and cars with their doors askew or torn off altogether. The doors and windows of buildings were either broken or left halfway barricaded from attempts to shatter them. They encountered a military checkpoint, though it had been ransacked and stripped of anything useful.

"Ain't a tenth as bad as New Orleans," D murmured. "Not after Katrina. It was hell on earth." She kept her thoughts to herself, but Brian caught a pensive expression on her usually chipper face. Her slight Adam's apple bobbed, the only remnant of a past she couldn't keep hidden. It didn't bother Brian; sometimes he wanted to be a different person too.

They passed over a canal connecting to the Mississippi and continued south past a ransacked supercenter with a surprising number of cars still in the parking lot. A downed streetlight crushed a red pickup truck. Birds skittered around the wreckage, chirping as they searched for food.

Brian eased when the scenery finally shifted to the rural flatlands he was more accustomed to. They slowed from their trot and D let up on the pedals of her bike.

He looked through a set of binoculars they salvaged from a sporting goods store. A group of pale figures swarmed in a field to the east. He handed the binoculars to Louis. "Is that what I think it is, or am I finally losing it?"

Louis took the binoculars. His lips tensed into a frown. "*Shit*—they're flockin' together now. What the fuck are they doin' out in a field?"

"Give me my gun—" D waggled her fingers from beside them "—and please tell me you left the shells in it."

Reminded of the swarm in the grocery store, Brian didn't hesitate. He handed D her shotgun despite any objections Louis might have. She pumped it and draped it over her lap.

Grimes whinnied. Brian caught movement from the corner of his eye and kicked her into a gallop that made him slide in his seat. Cans and jars rattled and clanged as they swung in their bags.

Louis buried his face in Brian's back and slung his free arm around him as tightly as he could. "What the hell, Brian?!"

"It was a fucking distraction," Brian choked out. "There's more. Shoot, Louis! Behind us, to the left!"

D's shotgun boomed before Louis could fire. Jonesy yowled and streaked past Grimes in a mad dash. Brian wanted to check on D, but the group of Stalkers was converging and moving toward them from the field.

Something blocked the road ahead of them: a huge tree that had either been sawed down or struck by lightning. Grimes reared up and sent Brian and Louis tumbling over her rump. They crashed to the ground in a disoriented jumble alongside their scattered groceries.

Brian lifted his head from whatever it had landed on—it pounded with a horrible ache like a migraine. He grabbed it in an attempt to ease the pain. When he removed his hand, blood colored it in gleaming blotches.

Louis got to his knees and coughed, clutching his gut with his left arm while he leaned on his right elbow. Grassy clumps of dirt fell from him. Grimes stood in front of them, squealing and rearing into the air. A Stalker crawled toward them, positioned to pounce at her.

Brian tried to lift his gun, but his head felt heavy and his vision went hazy. A dark shadow moved into it; he recognized the explosive sound of D's shotgun. White blurs mingled with red, gushing in streaks. Grimes backed up, her tail swishing.

Several unidentifiable voices warped into static as Brian's vision darkened.

Chapter Seventeen: Evergreen

SOMEWHERE OUTSIDE BATON ROUGE, LOUISIANA

Brian's eyes fluttered open, sticky with sleep. Light beams above him illuminated swirling specks of dust. He felt beneath him with his hands, fingers curling into a soft linen sheet. A plush pillow supported his head. The room smelled sweet, like flowers.

Like Eva.

A woman stood directly in front of him wringing a cloth in a bowl of water. For a moment, he had the delirious thought he'd died and gone to heaven and she was some sort of angel.

When he glimpsed Louis and D sitting on either side of him, he realized he was still in this realm, for better or worse. The relief he experienced upon seeing them transitioned into hesitation. *Where are we? And who the hell is this woman?*

"That was a nasty head wound. You're lucky you didn't need stitches." She smiled at him. "Praise the Good God. We've seen enough death."

Louis gave her a furtive look. D smiled at Brian and reached for his hand. "You feelin' okay, baby? Me and Jonesy was worried about you."

He noticed the cat curled against his left arm. Jonesy meowed and pawed him. Brian reached to pet him, still disoriented. "What happened? Is everyone okay?"

"Aside from your head and a few scrapes on me, we're good." Louis's shoulder had been re-dressed. "You were out cold. D shot the Stalker that came up from the left, but then the group came up on our right. D tried to get you up on Grimes while I covered you, but there were too many of 'em."

"It was a damn miracle." D clasped her hands as if she was thanking God. "Fire from the heavens came down and burned most of them up. But a Stalker come out all up in smoke and grabbed onto one of our saviors. Took him down. A couple other men tried to help him, but the fire got them. They got burned pretty bad."

"We lost one of our Guardians," the woman at the foot of his bed said. "The others will need time to recuperate—far more than you, I suspect."

"Who are you?" Brian asked.

The auburn-haired woman gave him an enigmatic smile. "Just shepherds tending the flock. Don't worry yourself. You need to recover and start things on a new foot. It's a new day and a new year."

Brian tried to sit up, but he cried out when pain shot from his head into his neck. Louis leaned out to catch him by the shoulder and ease him down. "Careful. It's been cleaned and stitched, but it's still gotta scab up."

D nodded. "We ain't leavin' until you're better. They let us keep our guns and goodies. Grimes is out in a field with other horses—goats and sheep too. They fed her fresh apples. Boy, did she nicker up a storm. Ol' girl probably had a damned horsegasm!"

Brian coughed, pain radiating down his spine. The short woman moved up to him and pressed a cool cloth to his forehead. "I can tell you're strong-willed, dear, but you should allow yourself to be vulnerable." She patted his shoulder gently before retreating. "Your friends can stay with you. We'll come check on you when supper is ready."

She left the room, shutting the door behind her. Louis went to check the knob—it twisted freely. They weren't locked in.

"This is weird," Brian muttered. "They came out of nowhere and saved us? Took us with them?"

Louis sat and tugged on his sling. "We didn't have much choice. They're set up on some plantation straight outta *Gone with the Wind*. We're in an old slave cabin, but they live in somethin' they call the 'Big House.'"

"Not the five-star hotel of my choice," D said, "but it's better than nothin'. We got a roof over our heads, nice springy beds with clean sheets, and the Big House has a tub to bathe in. We even got outhouses."

"How many of them are there?" Brian was still worried about the King's men showing up or having installations spread throughout the country.

"Too many," Louis said. "Way too much ground to cover too—there's no way we could shoot our way outta here. Can't sneak out easy, either: they got a wooden fence set up with barbed wire. I'm not sure if it's meant to keep things out or in."

D folded her arms beneath her ample bosom. "They lost someone savin' us. I don't think they'd risk it if they were up to no good."

"Do they have weapons?" Brian asked. "Guards?"

"They tossed a Molotov on that group of Stalkers." D removed the cloth from Brian's head and stood. She dropped it into the bowl at the foot of the bed. "Big Mama said they don't believe in violence, but they had Guardians or some such because it was necessary."

Louis swept Brian's wet bangs out of his face. "We're okay for now. We need to keep our heads on straight, not fall into this commune crap. After you've healed up, we'll keep movin'."

"What if they come in here with guns?" Brian asked. "What if they're trying to make us lower our guard so they can take us down when we're at our most vulnerable?"

"Once you're up, we'll scour the plantation and all its odds and ends," Louis said. "I don't think they'll do anythin' yet. They want somethin' from us: to fatten us up for dinner, to use us as runners, to barter us to some other group. I don't know exactly what yet. Point is, they want us here, alive, healthy, and we're gonna make sure we leave that way."

Louis's confidence made Brian's worries melt away instantly. He relaxed into the pillow, his pain ebbing as a pleasant haziness overtook him. "Louis, I love you."

Louis shrugged, but a smile betrayed the nonchalance he tried to affect. "I know."

D returned to Brian with the wet cloth and placed it on his forehead. "Uh-oh—the drugs are kickin' in. You got the feelin' good stuff in you now."

"I love you too, D." Brian smiled, reminded of his mother by D's tender care.

D gave his cheek a little pat. "I love you too, baby. It ain't been long, but you love fast when you ain't got much left to love. You a good-hearted boy—maybe *too* good. Got to dose your love out real careful like medicine. People get high off that shit—" she tweaked his nose "—like you are right now."

Brian shut his eyes, too exhausted and dazed for conversation or regrets.

A STUTTERING SOUND like someone trying to start a car roused Brian. He opened his eyes and lifted his head, looking around the moonlit room. D was asleep in the chair to his left, her head back and her hands clasped in her lap. Her mouth hung wide open, emitting the awful racket that had woken him.

Louis sat on the other side, fiddling with his phone since it still held some charge. When he saw Brian was awake, he straightened in the chair and leaned forward. "I wondered how long you'd take it. I about shoved that rag in her mouth."

A light knock came from the door, so Brian called for them to enter. Louis's hand moved to the pistol in his thigh holster.

The middle-aged woman from earlier entered alongside a tall, thin man with dark skin. Brian assumed they were the heads of this group, whatever it was. "It's time for supper. We thought we'd check to see if you'd like to eat with us."

"Thanks." Brian sat up, assessing the state of his head. "I feel a lot better. I think I was just shaken up. Tired too. Uh, I don't think I caught your name, Miss..."

"I'm Marie. This is Jacque." She indicated her partner with a sweep of her hand. He smiled and waved at Brian. "We were both pastors before this happened. Different churches, different religions, but similar beliefs. I'm Catholic and Jacque—"

"Might as well be upfront and tell you, though most people don't take well to it due to second-rate Hollywood writing." Jacque's accent reminded Brian of a more dignified version of Louis's. "I was a Voodoo King."

"A *what*?" Brian asked, raising his voice.

D stirred in her seat. Jonesy hopped onto her lap, finishing what Brian had started.

"It sounds strange, I know—" Jacque's dark eyes twinkled "—but voodoo is a combination of Catholicism and African beliefs. It's not all curses and dolls with pins in them and animals with their throats slit."

Marie clasped her hands underneath her modest bosom and above the slight swell of her belly. "Now more than ever, we need to put aside our differences and seek to understand one another. Humanity has been torn apart and needs to reconnect."

"Come to dinner," Jacque said. "Bring your weapons if it makes you more comfortable. We'll give you the grand tour on the way."

Brian removed his blanket, only to notice he'd been stripped to his boxers. He quickly tugged it back up. Louis tossed a set of clean clothes onto his lap, smirking while D rubbed her eyes.

"I apologize." Marie kept smiling. "We wanted to make sure you had no other wounds for your safety and our own. Your clothes are outside drying."

Brian asked them all to leave so he could dress. He slid on the pair of khaki board shorts and pale blue button-down Louis had tossed at him, and wore clean socks underneath the boots he'd grabbed from the fairground. One already had a loose sole.

He brushed his hair out of his face, opened the door, and stepped out into the hazy orange Louisiana twilight. Louis, D, Jacque, and Marie were waiting for him.

"Woah," he murmured as he spun, surveying the lay of the land. He'd been sleeping in a small wooden cabin, one in a row of many. Several white buildings surrounded the wooden shacks, but the largest one—which had two spiral staircases leading up to the porch—impressed him most.

Marie swept an arm toward it, her long white sleeve draping. "That's the Big House. There's a separate building for the kitchen to prevent a fire hazard in the Big House, and a Greek revival privy. We have stables, a barn, a carriage house..."

Brian half tuned her out, focused on people drifting by dressed in white robes and black snow boots. They smiled and nodded at him, carrying baskets but no weapons—that he saw. The land was so expansive Brian could only glimpse one side of the fence. Dead cypress trees lined the property, gnarled and bent, but he imagined they were stunning once spring rolled around.

"Our guests usually stay in the cabins," Marie continued, "since they offer the most privacy. But we congregate in the Big House, which is where we bathe and sup. Would you like to see it before we meet for dinner?"

Brian glanced at D and Louis. D shrugged, distracted by Jonesy as he pounced after a bug of some type. Louis's brows quirked, his bronze skin glowing in the flattering vermilion light. His dark complexion and clothing made him stand out from the others.

"Lead away." Brian followed Marie and Jacque as they glided through the lawn. D and Louis joined him, one on each side. Jonesy trailed after them.

"This is Evergreen Plantation." Marie ascended one of the spiral staircases ahead of them. "I was acquainted with it before, but it's not one of Jacque's favorite locales."

"For obvious reasons," Jacque said. D arched her eyebrows and nodded with a tight frown.

"But the past is the past," Marie continued, waiting for the others to slip through the doorway, "and now it's our saving grace. The name itself,

'Evergreen,' implies a beauty that remains despite whatever ugliness might surround it. Come spring, the flowers will bloom and the grass will grow, and moss will drape over the cypress trees once again."

"We converted the carriage house into a greenhouse." The wooden floor creaked as Jacque strode along faded rugs. "We've managed to grow enough to feed a handful of animals and ourselves. When the ground softens, we'll create a garden."

"How many of you are there?" Brian admired the cozy ambiance of the building, which retained a dusty scent as most old things tended to. Although he still caught himself inspecting every dark corner for Stalkers, it was nice not to see any there.

"About twenty, twenty-five," Jacque answered, his voice a calming, deep baritone. "We let people come and go as they please."

"You don't get robbed?" Louis traced a finger along yellowed floral wallpaper, leaving a clean trail in the dust that clung to it. Brian followed it with his own finger, pulling it away dust-free.

Jacque pushed through swinging French doors into a spacious foyer. A short set of steps led up to a hall that diverged into northern and southern wings of the house. A Greek or Roman god stared down at them in marbled silence beneath an ornate chandelier.

"Many people are lost and frightened and just want a sense of security and companionship," Jacque said. "The few who wanted more were dispatched by the Guardians. As for the Turned, there weren't many in the winter, but now that the air has warmed and the snow is melting, they're returning."

"We appreciate you savin' us and all," D said, "but why'd you do it?"

Jacque smiled at her, baring faintly yellowed teeth. "We'll discuss it with you after you've eaten. You can take a bath after that and sleep for as long as you like. You needn't rush."

The serene setting lulled Brian into a dangerous state of contentment. Aside from his aching head and back, he felt more relaxed than he had since his brief foray into the skating rink and his game of cards with Louis.

Compelled by nostalgia, he reached for Louis's sleeve and gripped the crass fabric between his fingers. Louis glanced at him as they followed Marie, Jacque, and D across the spacious foyer.

Louis leaned close to Brian, his nose tickling Brian's hair. "Does it feel hinky to you?"

Brian shook his head, smiling as D threw back her head and laughed at something Jacque said. Brian's hand fell from Louis's sleeve, but Louis nudged Brian's side with his arm. "You're not all drugged out still, are you? You gonna tell Marie and Jacque you love 'em too? Propose to the cat?"

"Shut up." Brian shoved him back, but they dropped their conversation as Marie pushed open a pair of French doors. They followed Jacque and Marie into a dining room with a long table set for at least two-dozen people. The elaborate lace tablecloth made D squeal with delight.

"Sit wherever you like." Marie stretched her arm toward the table, hazel eyes twinkling in the light shining through several windows. Jonesy dashed underneath the table to swat at the lace. D scolded him and sat at the end closest to the door. Brian plopped alongside her with Louis on his other side.

D tried to pull her chair closer to the table, but it jerked against the floor with a grating screech. She looked around guiltily and tucked her napkin into the collar of her shirt. Louis left his alone, toying with the steak knife instead.

Brian examined his surroundings while D's toes tapped on the tiled floor. Copper pots and pans dangled in front of cream walls, joined by wooden shelves with knickknacks stored on them. A pale blue armoire painted with sunflowers encased prized dishes. The scent of burning wood from a fireplace in the next room filled the air. Laughter and clatter drifted in along with the smoke. Brian had been so conditioned to fear laughter he tensed as soon as he heard it.

"They'll be done soon," Marie said. "Jacque and I will help them bring things in. You can wait here."

As soon as they left, Louis slid his hand along Brian's back, digging under his shirt for the revolver tucked in his waistband. His fingers tapped the grip, anticipating the worst. D's hand moved to the shotgun across her lap, which she kept pointed at the doorway Marie and Jacque left through.

The chatter intensified as people approached. A shadow curved around the doorway. Louis's fingers tightened around the gun.

A parade of people filed in, carrying serving dishes filled with delectable smelling foods: steaming mounds of corn and green beans, some sort of stew, and roasted meat of anonymous origin. Marie and Jacque held up the rear, sitting at either head of the table once all the empty seats were filled. They bowed their heads and held out their hands. D's hand abandoned her shotgun for Brian's. Louis moved his hand from the revolver and laced his fingers with Brian's. The tight sensation was warm and reassuring.

"Thanks be to our Good God—" Marie placed her hands together in prayer "—for this bountiful meal and the health of our new guests."

"And thanks be to the three spirits for passing on the Good God's gifts. May there be merriment, satiation and peace, and rest for our fallen brother." Jacque opened his eyes. Everyone else followed, aside from Brian, D, and Louis, who'd been watching. It was like being at holiday dinners with extended family and their polite but unfamiliar smiles.

Before Brian grabbed any food, he watched to make sure everyone else ate and drank. Once they started eating, he helped himself. A young blonde woman caught his eye and smiled. He smiled back before shoveling a forkful of beans into his mouth.

The food was delicious, better than any restaurant his parents had ever taken him to. Better than anything he'd ever eaten, in fact. He shut his eyes in bliss, melting into his seat as the warm food slid down his throat.

"I don't know who the cook is, but bless you, baby!" D shook her head, making a satisfied "mmm" sound. "Used to be I had manners, but when it this good, I gots to get it in my mouth quick as I can!"

Something brushed Brian's leg. He lifted the tablecloth and saw an orange tail swishing next to it. The cat anticipated a meal of his own.

Louis wiped his mouth with a cloth napkin and dropped it to the table. "I'm not a big fan of religion or strangers. You're lettin' us stay here because you want somethin' from us: what is it?"

Jacque dabbed his mouth with his napkin. "We can have that conversation after you've eaten and washed—"

Louis struck the tabletop with his fist, startling everyone. "We'll have it *now*."

Jacque placed his napkin on the table and laced his fingers atop it, a focused expression on his congenial face. "We have weapons but no hands to wield them. We must replace those we lost. The others here aren't fighters. They are capable in other ways but not the violence that's necessary for survival."

"You got to pay mercenaries, you know." Louis leaned back in his chair with a prolonged creak. "What're you offerin'?"

"Louis-boy—" D glared at him past Brian "—they already saved our asses and lost someone in the process. They don't owe us nothin'!"

Louis angled toward D, resting his good arm over the back of Brian's chair. "You're sayin' *we* owe them for somethin' we didn't even ask for?"

Brian ate silently, not thrilled to be trapped in the middle of another argument.

D leaned back in her seat and set her cutlery down. "If they hadn't showed up, we woulda had to leave Brian behind. You wouldn't have stayed with him, let those things tear you both apart. All you care about is survivin'."

Louis made scratching noises on the plate with his knife. "Survivin' isn't everythin'—you gotta have a reason for it."

D's eyes brightened as if she'd conjured a revelatory thought. "You act like you in control, but only because there's somethin' inside you got no control over."

Rage radiated off Louis like a corona of heat. Brian reached under the table and gripped his knee, giving him a cautioning look. He whacked D's leg with his free hand.

"Jacque, Marie," Brian said to the two, who were watching with wary, rapt attention along with the other diners, "I don't know how much you have, but we need to get to New Orleans. Any supplies you can offer will help—especially fuel. Let us know what you want in return."

Louis snatched Brian's hand from his knee as Jacque leaned forward into the light. "We need to test your devotion to our cause—think of it as a rite of passage. If you retrieve three Turned for our Cleansing, we will send you on your way with whatever we're able to part with. Should you wish, you may return here after you find what you seek in New Orleans. In the meantime, feel free to stay until you are well enough to undertake the endeavor. You'll be bathed and fed and have beds to sleep in."

Brian cradled his hand in his lap, glancing at D. "What do you think, D?"

"I got to look for my brother, but I know we need those supplies. And as I said before—" her eyes narrowed and shifted to Louis "—we owe them."

"Say we grab these Stalkers for you." Louis started fiddling with his knife again. "Do we have to bring 'em back alive?"

Marie folded her hands together. "Yes. Otherwise, we cannot cleanse their souls. Their bodies need not be intact; we understand the difficulty catching one requires."

"Take some time to think about it," Jacque said. "Help us ease the suffering souls of the Turned and satisfy the Good God's pleas for peace. In return, you will have our sanctuary and hospitality."

Louis dropped his knife and stabbed his fork into a chunk of meat. "This 'Good God' any different than all the others?"

"The Good God is the same God most other religions believe in. It's just one of His many names," Jacque explained. "He's different things for different people."

"The Bible's nothin' more than a book of fairy tales. Heaven doesn't exist, and Nirvana can't be achieved—even the Happy Huntin' Grounds my ancestors believed in is a load of delusional bunk people conjured because they're scared of death." Louis dropped his fork onto the plate and pushed his chair back to stand. "I think I'll have that bath now."

"Fred will escort you and show you how to operate it." Despite Louis's challenging attitude, Jacque's voice lacked anger. A softness more akin to sympathy took its place.

Louis fixed his dusky eyes on Brian. "Come help me out—I'm workin' with one arm."

Brian dropped his napkin to the table and stood, unable to say no from the spotlight he'd been thrust in. "Uh, okay." He looked at D. "D—"

"I'm still stuffin' my face, Sunshine." D tapped her shotgun. "Me and Mr. Jones'll be okay. Come get me if you need me."

Brian and Louis followed Fred, who didn't look much older than either of them—and definitely not old enough to be cursed with "Fred" for a name. He led them down the hall in silence, shuffling his feet.

They entered the bathroom. An oil lantern flickered from a table in the center of the room, bathing the brick walls in a warm glow. The shelves on the wall were lined with hotel soaps and shampoos; loofahs dangled from hangers nearby. Between this wall and the table, a copper tub sat over a fire pit with a row of gallon trash cans next to it. Brian leaned over one and glimpsed his reflection in the glassy surface of still water.

"It gets hot, so try not to sit directly in the middle." Fred grabbed a grill lighter from the table and held it to the pile of wood and kindling. The embers sparked as it ignited. "When you're finished, use the bucket to scoop the water into the empty can so we can repurpose it. I'll leave you to it."

Fred gave them a furtive look before he shut the door behind him. Louis unbuttoned his shirt and pointed at the trash cans. "There's no way I'm liftin' that with one arm. Think you can manage?"

Brian went to a can and fumbled with it. He managed to lug it over to the tub and tip it in. A good deal of it splashed onto him, soaking most of his clothes.

Louis scoffed. "Guess you already got *your* bath." Brian ignored him and left to grab a loofah and a bar of Best Western soap, wanting but not wanting to watch him undress.

After Louis splashed into the water, Brian approached the tub. He dragged a stool next to it and sat, eyeing the puckered wound on Louis's shoulder blade. His finger traced it in a light, circular motion. "How does it feel?"

Louis flinched away and leaned forward. "Leave it alone. It's fine."

Brian grabbed the soap from his lap. "Are you mad at me?"

"Your new best friend tried to put words in my mouth and you didn't do a damn thing to defend me."

"It's hard to get a word in between the two of you." Brian cleared his throat. "You want this soap or not?"

Louis held out his hand. "The problem is you don't *try*."

Brian dropped the loofah and unwrapped soap into Louis's slick palm. "I *did* try: I tried to calm you down and change the subject."

Louis rubbed the soap into the loofah and scrubbed his chest. The suds dripped down in white streaks, making patterns on his skin like rain tracks on a window. "We can't waste time when we got places to go and things to do."

Brian tapped his fingers on his knees, not entirely sure why he was in here with Louis other than to be scolded by him. "We can leave tomorrow. I don't care. I thought you'd be happy they're willing to give us supplies."

"I'll be *happy* to get D where she needs to go so it's the two of us again." Louis slunk farther down into the tub, dragging the loofah under with him. "I want hot sun and cool water, no Stalkers, no people: just you and me."

"Well, it'll be easier to get a head start on that with supplies. All they want is three Stalkers: we can manage it. And if we can't make it to the island, we can come back here."

"Why? So you can keep eye-fuckin' that blonde chick, do some more of your awkward fumblin'?"

"What?" This random comment took Brian aback. "What girl are you talking about? The one who smiled at me during dinner?"

Louis shut his eyes and leaned his head back, dipping his hair into the water. "The only reason you're with me is because you lost everyone else. But now you got D, so if you wanna leave me, leave. I'll be fine on my own."

Brian gripped the rim of the tub, surprised by how much heat it conducted. "That tough guy act doesn't fool me anymore. Deep down, you're scared of something—something you can't control, like D said. But what *is* it?"

Louis's fingers curled over Brian's and squeezed hard. "When you get hungry, you hunt. But you go slow and quiet so you don't scare the prey off. Sometimes you get *so close,* but it senses you and runs off and you never end up catchin' it. I want fresh meat—even just a taste of it—but you never let me have it. I figured I'd back off so I wouldn't upset you, but I'm *starvin',* Brian."

Brian's fingers ached, but he couldn't move them.

I didn't read him wrong back in the RV. He wants me to acknowledge this tension between us, wants me to give into it. But if I do, there's no going back.

Brian wasn't ready for the last of his walls to crumble. "Are you still mad I wouldn't let you shoot those animals?"

"Don't play dumb with me." Louis lifted his head from the water. "It's so easy for you to make people want to take care of you, isn't it? You're young and cute and you know how to play it up, just like Eva. But you've been takin' advantage of me to make things easier on yourself—"

"Fuck you!" Brian stood, knocking the stool onto the ground. He wanted to leave, but the goading expression on Louis's face enraged Brian. He leaned across the tub and angled a fist at Louis's face. "You only make things harder on me, asshole! You think it was easy to take a bullet out of you, huh? I did it because I love you!"

Louis snatched Brian's wrist. "You only told me you loved me because you were high as a kite. You told D too—and she hasn't been watchin' your ass for a fuckin' month. And now you're just tryin' to save face. Everyone who ever told me they loved me was lyin' through their teeth, and you're no different."

"I'm not lying!" Tears brimmed beneath Brian's eyes, sparked by his frustration at Louis's glaringly incorrect misconception. "I lost my family, Rocky, then Eva—if I lost you too, I'd lose *everything.* Don't you get it? I can't—"

The door crashed open. Louis released Brian's hand, and Brian sprang up from the tub. He withdrew and aimed his revolver—but it was only D. She cringed and lifted her hands, one still curled around her shotgun. Jonesy streaked past her legs into the room. "Sorry—I knocked, but I guess you ain't heard me. You been in here a while, so I wanted to check on you..."

Louis stepped out of the tub and snatched a towel without bothering to wrap it around himself. He stalked out of the room, leaving a trail of water droplets on the granite floor.

D looked from the door to Brian. "What's up *his* fine ass?"

Brian shook his head and relaxed his fist. His nails left crescent impressions in his itching palm. "The, uh, trash cans have water in them. We have to use this bucket to scoop the water into the empty can, and..."

"Mm-hm." D went to grab the bucket while Brian flexed his hand. "You wanna give me the deets on just how close you two are?"

"We were childhood friends—"

"Friends might take baths together when they kids, but not when they grown-ass adults. Y'all taken it *way* past friends."

Brian sighed while D scooped the dirty water into the empty can. "It's complicated." He explained their history to D, from their falling out to Louis's gunshot wound. "Don't say anything to him, but he has a personality disorder—Borderline, I think."

"Explains a lot." D shook her head. "I was feelin' him out durin' supper. I knew he cared about more than survivin', but I wanted to get him to admit what. I got pretty close—pissed him off 'cause I think he figured out what I was up to. He's sharp, I'll give him that."

Brian helped D lug a fresh gallon of water over to the tub while the fire still burned beneath it. "Yeah, well, I figured out what else he wants—you don't have to spell it out to me."

"Don't tell me you don't want it too, 'cause I'll *know* your ass is lyin'. It don't take a psychic to see the signs: just a pair of eyes and two bits of sense."

"I can't tell him." Brian leaned against the tub, gripping the warm rim and remembering that thinly veiled speech about fulfilling Louis's appetite. "Taking it anywhere past where it is—even if I want to—would make losing him unbearable. I think I'd give up."

D tugged on the gauzy sleeves of her blouse. "You shouldn't rush into these things—especially with someone as volatile as Louis. Bein' as young as you are, it's hard to tell if it's love or lust. You should let it simmer, absorb the flavor of y'all's relationship. I don't know if givin' him a taste will fill him up or make him want more. You got to seriously consider what he's got wrong with him and if you can handle it."

Brian moved back to pour the water in and set the can beside the tub. "We've got too many other things to think about right now. Dealing with these people, for one thing. I don't think they're asking too much. Do you?"

Jonesy hopped atop the rim of the tub and nosed at the water, his tail flicking into D's face. As she started to answer Brian, Jonesy slipped into the tub. He jumped out and dashed past them, shaking and spraying them with water. D sighed and picked at her soaked shirt. "Baby, I'll come talk to you later. I wanna take my bath now that Jonesy's started it for me."

Brian nodded and gave her a quick hug before he followed Jonesy out. He hurried across the lawn toward his cabin. Others passed him, going about their business with ease. Some flashed him friendly smiles—he recognized one as the smile from dinner that had gotten him into trouble.

Brian tried to rush past the blonde girl, offering a strained smile, but she started talking to him. "Hi! You're new here, right? I saw you at dinner."

"Hi. Uh, yeah." Brian looked around. The last thing he wanted was for Louis to show up and see him talking to this smiling blonde girl. "I'm Brian."

"I'm Cecilia, but everyone calls me Cill." She stuck out her hand. He shook it, thinking she looked close to his age. "I want you to know we aren't cannibals or into crazy sex parties or anything weird like that. I'm a college student—well, I used to be. I was at LSU when everything went to shit. I managed to get out of there, but there were barricades and traffic was jam-packed, so I went to a shelter with my friends since I couldn't get home. I still don't know what happened to my parents, but Marie and Jacque were at the shelter and took us with them. We found this place pretty early—it was empty, and people weren't looting it 'cause it's just a bunch of old houses. No one cares about history anymore, right?"

"How'd you survive?" Brian dropped her small, lukewarm hand. "Didn't Stalkers come after you, or people?"

"My friend had a gun. He was one of the first to look after us here." She skirted his gaze, eyes shining. "He died saving you. But he believed in Jacque and Marie, and so do I."

Brian's gut tightened. He reached for her shoulder and squeezed. "I'm so sorry. There's no way I could ever thank him enough—all of them. I don't want to seem ungrateful... it's just that we've been through so much it's hard to trust anyone."

He glanced around, his eyes following a balding, older man in a robe as he passed by with a guileless smile.

"Are you looking for your friends?" Cecilia tucked a strand of straw-colored hair behind a pale ear. "That guy gave me a dirty look during dinner. It was an ugly look on such a handsome face." She sighed like this had been some sort of disappointment to her.

Brian scratched the back of his head, cringing when he was reminded of his wound. "Let's talk in my cabin. It's getting dark out."

She tilted her head with a sly smile. "You don't want him to see us together, do you?"

He snagged her arm and escorted her to his cabin. They sat on the bed, and he explained his history with D and Louis to her. He went further back, digging up buried memories of his lost family. There was a reason Cecilia was such an attentive listener.

"I majored in Sociology," she said. "I'm pretty good at feeling people out, so Marie and Jacque have me go around and talk to the new folks. I help 'weed out the bad seeds.' Of course, if someone's on edge, I don't go anywhere with them alone..." She drifted off, clear blue eyes flitting to the floor. Her shoulders slumped, and she tugged on the hem of her bunched-up robe. "Should we worry about your dark-eyed friend?"

A knock interrupted Brian's answer. He headed to the door, which didn't have a peephole. "Who's there?"

"Open the damn door. We need to talk."

Speak of the devil and he shall appear. Brian's hand hovered around the doorknob as he looked at Cecilia. She exhaled, a loose strand of hair fluttering around her face.

Brian opened the door to Louis. His wet hair clung to his face, but he'd dressed in a barely buttoned black shirt with the sleeves rolled up. The shirt tails dangled over tight jeans that were starting to thin over his knees. Brian wasn't used to seeing him in such casual, sparse clothing.

"You gonna stand there starin' at me all night or let me in?"

Brian stood aside. Louis's arched eyebrows furrowed when he spied Cecilia behind Brian. "Oh, it's you. From dinner."

She stood, smoothing her robe. "I'm Cecilia—"

"I don't care." Louis shoved past Brian and stepped into the cabin. "Don't you have an orgy to get back to or somethin'?"

She stalked up to Louis and looked him in the eye, though she had to look up since he was a good five inches taller than her. "Look, my friend didn't die so you could come here and act like a jackass—"

Louis leaned toward her, making her flinch. His eyes gleamed with menace as his lips lifted into a sneer. "If you don't want me here, go ahead and kick me out, *peeshwank.*"

Brian was about to step in and say something when he heard yet *another* knock at his door. He approached it and asked who was there, a touch of exasperation in his voice.

"It's D. I came to talk, as promised."

When Brian let D in, Cecilia took the opportunity to dart through the door. Brian shut it, eyes moving from Louis's self-satisfied grin to D's utterly befuddled expression.

"What the hell I miss? Who was that, and why'd she run outta here like she had a fire to put out?"

"You ain't gonna get any answers if you keep askin' questions." Louis leaned against the wall with his arms folded. "We don't need to waste time gettin' to know these fuckers, anyway."

D sat on the bed and massaged the balls of her feet. Water dripped from the coils of her wet hair. "You're in a rotten mood, *massisi*. You need to make like a hurdler and get over it."

"*You* need to learn when to keep your big mouth shut—"

"Louis," Brian cut in before D's open mouth could form a reply, "you don't have to help us. D and I can do it alone. You can stay behind or...or leave if you want. I don't care." He pressed his lips together, knowing this was a mistake as soon as it came out of his mouth.

Louis was usually quick with comebacks, but this took him aback. He caressed the elbow of his right arm for a moment, trying to buy time. "Well, I guess I shouldn't care if you go get yourself killed, then. This is your fool's errand, so have at it."

D threw back her head with a sharp laugh. "Boy, *please*—you a lot easier to read than you think."

Louis's guilty expression made him look like a child who'd been caught in the middle of some naughty act. "Butt out, D: you're the reason we got mixed up in this shit, anyway. I wanted to get while the gettin' was good. But no, you got a guilty conscience over somethin' they did on their own—"

"Just stop this shit and help us before I knock your skinny ass out." D stood and approached Louis. She towered over him as if daring him to do something about it.

Louis narrowed his eyes and clenched his left fist—but it seemed to remind him his other arm was impaired. He sighed and slunk down with his back against the wall, running his hand through his bangs. "What's the fuckin' plan then?"

Brian exhaled, his shoulders slumping. "We should look for Stalkers in places where large groups will be less likely—so no grocery stores, hospitals, or anything like that. We can cut their hands off, rip their lower jaws away so they can't bite. We have to make sure we're covered—we can't have anything exposed since we'll be getting closer to them than normal. One of us can lure them out while the other two ambush them. You should be the bait, Louis, since your arm—"

"That's fine. I see how it is." Louis looked outright offended. "You're ready to get rid of me now that you got D and these crazy cult assholes."

A scorching surge of adrenaline encouraged Brian to step toward him and roll up his right sleeve. "I've had it with this childish bullshit of yours—"

"Woah, woah!" D moved between them, physically blocking their view of one another. "I know tempers are hot right now, but let's cool this shit off—y'all still friends, right?"

Louis stepped aside and gave Brian his most withering, condescending look, like he was some haughty British aristocrat. "That's up to him." He stalked out of the room and slammed the door behind him.

Brian flopped back in the bed, wincing as his injured head hit the pillow. He rubbed his eyes until he saw kaleidoscope-style patterns, replaying his dialogue with Louis in the bathroom so he could figure out where it had gone so wrong.

"You wanna talk about it?" D asked.

"Not now. I'm exhausted."

"As my moman used to say, 'Love is blind, and lust makes you cross-eyed.'" D tugged at a sheer lavender sleeve. "They got me set up next to you, so holler if you need me. Sweet dreams, Sunshine." She gave him a faint smile before she shut the door, briefly letting the chirp of crickets into the cabin.

Brian hadn't gotten a bath yet, but the thought of Louis in that damn tub was enough to keep him in bed.

The ache returned, throbbing harder than ever.

Chapter Eighteen: Storm Clouds

EDGARD, LOUISIANA

Evergreen Plantation
Morning

They accepted Jacque and Marie's offer in the morning. In exchange for the three "Turned," they would receive a saddle with saddlebags and as much fuel, food, and water as they could stuff into them.

The offer was too good to pass up, even for Louis. The folks at the plantation also had some equipment a prison guard had brought with him, along with some football gear from a player at ULA. It provided decent coverage, but they all looked ridiculous when they put it on.

Brian was none too happy about sitting in front of a sulky, bulky Louis, but he felt worse for D, who had to pedal in the riot gear and the Louisiana sun. Her hair poked out from the helmet in a shape that reminded Brian of an inverse mushroom.

Their destination was a golf course fifteen minutes from the plantation but still isolated from any large cities. Withered brown weeds surrounded bright turf-grass beneath a clear sky streaked with wispy clouds. A scenic lake glittered alongside a driving range with golf balls still scattered on the rolling green hills. Two large buildings, one with metal shutters, connected to the parking lot they were currently in. Grimes wandered in search of real grass after discovering the turf-grass wasn't edible.

Louis put his hand on his hip. "We look like a buncha fuckin' jackasses."

"It ain't the best I ever looked—" D straightened her helmet "—but I feel a whole lot safer in this get-up."

Brian fingered a machete in his belt loop. D had also borrowed one so they could dismember Stalkers instead of killing them.

D spied his antsy fingers. "You get one arm, I'll get the other. If it comes up snappin', we hack at its jaw or strap a muzzle on it. Our gloves should take a nick or two."

First, they explored the interiors of the buildings—but aside from some golf paraphernalia like clubs, tees, and balls, they didn't find anything noteworthy. No Stalkers. They gravitated toward the dark; if any were here, they'd be in the garage.

Louis approached the open garage while the others held back. "You ready?"

Brian and D nodded. Louis banged on the metal shutter with his fist. "Hey, motherfuckers, got any arms to spare? I'm short one."

Brian chortled at this poor joke despite his nerves. Louis said "motherfucker" with an emphatic "uh" at the end instead of "er," which always tickled Brian.

D stood ready with the machete as Louis stepped back, the PPK clenched in his hand. Nothing moved. They lowered their machetes and glanced at one another while Louis fidgeted with the strap of the football helmet, scowling.

Brian grabbed a flashlight from his belt loop and clicked it on, aiming into the dim garage. The circle of light illuminated a row of golf carts on a fractured concrete floor. Some were missing, but Brian imagined they didn't make good getaway vehicles because of their slow speed and poor tread.

Something in one of the gaps looked out of place. *A face?*

It moved toward him in a blur. He yelled a succession of every curse word he knew and dodged left, swinging the machete in a downward motion until the blade sank into decaying flesh and stopped. He'd hit bone.

Brian pressed his foot against the body and tried to tug the machete free. He managed with a rough jerk as a hand clawed for his face. He sliced again, and the hand disappeared.

"I got you, baby!" D swung from the other side. The confused Stalker twisted toward her, snapping like a rabid dog.

A bullet exploded through the Stalker's knee and sent it to the ground. D walloped at the other hand, separating it with two adrenaline-charged whacks. It rolled from side to side on its stomach, unable to crawl. Brian kneeled over it and strapped the muzzle over gnashing teeth.

D retreated, huffing behind her helmet. "Should we...get the feet too?"

Brian nodded. "Let's do it." They worked in unison, each chopping at one crusty, sore-covered foot. He still felt a degree of guilt and disgust over what he was doing. The moist noises and the splashes of blood sailing into the air disturbed him most of all—and that it still laughed while they hacked into it as if it couldn't stop itself.

Brian and D tied the Stalker's arms behind its back, leaving a length of rope to drag it with. He looked around, noticing Louis had disappeared.

He shot it, then what?

D stood, her hands on her knees as she struggled for air. "Fuck! Tell me again why we agreed to this shit."

"Where's Louis?"

"Fuck if I know!" She gasped, her breaths ragged. "I ain't had a workout like that in years! I'm burnin' up in here!"

Brian glanced away from the wriggling Stalker. The muzzle muffled quiet giggles. Now that he wasn't in mortal danger, Brian noticed the Stalker wore tattered remnants of the preppy golfing attire he loathed. "Are you okay, D?"

"Sure am, Sunshine. I was more worried about you. How you holdin' up?"

Brian's heart raced, and his head throbbed. The tight pants and padding strapped to him made him feel awkward and sticky. "Fine. No injuries." He glanced down at the dripping machete in his hand and scrunched his nose.

"You handled yourself pretty good." D straightened and grabbed her lower back with a light crack. "Nasty mother jumped out so fast I wasn't sure what I was seein'. You got good reflexes, thank goodness! Wonder if it knew we was tryin' to distract it somehow, didn't fall for it?"

The purr of a motor emerged from the garage. Louis emerged behind the wheel of a golf cart. Now he *really* looked ridiculous. "Load that thing up and let's haul ass. I wanna change outta this shit—I'm sweatin' like a sinner in church."

They dragged the restrained Stalker to the rear of the cart, heaved it onto the seat, and tied it to the metal bars on either side. It struggled a little at first but soon calmed and quieted. Its eyes locked on Brian's, a slight wheeze seeping through its muzzle like *eee eee eee.*

Are they aware but unable to communicate? If they know they're doing all these awful things but they can't stop it...

Even if there is someone in there, they're still trying to kill me. Better them than me.

They headed back to unload their foul cargo, eager to return to the delusion of normal surroundings.

1/15

We've been at Evergreen for a couple of weeks now. The people here call themselves the "Blanc et Noir," or B.E.N. for short. It means "black and white," but I'm not sure if it's because of Jacque and Marie or because religion has different angles or whatever.

Life is simple here. We wake up, eat breakfast, tend to the animals and greenhouse, and scavenge outside the plantation. Then we come back, eat dinner, take a bath every few nights, and retire to our cabins. There are communal activities in the Big House that D always goes to. I only go if she or Cill drag me. Lou spends most of his time sulking in his cabin or moodily prowling the grounds. I bet he's trying to find some evidence of insidious goings-on so he can convince us to leave.

D would love to come back here, but he's set on that island. Both seem appealing in different ways. If I stay, I have a roof over my head, a bed, food and water, even a tub to bathe in—and I'd have a new family. But if I go to the island with Lou, we can live how we want and not have to help other people or deal with them. Plus, Louis is almost an entirely different person when the two of us are alone...

Ugh. If I start writing about that, it'll turn into an essay. Let's just say the river runs both ways. As much as you might love someone, you can hate them just as much. He tolerates D, but he treats poor Cill like she doesn't exist. I'm not oblivious—I know why. But that's a really awkward conversation to have, and I'm not ready to have it yet. Besides, he needs to learn how to act like an adult and not some spoiled child. The best things are worth waiting for, right?

1/20

We got the other two Stalkers from a gas station and a library. I'm glad that's over with. It seems so easy on paper, but trust me, it was not fun.

Now they're getting ready for the Cleansing. In the meantime, I've been watching the Stalkers we caught. The first one we captured is skinnier now. Almost like a skeleton with skin. I guess if they don't eat, they'll die eventually. Good to know.

I keep telling myself they're animals, not people—but are people really any better?

Speaking of animals, Jonesy ran off or something. D hasn't seen him for the past day or so. Louis says he's sowing his oats, but D thinks Louis finally got tired of Jonesy and took out his aggression on him. As stupid as he's being right now, I still don't think he'd go that far. But D's convinced herself and there's no unconvincing her.

P.S. You know why I never sign off on these? I hate my initials. Nana once bought me a shirt that said "I ♥ BJ" on it and my dad made me wear it when we'd visit them. A. Why would I wear a shirt boasting how much I love myself? And B. I'd never go around telling the world how much I loved the other kind of BJs. Which I'm sure are amazing, but I couldn't say. I guess that's one of the many things I should experience before I get shot or bitten, ha ha ha...

1/23

So the Cleansing is today. I'm kinda curious what it's all about. I'm supposed to go meet D and Cecilia. I'm still on the outs with Lou, though... Well, fuck him. Or not.

Cecilia told me: "A sheep spends its life fearing the wolves only to be eaten by the shepherd." She's obviously implying Louis is the shepherd, but unless he gets infected (not gonna happen, better not happen), he won't eat me.

Even if he does have an appetite, I'm not on the menu.

Brian abandoned his rambling train of thought and headed to D's cabin to meet her and Cecilia. No one answered his knocks, so he went a few cabins down to try Louis's.

Raised voices mingled behind the door. Louis's distinct accent was among them, nearly indecipherable because it intensified when he was aggravated. Brian recognized the other two as D and Cecilia's.

He cracked the door open to see what was going on. Cecilia sat on the bed in her robe, clutching another robe on her lap. D was in hers as well, but Louis wore black as usual. D thrust an accusing finger in Louis's face. "If you didn't have nothin' to do with it, where is he?"

Louis swatted D's arm away. "Fuck if I know—I ain't your cat's keeper!"

"If he's dead," D started to say, her eyes flaring with fury—but she showed something rare for her: restraint.

It didn't matter; Louis knew what she'd been about to say. "I'd like to see you try. Anyway, if he shows up dead, who's to say some Stalker didn't catch him? Or a *cocodrie*? Hell, you might never find a body at that rate!"

Cecilia stood beside D with a flourish of her robe. "You took out your anger on him instead of us, right? You're on edge, suppressing something you're scared to let out."

Louis took a step toward her. "You run your mouth like this 'cause your daddy never slapped you? My père used to slap me and my mère around—he'd belt me too. You might need some discipline to keep you in line."

Cecilia stared at him, stunned. Brian knew he needed to step in before this escalated.

The door creaked as Brian pushed it open. All eyes moved to him. The fire in Louis's eyes dulled and he stepped back from Cecilia.

His gaze returned to D. "You're gonna feel fuckin' stupid when that damn cat comes back. It's not fair to gang up on me when I've done nothin' wrong." His eyes flashed to Brian. "I know you heard some of that—and once again, you don't dare stick a foot in it. I've been with you almost since the beginnin', but you're lettin' two women you just fuckin' met accuse me of some shit you *know* I didn't do. Or do you think I did it because of what happened with your dog? Have you been holdin' it over my head all this time? Is that why you keep your guard up with me?"

Guilt plunged through Brian's heart like a knife.

Louis twisted it more. "You're the only person I got in this godforsaken world and I can't even trust you to have my back!"

"Louis, calm down—" Brian reached for him, but Louis snatched his wrist away.

"I know you think you got some kinda magical effect on me, but you're makin' this shit worse. You really think you can avoid me for weeks and things'll go back to how they were? They won't. There's too much out in the air now for us to clear it."

The hard edge to his words snapped Brian out of his guilt-soaked fog. He had to remind himself that Louis had a personality disorder, that he wasn't like everyone else—that he wasn't as logical and detached as Brian once thought. In fact, he'd come to see Louis as quite the opposite of the image he projected.

Cecilia's tiny but firm voice cut the taut silence: "Louis, I think you should let go of him and have some time to yourself. We'll all go to the Cleansing—"

"Stay out of it, bitch."

Brian decked Louis square in the face. His knuckles stung, skinned by the impact, and his skin burned as if his blood was boiling beneath it.

Louis caught his balance and clutched his mouth. His eyes might as well have been blazing with hellfire. He dragged a finger through the blood trickling from his nose and pressed it between his lips, sucking. "You drew blood a second time, *enculé*."

Brian didn't have time to wonder what this meant—a weight on his chest knocked him onto the bed and hot pressure crushed his waist. A blur of beige flew at his face, slamming into the mattress next to his ear with an audible *whoosh*. Cecilia cried out for Louis to stop as he clenched Brian's collar in his fist and tore down the length of his shirt. The buttons flew into the air and clattered to the ground.

"What the hell are you doing? Snap out of it!" Brian smacked Louis hard on his scarred cheek, leaving a flushed print in the shape of his hand.

Louis's constricted pupils dilated. His brows knit above them as if he'd just realized what he was doing—or about to do. When a trickle of blood entered the cranny between his lips, he pressed them together. Heavy breaths puffed from his flared nostrils.

D's arms snaked around Louis's torso to pull him off Brian. Louis jerked out of her grip and wiped his nose with his good arm, sniffing. His furious expression shifted to reflect the confusion swirling within Brian. Before anyone could say anything, he shoved past D and stamped through the door into the murky Louisiana twilight.

Brian's head flopped back onto the bed. He stared at the ceiling, trying to catch his breath and process what had happened.

"You okay, baby?" D fumbled for buttons that weren't there. "I knew *somethin'* physical had to happen, but I didn't think it'd be like that."

"I don't know." Brian flexed his bloodstained knuckles.

"We should go to the Cleansing." Cecilia smoothed her hair, still trembling from the residual tension of the encounter. "Let's enjoy the rest of our time together since you're leaving tomorrow."

"I'm not leavin' 'til I know what happened to my cat," D said. "If Louis did somethin' to him, I'll—"

"If he didn't, we all owe him an apology," Brian murmured, sitting up. "He owes us all one for being a dick, but you both accused him of murder and I didn't speak up for him."

"He'd never let us live that shit down," D said. "Especially you, Sunshine. He'll hold it over your head like mistletoe on Christmas—'cept the only kinda kiss he'd get is a kiss with a fist."

"I forgot Christmas existed." Brian took the white robe Cecilia handed him and threw it over his busted shirt. He felt like he should break into carols and start ringing a bell. "The last Christmas I remember was after my mom got attacked. God, everything's changed so *much* since then. I know they're gone, but sometimes I forget they're never coming back ..."

D and Cecilia seemed to sense the melancholy mood he'd descended into. They grabbed his arms and strolled to the lawn with him in silence.

Thick gray clouds painted the canvas of the sky. Moist air soaked into his skin as he approached a courtyard once filled with patterned hedges. The three captive Stalkers took their place, tied to a series of fence posts. Marie and Jacque stood in front of them, facing their congregation. A variety of shapes and faces formed it, ranging in age from children to the elderly. Short, tall, wide, thin—blue, green, and brown eyes flitted to Brian and the others, lips lifting into accepting smiles.

It wasn't hard to spot what he'd been scanning for: the lone dark spot in a sea of white.

Marie clasped her hands in front of her, a smile on her dignified face. "Thank you all for attending our third Cleansing. Now we may lay bare our transgressions before our brethren and bid farewell to these cursed souls before us. Is there anything any of you would like to say?"

D lifted her hand. "Any of you seen my cat yet?"

The mundane question seemed out of place in the pseudo-ritualistic setting. Most of the congregation shook their heads or shrugged.

D's shoulders slumped. "Shoot. He's the only thing I got after I lost my man..."

"Tell us about him, D." Marie gave D an encouraging smile. "You may find it liberates you from the weight you carry."

D sighed long and deep, deliberating over what she wanted to reveal. Even Brian didn't know much about her past aside from her time spent in New Orleans with her brother. She talked about a lot of trivial topics—movies, especially horror, were a favorite—but she remained tight-lipped when it came to her personal issues. As she liked to say, "I keep my baggage zipped up."

"I might as well start from the beginning. My name, as most of you know, is Dionne Etienne. I come up from New Orleans where I lived with my brother. I left my popa and moman because they had trouble acceptin' me for who I was. I still remember Moman's Sunday dress and her straw hat with the little purple flowers. I used to dress up in them and run around the house like a little fool. Put on her heels too—didn't know how to run in 'em, so I fell into a table and that put a stop to that.

"Popa didn't take to the dressin' up. When I was sixteen, he told me he didn't want no nancy livin' in his house, so he threw me out. Moman tried to convince him to let me stay so long as I prayed for help and tried to change my ways. They couldn't see I was tryin' to change for myself, not them, so I took up with my brother, Antoine. He was the only person who accepted me the way I was. That's why I got to find him. We made it through Katrina together, and I know he made it through this too."

A drop of rain plopped onto Brian's arm. Another rolled down D's cheek. "I met my man, Gustave, durin' Katrina—kinda ironic, since Gustave was a hurricane too. Anyway, he been a friend of my brother's since high school. He come over to help board up for Katrina. I was in awe of his muscles and his big, bright smile. When he smiled, you couldn't help but smile with him. He was the nicest man you ever met, handy with tools, and well read. Once the storm came, we got to talkin' books. I coulda sat there listenin' to him for hours with that Barry White voice of his. Then we got to talkin' about our families, life, love...everything we could think to talk about.

"I could tell Gustave was givin' me the sweet-eye. I tried to play it cool even though I felt the flutters every time I was in a room with him. All the meanwhile, that storm come in—not too bad, at first. We been through a few, thought it'd be just another bump in the road. Then it started to sound like dinosaurs roarin' outside. The ground shook somethin' awful, and rain bounced off the tin roof like bullets. I got scared, so I told Gustave, 'Gus, we don't know each other too well yet, but we weatherin' this storm together, so I might as well see if you can weather another one with me.' He told me he could take anythin' that got thrown at him, so I blurted out, 'What about a woman tryin' to get out a man's body?' You know what he said? 'You fall in love with a soul, not a body.' To this day, I ain't never heard no sweeter words."

She threaded her fingers together and looked up to the darkened sky, trying to hold back tears. Eventually, her shaking hands reached for Cecilia and Brian's. "Me and Gus was together over ten years after that storm. We made it through a few others, but this the one that done him in. One of those Turned come at me out a car when we was tryin' to make it outta Monroe. He got between us and shot it, but it scratched him on the arm. We knew it was gonna turn him. He told me, 'D, I can die happy knowin' we shared a love no one else will ever share.' When I aimed the gun at him, all I could think about was how much I'd miss him. I aimed at myself instead, but he snatched it away and yelled at me, tellin' me I had to live on for him, else he'd haunt me as a spirit in this world or the next. He was stubborn to the end—always had to have his own way. So I...I aimed the gun at him. I tried to think up every memory I could of our time together, every argument, every laugh, every smile we shared and the lovin' glint in his eyes. That glint was there when I told him I loved him one last time and pulled the trigger. It gone away right in front of me, flyin' away with his soul up to heaven."

D's impressive composure crumbled under the weight of her agony. Cecilia and Brian embraced her. She sobbed and wailed, her sturdy body quaking against them. The entire group converged on them in a surreal circle of white bodies.

"Thank you for sharing with us, D," Marie said within the comforting circle. "I know it wasn't easy for you, but it's best not to suffer grief on your own. Don't bottle your feelings up—let them fly so you have room for new ones."

D's choked sobs and gasps died into dry wheezes and sniffles. The group backed away to give her space. She rubbed her eyes, smearing mascara in streaks. "I'm sorry I went and blubbered all over y'all. I ain't told anyone about how I lost Gus until now."

"As long as we're here, you always have a home to return to and a family who will accept you." Jacque gripped D's shoulders. "All of us have lost someone. Some have lost their entire families. But now that we're together, we can share in each other's joy and suffering all the same."

D nodded and managed a shaky smile. Wanting to spare her another emotional scene, Jacque and Marie left her with consolatory embraces and went over to the helpless Stalkers to proceed with the Cleansing. A light drizzle of rain filled the air with a pleasant earthen scent.

Brian fixated on the scabs forming on his knuckles. He thought back to their first dinner here and how he'd held D's hand in his left hand, same as now, and Louis's in his right. They'd been unified then, weathering the storm together.

Jacque stood a pace ahead of Marie, positioned in front of the Stalkers. He sprinkled powder from a small cloth bag onto the ground in some sort of pattern. A thin older woman went behind the posts the Stalkers were tied to, setting a candle atop each and lighting them with a match. Behind her, a stocky middle-aged man showered ground green herb over the bodies of the writhing Stalkers.

Jacque chanted something in an unfamiliar language while his assistants dropped lit matches onto the herb-covered Stalkers. The dry vegetation caught aflame, but the Stalkers didn't react to it. Three people stood by with buckets filled with water from the well, waiting to pour it on the blazing Stalkers. The rain intensified, doing most of their work for them.

The rancid sweetness of burning meat filled the air and brought tears to Brian's eyes. Some people coughed. Others gagged.

Drums pounded while Jacque's frenzied speech continued. Thunder rumbled, low and ominous. The repugnant smell intensified as taut skin cracked and the fat beneath it popped.

Brian was on the verge of leaving when D squeezed his hand and let out an excited little gasp. "Jonesy!"

Sure enough, an orange cat emerged from a thicket of shrubbery. He jogged toward them, nearly bouncing as he let out a high-pitched meow.

D bent to her knees. Jonesy rubbed along them, his tail straight up as a low purr thrummed in his chest. His fur was covered in thistles and twigs. "What kinda adventure you been on, asshole? You smelled meat, didn't you? Or maybe you wanted to—" Jonesy dashed away from her and headed for the Big House, streaking onto the covered porch to escape the storm. D's lips stretched into a broad grin. "—get out the rain."

Brian was relieved to see D smile again, and Jonesy too, but his stomach lurched with guilt—and from the stench lingering in the air.

"I know what you're thinkin'." D stared off into the distance as rain drenched her robe. "Never thought the day would come when I'd be apologizin' to *his* ass."

"Go on—we'll see you at supper." Cecilia leaned close to Brian and whispered, "Even though Marie and Jacque think the rain is a sign the Good God is pleased, the rest of us are *miserable*. We'll leave as soon as we can."

Brian headed for his cabin, hoping his curdling stomach would settle in time for supper. He twisted the doorknob and cracked the door open, pausing when he spied a black object reclining on his bed.

Louis lifted his glasses to reveal the beginnings of a black eye and a nasty bruise on the bridge of his nose. "I'll be lucky if you didn't leave another scar on my face. Impressive."

Brian stepped inside and shut the door. He stripped the wet robe from his body and tossed it to the floor. "I'm glad you're here: I wanted to talk to you."

Louis set his sunglasses on the bedside table and stood. He approached Brian and tugged on both sides of his open shirt. "I really busted this, didn't I? I'm sorry... I don't know what came over me."

Brian glanced down at the pitiful threads that poked out opposite his buttonholes. "Well, if we get to that island, I can get by without shirts."

When he looked up, Louis was staring at him intently, his mouth screwed to the side like he was chewing on the inside of his cheek. "You can always wear mine if you run out."

Brian laughed. "All your shirts are black, and I don't think I'd pull them off half as well as you do."

Louis let go of Brian's ruined shirt. "Don't sell yourself short."

An awkward silence engulfed them as they struggled with what they wanted to say. Lightning flashed outside the window, followed by a sharp crack like the fireworks Spike had set off what felt like a lifetime ago. The rain pattering atop the rooftop strengthened into a persistent downpour.

Brian cleared his throat. "Jonesy came back. I never thought you did anything to him, but you were right—I should've stood up for you."

Louis sat on the foot of the bed, his hands hanging over his knees. He sighed and looked down at the floor, his eyes hidden by his dangling bangs. "I let my temper get the best of me. I shouldn't have said that stuff to you. Cecilia, either."

Brian sat beside him, the springs squeaking beneath his weight. "You could always tell them what you told me. They try not to be judgmental." He lifted his hand so it hovered behind Louis's back, conducting the heat of his body through his damp shirt.

As if sensing Brian's hand, Louis leaned back and closed the distance between them. "But they'll never understand me like you do. You're the only person who ever put up with my bullshit long enough to get past it— the only person who ever called me out for it and tried to help me talk about it."

Brian's hand rested against the small of Louis's back. "You've helped me too. More than you can ever know."

Outside, lightning continued to flash. Rain beat against the roof.

Louis looked at his knees. He scratched the thin fabric, picking at the fraying threads with his short nails. "I want to get away from it all. My papère, Eva—even here, I'm reminded of them. Cecilia and Eva woulda been best friends: they're both sharp as a whip but they hide it behind a Goody Two-shoes act."

He still talks about her like she's alive. It hasn't sunk in for him yet.

Sometimes I forget Becks is gone too. It's easier to forget something when it's painful to remember.

Brian swirled his hand in light circles against Louis's back. "I'm sorry." He let it linger, stroking with his thumb. "You really think the island will help?"

Louis's hand moved to grip Brian's thigh. "I want it more than ever. Ever since I've been here, my head's gone all murky. I feel angry all the time. I can't deal with all these people—but worst of all, I couldn't deal with you not bein' with me. You kept me in check, calmed me down. You did more for me than my meds ever did."

Brian glanced at the fingers tapping his outer thigh. "Even though I've been surrounded by people here, I felt lonelier than ever. Sometimes I'd close myself off in my cabin and listen to music that would make me cry. I *wanted* to. I wanted to give in and feel sorry for myself. The part of me I inherited from my dad was taking over. Being around you kept my depression from getting the best of me. You were always so driven, so bold and confident..."

"Not really." Louis's hand tightened around Brian's thigh. "I only wanted to look like I was. I'm not really anythin', I think. Lately, all I am is wrapped up in you. It's been drivin' me nuts—that damn thing D was talkin' about that I couldn't control. When you said you loved me, I felt...I dunno. Validated? I think it was the first time someone said that to me and I believed it. I almost didn't want to because I didn't know how to handle it."

Louis caressed Brian's cheek with his other hand, stroking it as he searched Brian's eyes. Despite the return of the flutters and tingles that plagued him, Brian couldn't look away from those magnetic eyes.

"I don't think I'd ever *really* felt it before, so I didn't know what it was. But..." Louis blew air through his lips, making the tips of his bangs flutter. He looked up at the ceiling, a flush coloring his cheeks. When his eyes met Brian's, he exhaled and blurted out, "I'minlovewithyou" in one rushed breath. At first, Brian thought he'd said some new slang term, but once he processed it—latching onto the "in" and "with," specifically—he couldn't slow his racing pulse. He couldn't control the high arch of his eyebrows, force his eyes from Louis's, or get a reply through his gaping lips. His mind couldn't even put the words swirling through it into a sensible order: "me," "long," "serious," "time," "too," "you."

When the heat vanished from his thigh and cheek, the charged air of anticipation fizzled into disappointment.

Louis bolted from the bed, an embarrassed expression on his rosy face. He paced the room and kept ruffling his hair. "Fuck. Forget I said that. You look terrified." He slumped against the wall and covered his face with his hands, groaning through them. "I'm not good at this emotional shit."

Brian found it endearing how a sensitive confession rattled Louis more than dealing with deadly cannibals. He stood and moved to Louis, then gently lowered his hands from his face. "I'm not terrified—I'm just surprised you have a weakness."

Louis scowled and glanced at the window instead of Brian. "Don't rub it in." His lips parted to allow a deep sigh through them.

Impulse overwhelmed inhibition. Brian reached out and snatched Louis's cheeks. He pressed their lips together for what might've been a second or an eternity—a perfect, timeless moment. The entire world went out from under him. Louis kissed Brian like he was the air he needed to breathe. All Brian could think was, "Oh...*this* is how this is supposed to feel." It took him out at the knees, a freefall into an abyss he could never return from.

He rocked back on his heels and rubbed his cheeks, which burned with the heat of a thousand suns. "I assume that was the taste you were craving."

The hands clinging to Brian's hips kept them agonizingly close. Louis's parted lips closed into a crooked smile. "It was an enticin' *gouté*, that's for sure. But I've still got an *envie*."

In one sudden motion, their bodies collided again—but a sharp rap on the door nearly made Brian jump out of his skin.

Louis arched his eyebrows. "Don't answer that."

"Brian, you in there?" D called, banging on the door again. "It's pourin' out here—you better hurry over to the Big House before this place turns into a bayou!"

Brian broke away to head for the door, but Louis caught his sleeve. "We don't have to go."

As tempting as this offer was, Brian's sense of responsibility overwhelmed his curiosity. "She'll keep knocking, probably even bust the door in if I don't answer—and we don't want that." He slid his hand along the inside of Louis's collar, lightly tugging the tip of the V with one finger. "I should break *your* buttons someday."

Louis pressed himself to Brian and nuzzled his nose into his hair. "Maybe you should." Sultry breath tickled Brian's ear, sending a ripple of pleasant shivers into the tips of his fingers and toes. A sort of itchy heat simmered underneath his skin.

D's persistent pounding resumed. "Brian, come *on*—we need some sunshine out in this damn storm! Are you done makin' up with Louis-boy yet?"

He wanted to say, "It isn't food I want right now, so go away," but he reluctantly withdrew from Louis and opened the door instead. D's drenched robe clung to her, her hair flattened into a soggy mess by the rain. The setting sun cast a lustrous glow through the storm clouds behind her.

"You two are all red in the face, but I'm too wet and too hangry to care why—as long as y'all done kissed and made up." She snagged Brian's hand and tugged him into a jog. "Let's get!"

D might have been more of a psychic than she thought.

Chapter Nineteen: Bon Voyage

1/24, EDGARD, LOUISIANA

Evergreen Plantation

Louis spent the night in Brian's cabin. Although they picked up where they left off and fooled around a little, they never went past second base. The possibility of D knocking on the door kept them from engaging in anything too intimate—but her words also lingered in the back of Brian's mind.

"You should let it simmer, absorb the flavor of y'all's relationship."

Louis didn't push Brian. He was content to curl up alongside him, settling his chin into Brian's shoulder with a content sigh and an arm draped over Brian's torso. The storm diminished into a drizzle that lulled them into a deep slumber throughout the night.

They packed their things and left in the morning. Grimes trotted alongside D's bicycle, shadowed by an overhang of dead limbs reaching for each other as if they were trying to merge. In the distance, sunlight dappled the bucolic mansion while white-clad figures waved goodbye. Brian relived memories of sitting in the back seat of his parents' truck, looking through the window as his grandparents waved goodbye from their porch. Tears stung his eyes.

Adjusting to being back on the road was strange at first, but old habits kicked in and they settled into their routine: D on the bike with the cat and shotgun, Brian and Louis on Grimes with Brian in front, both with a gun close at hand. Louis's fingers would stroke Brian's stomach on occasion, slow and teasing, sometimes lowering to his waistband but always skittering back up like a spider. Acting on their attraction did nothing to ease the tension—it only served to make it worse.

Their arrival at the fringe of New Orleans brought an end to this agony and a beginning to another.

D stopped in front of a collection of signs pointing out destinations of interest to travelers. She attempted to straighten one out, but it refused to budge. The bent sign swayed as she stepped back and shook her head.

"It's been over ten years, but you still see signs of it. I'm only survivin' this storm 'cause I made it through that one. But I had Gus and 'Toine. When I had to travel on my own, I was so lonely. Jones was the only thing that got me through."

Brian patted Grimes as she foraged in the dirt on the side of the highway. "When was the last time you talked to your brother?"

"The middle of October, before the phones went down. He told me he'd wait for me. I'd gone to check on my parents—" She brought a fist to her mouth and screwed her eyes shut. "They went together. Think my popa shot my moman then hisself. Curled up in the bed lookin' just like I remembered 'em, 'cept their heads was in pools of brown stains and old hamburger."

"I'm so sorry, D." Brian knew no words could properly express his sympathy, so he squeezed her arm instead. "We'll find your brother. Even if he isn't there, he probably left a note for you or something. Where should we start heading?"

"He got this bougie house in the French Quarter, bought it after he won the Powerball. Katrina hit three years later, did almost as much damage as the house was worth—talk about goin' from good to shit luck. Me and Gus helped him fix it up—now it's right as rain. I hope it still is. Him too." She patted Grimes and grinned at Brian. "Better get movin': that ol' storm's comin' back for round two."

The dense air and ominous clouds from the prior night never dissipated; they only retreated, beat back by the sun in a short-lived victory.

To reach the French Quarter, they had to travel through the city—their largest yet. Everyone had a weapon in their hand and an eye out for movement. Darkening clouds cast shadows on roads cluttered with remnants of a bustling city: businesses with busted windows, dented cars without tires and windshields, spent ammo casings, and pieces of skeletons scattered around. The disorder limited their path.

"Used to be music pumpin' outta about every joint in town." A bittersweet smile accompanied D's forlorn sigh. "Now it's just an empty shell that's lost its shine."

The quiet was peaceful yet foreboding. Revving car motors speeding by and whistling trains were once inherently reassuring, a reminder that people were going somewhere, and that life went on.

As they passed the glass exterior of the Audubon Aquarium, Brian pictured hordes of tourists flocking down the street. A distasteful part of himself was thankful nobody could knock into him while they stared at their cell phones, tried to console their squalling children, or walked in an obnoxious wall of discordant chatter. It hadn't truly hit him until he was in a city this large that he was one of the lucky few who'd survived what millions of others—maybe billions—hadn't.

"Let's see...we on Conti right now... I think we turn right at this corner by the spirits shop." D sat on her bike, peering around the tight intersections. "That's it: down Chartres. Antoine's place is a few blocks from there."

After they turned and followed the road, they encountered a building resembling a castle across from a vast park with a statue at its center. D informed them this was St. Louis's Cathedral, which was hundreds of years old.

One day, something will destroy it like the virus destroyed us. Time will destroy everything.

Brian peered through his binoculars at the area ahead of them. Something glinted in one of the buildings. He assumed it was broken glass until he caught movement behind the window.

"Get down!" He snapped the reins and squeezed his feet, guiding Grimes toward the park across from the cathedral. D pedaled in the opposite direction as a shot zipped through the air, plunging into a statue between Grimes and D's bike. Chunks of concrete sprayed into the air.

D cursed and skidded into a bush, clutching Jonesy to her. Louis's voice was muffled, but Brian heard him say: "Fucker must have a rifle!"

"Take Grimes and go," Brian whispered. "I'll get them with the bow."

Louis dug his hands into Brian's sides. "What? Are you crazy? I'm not leavin' you!"

Brian jerked free of Louis's grip and slid down. He smacked Grimes on the rear, sending her galloping as another shot boomed.

Brian scrambled for cover, snatching the bow from his chest and withdrawing an arrow from the quiver. D stayed hidden in the bushes, her shotgun useless against ranged weapons.

I don't think she's hit. Whoever that is will look for Lou. I have to get them while they're distracted.

Brian snuck into the burnt-out diner the sniper was holed up in, creeping beneath singed paintings of musicians. The broken bottles scattered on the ground left a perilous trail to navigate around.

A shot boomed from above him, shaking the ceiling. He snatched one of the bottles and flung it as far as he could through the shattered window. It crashed into the street as he stepped onto a creaking step.

Fuck. They'll hear me.

He moved slowly, placing each foot as gingerly as Jonesy had pawed at the rat trap. Sweat beaded on his brow and clung to his hands as he emerged onto the second floor and knelt behind a ruined bar.

The sniper aimed through the edge of the busted window. The figure was slight, a young man or a woman. Whoever they were, they'd opened fire without question: there'd be no negotiating.

Brian aimed his arrow over the counter. He kept his breathing steady, angling the tip toward the person's head.

Don't fuck this up. You fuck it up, you're dead, Lou is dead, D's dead, Grimes and Jonesy are dinner.

Brian pictured the arrow sailing into the sniper's skull and released the string. The arrow struck its target, making a strange sound between a *fwump* and a *crack*, and the sniper tumbled over the window ledge. Their body crashed into the pavement below with the unmistakable squish of tissue exploding on impact.

He lowered the bow, exhaling.

Something crunched behind him.

The bow fell to the ground as he reached for his knife and spun around with it slashing in front of him. He peered into the wild-eyed stare of a stranger lifting a baseball bat rimmed with barbed wire.

How the hell am I gonna beat that with a knife?

He dodged and stepped back as they swung, stumbling toward him.

The guy's heavy. Slow. I can wear him out, get him off-balance.

Brian let him get a few more swings in before leaping over the bar and skidding off with shattered glasses. He plunged the knife into the man's shoulder, making him cry out.

"You killed my daughter!" The man yanked the blade out and held it in his free hand, acting as if he'd fling the knife back through the air.

"She shot at us!" Brian shouted, out of breath. He kicked a chair forward as he backed away from the crazed man. "I had no choice!"

"This is my town! *My town!*"

The knife sliced through the air. Brian fell to his knees and turned a table onto its side. The tip of the knife sank through the table, gleaming next to his eye. He tried to snatch it out, but it was wedged in the wood.

"My Town" bore down on him from above. The table Brian kicked above him cracked with the impact of the bat. He rolled away, searching for anything to use as a weapon or a shield.

While the man struggled to separate the table from the barbed wire, Brian swept his leg out and knocked him off balance. The man grunted and stumbled. Brian reached for the knife, his glove slipping around the metal. "Fuck!"

"You're fucked all right!" The man lunged for Brian with a guttural war cry.

Something strange happened: he fell flat on his face. Someone was above the downed man, putting a knee to his back and holding his arms behind him. Not Louis, not D.

The bat skittered onto the floor. Brian picked it up and lifted it overhead.

"I'll do it, kid." The man in black gestured for the bat. "Fucker always thought this was his town, but it's *mine*."

Brian handed it to him and scrambled to yank at his pocketknife, cringing as wood crunched into bone and flesh. The man's agonized cries chilled him. He couldn't bring himself to look.

Eventually, the screams quieted to gurgles. Brian's savior stood. "You okay? What you doin' here alone?"

"I...I came here looking for someone." Brian bent over, his hands on his knees as he caught his breath. "Antoine...Etienne."

The stranger lifted the helmet that covered his face. His dark face flashed a bright smile at Brian. "No shit. You found him."

"What?" Brian wiped his sweat-beaded brow. He was still so dazed this revelation seemed perfectly normal. "Uh, your sister's looking for you. She's with me. Well, she was—"

"D?" Antoine's jaw fell. "Where is she?"

Brian pointed behind Antoine. "Hiding in a bush across from the cathedral."

Antoine smiled and slipped into booming, contagious laughter. He laughed until he cried, wiping away tears from his angular cheeks. "What's your name, kid?"

"Brian. Brian Jameson."

"Well, Brian, Brian Jameson: take me to my little sister. I been waitin' for her ass a *long* time."

Brian plodded down the stairs after the tall man, who was built like a football player and wore dark riot gear. Brian envied him—as generous as the B.E.N. were, they remained reluctant to part with their protective gear since they'd need it for new Guardians.

Antoine withdrew a shotgun from his side as they approached the door of the café. Brian watched him, a little wary but mostly flabbergasted. *I guess if he'd shot him, he might've hit me. Good thing he knew another way to incapacitate him.*

Brian heard the clop of hooves before they made it to D. Louis jumped down when he saw Brian and Antoine. He jogged over to Brian and snatched his face in his hands, smoothing back his sweaty hair. "Are you all right?" His eyes scanned Brian's face intently, his furrowed brow conveying rare concern.

Brian nodded, but he wanted to cry now that he had time to process what he'd done. "I killed the sniper. It was only a young girl... But I had to do it. Right?"

Louis pulled Brian to him and held him tight. "Of course you did—she shot first." He lifted his head from Brian's shoulder and glanced at Antoine. "Who's the jolly black giant?"

"Antoine. D's brother. He saved me from a guy with a baseball bat wrapped in barbed wire. The sniper's father."

"No shit." Louis withdrew from Brian and offered his hand to Antoine. "I'm Louis. Thanks for helpin' Brian. I owe you one."

Antoine took it and shook. "Think nothin' of it, son."

Before he could say more, D emerged from the bush with Jonesy in her arms, both covered in twigs and leaves. "You got to be fuckin' *kiddin'* me! Bro?" She jogged up to him and smashed the cat between them as they embraced. "Thank God. Oh, thank *God!*"

Antoine withdrew, gripping his sister's shoulder. The broad smile on his face shrank slightly. "Where's Gus?"

D shook her head, her lips quivering. She burst into tears and buried her face in her brother's neck. He held her until her cries died down.

"We should go back to my place." Antoine kept an arm curled around D's shaking shoulders. "Won't take long to get there."

Antoine spoke quietly to D as he led them to his house. Brian's exhaustion mingled with nausea when they passed the splattered body of the sniper. Louis squeezed his side and told him not to look, but it was impossible to ignore. It became another image seared into his brain, one of many photographs filling the album of his mind.

Flip the page.

Antoine's house was a pink, two-story building with a balcony. The front door and window frames were painted navy-blue, but they were all boarded. An iron fence to the right protected a blue SUV.

Antoine parted from D to unlock the gate. "Come on in. It's gonna drown some frogs soon."

"Thanks," Brian said. "What should we do with Grimes?"

"Grimes?"

"That's the ol' girl right there." D pointed to the horse, who huffed as if she was exasperated. "She Jonesy's best friend—took my place."

"All right, then. Best take care of her." Antoine locked the gate behind them after they were all through. "You can let her walk around here or tie her up if you want. She'll be safe." Brian let her wander, unable to bear the thought of her tied up and alone.

Antoine unlocked a series of metal bars first, then a screen door—and finally, the actual front door. Jonesy dashed past Antoine and D as they tried to step in, causing them to stumble and curse.

The spaciousness of the house surprised Brian. Vintage ads for jazz and classical African paintings adorned soothing pastel walls with exposed brick façades. Extravagant chandeliers dangled over a cedar kitchen table and an ornate Oriental rug in the living room. The tight but lavish rooms projected an air of class that would've been at home in any swanky New York apartment.

"Let's go get some air before it storms," Antoine said after their tour concluded in his bedroom. He removed a layer of particle board from the patio door and took them out onto it. Brian approached the railing and surveyed the French Quarter's cramped but quaint streets. St. Louis's cathedral loomed proudly in the distance.

This must have been a prime spot for viewing Mardi Gras parades.

He pictured a colorful procession with trumpeters playing jazz and people throwing beads, all clad in elaborate costumes and painted masks. The vivid image faded as he focused on the barren street, a final image of discarded beads melting into it.

And a broken, bloodied body with an arrow in the head.

"Used to be real lively here." Antoine slid into a metallic patio chair, resting his hands on a matching circular table. Jonesy promptly hopped onto the table and groomed himself. "You could watch people go by— tourists, mostly. Sometimes it'd be the locals: bartenders, shopkeepers, artists, musicians. Yes, sir, used to be you heard music until the wee hours of the morning. I got so used to it I slept better with it. Now that it's quiet, I don't sleep so good."

Louis leaned against the railing with Brian. Antoine chuckled as D sat across from him. "Guess I should blame the not sleepin' good on that 'My Town' guy. I'd be dead out and wake up to one of my trip wires activatin'—it was hooked up to empty beer cans, so they'd jingle like Christmas bells. When I ran down to whatever door or window the wire was wigglin' in front of, I'd pump my shotgun and yell at him to go away. 'This is *my town, my town*,' he'd yell, then go runnin' off with that skinny kid of his. Fucker went around all day killin' Stalkers to clear out his damn town, but he was just doin' all my work for me. When he got bored with them, I guess he tried to entertain himself by rootin' me out. I didn't want to fuck with him none—you don't fuck with crazy—and that trigger-happy kid was too much to mess with. At least until Robin Hood showed up."

D reached over and socked Antoine in the arm, her eyes softening as they shifted to Brian. His gut ached, but Louis's warm touch on his shoulder eased the pain.

"I wondered why the town was so damn empty. He mighta wandered down from Baton Rouge. We found a group of people set up at a plantation there—" D clicked her tongue when Antoine scrunched up his face. "Don't give me that look, it ain't like that. They all joined up to contribute supplies, got them a well and a store of water, and they're growin' a garden in a greenhouse. Got them some animals too, and some land that's gonna look beautiful come spring."

"That sounds real nice, baby girl, but I been fine here. I got everything to myself, hoarded plenty of food and supplies, get to be in my own home. And—"

"You gonna run outta food and water one day. And you gonna be outnumbered if a gang of raiders come in. Brian told me he and Louis-boy barely got away from one in Missouri. Safety in numbers, big brother."

Antoine's narrowed eyes mirrored his sister's. "Yeah, but how long before that big gang of raiders goes after your gang of plantation hippies?"

Louis smiled slightly as he stared at the empty city, his windswept hair concealing his eyes. Brian tried to stay out of it; he'd had enough of being caught in other people's arguments.

Antoine and D continued their staring match until Antoine caved with a heavy sigh. "How we gonna get me to this plantation you talkin' about? My fat ass is gonna break that bike if you try and fit me on the handlebars! Where you even get it? You must look hella silly ridin' that thing."

"I picked it up from a driveway," D said. "It was just layin' there—guess someone dropped it and ran off somewhere. I got to say, I like their taste. I even put ol' Jones in the basket!"

"You can take Grimes," Brian said. "She was happy at Evergreen. Besides, how can I part her from Jonesy?"

D's mouth hung open until a fond smile lifted her violet lips. "The hell am I gonna do with a cat and a horse? Horse's always the first to go in scary movies, then the black guy." D winked at Antoine. "Just joshin', big bro. I'll take care of old girl, Sunshine, as long as you sure."

"Only if you're sure you don't want to come with us." Although Louis shot Brian a sharp look out of the corner of his eye, Brian continued. "Antoine can come too."

"What's this you talkin' about?" Antoine asked. "You ain't headed to this plantation?"

Brian shook his head. "We want to take a boat to a resort off the coast of Cuba. Louis's aunt and uncle have a condo in the Garden District. The key for their boat might be there, even if they aren't."

Antoine looked up at the sky while Jonesy hopped down from the table. "Jones knows what's up. Best wait out the storm. Once it's cleared, we'll help you look for that key. I don't know about no island—me and Dee ain't too fond of water."

The first drops of rain tickled Brian's skin as the moist scent of the imminent storm drifted into his nose. He inhaled heartily while Antoine let the cat in. D hurried in after him, but Brian lingered, enjoying the dark beauty of the weather as the wind tousled his hair. Louis remained beside him, leaning against the railing overlooking the city.

Louis moved a lock of hair out of Brian's eye. "You sure you're all right?"

Brian furrowed his brow and wiped away the phantom tickle of his hair. "I'm sore all over from fighting that guy off. But what hurt most was him yelling that I'd killed his daughter. She couldn't have been older than me. She was trying to survive too."

"You did what you had to do. We're alive because of you. But I shoulda been the one to do it; I don't mind killin', but I know you hate it." Louis turned away from the railing. A drop of rain rolled down his ruddy cheek. "I'm sorry I wasn't there to protect you."

"It was just my turn to protect you, is all. To protect D and Grimes."

A peal of thunder cracked the air, making it sizzle with electricity.

Louis sighed and stepped forward from the railing. "Better get inside unless we wanna get soaked again." He reached for Brian's arm and tugged him into Antoine's room, which smelled pleasant, like a mild cologne.

Brian tried not to worry about the condo, the boat, or the island. But as they settled down to share a meal, all he could think about was the young girl's body splattered onto the sidewalk—an entire life and future he'd destroyed.

AFTER A LEISURELY breakfast, they planned their path to the condo in the Garden District. D and Antoine were too hefty to fit on the bike together, so they rode Grimes instead. Brian and Louis had to share the bike. Fortunately, it was only a fifteen-minute ride.

A strange mixture of elegiac mansions, modern housing, and businesses filled the Garden District. Aside from the gardens at the old-fashioned manses, Brian couldn't see what the name had to do with it. D explained there'd been more gardens in the days when the district was created, but expansion had eliminated most of them. She also eagerly pointed out where famous people once lived.

A metal fence with pointed posts surrounded the three-story condominium. The group disembarked from their rides and entered through the busted gates, letting Grimes mosey in a sparsely vegetated courtyard. Louis led them left past patchy topiary and two battered palm trees. The stink of decay drifted through a busted front door.

"Whatever happened was recent," Antoine whispered. "Might be some people were holed up in here, got slaughtered."

"But is what slaughtered them still in there?" D whispered back. Louis glared and shushed them.

Brian's nose crinkled, but it didn't block out the stench. He was on the verge of retching; it never got any easier to deal with.

The group entered cautiously, pulling their coats over their mouths and noses. The Etiennes gripped their shotguns while Brian prepared his bow. Louis grasped the PPK in one hand and the flashlight in the other—but it was flickering again and the PPK only had three bullets left. The revolver still had plenty, but it could only hold five bullets at a time.

The cone of light swept over a set of keys, a beach towel, and a weathered romance novel scattered on the lobby's floor. Mailboxes hung open, some still stuffed with white slips of paper. A phone dangled from a cord attached to a wall-mounted receiver. No dial tone, no one to call anymore. Digital connections ceased to exist.

"Second floor." Louis settled a foot onto a step beside a broken green flip-flop. It creaked loudly, the splintering wood warped by people tracking in water. Brian followed while D and Antoine took up the rear.

The smell thickened to sickening levels upstairs. Minimal light entered through the busted boards of a window. A streak of blood on the floor swerved into an open apartment door.

"Not theirs," Louis whispered. Brian was relieved, even if it wasn't *his* aunt and uncle. "We want 3B."

Brian approached the door labeled "3B" with an arrow drawn. A scratching sound came from inside—not next to the door but deeper within the apartment. He nudged the door open with his elbow and stepped back. Nothing.

The scratching sharpened as he tiptoed past a couch, a busted TV, and an empty pet bed. A shadow moved in the kitchen window—but it was only a palm tree scraping the glass.

Brian lowered his arms slightly, but he sensed movement to his left. He swiveled and released the bowstring as soon as he saw a Stalker's telltale grin.

But it ducked.

The Stalker streaked past him, past Louis—and straight for D. Her shotgun boomed and flashed in the darkness.

Brian quickly strung another arrow and aimed at the head of D's assailant. The arrow sank into the pulpy head with a wet sound and the body fell forward against a disgusted D.

Louis aimed his flashlight past her at the door. Antoine pressed himself against it, using his weight to keep something from getting in. A white hand reached around and clutched for his arm. Brian cringed at the grating sound of nails scraping the riot gear and hurried over to Antoine, dropping the bow. He withdrew his pocketknife and sawed through the decrepit wrist. Antoine was finally able to shut the door when the hand plopped to the ground, still clenching and opening like a disembodied snake head.

Brian slumped against the living room couch, catching his breath. "Everyone okay?"

Antoine nodded, sweat beading on what was visible of his face. "It come up behind me, sneaky motherfucker, but I heard it and whipped around in time to give it a kick and slam the door shut."

D pressed a hand to her chest. "That other one 'bout gave me a heart attack! Thank God for you, Sunshine!"

Louis aimed the flashlight at the ground. Blood pooled around the Stalker's head. He approached the body and kicked it. "No wonder he went for you, D."

"Huh?" D undid her bandanna and wiped her sweating brow with it. "What you mean?"

Louis kneeled and dug into the stained cargo shorts the Stalker wore. He withdrew a wallet and opened it to inspect the driver's license. "My nonc always did like dark meat."

"What kinda racist shit is that, you Cajun-Injun?" D folded her arms underneath her bosom and huffed. "You—you Cajunjun."

Louis lifted a ring of keys on his finger. A bright red floater dangled from it. "Don't get your panties in a twist—my tante was black." He swiped the keys into his palm and stuck them into his pocket before standing up.

"There any point to lookin' for her?" Antoine asked.

"He came outta the bedroom. I got a feelin' that's where she is." Louis handed Brian the flashlight. "Brian, shine this, *s'il vous plait.*"

Brian obliged. Smears of blood stained most of the rank bedroom. A figure lay half under a dangling duvet as if it had been dragged out. The flashlight caught the glint of a gold bracelet wrapped around a skeletal wrist.

Louis walked in and bent near it, wincing. "It's her. Must've been too crazy out there for them to try and take the boat. Probably waited it out but my uncle got infected. Got a hold of my aunt."

"If they were waiting it out, wouldn't they have boarded the door?" Brian asked as Louis shut the bedroom door on his aunt's corpse.

"Maybe somethin' got in. Doesn't matter, anyway. I got what I needed." Louis skirted his uncle's body. He approached Antoine, who had his ear to the door. "You hear anythin'?"

"Not a damn thing."

Louis shook his head. "We step into that hall, that wood's gonna creak. Antoine, you take point. D, you cover the right side of the hall. Brian, you get the stairs. I'll take over flashlight duty from the rear."

Antoine nodded and turned the doorknob. The door squeaked open, gradually unveiling the dim hallway. Louis shone the light into it, highlighting swirls of dust and the dried blood smeared across the wooden floor.

One by one, the apartment doors crept open. Alabaster faces with crimson smiles gleamed in the darkness. It took a split-second for everyone to realize they were surrounded.

They pressed their backs together. Brian focused on the faces in front of him as he aimed the Magnum. Mocking laughter surrounded them even though the gunfire nearly deafened Brian. He put down one, two, three of them as they scrambled out from their apartments.

Louis scrambled for Brian's hand. "I'm out—give me the Magnum!"

"There's only two bullets in the chamber!" But he handed it over and wrestled with the bow, struggling to line up a shot in the limited space he had. He elbowed someone but didn't care. He launched an arrow at the only Stalker remaining in front of him, its teeth so close to his face he saw gristle in them and got a whiff of its rancid breath.

All fell silent and the smoke settled.

Brian swallowed and lowered the bow, turning. Louis was behind him, staring in stunned disbelief at the circular pile of corpses around them. D and Antoine stood beside them, heaving and exhaling.

"Anyone hurt?" Antoine asked.

"No," Brian said. Louis shook his head.

"One grabbed me." D held out her shaking arm. "I-I think it got my sleeve."

Once they were confident they had a moment of safety, they examined D's arm. The tear in her coat sleeve didn't extend to the shirt sleeve beneath it.

Brian and Antoine seemed to exhale at once.

"They planned that," Louis said. "They fuckin' *planned* that. And the one Brian took out *ducked*."

"The one we shut out let them know somehow." D smoothed back her hair. "Like a gotdamn messaging service."

"Are they adapting, or are they recovering some of their brain function?" Brian asked. No one acknowledged his question. Something deep within the bowels of the building creaked.

They scrambled down the stairs and dashed through the door into the courtyard. Grimes awaited them, summoned by the raucous gunfire. The Etiennes clambered onto her while Brian and Louis sat on D's bike. The group rushed out of the complex and shot down St. Charles Avenue past cars and buildings. They turned left onto an expressway packed with the twisted remnants of both bone and metal skeletons, some warped by fire as if they were abstract sculptures in an art museum.

Marconi Drive took them past a more visually appealing and relaxing route with fewer buildings and more trees. Brian could tell they were entering what had been a more upscale housing area, which made sense because it was near a private marina.

Exhaustion forced them to slow down. Laconic trees draped with moss beckoned them to stop and rest beneath their shade. The pillared porches of upper-crust houses invited them to laze on swinging benches.

Brian didn't succumb. Instead, Louis offered to take over pedaling duty. Grimes trotted on, drinking from a bottle of water Brian tipped over for her. When they reached the marina, the island dream took a giant leap toward reality.

We might actually make it out of here.

"Let's split up and look for this boat," Antoine said. "Maybe we'll find some more supplies. Wouldn't hurt to look for more fuel too. We still got about an hour and a half of sunlight left."

Louis explained what the boat looked like, but D snagged Brian by the arm and pulled him away. "Sunshine, come with."

Brian shrugged, happy to go with her. Louis gave her a suspicious look but didn't say anything. He and Antoine headed west to search the first three docks while D and Brian headed east to search the last three.

While they tried to spot a boat matching the description Louis gave, Brian asked D what she'd wanted to talk to him about.

She kept walking and talking. "I just want to make sure you still want to go."

"Why wouldn't I? We came all this way."

"You don't know what's on that island, but you know you got a safe place waitin' for you. Come with us. If you're worried about Louis, he'll go with you—he's stuck to you like a burr on a boot." A stern look knotted her round face when Brian didn't reply. "You two seem like you're welded back together, but I want to make sure you didn't just slap some tape on the crack."

Brian tuned her out, distracted by the squawks of seagulls and the gentle lapping of waves against the dock. The air smelled of fish and salt. He was imagining that he was on that island, not on a dock in Louisiana.

D snapped her fingers, drawing him out of his daydream. "You got your head there already, don't you?" She sighed and put her hands on her hips. "Baby, I know you spent that last night at Evergreen with Louis. I'm sure he sweet-talked you in French, that he's good with his hands—"

"D!" Brian shook his head and dragged his hands down his face, mortified. "Not that it's any of your business, but we didn't go all the way. Okay? End of story."

"*Not* end of story." D's honey-hued eyes pierced Brian's. "The thing is, I don't doubt he's in love with you—you the only thing that makes those dead eyes of his light up. But you need to make sure you love *him* before you commit to sailin' a damn boat to an island with him."

Brian folded his arms, glancing at Louis and Antoine while they moved from boat to boat. "I know what a crush is—this is more than that. I've never felt anything like this before. I've never *needed* anybody like this before. It's gonna sound awful, but if the rest of the world didn't exist and the only world I knew was him, I'd be happy. But if I had the rest of the world at my fingertips but didn't have him, I'd be miserable."

D spun a finger with chipped sparkling polish. "Y'all got yourselves wound up so tight there's no you without him and no him without you. That's some dangerous shit, baby. I don't know if he got you thinkin' it or you done it yourself, but you don't *need* him to survive."

Brian shook his head, ready to move on from the conversation. "D, if you're so worried about it, take Antoine and come with us."

D crossed her arms and narrowed her eyes. "I don't like water and I don't like Louis. *That's* the end of the story. Now let's find this damn boat so you can sail off into the sunset and have your happily ever after with Prince Not-So-Charming."

D seemed agitated, so Brian let her be. He chalked most of what she said up to her bias against Louis. Brian was fully aware of Louis's volatile temperament, but D's blunt attitude only added fuel to the fire. On the other hand, Antoine had such an amiable personality even Louis didn't mind him.

D kept muttering things to herself while they strolled along the dock, but Brian didn't press it. The setting sun cast auburn radiance over the ocean that rippled into golden waves. Brian had been to lakes and rivers, but he'd never been to a real beach before. The illusion of infinity created by the meeting of sky and sea awed him.

Louis ended up finding the boat. He called them over and climbed aboard, Magnum in hand since the PPK was out of ammo. The Etiennes watched with Brian while Louis searched the deck of the modest vessel.

"This is an Albatross 37." Louis lost his balance a little as he scrambled to the front of the boat. "It's got a cabin with a bed, shower, and toilet;

plenty of room for our shit—our things, I mean. It's even got a sink and a stove. Plus, it's got a deck up front for sunnin'. It's a good size for ocean cruisin'—I sailed it before with my family."

Grimes wandered up to them, curious what all the hoopla was about. Brian gave her a reassuring pat and sighed. "I guess we should load everything on."

During their search, they'd found remnants of people's sailing trips—mostly clothing or swimsuits, or a straw hat and ball cap. A cooler with cans of soda and beer had been buried by life vests. Another boat had fishing poles and a rusted tackle box still aboard it. Most of the fuel had been drained by opportunistic scroungers, but they were able to siphon the scanty remnants out of a few tanks and into some of their fuel cans.

They worked together to load the boat, which wasn't as cramped and unpleasant as Brian had imagined. The stove, toilet, and shower were exciting amenities. The bed, on the other hand, intimidated him. The white sheets were a blank canvas waiting for something to be painted on them.

"I think that's it." Louis stuck the key into the ignition: the motor thrummed to life like a victory cry. A huge smile curved his lips. "We can finally leave this fuckin' country and this fuckin' winter behind."

That isn't all we're leaving behind.

Brian threw his arms around Grimes's neck and pressed his face to her side, inhaling the sweaty but pleasant scent of her skin. "Thanks for everything, girl. We couldn't have made it without you. D and Antoine are going to take care of you and bring you back to the place with fresh fruit and vegetables and room for you to run. You can be with Jonesy and all the other animals." Grimes reached around and nuzzled him with her nose, exhaling a warm cloud of breath.

Antoine opened his arms for a hug, a broad smile on his face. "I ain't known you that long, but I can tell you a good kid—my sister speaks so highly of you she might as well be tokin'. You be safe, now."

Brian embraced him while Louis fiddled with the instrument panel, turning on the lights to make sure they worked. D watched him, a stoic expression on her normally animated face. When she looked back to Brian and her brother, her stony façade crumbled.

"Aw, let me in on that action, now!" She wrapped Brian up in a hug from behind, her hands gripping her brother's arms. "The Lady's gonna miss you more than Bro and that ol' horse! When we get back, Jones gonna be lookin' for you too."

When Brian managed to wriggle out of the comforting but nearly suffocating hug, D dug into her backpack and pulled out a sheet of paper. Her eyes gleamed as she offered it to him. "As long as I'm around, you got someone to go back to if this island ain't the paradise you hope it'll be. Don't forget that."

Brian took the paper. It advertised "Lady D's Psychic Readings" with bullet points listing the services she offered. An image of D smiled from it, dressed in a purple and gold smock and headwrap. Tarot cards and a crystal ball sat on a table in front of her. Jonesy was curled up behind her on a table beside a strange model of a hand with lines drawn on the palm.

A surge of panic struck Brian when he realized how much he'd miss her—and how much he'd miss the makeshift family he'd made over the past month. He tried to dull the edge with humor. "I'll miss you most of all, Scarecrow."

Louis approached the dock and extended his hand. "Get to say your goodbyes?"

Brian nodded, looking back at D and Antoine. Antoine's expression was friendly enough, but D fixed Louis with a firm glare. "You better not let anything happen to him, Louis-boy. He's one of the only bright lights left in this dark-ass world."

Louis kept his eyes on hers, neither frowning nor smiling. "I know."

Witnessing this strange exchange was awkward for Brian, but it also reminded him of his grandfather telling him he was the only beautiful thing left in this ugly world. It led to a moment of introspection where he contemplated why Poppa, D, and Louis saw something in him he didn't. *They all think I'm so sensitive and naïve, that I need protecting. But I don't.*

D and Antoine gave Brian another quick hug. Grimes joined them as they headed toward the shore, cloaked in twilight shadow. Brian caught the glint of what D called her "thrift store glitter coat" and missed her already.

Louis wrapped his warm hand around Brian's. He smiled, his angular face lit in a soft halo by the sinking sun. "Once we're there, you won't miss any of it."

Brian glanced back at the Etiennes and Grimes a final time, a potent, bittersweet mixture of regret and affection stirring within him. He wanted to believe Louis, but he still missed his family. He missed Eva, and he'd miss D and Antoine. He'd even miss the B.E.N. and the animals.

Why am I leaving that behind?

He looked at Louis as their fingers locked together. Relief and anticipation were etched in the luminous terrain of his face. He didn't smile often, mostly smirked, but the boyish grin spreading across his face dazzled Brian.

This irresistible attraction, this all-consuming adulation, this overpowering *need* hadn't hit him like a punch to the gut—more like a poison slowly diffusing throughout his system.

It wasn't love—it was *everything*.

Chapter Twenty: No Going Back

1/25, LAKE PONTCHARTRAIN

Night

Although the excitement of leaving kept Brian awake a bit longer, the exhaustion from the trip and their encounter in the condo took its toll. He crashed on the cushions of an enclosed bench behind the cockpit, lulled into sleep by the gentle breeze tickling his skin.

When he woke, the air was chill and crisp, and stars twinkled in the clear sky. Louis was at the wheel, dressed down to board shorts and an open button-down that fluttered in the breeze. He'd even switched to flip-flops.

Brian sat up and stretched, yawning. "Hey. How long was I out?"

"About three hours. I wanted to let you rest."

"I needed it." Brian stood, swiveling his torso to crack his back. "How far out are we?"

"I took us down the industrial canal and crossed over the Mississippi to Grand Isle. We're in the gulf now. The water is calm, so I'll cruise until the wind picks up." Louis jerked his head, gesturing for Brian to join him. "I should teach you how to operate this thing so I can sleep too."

Brian shrugged. "Sure. It can't be much different than driving a car, right?"

"Operatin' the boat itself isn't too hard. But navigatin' is tough: the built-in GPS doesn't work anymore. Got to do it the old-school way, like pirates. Bet you don't know how to work a sail none, either."

Brian frowned and stepped up beside Louis. "I'm not an idiot. My grandfather taught me how to navigate using the positions of the sun, moon, and stars." He elbowed Louis. "Or do you not remember that from my journal, either? If you read it while I was asleep, I might punch you again."

Louis's lips quirked. "Why? You write about me in there?"

"Shut up and show me how to work this stuff."

Louis moved behind Brian and pointed to the instrument panel, instructing Brian on what all the gauges were and where their needles were supposed to aim. Brian tried to pay attention, but the breath tickling the back of his neck and the occasional brush of Louis's front against his back distracted him.

Fortunately, Louis moved on to navigation using the compass and the North Star and Southern Cross, testing Brian's knowledge until he seemed satisfied with it. He set the boat on autopilot and strolled around explaining all the parts of the boat, from things like the deck and the cabin to the anchor and sails.

Once Brian assured Louis he'd be fine on his own, Louis hugged him and retreated into the cabin for a nap. Everything was silent: no birds, no wind, no waves. Only dead salt air. The expansive ocean merged with the night sky, no land in sight.

The vast emptiness terrified Brian like that incomprehensible thought of dying and disintegrating into *nothing*. His heart raced, but he tried to tell himself he was being silly—that he was alive here, now, and that he wasn't alone after all. Louis was asleep in the cabin, out of sight but never out of mind. Louis had become his center of gravity in this universe of fear and uncertainty.

ABOUT SIX HOURS later, Louis woke and took over so Brian could finish sleeping. But Brian was too wired by his earlier thoughts to drift off. He lay in bed, tossing and turning in sheets and pillowcases infused with Louis's scent. The dark cabin made it impossible for him to tell the time, but he was certain the sun had risen by now.

Fuck it.

He climbed out of bed and joined Louis on the deck, wincing at the abrupt transition from complete darkness to the overpowering brightness of the morning sun. A group of squawking gulls soared overhead, and a cool sea breeze chilled the warm rays of the sun.

Louis grabbed both sides of Brian's head and attempted to detangle the mess his hair had become. "You look awful. You get seasick?"

Brian was too exhausted to enjoy this. "No. I couldn't sleep."

"Ah. I slept like the dead." Louis clicked the "nav" button and circled around to the kitchen, stretching his arms. "Let's get some food in you."

Brian followed him, rubbing his eyes as the sun continued to cruelly assail them. At some point, while Brian was *trying* to sleep, Louis had arranged some of the food from the B.E.N. in the kitchen. He dug into cabinets and retrieved cookware, familiar with the layout of the boat. Brian slumped onto a bench and leaned onto the table, struggling to rouse some energy for conversation.

Thinking back to his first meeting with Louis and Eva, he blurted out the first thing that came to mind: "You only cook when you wanna get laid, right?"

Louis sputtered and spun, his eyebrows quirking. "Wow, you dug that one up from pretty far back. Mère taught me and Eva how to cook, but Père told her that was a woman's job. I don't mind it, but I only do it on rare occasions—even rarer, now."

"He sounds like a peach." Brian buried his face in his arms, trying to hide his flushed cheeks.

"Now you know where *I* get it." Louis opened a can of corned beef hash and dumped it into a sizzling skillet. The savory scent of cooking meat made Brian's stomach rumble. "But I'm nice sometimes, right?"

Brian sighed and looked up, watching Louis bustle around in the tight kitchen. "You're overflowing with sugar *and* spice."

When Louis finished, they sat and ate, engaging in sporadic conversation. Neither of them was used to this feeling of ease, of not having to watch every angle for movement. Brian still shuddered whenever Louis's feet brushed his under the table, but his shivers soon shifted from anxiety to pleasure.

After breakfast, Brian took Louis up on his suggestion to go for a swim. He hadn't been swimming since the summer before his mother was attacked. They dropped anchor and leaped in with a cathartic splash, staying close to the boat. Brian breathed in the refreshing salt air. The sun's heat soothed his skin even though the water was still a little chilly and the occasional thought of a shark drifted through his mind. Louis was in a playful mood now that he could drop his guard. It seemed so normal—but "normal" no longer *felt* normal.

When they climbed back on board and dried off, Louis took over at the wheel while Brian sat behind him listening to music. Salt breeze sprayed them as they thumped against the waves into the endless sea and sky. The descending sun sent soothing rays of heat into their exposed skin. Brian didn't miss the layers of clothes, the wet snow and the sting of cold air on his skin, or the stark deluge of white and gray landscapes. The entirety of winter seemed like a nightmare he'd finally woken up from.

The soothing synths of a lush song pulsed through Brian's earbuds. He watched Louis's dark hair whip in the breeze as he drank from a can of beer. Some of it dribbled down his chin. Covertly, Brian lifted the tablet and snapped a quick shot capturing Louis with the endless expanse of ocean beyond him.

He scrolled through photos he'd taken during the downtime of their travels, going from most recent to oldest: a grinning D clinging to Antoine inside his living room; D cradling Jonesy while Cill wrapped her arms around Grimes's neck; a picture Marie took of Brian with D and Cecilia; the one selfie he'd ever convinced Louis to take (he wasn't even looking at the camera); a selfie with Parker and Spike that must've happened during his drunken haze; Eva pretending to strangle Louis with an expression caught between faux-aggression and a laugh; Poppa bending down to pet Rocky with Nana standing behind him, her hands on his shoulders; and his smiling parents on the couch with Becky squished between them, sticking out her tongue and putting her thumbs in her ears.

When Brian looked up, a blurry image of Louis holding out the beer can filled his field of vision. He paused the song. "What? Sorry."

"I was tryin' to ask you if you wanted to finish the beer."

"Sure. Thanks." Brian wrapped his hand around the can and took it. He pulled it to his lips as Louis clicked something on the dashboard. His thoughts flickered back to the image of Louis drinking from the can, which made the yeasty beverage more appealing when he swallowed it.

Louis squeezed next to Brian in the cushioned alcove. "What're you doin'? You were all misty-eyed when I came over."

"I was looking at pictures I've taken over the past year or so."

"Show me."

Brian swiped in the opposite direction, remembering to stop before the candid shot he'd just taken. He watched Louis's expressions as he absorbed each image. For most, he remained neutral or smiled slightly, but his brow creased when he saw his sister. Brian swiped past that one quickly.

"Funny how you can capture a moment in time," Louis said. "It's like the people in those photos are here with you."

The heat their arms generated as they sat pressed together made Brian sink into a contented drowsiness. "Yeah. Sometimes it comforts me. Other times, it makes me sad because they aren't really here—and some of them don't even exist outside those photos anymore."

"You got nothin' to be sad about, *beb*—we're leavin' it all behind." Louis took the can from Brian and swigged the last of the beer, wiping his mouth before tossing it to the floor. It rolled around with a tinny *clink*. "I hope I didn't build it up too much, though. I don't want you to be disappointed."

"I don't think I'll be disappointed—unless it's infested with Stalkers or some kinda stronghold for another gang of masked freaks." Brian laughed at the ridiculous images he conjured of costumed men brandishing machine guns in some island fortress. "But as long as you're there with me, I'll be okay."

Louis looked at Brian without so much as a quirk of his lips, his intensity verging on intimidating. "I'm not goin' anywhere without you."

Brian searched Louis's sable eyes, losing all sense of time and location. The sun retreated behind the clouds, cloaking them in shadow. Brian's skin rippled with goose bumps and his shoulders shuddered.

Louis's eyebrows and lips lifted. That one sharp canine snagged his lower lip. "Cold?"

"A little."

Louis leaned forward, but a sharp jolt shook the boat. Brian fell back and collided with the armrest of the cushioned bench. Louis scrambled to the steering wheel, feet slipping as the boat shifted.

Brian stuffed his tablet into his backpack and joined Louis, looking around to see if they'd hit something—or been hit *by* something. "What *was* that?"

"Probably just a big wave." Louis examined the console. "I thought it was gettin' dark because the sun was settin', but we might be in for a storm."

Brian looked up at the darkening sky. Choppy waves made the beer can roll all over the deck. The sails swelled, tossed by the building breeze. "Have you ever sailed through one?"

Louis scurried along to undo the sails. "Not a strong one, but I'm always up for a challenge. First things first: help me with the mainsail and jib. We're gonna heave-to."

"What's that mean?"

"It's like parkin' your boat without droppin' anchor," Louis explained as they worked with the ropes of the sails. "You do it right, you can weather the storm while you're snug as a bug in a rug below deck."

Brian hustled to help him, pressured by time. Louis seemed eager to tackle this hurdle, but the interruption irritated Brian.

"Secure anythin' that can go overboard in the cabin," Louis said. "And make sure we have life vests close by."

Brian stowed their belongings in the cabin, locking whatever would fit in a small closet. The boat wasn't rocking enough to make him uncomfortable, but he was noticing movement he hadn't before. He pictured a series of horrifying events where the boat capsized and they lost all their belongings, forced to drift in the ocean until they got eaten by sharks or perished from dehydration. Out of one hole, into another.

When Brian returned to the deck, Louis was holding a finger into the breeze. "Hard to say how bad this storm'll be. If there's lightnin', it could fry the electronics. We'll shut them off, keep our bow to the breeze, and hunker down in the cabin."

"You're not supposed to steer and avoid waves?" Brian asked as Louis ambled over to the wheel and turned it, angling the boat's bow. "Aren't we going to drift off course?" He looked up as a drop of water rolled down his cheek. The sky was so hazy he couldn't see the sun at all.

"*Beb*," Louis said sharply, drawing Brian's attention back to him, "it'll be okay. Why don't you go down into the cabin? If you manage to fall asleep, you might sleep through the whole damn thing."

"What'll you do?"

"I'll be down momentarily." Louis squeezed Brian's shoulders. "Go on—I got this."

Brian descended into the cabin. The waves seemed worse when he was down there, but he told himself it was mind over matter.

Music. I'll turn on music.

He opened the cabinet to grab the lantern and tablet from his backpack and plugged the solar charger and auxiliary cable into it. He switched the lantern on and opened a drawer in an end table next to the bed, intending to put the tablet in it. His eyebrows arched when he saw a tube of lube and a sleeve of condoms.

That's not awkward at all. I guess this really was *a pleasure cruiser.*

Brian plugged the cable into the radio and attempted to lose himself in the music, writing to keep himself occupied.

When Louis finally arrived at the foot of the steps, Brian looked up from his journal. The lantern lit Louis in a soft halo of white light as he meandered over to the smudged mirror above the dresser. "How bad is it?"

Louis swept his wet bangs out of his face, glancing at Brian's reflection in the mirror. "It's gettin' a little worse, but I think we'll be okay. Be thankful you don't get seasick—this boat's gonna rock."

"I think it's been rocked plenty already," Brian said drily, glancing at the open drawer and its contents.

Louis turned and leaned back against the dresser. "What do you mean?"

"Your aunt and uncle left sex stuff in here."

Louis scoffed. "Doesn't surprise me." He stripped his soaked shirt off and shuddered, muscles rippling in the light. After he kicked his flip-flops off and tugged his swim trunks down, he jumped into bed and tugged the covers over him. "I'm not gonna lie—I felt like I was in a monsoon out there. It's nice to be in a dry, warm bed."

"I haven't been on a lot of boats," Brian said. "Only little ones on lakes. I fell out of a canoe once when I was younger, so I didn't go out much on the water after that."

"It'll feel worse than it is." Louis looked up at the white ceiling, his feet fidgeting underneath the covers. "Especially if it's your first time."

The dual meaning of this wasn't lost on Brian, but he wasn't going to point it out. Their conversation only seemed to be postponing the inevitable, which had already been postponed several times by raccoons fleeing from Stalkers, a wet, hangry D, and the storm itself.

It's simmered long enough—hasn't it?

Brian's tablet and charger slid to the opposite side of the drawer. The pencil he'd poised over his journal jerked in a diagonal line. He tossed them into the drawer as the cabin rolled with the intensifying waves.

"I've never been through this before." Brian slunk down and tugged the covers over himself. "How long will it last?"

"Could be half an hour, could be all night. Only time'll tell."

The boat jerked abruptly. Their things clattered against the inside of the cabinet. Brian wanted to pull the pillow out from under his head and put it over his ears to block everything out. He inhaled the scent of sea salt mixed with Louis's smoky-sweet cologne and exhaled slowly to calm his shaky nerves.

Louis found his hand under the blanket and laced their fingers together. "You know, there's one nice thing about bein' stuck in a boat cabin durin' a storm."

Brian twisted to face Louis. His pulse throbbed in his ears as the waves pounded against the hull. "What's that?"

"Nothin' and no one can hear you. You can be as loud as you want." Louis's voice dripped with honey but burned like cinnamon. "The moment you kissed me was the happiest I've been in my entire life. That night was just icin' on the cake. Now we have the privacy to improve on those memories—and all the time in the world."

A warm sensation fluttered inside Brian, evolving into a persisting throb throughout the entirety of his body. Louis gripped his neck and pulled him closer, closer still until the energy radiating from them merged into an atom bomb.

Their accumulated tension culminated in a series of far less awkward fumblings without anything to interrupt them. Even if there had been, Brian wouldn't have noticed—the cabin was everything, the entire universe, and only he and Louis existed within it. The storm raged on throughout the night, leaving them adrift in a tangle of sheets and limbs.

THEY DIDN'T EMERGE from the cabin until the waters were still. When they climbed up to the deck, they surveyed the scene. The boat was dotted with drops of rain and puddles on the deck, but everything looked intact.

Louis examined the connections, including the fuel tank and battery. They'd been lucky; everything still worked. It'd only been a squall. A gull streaked beneath the diminishing clouds, and the still water glittered.

Brian slumped onto the seat behind the steering wheel. He moved his hand to the lingering ache on his neck and caressed a fresh bruise coloring his skin. A dull pain pulsed within him from head to toe, but it wasn't unpleasant: it was a reminder that what had happened wasn't a dream.

Louis spun to give him a butter-smooth smile and leaned back against the console, his arms spread over the plexiglass shield. "Told you it'd work out. We only got about a day and a half before we're there."

"Oh, yeah? You didn't check to see how far we drifted off course, did you?"

Louis's eyebrows arched. "So go check, smartass." The smirk that followed carried the teasing intent of this insult. Louis had said a lot of things during the night Brian didn't understand, but all he needed to pick up on was the *way* he said them. Like D said, a series of French sweet nothings whispered or moaned against his ear and into his neck.

A pleasurable echo of the sensations he'd experienced followed him into the cabin. So did Louis. His attempts to help Brian decipher their location only ended up taking them farther off-course.

THE NEXT MORNING, Brian woke to Louis shaking his shoulders. "Come with me—I got a surprise for you." He snagged Brian's hand and dragged him out of bed. Brian jogged after Louis, roused by his contagious excitement.

Louis covered Brian's eyes with his hands and guided him up onto the deck. Brian couldn't see anything but darkness, but he smelled the salty sea air and felt Louis's shuddering warmth pressed against his back. A gentle breeze tickled his skin as Louis's hands withdrew, removing the blindfold.

A thin strip of green lined the horizon. Brian grabbed the binoculars from the center console Louis had guided them to. He looked through the lenses and focused them, revealing white sugar sand, windswept palm trees, and thatched bungalows exactly as Louis had described.

Louis slid his arm around Brian's torso and nestled his chin into Brian's shoulder. "Is it everythin' you hoped it would be?"

"I won't know until I'm there, will I?" Brian reached up to grab Louis's hand. He toyed with his fingers, trying to ward away anxious thoughts—and failing. "It can't be uninhabited. There's got to be people there. Or what's left of them."

"So what? We'll take care of it. We made it this far together—" Louis snaked his other arm around Brian's shoulder "—we'll make it there, too. We can do all the things I described and so much more." He pressed his nose to the sensitive skin of Brian's neck, inhaling. "I always thought you smelled like the ocean even before we got to the boat. It just made me want the island more. I think I came to associate it with you."

Brian leaned back into Louis and shut his eyes. "Oh, yeah? And why's that? Am I your idea of Paradise?"

"Sandy hair, ocean-blue eyes, sun-kissed skin ..." Louis tightened his arms around Brian, pulling them together. His lips left a warm, wet sensation on Brian's neck. "You even *taste* salty. I guess people don't know what their version of Paradise is until they find it."

Brian twisted in Louis's arms and linked his hands behind his neck. "I never took you for such a sap."

"*Touché, beb.*" Louis leaned forward and pressed his lips to Brian's, cutting off Brian's reply. He didn't mind—he enjoyed the tension when he knew where it would lead.

Everything led to this: the island, a literal Paradise or a metaphorical one where they came together, united by their arduous journey. Regardless of what lurked behind those bungalows and palm trees, the island would be theirs forever.

Chapter Twenty-One: Isolation

1/28, CAYO LEVISA, PINAR DEL RIO, CUBA

Warm grains of sand crunched beneath their bare feet. The waves crashed against the shore, spraying the air with moisture. Azure sky and cerulean sea surrounded them. Vivid green palm fronds swished in the refreshing breeze, reminding Brian the worst of winter was already behind him.

They'd made it. Cayo Levisa, their island paradise.

Now what?

Brian turned to Louis to pose that exact question.

"We get to business," he replied. "And by that, I mean we scour this island from coast to coast—every bungalow and every inch of land until we're sure it's clear or we *make* sure it is."

Louis's blissful haze from the boat had sharpened into his survivalist mindset once more, but Brian found this equally appealing.

"Let's clear one of these bungalows for now." Louis set his backpack down and exchanged his swim trunks for his usual pair of jeans and a long-sleeved shirt. He tied a bandana around his neck and swapped his flip-flops for combat boots. The outfit didn't suit this tropical climate, but comfort needed to be sacrificed for safety. Brian followed suit, not thrilled to transition back into survival mode. But he thought back to President Roosevelt's words: "Nothing in the world is worth having or doing unless it means effort, pain, and difficulty."

What was a little more effort and difficulty in the scheme of things? Especially if it meant living on an island far-removed from everything they wanted to escape?

Thus far, the only signs of life were the echoes of a solitary seagull's cry. Brian hadn't even seen a crab scuttling on the shore. He imagined they retreated underneath the sand into their little hovels like people had retreated into their homes during the pandemic.

This sense of desolation diminished when they approached the brick and wood bungalows. They were grouped together and lined along the shore for optimal views of the sea from their porches. Lounge seats sank into the sand in front of them, dragged out during high tide.

The first door they checked was locked, but they searched every inch of the exterior until Brian chanced onto a potted plant. He thought this might've been *too* obvious, but he still turned the pot over. Nothing. However, when he tugged out the plant—which was silk and plastic stuck into a foam base—it revealed a key underneath it.

They unlocked and opened the door. The interior was what Brian expected: somewhere between a rustic and tropical aesthetic. Wooden walls, tiled floors with a few patterned rugs, and a few chairs, tables, and lamps. Sheer curtains filtered the sunlight beaming through the window. An elaborate brocade comforter covered the bed in the combined sleeping/living area. Two other rooms connected to it: a bathroom and a kitchen.

Once they poked their heads into every nook and cranny—which wasn't difficult in a three-room building—they hurried back to the weather-beaten dock where they'd anchored the boat. They grabbed everything they could carry and brought it to the bungalow for safekeeping.

Louis brushed aside a net canopy and sank onto the bed. "One down, a bunch more to go." He scrunched his nose. "Ugh—this comforter's all scratchy." He stood and stripped it, tossing it to the ground.

While he flopped onto the bed to rest, Brian kneeled and started inventorying their belongings. It reminded him of camping or going on an extended vacation—it didn't seem *real*. This was the kind of place where he'd usually try to go out on the beach, get bored, and wind up back in the bungalow playing games or watching TV. He'd wasted so much time on digital distractions he'd neglected the natural beauty of the world.

"This PPK is useless now." Brian stuffed it back into a duffel bag Antoine had given them. "And the revolver only has a box of bullets left. I still have a few arrows for my bow. A couple broke, and some were too nasty to reclaim. I can carve more, though."

"How's the food for now?"

"Okay... It'll run out pretty quick. We burned through a lot. But we have the fishing rod and tackle box from the other boats."

"Water?"

"One gallon jug and six bottles. Eight if you count the ones with filters." Brian lined everything up in neat rows, separated by types of items. "If there's no water source here, we'll need to desalinate some. They teach you that in Boy Scouts, Lou?"

"You take a pot, a cup, and a lid, turn the lid upside down and boil the water—right? Condensation drips from the pot handle into the cup, stripped of salt by the heat."

"Clever as always." Brian sighed. "I guess the ocean'll do for bathing, but we'll run out of toiletries and our clothes are thinning—"

"Beb—" Louis sat on the edge of the bed "—stop worryin'. When it becomes a problem, *then* we worry. Hell, if we wanted to, we could run around in our underwear."

"The sun would make that problematic." Brian arched his eyebrows. "If we run out of sunscreen, we'll have to slather mud on ourselves. Pretty soon, we'll end up running around with spears like we're in *Lord of the Flies.*"

"Sounds fun." Louis sank to the ground in front of Brian and crossed his legs. "I think you've done enough of this. Let's put it up somewhere out of sight and check the rest of the bungalows for now. Come nightfall, we'll break this bed in." He slapped his hands on his knees and stood. "Hand me the Magnum and whatever ammo we have for it, *s'il vous plait.*"

Brian handed the revolver to Louis and tossed the ammo to him. While Louis stuffed it into his backpack, Brian strapped his own on and followed it with the quiver. He snatched his bow and kept an arrow in one hand. "Let's do this."

They spent the bulk of the day searching the bungalows lining the beachfront. They took anything they could fit in their backpacks: pens, sheets, pillowcases, empty soda cans and bottles, notepads, half-empty tubes of sunscreen, and batteries from remotes.

No signs of life lingered. Either the island had been evacuated and closed off or the survivors had retreated into the forest. Brian suspected any remaining people would do exactly what he and Louis were doing: set up in one of the bungalows for the long haul. Therefore, he concluded the chance of normal people being here was slim to none.

As for Stalkers? That remained to be seen.

BRIAN WASN'T RELAXED enough to break the bed in, so he stayed up while Louis slept. He wrote in his journal and read a few magazines they'd grabbed in the bungalows. Sometimes he glanced up, reassured by Louis's face in the soft glow of the lantern.

When Louis woke, Brian slept. A dark, dreamless void closed the gap between night and day. His eyes opened to light streaming in through the diaphanous curtains.

Brian rolled over and found Louis next to him. His tawny features softened into a reverent expression as he stroked a stray lock of hair from Brian's forehead. "*Bonjour, mon amour.* Sleep well?"

Brian rubbed the sleep out of his eyes. "Yeah, but not long enough. It'll be nice when we can both get a full night's rest." He turned so Louis wouldn't see him yawn.

Louis curled his arms around Brian and buried his chin in his back. His sinewy warmth pressed against Brian's body. "You look so peaceful when you sleep. Makes me wonder what you dream about."

"I'm sure you want me to say 'you,' but I don't want to inflate your already massive ego." Brian wanted to shut his eyes and drift off in Louis's arms. But the threat of the unknown lingered in the back of his mind, so he forced himself to rouse from this daydream. "We should go. The more daylight we have, the more we can cover in one go."

While Brian stood, Louis rolled out of bed and grabbed something from the bedstand next to him. "One of the bungalows had a brochure in it. Doesn't help us any with the forest, but it points out where all the buildin's are. There's fifty-six bungalows and a restaurant." He stood next to Brian, pointing out these buildings on the cartoonish map. "We covered a good chunk of these, but we should finish checkin' out the bungalows and the restaurant before we explore the natural splendor. This bit's written in Spanish, so—"

"It says the cay is 4.2 kilometers long and ranges from 280 to 750 meters in width. Swamps cover more than three-quarters of the surface and the south is inaccessible due to a forest of mangroves."

Louis shoved Brian's shoulder. "How the hell you know Spanish but not French?"

Brian laughed at Louis's incredulous expression. "My mom taught it to me when I was homeschooled."

"*Muy caliente.* Did I say that right?"

"Oui." Brian dragged a finger down Louis's bare chest, making goose bumps ripple along his sun-darkened skin. Recognizing the heavy look in Louis's eyes, he turned and hurried to pull on his jeans before he could cave to his own impulses. "Better get dressed so we can get this over with."

Once they dressed and armed themselves, they set about exploring the remaining bungalows. Much like the others, they remained perfectly preserved and uninhabited. A parrot burst out of one and startled them, but nothing else popped out. They scavenged anything they could carry, but aside from the décor and the garbage left behind, the bungalows had been stripped of all personal touches. In other words, no food, no water, no clothing.

By midday, they'd finished exploring the northern coast of the island. The only building left was the restaurant. Their treks along the sandy coast made Brian miss Grimes, and the silence made him miss D and the others. The island was exquisite but isolated—if he didn't have Louis for company, Brian doubted he'd enjoy any of it regardless of how majestic and serene it was.

They ventured along an aged wooden boardwalk toward the inland restaurant. Lush green foliage surrounded them on either side. Some of the palm trees had ripening coconuts on them. On occasion, a bird squawked— probably that parrot or a gull, not the pleasant songbirds from the US. Insects buzzed like cicadas on a hot summer day. Brian looked down at the shallow water glimmering beneath the walkway and imagined he was a pirate touching down in the Bahamas.

A straw canopy stretched over the deck surrounding the restaurant. Empty tables and chairs sat beneath it on a tiled floor. In the corner, someone had left a bizarre chess set.

When Louis wandered up to it, the pieces reached up to his knees. "Cool—now I can get you back for that game of pool I lost."

"That's what you think."

Louis clicked his tongue. "Cocky." He brushed by Brian and approached the restaurant's lone window, which hadn't been boarded or broken. A pale blue mural with painted fish swimming along it spanned from wall to wall. Stacked dishes sat atop buffet tables. Netting speckled with seashells and starfish hung from the ceiling. The set of double-doors in the back led to the kitchen, presumably.

When Louis applied pressure to the front door, it swung open. Natural light penetrated the window and cast a bright rectangle along the ground, wall, and some of the tables. They picked their way through the dining area but didn't find anything until they entered the kitchen. Amidst the clutter of pots, pans, dishes and utensils, they discovered a locked cabinet. One shot from the revolver took out the lock, revealing shelves stocked with non-perishables such as canned vegetables, boxed pasta, and some prized beef jerky. Louis and Brian looked at each other, their eyes wide—regardless of why it hadn't been taken, it was theirs now.

Everything was. Here, they owned the world.

They stuffed as much as they could carry into their bags, which they'd emptied save for bullets, bottles of water, and sunscreen. After they'd finished, they made a beeline for the bar outside. Most of the liquor had been removed, but Louis lucked onto a bottle of rum that had rolled underneath the ledge of the lower cabinets.

Brian and Louis lugged their haul to one of the tables for lunch. A gorgeous panorama of the shore and horizon provided them with a view better than anything a screen could've displayed.

"Where do you think everyone went?" Brian asked as he tore open the bag of jerky.

Louis twisted the cap off the rum. "My guess is the island got shut down at some point before things spiraled outta control, sent everyone away. They took all their things with 'em, 'cept for what we already found. Tourist-types wouldn't stand a chance here."

Brian scanned the area around them while Louis took a swig from the rum and crinkled his nose. "So you don't think there are any Stalkers here? All I've seen is that stupid parrot that screeched at us. I swear it said, 'Get out!'"

Louis scoffed and screwed the cap back onto the bottle. "You and that imagination of yours... I'm sure there's more here than we've seen. Probably all kinds of lizards and snakes and shit. Some giant rodent thing came up to Eva. She thought it was cute, but Père made her cry 'cause he threw a rock at it, said it was diseased vermin."

"I think they're called 'hutia.'"

Louis lifted his sunglasses into his hair. "Okay—you can't tell the difference between a buffalo and bison, but you know the name of some rodent from an island you never been to until now?"

"I remember it from school... The only ones remaining all live on the Caribbean islands. The locals call them Banana Rats."

"You're just full of surprises." Louis shook his head. He grabbed the can opener they'd found in the kitchen and tore through a can of mandarin oranges.

As always, his efficiency impressed Brian. "You would've done really well in the military, you know."

"I considered it. But I didn't care about my country enough to risk my life for it. I mean, they stole the land from my ancestors and all that, so why should I? My mamère's family grew up on a reservation—I'm lucky I didn't."

"I guess I didn't realize how privileged I was as a white guy in a middle-class family." Brian exhaled, thinking back to his childhood. "My problems seemed like they were the end of the world until the *actual* end of the world happened. Or civilization, I guess."

"Weird thing is, I'm kinda glad it happened. I mean, yeah, I wish all those people hadn't died...but I dunno if we woulda met up again otherwise." Louis held an orange slice out to Brian. He leaned forward and took it, savoring the juice that coated Louis's fingers. "Even if we had, do you think things woulda ended up the same way? You and me together like this? I always liked you, but this situation stripped away a lotta hang-ups that came from growin' up in the rural Midwest."

Brian tried to imagine this alternate reality. He highly suspected his reunion with the Lavellés wouldn't have thrilled his parents—especially what developed with Louis, who was the stereotypical Bad Boy every parent dreaded their child bringing home. "Did you think about me sometimes? It sounds bad, but I think I tried to forget you guys because remembering hurt too much...and I was afraid you hated me."

Louis smiled at Brian. "I did think about you now and again, wondered what you were up to. Eva and I tried to look you up, but neither of us could ever gather the courage to call your house or send an e-mail. We kinda thought the same thing, that you might have bad memories we shouldn't stir up."

The return of the butterflies and tingling fingers plagued Brian. "I wish one of us had the guts to reach out before all this, that our families were still around, but I'm glad I'm with you right now. I don't want to lose you again."

Brian stretched his hand toward Louis's, reminded of the times he'd clung to it in search of security. Louis laced his fingers through Brian's and squeezed. A moment of silence passed while they enjoyed the vista before them. When a breeze blew through the swishing palm fronds, Louis's hair fluttered, revealing a peaceful expression new to Brian. Heat radiated throughout him like the throb of a fresh sunburn.

"*Je t'aime*, Louis."

"*Je suis amoureux de vous*, Brian."

The eye contact between them made the world spin into oblivion. Nothing else existed—not the island, not Earth, not even the universe. The only universe that mattered swirled in those nebulous eyes.

Louis cupped a hand around Brian's cheek and leaned across the table. The heatwave within him escalated until his muscles seemed to melt. The sugary syrup of oranges swirled within his mouth, lingering when Louis parted from him.

"All good things must come to an end." Louis stuffed the rum into his backpack and zipped it up. He stood and faced the ocean. "Even though the sea and sky look infinite, they'll meet their end one day, too."

Brian packed the rest of the food into his backpack and shrugged the straps over his shoulders. Even though he didn't need to, he pushed his chair underneath the table. He walked up next to Louis and slid his hand along the taut contours of Louis's arm. "Maybe. But not in our lifetime. Not today, not tomorrow. Now let's go secure this island so we can enjoy ourselves."

He snagged Louis's hand and tugged him away from his contemplations.

WHEN THEY RETURNED to the bungalow, one of the windows was cracked open.

"The Stalker that got your mom," Louis whispered, "it crawled in through a window, didn't it?"

Brian nodded, only slightly reassured by the bow in his hands.

Louis jerked his head. "Let's check the outside first."

After a brief inspection of the perimeter, they discovered a set of footprints in the sand that led from the open window toward the walkway.

Louis approached the front door and started twisting the knob. Brian tightened the bowstring and aimed an arrow at the entrance.

The door creaked open. Nothing jumped out at them or appeared to be out of sorts—until Brian caught a blur of white and red crawling out of the side window. Brian loosed the arrow and strung another one, but the intruder dodged and bolted for the wooden walkway.

Brian watched the hunched body weave a jagged path into the distance. He kept the tip of the arrow lined up with it, intending to wound them so they'd leave a trail of blood. The arrow hit its mark and stuck out of the shrinking figure's back.

"Nice one." Louis lowered the revolver, unable to get a clear shot at this distance. "We should track them before we lose the trail."

"What about the bungalow?"

"It'll be here when we get back." Louis jogged toward the walkway. Brian joined him, still trying to piece together what he'd seen. *Why would it break in if it didn't want to hide and wait for us? Did it make a kneejerk decision to run for it when it saw it was outnumbered?*

It might've been a frightened person. Anyone would look rough after a while on this island if they didn't know what they were doing.

Something rustled in the foliage surrounding them. A blur of red burst from the trees, soaring over their head. Louis aimed his revolver at the screeching parrot. "I'm gonna kill that fuckin' thing, I swear it!"

"Don't fire unless you have to. Let's keep going." Brian exhaled, certain he'd heard it yell "Get out!" this time. Someone's pet parrot, or a wild one that had picked up a thing or two from the tourists. Although it kept startling him, he found it comforting to know there was another semi-friendly lifeform on the island with them.

The walkway emerged at the other side of the island. It continued past the sugar-sand shore into a pier with an archway of two carved palm trees and "Cayo Levisa" painted on it. A large ship still drifted alongside it. The blood streaks along the exterior—some in the shape of handprints—meant they were on the right path.

After Louis scoped it out with binoculars, they advanced toward the impressive vessel. Although theirs was comfortable enough for a long trip, it wouldn't have been suitable to live in. This was. It wasn't the size of a cruise ship—thank God—but it dwarfed their own respectable cruiser.

Brian's nose scrunched to block a familiar scent. *Something dead or rotten.*

He climbed onto the deck and lifted the bandana from neck to nose, his eyes watering. Louis's face crinkled when he followed. They tiptoed along the fiberglass deck, keeping their backs to the railing. Russet swirls and smudges stained the white décor, leading from the deck down to the cabins below.

This is way more blood than there should be. What the fuck have we gotten ourselves into?

They canvassed the deck from bow to stern. Satisfied that it was clear, they descended below deck. The already-repugnant stench became unbearable to the point Brian's cheeks swelled with bitter fluid. He swallowed back the lunch trying to force its way up from his stomach. Despite his strong constitution, even Louis retched.

The sun didn't reach below deck, forcing them to use the flashlight. The sour feeling in Brian's stomach deepened when he decided no sane person would ever retreat into this squalor. They were either on the trail of a lunatic or a Stalker.

Louis focused the sphere of light onto the floor, following the substantial trail of blood. It stopped in front of a door. Their eagerness to return to fresh air impaired their vigilance. Louis tried to turn the knob, but he made a face that meant the door was locked.

Mom locked the door.

Louis kicked the door above the knob. It cracked but didn't budge. When Brian joined, there was no give beneath his foot.

Mom barricaded the door too.

Louis withdrew a souvenir from Evergreen: one of their machetes. He hacked into the wooden door with a furor powered by determination. The wood splintered, the lacquered paint cracking and peeling where the blade struck. Heavy exhalations slipped out of him as he wore himself to the point of exhaustion.

Brian stepped in and took over. Louis aimed the flashlight through the gap he'd torn into the door. He muttered something and snatched Brian's arm, drawing him back. "Stop—stop."

Louis's bandana swelled in and out as he exhaled through his mouth. His eyes had gone wide and glassy, his brows arched high above them. Brian peered through the jagged gap at the contents of the room. The expression his face formed was an exact mirror of Louis's.

Fully and partially skeletal bodies filled the room. Some were small, obviously animals, but the rest were human. The thick odor of sweet, pungent rot clung to the stagnant air. A figure huddled in the corner, dressed in a tattered white uniform. Well, it had been once—stains ranging from dirt to blood had soaked into it.

A pair of cloudy eyes looked up at them. It held up its hands as if it was surrendering. "Nuh-no." Although its speech was slurred, there was no mistaking the word it managed to form. Unlike the others, it didn't laugh.

"The *fuck*?" Louis managed to murmur. When Brian forced his eyes from the figure in front of them, they locked onto Louis's. His brow furrowed into them, crinkling the bridge of his nose.

The Stalker's pallid fingers curled around a blue tin—one of their cans of SPAM from the B.E.N. If Brian hadn't been so stupefied by its prior behavior, the ridiculous image of a Stalker shoveling SPAM from the can into its grinning mouth would've made him laugh.

"It's been livin' here, draggin' its food here—probably sailed the damn ship here. Must be why there's no other Stalkers or people on the island: it's the lone survivor." Louis's thumb lingered on the hammer of the revolver. "Part of me almost admires it."

"I don't." Brian lifted his arms and drew the bowstring back with the arrow. "I pity it."

He let go. The arrow soared into the top of the Stalker's skull, putting an end to its mournful whimpers.

"Let's get out of here." Brian turned his back to the Stalker, ready to leave it all behind.

NO MORE INVASIONS or encounters happened the next few days. They explored what they could, excluding the southern coast with the mangroves. Not much could live in that—at least that would threaten them.

Concluding that the Stalker living on the boat had eaten any other survivors or Stalkers, they started to let their guard down and focus more on preparing than exploring. The kitchen had plenty of cookware to desalinate the ocean water with, but it was a laborious process that bored Louis. Tired of Louis pestering him, Brian sent him away to fish or hunt.

Although they were 99 percent certain any threatening lifeforms were absent from the island, that didn't mean no more would show up. They stripped wood and nails from the other bungalows to barricade the window to theirs. Fortunately, plenty of courtesy soaps and shampoos littered the bungalows, and Brian recalled a method Poppa taught him where he could make soap with ashes from a fire, rainwater, and leftover cooking fat. If their toothpaste ran out, pine needles would scrub away debris and refresh their breath. The one concern he'd been most preoccupied with was solved—for the time being—by the toilet paper remaining in the bungalows and a reserve in the kitchen storeroom.

After a week passed by, Brian lost track of time. His life became the vacation most people dreamed of. Complete freedom, gorgeous scenery, pleasant weather, and the only company he wanted or needed. Sometimes they played chess with the giant set outside the restaurant. They jury-rigged a game of horseshoes out of driftwood and woven vines. The temperature of the water made it ideal for swimming. When they felt lazy, they laid out on the lounge chairs and tanned. Brian didn't have anything to read, so he scribbled in his journal or on the notepads they'd found in the bungalows. Louis continued to teach Brian an impressive amount of French. They broke the bed in—along with several other areas.

The "get out" parrot still flitted around now and then. Sometimes it settled onto the umbrella above them, curious about what they were doing. Louis always shooed it away, but it never stayed gone. Brian saw a few other things: a huge, glistening snake for one. When he told Louis, Louis got all excited and set about turning it into dinner. He succeeded.

Every now and then, the hutia popped out from the forest. Brian found them cute and convinced Louis not to kill them unless they got desperate. Tree frogs sometimes croaked within the jungle. Other birds flitted by with musical chirps. Once, Brian saw a hummingbird hovering outside their bungalow. Its minuscule size impressed him as much as the girth of the snake had.

Although Louis had been antisocial back on the mainland, he talked more than Brian now. Brian listened and replied, carrying on conversations about the gaps in their adolescence when they'd lost touch. Louis discussed his upbringing, his relationship with Eva and his grandparents, and the fire. He didn't touch on some aspects—his conversation was somewhat detached, and he never revealed how he *felt* about the things he brought up. Brian, on the other hand, blurted out every lifechanging event and how it had affected him. But Louis listened as well as he conversed, so Brian was sure it sank in.

Louis resented the entirety of his family for not giving him the attention he needed—which was more than usual because of the illness they didn't understand. His father took after his grandfather—an abusive alcoholic with a turn-screw temper. Eva adapted by being obedient and staying out of trouble. When she did something, they always blamed Louis. The straw that broke the camel's back was her blabbing about Brian cutting Louis and their parents forcing them apart for all those years.

This led Louis to reveal a rather momentous truth: "I set the fire."

As shocking as this was, Brian had no trouble imagining Louis doing this. "Did you mean to kill them?"

"No. I didn't even know they were home. Their truck was in the shop, so our neighbors took me and Eva to school and would take them to work. When I decided to ditch school and head home, nothin' looked out of the ordinary. But Père was sick, and Mère stayed home to take care of him. They were closed up in the bedroom, so I didn't see 'em. I poured lighter fluid all over the livin' room and struck a match, thinkin' of all the times Père belted me and Mère stood there lettin' him."

"Would you take it back?"

Louis nursed his glass of rum, which he'd been mixing with coconut milk to cut the burn. "Honestly, no. I didn't love them. I don't think they ever loved *me*. If they had the choice, they woulda just had Eva. My grandparents felt the same way, only took us in because they had to. Out of one hole, into another: my papère was just as mean and nasty as my père." Louis dug his feet into the sand and started tapping his nails against the glass in his hand. "I killed him, but he wasn't infected. I hated him."

Brian tensed a little, but mostly because he sensed the anxiety in Louis's voice. "Was all that stuff you said true? About him wanting to take our stuff and leave us?"

"Oh, yeah. He was a nasty piece of work." Louis snatched Brian's arm. "But I wasn't gonna let him do that. You were the only good thing about my childhood—I wanted to get that back and I wasn't gonna let him take it from me."

The tight grip around Brian's arm loosened. "I didn't really know him, but if you say he was that bad, I believe you. I mean, I can *feel* how much you hate him and your dad when you talk about them."

"You hated yours too, didn't you?"

"Kind of. But I shouldn't have. I should've tried to understand why he did what he did, and that he didn't do it to hurt me and Mom." Brian twisted onto his side, face pressed against the vinyl strips of the lounge chair. "He was sick like us. Like your dad and grandfather were. And he tried to fix things—I just wouldn't let him."

It surprised him how distant of a memory that already seemed: a fading dream gone entirely by the end of the day.

"I shoulda patched things up with Eva, I guess." Louis chugged the rest of his drink and started to mix another one. His already-thick accent was starting to slur. "She pissed me off when she accused me of ditchin' her for you. Then she kept pushin' it by insultin' me in front of those actors..." Louis drifted into an extended silence, during which he downed the drink he'd just mixed. Brian took the bottle and set it on the other side of his chair so Louis couldn't reach it. "I saw her kiss you in the warehouse, you know. It felt like she was doin' somethin' behind my back, like some kind of betrayal. I guess I was scared you'd like her better than me—everyone else did."

Louis stood and grabbed both of Brian's hands, pulling him into an upright position. "I'm tired of sittin'. Let's stretch out and look at the stars."

Although Brian had partaken of his share of the rum, his ratio of coconut milk was much higher than Louis's. While he fanned out a towel, Louis stumbled over his own feet and crashed into Brian. "But you didn't wanna kiss her, did you? Bet you wanted me all along. I started to pick up on it at that skatin' rink, but I didn't know how to handle it with Eva around."

Brian struggled to keep Louis upright and set the towel down. He succeeded at both, but only barely; Louis slumped onto the towel as soon as Brian got it down. Brian snagged a bottle of water and extended it to Louis. "You'll want this. Trust me."

"I don't wanna sit up."

Brian sank onto his backside and unscrewed the cap. He lifted Louis's head and forced the bottle to his mouth. "Don't be a baby. You'll thank me later."

Louis finished chugging the water. While Brian screwed the cap back on, Louis reached over and slipped a finger underneath the waistband of Brian's swim trunks. "I could thank you *now*."

"Not when you're sloppy drunk, Lou." But the finger persisted, trying to wriggle the waistband down. Brian grabbed Louis's wrist. "I really think you should get some rest."

Louis furrowed his brow and frowned, on the verge of a pout. "Don't you want me?"

By now, Brian had been around Louis long enough to read both his expressions and vocal tone: desperation, fear, and insecurity were written in bold print.

Brian stroked Louis's scarred cheek with the back of his hand. His skin was sticky from the sweat attempting to push out the alcohol. "Of course. But I'm not gonna take advantage of you while you're drunk."

Louis's head flopped onto Brian's lap. Brian stroked his hair, mesmerized by the clear sky above them. The ocean was so still he could see a perfect reflection of the stars in its surface.

"I'm scared you're gonna leave me."

Brian stopped stroking. "Why do you say that?"

Louis popped up from Brian's lap and kneeled in front of him, his hands balled into fists between his knees. "Listen, I can't keep this from you anymore. I wanna be honest with you. You deserve it, and I don't deserve you."

Brian's eyebrows furrowed. "Where's this coming from?"

"I left her. Eva. I took the knife from her and locked her in an electrical closet at the arcade."

Brian nodded. "You told me."

"She wasn't dead. She wasn't even injured. I just didn't wanna deal with her anymore. I didn't wanna be reminded of that part of my life."

A *whooshing* sound drowned out the ambient noises of the island. Brian tried to process what he'd been told, in denial at first, but this swiftly transitioned into anger. "You came all this way knowing she was still alive? And that you *left* her?"

Louis smacked his hands against his head and covered his face with his arms. "If I told you, we never woulda come here. None of it ever woulda happened. I made a fucked-up decision in the heat of the moment and was too much of a fuckin' coward to say anythin' until now."

Brian stood and backed away from Louis. "I can't stay here knowing you left her to those assholes—they'll do the same thing to her they did to Parker's sister!"

"That's why I tossed the grenade in: to mess up their shit and scare 'em away. They weren't gonna stay there after that. I shoved an arcade game in front of the door—they wouldn't even think to look there for her. When she got desperate enough, she'd have no problem shovin' it away so she could get out—"

"You tried to make me think Parker and Spike had something to do with it!" The ground beneath Brian's feet seemed unsteady, either from the alcohol or the truth sinking in. "Jesus, Lou! What else is there? Are you gonna tell me you're the one who shot my grandfather, too?"

Louis's plaintive expression cut off Brian's incredulous laughter. "He didn't believe me. About what I did to Papère. And he was already pissed about me shootin' his dog. I knew if he was anythin' like my Papère, he wouldn't hesitate to take me out. I only wanted you to stay with me, but I felt all those horrible, wonderful things and I couldn't...I couldn't keep this from you."

Too many things whirled in Brian to separate—too many thoughts, too many feelings. The affection he felt toward Louis didn't diminish, but unpleasant sensations joined it: the sting of betrayal, the numbness of denial, the inferno of rage. None of these awful things had happened since Eva, but how could Brian know what Louis did or *didn't* do at this point? For all he knew, he took Jonesy to fuck with D and let him back out while they were distracted. He probably *did* go out in the middle of the night and hack Henry's "family" to death.

I never should've given my heart to someone who shot my dog.

"I knew you had some issues, but this..." Brian scoffed, his eyes burning. "God, all the things I did with you! All those things I let you do to *me*. I feel so stupid. I knew it couldn't last—everything was so perfect, but you just had to go and fuck it up." He stepped back, grabbed hold of his lounge chair, and hurled it toward Louis. "I wish you'd never said anything! I just wanna be blind again, ignorant, happy—anything except this-this anger and *pain*." He bent down to grab the bottle of rum and started to chug the rest of it, pushing on despite the burn, seeking an escape from this unbearable reality.

Louis stumbled to his feet, rushed over to Brian, and snatched the bottle. He tossed it into the sand and grabbed Brian's sticky cheeks. "Don't you try it. Your Daddy tried escapin', but it didn't work. Messed you up instead."

"*You* messed me up!" Brian tried to take a swing at Louis, but Louis dodged it and tackled Brian into the sand. He shoved a knee into Louis's gut and rolled out from under him, then bolted for the bungalow. "Fuck you—I'll escape another way!"

He stumbled into a hole obscured by the shadows of the towering trees. Louis grabbed his ankle, but Brian kicked him in the face and got to his feet. He scrambled onto the porch, flinging the patio furniture into Louis to slow him down. Brian didn't even know what Louis wanted—to reconcile, to apologize—but he knew he *needed* to get away from him.

After he made it through the door, he rushed to lock it and shove a bookcase in front of it. Louis couldn't make it through the barricaded window—but he was desperate, and Brian knew full well that a desperate Louis was a terrifying thing.

He shoved as much of his belongings into his backpack as he could, taking whatever food and water would fit. The bow sat in a corner with a full quiver, long-abandoned, but Brian took both. When he didn't hear banging against the door anymore, he started to panic. He tried to think where Louis would've put the boat key and checked the hanger by the door and inside both bedside tables. Nothing.

Fuck.

The other boat didn't have a key that he knew of, and he wasn't frantic enough to rummage through the Stalker's pockets for it. If Louis was, God help him.

Brian paced amidst the ominous silence, raking his trembling hands through his hair. *He wouldn't hurt me, would he? But he's fucked up right now—his emotions are at their boiling point and the alcohol isn't helping. I need to get away from him, have time to process this, get distance from this island and all the memories I have of him.*

I can't kill him. I don't even want to hit him with an arrow. It might feel nice for a second, but I know I'd regret it. I need to find something else, some way to knock him out. I'll dig the key out of his pocket and run for it.

Brian snatched one of Louis's belts and several pairs of tube socks. He stuffed them into his pockets and clung to the belt. After he moved the bookcase out of the way, he unlocked the door and tried to prepare himself for the worst.

The door swung open into the night. Patio furniture littered the porch and the foot of the steps, but Louis was nowhere in sight.

Brian swallowed. *He knows. He knows I'll go for the boat. For all I know, he's already flung the key somewhere I'll never find it.*

Brian pressed his back to the door, pulse racing as his vision adjusted to the murky moonlit night. He scanned the shore for movement but only saw the umbrella and two lounge chairs, one of which still lay on its side. The empty bottle of rum glistened.

He can't have gone far. He'd be waiting for me somewhere out of sight. Out of sight but close—where wouldn't he expect me to look?

Up.

Brian stepped forward and turned. A shadow leaped down and tackled him, sending him crashing down the steps. His head smashed against something, made his vision blur, but he knew that scent—leather and tobacco, sweet but piquant. He'd buried his nose in Louis's hair enough to memorize it.

"I don't wanna hurt you, but you're not thinkin' straight." Louis's weight burrowed into Brian's waist, keeping him pinned to the sand in front of the foot of the steps. "What were you gonna do with this? Spank me?" While Louis tried to yank the belt from Brian's hand, Brian punched him in the throat. He made horrible gurgling noises and lost his center of gravity, giving Brian an opening to slide out from underneath him.

Brian circled around to Louis's back while he fell to his knees, grasping his throat as uncontrollable coughs shook him. Brian thrust his knee into Louis's lower back and pinned his arm behind him, shoving him onto the ground. "I'm gonna go back for her. Where's the key?"

Louis could only cough when he tried to talk. Brian had held back his full strength for that punch, aware of how much damage it could do. All he'd wanted was to get Louis off him.

"Point."

Louis gestured to his swim trunks with the hand pinned behind his back. Brian kept one hand on the back of Louis's neck and his knee in Louis's lower back. He tried to feel around for the key with the other hand but ended up groping anatomy he'd familiarized himself with long ago.

Louis spun, swiveling his free arm and striking Brian's side with his elbow. It knocked the wind out of him long enough for Louis to slither out and get to his feet. Brian scrambled onto his, gasping for air while Louis continued to struggle with his throat.

"You...asshole... You've...hidden it somewhere...haven't you?"

Louis's resulting smirk enraged Brian. He racked his brain for some alternative to a physical altercation, trying to hone in on Louis's weakness since his instincts remained formidable even when his thinking was impaired.

"Louis." Brian stepped forward. "If you love me, you have to let me go."

Louis shook his head. "I'll never...see you again." The hoarseness of his already-raspy voice pained Brian—he could scarcely imagine how much it hurt Louis to talk.

Brian held up his hands and dropped the belt. "You're the one who got drunk and decided to tell me everything. I-I appreciate your honesty. It must've been hard for you. But you know what you did was wrong. My grandfather might've acted irrationally—I was afraid of that too. For lack of a better word, he was cutthroat. But Eva did nothing to you. She counted on you to *protect* her, and you shattered that trust. You shattered the trust *we* shared."

Louis lowered his eyes from Brian's.

"I can't leave her behind," Brian said. "If there's a chance they got a hold of her, I won't be able to live with myself. I have to go clean up your mess."

"I should go...with you—"

"No." Brian thought back to his final conversation with his father and his inability to forgive him until it was too late. "I can forgive you. But I can't trust you."

Louis's shoulders started shaking. This cut the words from the tip of Brian's tongue. He'd never seen Louis cry. Not once. Not even a tear.

His trembling hands curved over Louis's shoulders. "I don't wanna hurt you more and I'm sure you didn't enjoy hurting me. Tell me where the key is—*please*."

Louis's cheeks and eyes gleamed in the fading moonlight. An emerging sunrise started to take its place, creating that strange indigo moment when light and dark met. "Bungalow...next door. I'll show...you."

Brian yanked the tube socks from his pockets. "I'm going to tie your hands—you know why, right?"

Louis nodded. Brian circled behind him and pulled Louis's hands behind his back, catching a whiff of that captivating scent he knew would haunt him while he was alone on the boat. Brian struggled with the intimacy he'd grown accustomed to and prepared himself for any tricks Louis might have up his sleeve, knotting the socks in tight, quick motions.

He marched Louis over to the bungalow and retrieved the key from an empty toilet tank, keeping one hand on Louis to make sure he didn't make a run for it. He could *feel* the strength going out of him, whether from physical exhaustion, the effect of the alcohol, or sheer depression. Brian knew it all too well, that feeling of *globbiness* where he wanted to puddle onto the couch or in his bed and do nothing, not even *think*.

Once he'd secured the key, he towed Louis back to the dock where their boat drifted. A shuffling gait replaced Louis's confident strut. When they approached the wooden walkway, Louis sank to his knees like a petulant child who didn't want their parent to drag them out of Disney World.

Brian kneeled in front of him, smudging the tears streaming down Louis's ruddy cheeks with his thumbs. "Louis, I've left your things and some of the supplies in the bungalow. I'll even leave you something to help you get out of the knots I tied you up in." He traced the scar he'd left on Louis's cheek so long ago. "It might be a long time before we see each other again, but I'm sure it won't be another nine years."

Louis's knit brow and quivering lips signified an outburst of tears was imminent, that emotion had come out the victor in this battle of willpower—Brian had seen this expression many times on his sister's face. Louis shuddered into full-on sobs even though it must've been agony on his injured throat.

It bothered Brian that he'd put that Stalker down out of pity but couldn't do the same to Louis. He wasn't sure if it was because he wanted him to live with what he'd done or because he simply loved Louis too much to ever kill him. The building tears blurring his vision indicated the latter.

He dug into his back pocket and tossed the pocketknife just out of Louis's reach. Although he was glad to be rid of the thing and the memories attached to it, he suspected he'd come to miss it sooner than later.

Reverence for the past softened Brian's bitterness. He smoothed Louis's bangs back and pressed his lips to his forehead. "*Au revoir, mon amour.*"

Brian tried to tune out the haunting wails and pleas that followed him as he turned and rushed toward the dock. He climbed aboard the boat and twisted the key in the ignition. The engine sputtered to life, mercifully drowning Louis's anguished voice and churning the water behind him. The breeze caressed Brian's face as he pushed up on the throttle and reversed from the shore. Moisture clung to his skin; when he pressed his lips together, he tasted salt.

Don't look back. Don't give up.

There's still so much to live for.

Like spring.

Like summer.

After all, I made it through the dead of winter.

And if another storm rolls in, I'll weather it—because the clouds always clear.

Eva

Sunshine and Shadow

Spike and Parker Playbill

Acknowledgements

I'd like to thank Justin, Violet, and Tonya for their excellent critiques, which shaped this into the work it is today. And, as always, Bryant—my perpetual partner in crime (and beta reading).

About the Author

As an only child, I was allowed plenty of freedom to explore my interests—namely reading, writing, and art. My parents encouraged me to pursue these and never discouraged me from the diversity of the world. I like to think my work today reflects my interest in exploring and appreciating such diversity. Ultimately, I wanted to create and inspire as so many others have done in my life, and to tell stories people might take something from.

Compared to the rest of the world, I'm not all that interesting! I love animals, Fall/Halloween/Horror, coffee, board and video games, and the occasional Anime. And yes, I owe the world of fanfiction a debt for being my stomping grounds as a teen. I sometimes call myself the "Mother of Rats" because I own three—they're clever and sweet and don't deserve the bad rap they get! Beyond that, I count myself lucky to be able to share my love of writing with anyone interested enough to read it—so thank you!

Email: ikebukuroinfobroker@yahoo.com

Twitter: @LolaInSlacks69

Website: www.lola-in-slacks-88.tumblr.com

Also Available from NineStar Press

Connect with NineStar Press

Website: NineStarPress.com

Facebook: NineStarPress

Facebook Reader Group: NineStarNiche

Twitter: @ninestarpress

Tumblr: NineStarPress